BOOKING A KILLER VACATION

A Myrtle Beach Mystery #1

J.R. Ripley

Beachfront Entertainment

Booking A Killer Vacation

1

Kelly loved the beach, especially the gorgeous one here in Myrtle Beach, South Carolina. But she wasn't loving it so much at the moment. The tide was coming in. Her patience was running out. Work was piling up back in the Beach Lovers Inn office.

And a perfectly good pair of leather sandals were now soaking up warm salt water.

Why had she agreed to meet one of the guests—the weirdest one—Harry Leland, out here at the beach, around the corner and out of sight from the Beach Lovers Inn?

Did he think they were in some goofy spy novel?

She must have been out of her mind. She couldn't get enough of the beach but she had had enough of this guy.

Gullible, that's what she was. She was too gullible. Her brother, Sam, always said so. The fact that she was standing there proved Sam right. All because Harry Leland urged her to meet him someplace private.

Like the freaking beach was private. There were sunbathers everywhere.

Then again, maybe Harry Leland had a point. Beachgoers were more interested in their tans than in what two fully-clothed people might be talking about at the ocean's edge.

Harry Leland insisted he had something important

to tell her and that he didn't want "prying eyes" over-hearing their conversation.

What did that mean? Could eyes pry? Crow bars pry, not eyes. And they don't hear anything. They see things, thought Kelly.

A small wave sent a dead fish of some sort, which appeared to have been half-eaten by a hungry seagull or a crab or possibly both, up against her toes.

A growl vibrated in Kelly's throat. Her feet were wet and she was shivering. She'd probably end up with pneumonia on top of a wrecked pair of sandals.

Now she had fish guts on her toes.

"Did you hear what I said, Mrs. Green?"

"I heard you, Mr. Leland." Kelly raised her voice over the sound of the crashing waves and the brisk breeze blowing in off the Atlantic Ocean. "But why would any-body want to harm Aunt Ruth?"

Her aunt Ruth was a wee wisp of a woman. She'd never harmed anyone in her entire life.

The next wave rose over Kelly's ankles. Further in-creasing the damage to her sandals. On the bright side, maybe the salt water would wash away the fish goop.

"I don't know why, Mrs. Green," Harry Leland re-plied to her question. "It's my sixth sense, that's all." He crossed his arms over his scrawny chest. "Trust me."

"Trust you?" Kelly eyed him appraisingly. "Why should I?"

Kelly wasn't so sure Harry Leland had five senses in good working order, let alone a sixth one that alerted him to potential trouble. If he had, he would have known she felt like punching him for dragging her away from her work to have this idiotic and pointless conver-sation.

"I am somewhat of an expert at this sort of thing."

She narrowed her eyes at him. "What sort of thing?"

"Mysteries, intrigue." He paused for dramatic effect. "Murder."

"Murder!" Kelly grabbed him by the collar. "Are you crazy? What right do you have going around talking like my aunt is going to be murdered?"

Harry pulled away. But it wasn't without effort. Kelly easily outmatched him. "You forget. I write a detective series."

Kelly arched her brow. "I checked you out, Mr. Leland. You wrote two detective novels. Just two." She held up her fingers. "That's not a series. That's a novel and a sequel."

Harry staggered backwards. Was it her words or the stiff breeze?

"And the last one was over four years ago. Why haven't there been any since? Poor sales or have you run out of ideas?"

Harry winced. Kelly could see she had wounded him. This whole conversation was getting out of hand.

"Look, I'm sorry, Mr. Leland." She straightened his shirt for him. "I didn't mean to get carried away. But murder?"

Harry Leland was overdressed for Myrtle Beach in the summertime. No wonder he was sweating profusely. Since she'd been at the inn, Kelly had rarely seen him in anything less than long-sleeved shirts and baggy trousers.

"I feel it in my bones."

Kelly extricated her feet from the wet sand that had been gobbling her up. Why wasn't Harry Leland sinking? He wore boxy black shoes that looked like they weighed practically as much as him. "Thank you, Mr. Leland, for your concern for my aunt. Now, if you don't mind, I've got guests to attend to and a reunion to prepare for."

"Going to your reunion? Nice. High school or college?"

"Neither. The inn is hosting one. Now, if you don't mind?" She motioned toward the inn.

"Okay," said Harry. "But don't forget what I said."

"Oh, I won't," Kelly assured the young man. She plodded through the sand and over the dunes, silently cursing Harry Leland as she left him behind to his madness and own devices.

Back at the inn, she kicked off her sandals outside the kitchen door and inspected them. With luck and a little sunshine maybe they'd be salvageable. She set them on the stoop to dry.

"You'll never guess who I saw at the Golden Arms," began Aunt Ruth as Kelly entered through the side kitchen door.

"Who?"

"Oops!" Charles "Charlie" Barron, a new guest, cursed from the dining room.

"Sorry, sorry." Charlie Barron held up his hands as Aunt Ruth flew into the room.

"Charlie, really!" admonished his wife, Mary.

"I do apologize for my language," Charlie said, looking helplessly at the busted water pitcher laying sideways in the center of the dining table.

Aunt Ruth dabbed first at him then at the tablecloth. "I've heard worse. You can darn well curse all you want," she closed with a wink.

Dr. Barron laughed. "Besides, you bumped my elbow,

dear." Charlie Barron rubbed his elbow with his opposite hand while casting an accusing look at his spouse.

"Sorry, darling." Mary Barron apologized to my aunt as well and used her linen napkin to help soak up the spill.

Aunt Ruth picked up the broken handle. "No need to apologize. This is my fault. I should have replaced this old pitcher years ago. I thought I could get away with gluing the handle back on. I see now, I should have gotten rid of it."

Harry Leland entered from the other door. "Not too late for dinner, I hope?"

"Not too late at all, Harry." Ruth smiled at the young man. "Take your seat. I'll bring you a plate." She dropped the broken handle into the pitcher and carried both off.

Back in the kitchen, Kelly was holding the dishcloth helplessly over a geyser. "The faucet's broken again, Auntie!" Water thundered from the spout to the white porcelain sink, sending cold spray every which way. Unfortunately, very little of it remained in the sink.

"Bang on it, dear." There was a resounding crash as Aunt Ruth dropped the busted pitcher in the trashcan kept out of sight inside the pantry.

"Bang on it?" Kelly wanted it to stop leaking. She didn't want to snap the faucet off like a dead tree branch. The thing was a gusher already. "It might break." She eyed the faucet suspiciously.

"It won't break." Aunt Ruth pulled the string to the pantry light and shut the door behind her. She padded across the pink and white-tiled kitchen floor and calmly eyed the out-of-control faucet. "Trust me. If I've done it once, I've done it a hundred times."

Ruth took aim. "One, two, three!"

Kelly held her breath as Aunt Ruth proved her point by slamming her aged fist down three times in quick succession atop the spigot.

To top it off, she'd somehow managed to keep each and every one of the tiny blue and rose-colored petunias decorating her high lace-collared rayon dress dry while doing so.

"There," Aunt Ruth said with a smile. "See?" She turned the faucet on then off again. "All better."

Kelly squinted skeptically at the faucet, waiting for a telltale drip or, more likely in her opinion, a catastrophic failure.

But nothing bad happened.

"If you say so." Water trickled down Kelly's nose and dribbled from her hair to the counter. The kitchen window looked like a summer shower had unexpectedly formed inside the vintage yet stylish kitchen. Water dripped sluggishly from the fruit punch-colored curtains.

The smell of lemon-scented dish soap hung in the air along with a million miniscule bubbles. Two went up Kelly's nose and she sneezed.

"Oh, dear." Aunt Ruth made tsk-tsking sounds and pulled open the door to the white cabinet beneath the sink to reach for a towel.

"I'll take care of it." Kelly sniffed, reaching past her aunt and grabbing the towel that hung on a plastic hook on the inside of the cabinet door. "Why don't you go rest for a while?"

"Rest?" said Aunt Ruth, pulling herself up to her entire four-foot whatever. "With an inn full of guests?" She shook her head. "Not very likely. We have guests to attend to, plus that special party."

One of the Beach Lovers Inn's regular summer visitors had chosen to host a vacation reunion at the inn. Although the party was small in size, having booked four of their rooms for eight guests, it would be a real boon to the business's bottom line. With so many newer, fancier places in Myrtle Beach, the Beach Lovers Inn was feeling the financial strain.

"Not quite full, Aunt Ruth. We do have several rooms empty, remember? And a no-show. Not to worry, it won't be your problem much longer." It would be hers.

The corner of Aunt Ruth's lips turned down. "Oh, yes. The Nelsons. It's the first time they've been a no-show in nearly twenty years."

"Speaking of which," Kelly began, "what's with that weird guy in 209, Auntie?"

"209?" Kelly's aunt tapped her pink cheek. "You mean Harry Leland."

"Yes, Mr. Leland." She didn't dare bring up what he had said to her aunt. It might frighten her. Maybe she had some insight into his psyche.

"Oh, dear. I forgot. He needs his dinner." Aunt Ruth moved quickly to the range and pulled a warm plate from the oven. "I'll be right back."

While the inn didn't normally serve dinner or any other meals, except for providing a casual, daily breakfast bar, Ruth had prepared a special banquet that evening to which all guests and staff had been invited. This was intended as a welcome dinner for the vacationing reunion group and something of a farewell meal for Ruth herself.

Kelly had helped her aunt prepare the informal feast which they had laid out on the long buffet that normally held the breakfast bar. Many had taken advantage of the free meal. Harry Leland, included.

Of course, with Harry, that meant meeting his special dietary needs.

When Ruth returned from the dining room, Kelly was mopping up. "Careful," said Kelly. "It's wet. You were telling me about Mr. Leland."

"Was I?" The older woman stepped aside as her niece swabbed the floor. "There's not much to tell. Such a dear boy. What is it you want to know about him? He is single," she said with a twinkle in her eyes.

"No, no. Nothing like that." Kelly cringed. "How much longer is he staying?"

Aunt Ruth settled herself at the old hickory table occupying the middle of the kitchen. Its top was scarred by years of use and its legs wobbled. Ruth frowned as it jiggled under the weight of her hands. "Until he finds a place of his own, dear."

"Why do you rent to him?" Kelly leaned on the wood handle of the mop looking through the open doorway to the guest dining room. He sat picking daintily at his food. The brooding, gangly man reminded her of someone but she couldn't think who.

"We run an inn. That's what we do."

"Yes, but he's so...strange." Kelly rested the mop against the old-fashioned two-tone white and teal refrigerator.

Aunt Ruth was surprised by Kelly's assessment. "Whatever do you mean?"

Kelly stole another glance into the dining room at the thirtysomething man in question. "I mean that in the two weeks I've been here, I've barely seen Mr. Leland. He's always in his room."

Kelly plucked clean glasses from the drying rack at

the sink, wiped them meticulously and returned them to the cupboard. "With the curtains closed, no less."

She moved on to the silverware, dropping piece after piece into the tray tucked inside the drawer. "It's weird. Don't you think?"

"His money's as good as anyone's. Besides," Aunt Ruth smiled, "I like him."

"I suppose," Kelly said, though she was far from sure she felt the same. She laid the damp mop outside the backdoor. She noted her sandals were turning a salty brown. Maybe she'd buy a new pair and add the cost to Leland's bill.

"Are you sure you have to leave tomorrow? Couldn't you stay another day or two?" Kelly squeezed her auntie's hand. "Maybe one more year or two?"

"Sorry, Kelly. Sun City beckons." Ruth Evans would be on a plane for Arizona the next day—Kelly would be driving her to Myrtle Beach International Airport—to live out her years in a retirement community nearer her remaining sister. "Besides, I've taught you all I know. At least enough to get by. You call me if you get into any trouble."

Kelly mulled over her aunt's words. Though she had agreed to the schedule, two weeks had not been nearly enough time to learn the ropes.

"Are you sure you aren't going to miss Myrtle Beach too much?" Her aunt and uncle had been running the quaint fifteen-room Beach Lovers Inn for nearly forty years. When Ruth's husband, Kelly's uncle Jim, died unexpectedly of a ruptured aortic aneurysm the year before last, the business began to go adrift. At seventy-three years old, Aunt Ruth was finding it hard to manage the day to day operations without him.

"This place will always be in my heart. But it is time for a change." Feeling that it was time to move on, Ruth had put the inn on the market. The only potential buyer in the past year had been a hotel chain that had wanted nothing more than to knock the inn down and put up a steel and glass twenty-two story timeshare tower.

Aunt Ruth couldn't bear the idea and had refused the generous offer. The Beach Lovers Inn had been going downhill ever since.

Then Kelly had come along, fresh off her divorce from her second husband, Alan. Her ex-husband ran a big resort down in Hilton Head but had never let her help with the business operations. Now she was running the show at the Beach Lovers Inn—at least she would be starting tomorrow.

She may not have had an MBA like dear old Alan, but she had common sense and initiative, that's all it took to be successful—not a piece of paper.

After all, she and Alan had had a piece of paper—a marriage certificate—and their marriage had been anything but successful, although she had stuck it out for seven long years until she finally gave into the idea that Alan would always be more married to his work than he ever had been to her.

The choice to end the marriage had been a mutual decision, although the look on Alan's face when they had reached that mutual conclusion clearly showed relief, like the face of a weary general at the end of a long, drawn-out military campaign.

Kelly had initially resisted divorce despite knowing their separation was for the best. She had been married once before, however briefly. Theirs had been a whirlwind courtship followed by a hasty marriage and an equally speedy but reasonably amicable divorce.

Fresh out of college then, Kelly had met Tommy Johnson, a professional surfer—at least that had been his goal in life. The pair had first crossed paths at the University of South Carolina in Columbia. She had been majoring in advertising. Tommy had been majoring in athletic training with a minor in sport and entertainment management. They shared a course in media planning.

Tommy, all tan and teeth and oozing Southern charm, asked her out to lunch where they shared a pitcher of beer and a main course of deep dish pizza. Before long, they were spending all their free time together. Not long after, Tommy dropped out of college to join the pro surfing circuit while Kelly remained behind to complete her degree.

On one of his infrequent returns to Columbia, Tommy suggested they marry. Kelly had been young, impressionable and filled with optimism. Swept off her feet by Tommy's rugged outdoor looks and laid back attitude, Kelly said yes to his proposal. They were married at the Chapel Of The Beach in Daytona Beach in the middle of the *Surfari Surfing Competition*.

Despite having spent more time on his surfboard than he had in their honeymoon bed, Tommy didn't even manage to place in the competition. Through love-struck eyes, Kelly didn't see what the judges saw: Tommy was not a very good surfer.

The honeymoon, such as it was, hadn't lasted long. Tommy's *work* demanded plenty of travel. She mostly heard from her husband by phone, text or email when he wanted her to send him money, mostly to such locations as Bondi Beach, Playa Grande and Huntington

Beach.

Meanwhile, she had completed her BA degree and was stuck in a cubicle drafting ads for a small advertising firm in an office park on the outskirts of Columbia. Kelly quickly realized that Tommy was more of a sea sponge than a surfer, expecting her to work long hours while he hit the waves and hit on the ubiquitous beach bunnies.

She divorced him during his month-long surfing adventure in the south of Spain. She hadn't seen or heard from him since. Theirs had been a whirlwind courtship and a relatively pain-free divorce.

Lesson learned. Or so she thought. Vowing not to make the same mistake she had made with Tommy, Kelly took her time, dating a seemingly endless line of suitors until she met Alan on a blind date set up by her then best friend from her college days.

Alan Green looked good on paper. He looked good in person too. Thick dark hair, deep blue eyes and pale skin. He was everything that Tommy wasn't, including employed. All points in his favor.

Unfortunately, once Alan had what he wanted—a wife to bring to parties at the club—he paid her no attention. When she suggested she put her advertising expertise to use in helping run her husband's two hundred unit vacation property with eight clay tennis courts, a day spa and a championship golf course, he nipped the idea in the bud. Alan believed she would best serve them both by maintaining the home front.

So after seven years of loveless living, marriage number two ended, not with a bang and with barely a whimper.

Kelly had taken her small divorce settlement and,

with the help of a large bank loan, bought the inn. She wanted no help from Alan, although he had offered to come up and lend his expertise. At the time, it seemed like the perfect way for her to move forward with her life and she would be helping out Aunt Ruth at the same time.

Now she was beginning to wonder if she had been hasty in her decision to prove to herself, her exes and the world that she had what it took to run her own business.

As for marriage, she had vowed: Never Again.

Aunt Ruth yawned as if she'd been reading Kelly's mind and reliving her memories with her.

"Why don't you go on to bed and get some rest?" Kelly suggested once more. "It's after nine. I'll finish up here."

Kelly adored the vintage kitchen with its teal appliances and cabinets, butcher block counters and checkerboard floor. She was glad her aunt had retained its old-fashioned charm over the long years.

"I suppose," Ruth sighed. She pushed off from the table and rubbed the small of her back. Crossing to the doorway to the dining room, she called out, "Goodnight, Harry."

Harry Leyland looked up from his second helping of tofu loaf. He had come in to dinner late and was the last diner to remain. "Goodnight, Mrs. Evans. Will I see you in the morning before you go?"

"Absolutely." Aunt Ruth waved to the young man, pecked Kelly's left cheek and exited to the courtyard.

"That's one sweet old lady." Harry Leland dabbed his chin with a cloth napkin. Aunt Ruth insisted on using real linens instead of paper.

"That she is. Are you about done?" Kelly eyed the sliver of tofu resting on the edge of his plate.

"Yes, thanks." Catching her eye, he added, "That's for Sharky."

"Good idea." Kelly smiled and picked up the plate. "I'll take it to him." Sharky was the young Chartreux cat who had adopted the inn some months back, according to her aunt. Ruth said she had tried to bring him indoors but the cat was having none of it.

While he didn't mind the occasional foray indoors, the outdoors belonged to Sharky. The same way the Beach Lovers Inn did. Sharky treated the courtyard as his private domain and considered the beach his kingdom.

"Is the pie gone?" Harry Leland asked with hope-filled eyes.

As much as Kelly wanted to say yes and move the odd fellow along so she could finish cleaning up, she said, "I saved a piece. I'll bring it to you after I feed Sharky, Mr. Leland." She eyed the food scrap skeptically. "Are you certain he's going to eat this? It's tofu, not tuna."

"Definitely." Harry Leland licked his chops.

Kelly skeptically carried the scrap of tofu loaf to the door leading out to the courtyard. "Here, Sharky. I've got something for you!"

Kelly heard an excited mewl. A moment later, the beautiful gray cat came jogging toward her from behind the stairs. "I've got a nice treat for you. Auntie's homemade tofu loaf."

Ruth was always catering to everyone's needs, even when those needs included fare such as tofu for Mr. Leland whom she had learned was a strict vegetarian.

Kelly set the meatless treat in the first of the stainless steel dishes at the door. The second dish held fresh water.

Sharky took a tentative sniff—who could blame him? Then, to her great surprise, ate while she stroked the silky fur along his back.

The blue-gray cat was pleasant and placid and spent much of his days sunbathing in the courtyard. Aunt Ruth had read up on the history of the Chartreux a few days after the cat had taken up residency. Ruth had explained to Kelly that the breed was thought to have originated in Persia and been brought to France by knights returning from the Crusades.

Kelly believed it. Sharky had the attitude of a returned and very much retired ex-Crusader himself.

With the treat safely ensconced in his belly, Sharky resumed his nightly prowl. Kelly returned to the kitchen, washed her hands and took Harry his dessert.

While Harry Leland polished off his sweet potato pie, Kelly cleared the last of the tables. After licking his fork clean, Harry picked up his plate and glass. "I'll take these to the kitchen."

"You don't have to bother. I'll do it." Kelly hooked a damp cloth over her apron tie. "You are a guest."

Despite the dim yellow lighting of the lone chandelier, Harry seemed to color. His skin took on a jaundiced appearance. "I don't mind." He took his things to the kitchen.

"That is one odd bird." Kelly moved to the last dining table and began wiping her rag in lazy circles. She heard voices and laughter coming from the pool patio and peeked outside. The reunion crowd had gotten the party started.

She hoped they wouldn't party too late. Every little

sound was amplified as it bounced off the stucco walls and concrete deck. There were other guests to consider. Plus, Aunt Ruth was going to need a good night's rest before her long travel day tomorrow.

Making sure that the insulated stainless steel cold and hot water urns were filled, Kelly locked the doors to the kitchen and dining room. Only staff had access to certain areas after hours.

The small foyer, although locked as well, could be accessed with any guest key. Aunt Ruth liked to keep the foyer available twenty-four hours a day for her guests. Instant coffee, teabags, an assortment of sweeteners and, as often as not, a baked good or candy were regularly left out on the large serving platter. Guests could freely help themselves.

Tonight, there were stacks of fresh-baked oatmeal raisin cookies. She lifted the glass lid and took a whiff.

She also took two cookies.

Waist-high bookcases stood on the opposite wall, built by her late uncle. This was the inn's lending library for guests. Kelly scanned the titles and opted for *David Copperfield*. There was also a rack filled with DVDs but she was in a mood to read.

Climbing the stairs to her second floor room, Kelly waved to George Easterling, a part-time employee of the inn. George had been one of Jim and Ruth's first employees. Kelly used to visit the inn as a child and couldn't remember a time when George wasn't puttering around the property, tool in hand.

Recently, he had been putting in extra hours to assist with the inn's upcoming transition and the scheduled reunion preparations. At the moment, he was gamely trying to slide a heavy outdoor fire pit from nearer the storage shed at the rear of the property to the swimming pool at the request of one of the guests.

Kelly was about to run down and help when, mercifully, two of the male guests jumped from their seats, lowered their drinks and offered to assist.

Up in her room, Kelly tossed her book on the bed nearest the window. She washed up and exchanged her jeans and ocean blue Beach Lovers Inn polo shirt for a pair of light cotton pajamas. Taking out her contact lenses, she studied her reflection in the patinated mirror of the medicine chest.

Kelly saw a twice married, twice divorced woman of forty-one going on fifty. She had cut her hair after the divorce. But that was six months ago and now her brown hair was creeping back down to her shoulders.

The gray was back too. But it wouldn't be for long. She tugged at a silvery strand. "Tomorrow, you go." She had bought a self-coloring kit at the drugstore. She was going for *bronde*, a nice beachy compromise between her natural brunette and the all-out beach blonde that she didn't think she could pull off.

Settling in her queen-sized bed, Kelly picked up her novel and read to the accompanying clicking of the ceiling fan blades fighting their way through the warm, humid air. She wasn't generally a fan of air conditioning but, if she hadn't been so tired, she would have gotten up, shut the windows and switched on the wall unit for relief.

A dog barked somewhere far off, another answered, closer. A light breeze off the Atlantic susurrated through the palm trees. Somewhere out there, she imagined Sharky prowling his kingdom.

Kelly fell asleep in the middle of reading about David

Copperfield's fall into disgrace, with the bedside light glowing and the heavy book open on her chest.

Kelly slept fitfully, partly due to the heat and humidity, partly due to the enormity of the path she saw ahead of her.

She woke with a start. Sitting up quickly, half-forgetting where she was for a moment, the thick novel hit the floor. "Oh!"

The bedsheets were damp.

Bending to retrieve the book, Kelly heard a scream, followed by quick steps and urgent voices. A glance at the alarm clock told her that it was just past midnight.

Whatever it was, it couldn't be good.

Kelly threw her legs over the side of the bed and ran to the bathroom. She kept a knee-length bathrobe on a metal hook behind the door. She pushed her arms through the terry cloth sleeves and threw open her front door, stepping out on the balcony.

"What's going on?" Kelly demanded, hurrying along the walkway, pushing sleep-sculpted hair from her eyes. "What is it?"

The Beach Lovers Inn consisted of a U-shaped two-story building with the open end facing the Atlantic Ocean. The bottom of the U was broken at ground level by the eight-foot wide breezeway separating the northside wing from the southside. Rooms occupied both floors. Except for the bottom floor northside, there were four guest rooms on each floor of each wing, for a total of fifteen.

The northside also contained the first-floor kitchen and breakfast slash dining room, which was why there were only three guest rooms in that wing. The lobby and connecting office was on the ground floor on the southside. A small garage was also located on that side of the inn.

The hotel's architect had rightly chosen that no guest facilities be located in the front. Beach Lovers Inn sat along North Ocean Boulevard, one of Myrtle Beach's busiest roads. Much better to look at the ocean than the passing traffic.

The only thing Kelly might have changed about that inn was to have the kitchen and dining room beach-side, creating a restaurant with a view not only for the benefit of the guests but as a way of drawing in more dining traffic from non-guests.

The owner's quarters, Aunt Ruth's residence, was on the second floor, street side, in the north wing. She and Uncle Jim had kept the best rooms for the paying guests.

Aunt Ruth was not in her room now though. Kelly blew out a sharp breath as if she'd been punched in the gut by the heavyweight champion of the world as she leaned over the railing and peered down.

A small, tense group was huddled around her aunt who was lying in a heap at the bottom of the steps of the opposite stairway.

2

"There's been an accident!" a man's voice called up to her.

Kelly's frozen limbs snapped loose. She flew down the steps, running across the courtyard and jerking to a halt. "Auntie!"

Several people hovered over Ruth Evans where she lay in a puddle of arms and legs and blood. Her purple robe looked black in the low light cast by the few landscape lights that were in the garden beds scattered around the courtyard.

Aunt Ruth's blue-gray eyes were mere slits. Her left arm was twisted behind her and her long robe was pulled up to her waist. She wore white cotton pajamas underneath the robe. Her right knee was bent and her left leg, showing signs of heavy scraping was angled out. Her breath was shallow but at least she was still breathing.

"It looks like your aunt fell," suggested Dr. Barron. He knelt beside her and tilted his eyes towards the exterior stairway.

Kelly sank to her knees. "Auntie," she whispered, resting her fingers lightly on Ruth's right hand. "It's okay. Hang on." Kelly looked up wildly. "Somebody call for help!"

"Already done," Dr. Barron said calmly. He laid a hand

on Kelly's trembling shoulder. "The ambulance should be here any minute."

"Help me." Kelly gingerly took her aunt's arm.

Dr. Barron held her back. "I don't think we should move her."

"Right." Kelly's jaw tightened. "What happened? What is she doing out here?"

"She probably came downstairs to get something from the kitchen or the office," suggested Mrs. Barron, hovering over Ruth.

Kelly rearranged Aunt Ruth's robe around her. Her aunt deserved some dignity. "Why would she do that? She has a kitchenette in her apartment. And what could she possibly want from the office at this hour?"

Mrs. Barron shrugged. "I do hope she will be all right. What do you think, Charlie?"

"Let's hope for the best," said her husband, gently probing Ruth's injuries.

"I couldn't sleep and was watching the television," said a tall, thin man with red hair. Kelly thought his name was Irwin Brunner. "I heard the..." His tongue moved around the inside of his mouth as if rooting around for the proper word. "A thump," he said finally. "Felt it too."

Kelly shivered. She wished Irwin would shut up.

Mr. and Mrs. Dennis, one of the reunion couples, stood off to one side, leaning against an outdoor umbrella table. Mr. Dennis consoled his wife, wrapping his arms around her. Kelly heard their whispers but could not make out their words. Both wore long-sleeved pajamas and slippers.

George Easterling shuffled up from the street. Harsh red lights glowed behind him. The piercing sirens Kelly had been hearing suddenly cut off. "The ambulance is here." A large black flashlight dangled from the loop of his knee-length overalls. A thick shock of gray-black hair fell free as he raised his ball cap and wiped his brow with it.

"Thank you, George," whispered Kelly. "I thought you'd gone home."

"I stayed behind to clean up. I didn't want the place looking a mess first thing in the morning." He looked accusingly at the inn's guests. George liked things neat. "I'll check the utility closet." He loped off.

"Step aside, please." A determined man in a blue uniform strode into the courtyard.

George pulled a switch. More exterior lights blinked on, casting them all in a bath of light as if they were on a theater stage.

Two more men in blue rolled a yellow folding stretcher into the courtyard. They were followed by a firefighter in full gear and two police officers in navy blue uniforms.

From her vantage beside her fallen aunt, Kelly saw the ambulance and the nose of a firetruck. Several curious faces peered into the courtyard from the sidewalk. An officer kept them from coming closer.

The first EMS technician urged them all away from Ruth. Dropping to his knees, he felt Ruth's pulse at her wrist and neck. His lips formed a straight line.

"Is she—" Kelly knew it was useless to ask but she asked anyway. "Is she going to be okay?"

"She's in rough shape." The man stood. Despite his youthful appearance, Kelly thought she heard his knees crack. "Do you know her?"

"She's my aunt."

"Sorry." He motioned for the other EMS crew members and they pushed the cart beside her aunt.

A police officer approached Kelly. "I'm Officer Lowe. You say the woman is your aunt?" He had a strong chin and a deep tan.

Kelly nodded numbly.

"I'm very sorry." Officer Lowe faced the small crowd. "Does anybody know what happened?"

"She fell down the stairs," said Dr. Barron.

"Did you see her fall, sir?" The officer pulled a pad and paper from his front pocket.

"No, officer. But that seems most likely," Dr. Barron replied. He glanced at his wife who nodded. "We heard noises."

"Muffled noises," put in his wife, pressing her shoulder against her husband's.

Dr. Barron continued. "I came outside to have a look. That's when I spotted her."

"Probably tripped on her robe or just plain lost her balance," put in Mrs. Barron.

"I always told Ruth she should be more careful. She's not as young as she used to be." George had reappeared. He cleared his throat, resting his hand on the stair rail. "I always told her the stairs should be better lit too." The bannister rattled as he thumped it with his palm.

Kelly started to cry. A firefighter draped a wool blanket over her shoulders.

Officer Lowe pulled her aside. "I'm sorry, miss. There's really nothing more that can be done. We can talk about this in the morning."

He laid a tentative hand on her shoulder. "Why don't you go inside? Get some rest. I notice you are wearing pajamas. You are staying here, I take it?"

"I live here." The paramedics wheeled Aunt Ruth into the back of the ambulance. A moment later, they hopped in and sped off.

"I see. Would you like someone to escort you to your room?"

Kelly sniffed. He handed her a tissue and she blew her nose. "No, thanks. I need to get to the hospital. Where are they taking her?"

"Grand Strand."

"Where?"

"The Grand Strand Medical Center out on King's Highway." He pointed northwest. "It's only a couple miles or so. You can't miss it."

"Thank you." She looked at her rumpled robe and pajamas. "I'm going to change and head over." Kelly moved slowly, as if in a nightmare. More guests had gathered in the courtyard. Some gazed down from the second floor walkway. Others were watching out their windows.

Kelly hoped more than anything that this really was all a terrible nightmare and that she would wake in the morning, find Aunt Ruth happy and hale in the kitchen, drinking her treasured first cup of coffee of the day along with her single slice of buttered toast, and awaiting her trip to sunny Arizona.

Halfway up the steps, Kelly heard a honk and looked out toward the main street. A car, headlights glaring, idled outside. The driver stuck her head out the window. The police officer tried to wave her off.

Emergency vehicles blocked the small parking lot on the opposite side of the inn's property. Kelly called down to the first officer who had interviewed her. "That's the Rochesters," she explained. "They are guests here. I think the firetruck might be in the way."

The officer saluted and told her he would take care of it.

Hurriedly throwing on the clothes she had only removed hours before, Kelly grabbed her car key and drove anxiously to the medical center. The nurse occupying the desk in the emergency department told her that Ruth was still in surgery. Kelly paced for a while then curled up in a chair and dozed off.

Sometime later, a hand on her shoulder woke her. Kelly's eyes ticced up. It was the desk nurse. "Why don't you go home and get some rest?"

Kelly winced as she uncurled herself. "My aunt?"

The nurse smiled. "She's in recovery."

"Is she okay? Did she say anything?"

The nurse shook her head. "I'm afraid she hasn't regained consciousness yet."

Kelly rose, clutching her purse. "I need to see her."

The nurse patted her arm. "You need to go home and get some sleep. The doctor will call you in the morning."

"But—"

"I'm sorry, Mrs. Green. There's nothing you can do for your aunt now. She's getting the very best care."

"Thanks." Kelly shuffled wearily out to her car and drove the short distance back to the inn. She parked in the lot and said a silent prayer for Ruth as she mounted the stairs.

At the top of the steps, Kelly paused briefly then headed to her room. She'd left the door wide open. Light spilled out. Winged denizens of the night rushed in.

"Psst."

Kelly froze.

"Psst."

She turned. Harry Leland stood at the door to his

room, barefoot and bare chested. Even from a distance, it wasn't a pretty sight. Harry was average height, average weight and average looks.

If he'd ever gone to a gym in his life, it had to be because he'd punched a wrong address into a GPS.

Harry's hair was thick and brown. It didn't look like he owned a comb or a brush. His teeth were slightly too large, she thought, or maybe his chin was slightly too small.

His above-the-knee pajama bottoms featured tuxedoed kittens. His skinny legs featured knobby knees.

Good grief.

"What do you want, Mr. Leland?"

He scratched the top of his head. "What happened down there?"

"There's been an accident." Kelly really wasn't in the mood to say more.

"It was Mrs. Evans, wasn't it?" Harry moved closer to the railing. He had the room at the end of the building with an unspoiled view of the ocean. Being on the second floor and oceanfront, this was one of the most expensive and sought after rooms at the inn.

"Y-yes, it was."

A half-wall of decorative square concrete blocks ran along the edge of the walkway. Harry gripped his hands over the top of the wall and peered down. Kelly, though she would have rather avoided it, couldn't help but look too.

"Are you okay, Mrs. Green?"

"No, I am not okay. My aunt fell." Tears forced their way out the corners of her forest green eyes despite her best efforts to quell them. "She's in the hospital."

Harry padded closer on silent bare feet. Several

scraggly hair follicles sprouted along the sides of a white concave sternum.

Harry squeezed Kelly's upper arms. "That's what I thought." His breath smelled of spearmint toothpaste. "But your aunt didn't fall, Mrs. Green."

"What?" Kelly stared at Mr. Leland through tear-blurred eyes.

"Oh, no. Your aunt was pushed."

3

"What are you talking about, Mr. Leland?" Kelly was tired, depressed and angry at the world. It wasn't fair. Aunt Ruth had so much to live for. She had planned to start her new life tomorrow. Why did something so terrible have to happen today?

Aunt Ruth had been up and down those stairs a hundred times. A thousand times.

"It's Harry."

"I've had all I can handle tonight. Whatever it is you have to say can wait until tomorrow." Kelly warned him with a look. "Goodnight, *Mr. Leland.*"

"But Mrs. Green—"

Kelly held her finger to her lips. "Better yet, don't say anything, Mr. Leland." She turned on her heel and marched to her room. "And put a shirt on," she muttered under her breath.

Kelly slammed the door behind her, leaving her alone with a roomful of mosquitoes, moths, something slick and black with too many legs that was crawling up the wall near the desk and a head filled with sorrows and bad memories.

She grabbed the book from the night table and hurled it at the bajillion-legged bug on the wall. She missed it by a mile, not that she had expected to hit it. In fact, she would have been mortified if she had. She preferred sending such critters off to nature rather than to their deaths.

Kelly threw herself into bed and turned violently to the right, smothering herself with a pillow. She willed herself to sleep but sleep didn't come. Harry Leland's words penetrated her thoughts. "Darn you, Leland."

Kelly kicked the covers off her ankles and cursed some more as she climbed out of bed and cinched her robe around her waist. She shoved her feet into an old pair of open-toed leather sandals tucked under the AC unit beneath the front window.

Carefully closing the hotel room door behind her lest she gain any further roommates—the room only had two beds for goodness's sake—she tiptoed down the hall.

The courtyard was quiet now. George had turned off most of the outdoor lights before retiring, leaving only the landscape lighting, the oceanside fairy lights attached to a low latticework fence, and the blurry glow of the pool light down at the deep end.

Reaching the end of the deserted corridor, Kelly pounded on the last door. The ocean was a vast sea of ink with stars along its edge. A light breeze sent her hair dancing against her cheekbones.

"Hello?" A sleepy voice called through the thick door.

"It's me, Mr. Leland. Kelly Green." She closed her eyes for a moment, breathing in the warm, salty air.

A light came on. Kelly heard the sound of the security hook being released.

Harry Leland opened the door and peered at her curiously. He held a pair of reading glasses in his left hand. "Yes?"

A small smile formed on her lips. Young Mr. Leland

had taken her advice and put on a shirt. More dancing tuxedoed kittens. Still, it was an improvement.

"My aunt wasn't pushed, Mr. Leland. That would be attempted murder."

"She didn't exactly throw herself down the stairs, did she?"

"No. She *fell* down the stairs." Kelly watched him fold and unfold the thick black glasses.

Leland snorted. "If you are so sure of that, why are you here knocking on my door?"

What she wanted to say was *Because you are driving me crazy and I'm trying to get to sleep and deal with this tragedy*. Instead, what she said was, "Because you're a guest. I wanted to reassure you." She turned and watched the slow moving dark ocean. "We don't have murders at the Beach Lovers Inn."

"Oh, but you do. Not for the first time." Harry Leland stepped away from the door and pushed it open wide. "Come in, won't you, Mrs. Green?"

Kelly looked warily inside. "In the first place, I'm not Mrs. Green. I mean, I am—I was—but I'm not anymore. We're divorced." Why was she blathering? And to Harry Leland?

"Sorry." His gaunt cheeks reddened.

"Don't be. What about you? Is there a Mrs. Leland?"

"Only my mother. I never married."

Kelly didn't know why she had even asked. She was only being polite. It was either that or ask what sign of the zodiac he was born under, which she was equally disinterested in.

"I'm a Scorpio. We're shrewd and have powerful reasoning skills."

"What?" She narrowed her eyes as she entered the

room, lit only by the desk lamp. "How did you know...? Never mind. Tell me about yourself, Mr. Leland." Listening to him talk might distract her from more unpleasant thoughts.

One look inside Leland's hotel room and Kelly could see why he wasn't married. The king-sized bed, the dresser and carpets were littered with books, some open, some stacked six or seven high. Typed and scribbled sheets of paper lay everywhere. Others sat balled up in the vicinity of the trash can. "Were you burgled?"

"Huh?" There was a click as Harry Leland closed the door behind them.

"Has housekeeping been forgetting your room? Because if they have, I'll have a word with them in the morning."

"No, the room is fine."

"Are you sure?" The inn could ill-afford him posting a negative review on social media.

"Yes." Harry Leland took a swig of water from a plastic cup.

Atop the narrow desk beneath the window facing the ocean sat an open silver laptop computer. A legal pad lay to the right, with a Beach Lovers Inn pen beside it.

The corner of Kelly's mouth edged down. "You do know that housekeeping is included in the cost of the room, right?"

Harry Leland sat gingerly on the edge of his bed. "Won't you have a seat, Mrs., er, Miss..."

"Call me Kelly."

He squinted at her from behind thick glasses. "And *please* call me Harry."

Kelly opted to stand beside the desk. More typed

pages were strewn about the surface. "All this talk about murder, Harry. Are you a cop?"

"Nope."

"Lawyer?"

"No again." Lines of confusion deepened on Leland's dome-like forehead.

"So what are you then?"

"I'm a writer." Harry was puzzled. "You said you knew."

"Yes. But what I mean is, what do you do to earn a living?"

"I write crime novels." He scratched the back of his hand. "Traditional mysteries, thrillers. I'm trying my hand at a caper."

Unless Harry Leland's two novels had been block-busters—and from what she had learned on the internet, they had not—something about Leland was not adding up. The money this room alone was costing definitely was not adding up.

"Great." Kelly decided to save that puzzle for another time. "Well, Harry," she tilted the screen of the laptop for a closer look. "As a writer, you must have quite a vivid imagination."

"I'm not imagining that somebody tried to murder Mrs. Evans, if that's what you are implying."

Kelly pushed her fists into her temples. "Would you please stop saying that?"

"Sorry."

"I know. It's hard enough that Aunt Ruth is seriously hurt. Do you have to start imagining something more nefarious than an accident?"

Harry stood and went to the window overlooking the walkway. "I was working at my desk. I heard voices."

"What kind of voices?"

Harry shrugged without looking back. "I dunno. Just voices. I thought I heard your aunt." He wriggled his finger inside his right ear. "I went back to work." Now he turned to face her. Anguish was written there. "That's when I thought I heard a scream."

Kelly gulped. "A scream?"

"A short, sharp scream."

Kelly paced the floor. "If you heard this scream and were so sure somebody was about to be murdered, why didn't you open your door and see what was happening? Why is it that you remained in your room? You weren't with the others at the bottom of the stairs."

A look of sadness worked its way across his face and into his eyes. "I'm sorry. I-I was writing. It was an important scene. It could have been a TV. Besides, the noises stopped. How was I to know that Mrs. Evans was being attacked?"

She goggled at him.

"Maybe your aunt would be okay if only I'd checked to see what was happening." His face fell.

Kelly couldn't help but take pity on him. "Look, it's not your fault, Harry. Auntie slipped on the dark stairs, maybe she tripped on her robe like George suggested—I don't know." She grabbed him by the shoulders. "What I do know is that it was an accident. A terrible, terrible accident."

What she didn't understand and was not about to mention to Harry for fear of what preposterous theories he might propose was: What was Aunt Ruth doing coming down the opposite stairs in the middle of the night?

Even if she had wanted something from the kitchen, why not take the stairs in the north wing, closest to her apartment? Why walk all the way around to the south wing?

4

The next day, Kelly was dressed and downstairs early, five-thirty to be precise. She was running on only a couple hours of sleep but she was responsible for seeing that breakfast was set up in the dining room for the guests. Despite her aunt's accident, people had to eat. Breakfast ran from six to nine.

Plus, she was determined to keep as busy as possible. If she didn't, she would go crazy with worry for her aunt's health.

Despite the early hour, before heading downstairs and opening up, the first thing she did was telephone the hospital to check on Ruth. There had been no change. Ruth remained in critical care and was still unconscious.

She next called her father to tell him the news of his sister's accident. At the moment, he was staying on Siesta Key, off the west coast of Florida, near Sarasota. He was an early riser and this morning she'd caught him, so he said, with a fishing pole in hand.

While his permanent home was five acres in a rural western portion of South Carolina, Ben Walsh was in travel mode. A retired plumber with no more leaks to fix and his wife deceased, he had purchased a secondhand motorhome and was touring the southeast.

Her father had been devastated to learn of the accident. "How's Ruth doing? When will she be released from the hospital?" he bellowed, assuming that, because they were nearly a thousand miles apart, he had to shout to be heard.

"I'm not sure yet. A few days, a week..." replied Kelly from the inn's kitchen. "When I find out, I'll let you know."

"Fine. Have you phoned Angie?" Angie was Ben and Ruth's sister.

"Not yet. There's a time difference."

"Gotcha. Want me to call her, kiddo?"

"Thanks but I can handle it."

"What about Sam?"

"I'll drop him a note." Kelly's brother was doing the Thoreau thing, living off the grid in the Alaska wilderness.

"Okay." Her father promised to remain in touch and would head north as soon as possible to lend a hand.

After ringing off, Kelly laid out a breakfast spread for her guests. She then grabbed the spare key to the lobby from the wall of the kitchen and opened up the office. Her aunt's set of keys was probably upstairs in her apartment.

Then Kelly remembered she needed to call Angie, and give her the bad news. But with the time difference between South Carolina and Arizona, that call would have to wait a bit longer yet.

Through the window, Kelly noticed that somebody, probably George, had placed a collapsible yellow caution sign at the bottom of the stairs, for what it was worth now.

Kelly crossed the breezeway to the dining room as the first breakfast guests trickled in. Harry was among them.

Dressed in jeans and a rumpled heather gray tee shirt for a change, he was seated at the first table along with the Barrons and a pair of newcomers.

"She fell down the stairs," pronounced Dr. Barron. He had a head of thinning, wispy brown hair. His wife compensated for his lack of hair with a full head of shoulder-length red locks that framed her round face.

Mrs. Barron nodded her support for the theory. Both Barrons wore khaki shorts and electric yellow *Boardwalk Off the Beach* tee shirts. This was a popular shopping mecca. A light, floral scent emanated from Mrs. Barron.

"Fell or was pushed?" asked Harry.

"What's wrong with you?" Kelly turned on him from the sideboard where she had been cutting up more grapefruit and oranges. "We talked about this Harry. How could you think that? Let alone say it aloud?" She dropped the fruit slices in a bowl.

"Who would want to harm her? Auntie was the quintessential sweet little old lady."

"Trust me," Harry retorted, waving his fork at her. "Sweet little old ladies are often the first to go."

Kelly opened her mouth then shut it again. There was really no point replying at all. She turned and headed for the kitchen.

"Hey, where are you going? We need to talk about this."

"I have work to do, Harry."

Slamming pots and pans in the kitchen, Kelly made up her mind: paying guest or not, Harry Leland had to go. He was disturbing the guests and, more importantly, he was disturbing her.

Kelly turned at the sound of a knock. The newcomer was tapping his knuckles on the doorframe. "Yes?" She managed to smile. "Can I help you?"

"I'm Dr. Nelson. My wife and I have a reservation. I know it's early but I was hoping we could check in." He tugged at the collar of a mauve golf shirt. "Our flight was delayed."

"Dr. Nelson? When you didn't show up yesterday we thought you had cancelled." The doctor was of average build with a long angular face and close-set eyes.

The man seemed genuinely confused. "Cancelled? Why would we cancel? No, merely coming in a day later. We've been coming to the Beach Lovers Inn for many, many years."

He smiled broadly. "We wouldn't miss the annual trip for anything. Especially this year. A chance to see old friends and colleagues."

The Nelsons were part of the group.

"Of course. Let me see what I can do." Kelly dried her hands on her apron front. She untied the apron and hung it over the handle of the stove.

"I don't know what happened," Kelly said as they walked through the dining room, across the breezeway and into the lobby. Dr. Nelson held the door open for her. "I suppose Auntie was confused." Her aunt had admitted that her memory was slipping. Kelly had noticed small signs herself—a forgotten word, a misplaced pair of shears, not remembering the day of the week.

"Auntie?" He followed her to the counter.

Kelly pulled out the big leather-bound ledger. "My aunt Ruth."

"Ah, yes. She is a lovely woman. I was so sorry to hear about the accident."

Kelly pushed her knuckles into the corners of her eyes to quell the mounting tears. "Thank you."

She handed Dr. Nelson a pen and slid the ledger across. "You're in luck. Room 102 is available." It was far from the best room in the inn, close to the street and with no view to speak of, but it had been the Nelsons' room of choice all these years. Who was she to argue?

To each their own. And an occupied room was a paid for room.

"You said *we*. Was that your wife I noticed earlier in the dining room? Curly brown hair, blue eyes?"

"You're very observant. Yes. Jean is taking a stroll on the beach," Dr. Nelson explained. "I'm Ted. The sand and the seagulls are more Jean's thing than mine."

Kelly ran his credit card and checked him in. "Do you need some help with your bags?"

"No, thanks. The car is around the corner. And we travel light. At least, I do," he added with a friendly chuckle on his way out the door.

Drew Schiffer rumbled past with the housekeeping cart and parked it in the breezeway. Drew was the inn's head housekeeper. She and a couple of part-timers handled the rooms. "Good morning, Kelly."

"Hi, Drew. I just checked in the Nelsons. It looks like you and your crew will have a pretty full house for the next few days."

Drew was a very pretty brunette of thirty or so who enjoyed surfing and tanning in her spare time—despite the multitude of warnings about sharks and skin cancer.

"No problem. I thought I recognized him." Drew had been with the inn for several years. She squeezed the hem of her smock in her hands. "I wanted to tell you how sorry I was to hear about your aunt. We all were."

"Thanks." Kelly noticed tiny teardrops forming in the corners of Drew's brown eyes. It was like watching a bar of milk chocolate melt in the hot summer sun.

"Here's the checkout list." She handed Drew a small paper form showing that three guests would be leaving that day and two more checking in.

The housekeeper bobbed her chin and sniffled. "Got it. I'd better get to work. The patio needs clearing and the rooms don't clean themselves."

"George will help with the patio."

"Right." Drew stopped in the open door. "I almost forgot. I wanted to mention that the lock on the laundry room door is busted again."

Kelly sighed. "Thanks. I'll see it gets fixed. In fact, I'll ask George to install a padlock on the outside."

"Good idea. I wouldn't wait too long," Drew suggested. "I found a nest of bath towels on the floor when I came in this morning."

"A nest?"

"Yeah, you know, like maybe a vagrant made a bed and spent the night."

Kelly tapped her fingers on the counter. "Maybe I'll go take a look."

"You can if you want to," Drew replied. "But the girls already straightened the area up. The towels are getting a strong wash as we speak."

"Great." The phone rang and Kelly moved to answer it. "Hello, Beach Lovers Inn." It was a Georgia man inquiring about a room for the following week.

She wriggled her fingers at the Barrons in greeting as they entered the lobby.

Drew held the door open for them. "Welcome back."

Dr. Barron appeared confused. His wife hauled him over to the brochure rack. "I'm in the mood for some shopping," she said, snatching up brochures on several of the local outlet malls.

"When aren't you?" her husband replied good-naturedly. "How about if you shop and I sleep?"

"How about if you come along and carry my bags?" quipped his wife.

"Okay, okay. I gave it a shot." Charlie Barron winked at Kelly. "Was that Ted Nelson I saw checking in?"

"Yes," Kelly answered, replacing the phone in its cradle. The Barrons made a cute couple. "Dr. Nelson and his wife just checked in. It looks like you'll have a wonderful reunion." The phone rang once more. "Thank you for choosing the Beach Lovers Inn to host it," Kelly added before picking up the receiver.

"It wasn't my idea," Charlie Barron replied as his wife led him away by the hand. "All I wanted was a little vacation."

After dealing with the phones and making sure that breakfast was running smoothly, Kelly crossed the courtyard and climbed the stairs to the second floor of the southside wing. The laundry room was located in the southwest corner abutting North Ocean Boulevard.

A white industrial-sized washer and dryer stood on the right. Tall shelves rose to the left and held clean towels, linens, soaps, shampoos, tissue and toilet paper and anything else the housekeeping staff might require. A four-foot long by three-foot wide stainless steel table in the center of the room served as a workstation for the staff who used it mostly for folding fresh towels.

It wasn't a small room but with everything inside it, there wasn't a lot of room to move around. The laundry room was warm and humid with a slight floral smell that Kelly knew was due to the soap.

Kelly studied the worn yellow and black linoleum floor then scanned the shelves. Drew was right. There was nothing to see. Nothing amiss.

Thank goodness. The price of vandalism could be steep. The inn operated on a tight budget as it was.

Turning toward the open door, something shiny caught her eye. She bent down for a closer look. A small crumpled piece of cellophane wrapper lay between the wall and the leg of the standing shelf nearest the door.

She squeezed her fingers into the tight space and retrieved it. There was a whitish trace of something on the inside. She held it to her nose and found it sweetish.

Kelly shoved it in her pants pocket and went to clear up the remains of breakfast.

5

Two days passed and Kelly's life took on a new rhythm. Aunt Ruth remained in serious condition, in and out of consciousness, but stable. Kelly visited her every day and spent an hour talking quietly to her, filling her in on the action at the inn.

The Myrtle Beach police had searched the inn and grounds the day after Ruth's accident and found nothing suspicious. Kelly's aunt had had an unfortunate accident, nothing more—despite a certain someone's persistence in trying to make out like it had been something more nefarious.

At Kelly's instance, George installed some extra lighting at the top and bottom of each stairway. She had an inn filled with paying guests and didn't want to see anybody else getting hurt.

When she found time, she vowed to start a checklist of projects: things that needed updating, repair or replacing. She had had no idea of the enormity of work involved in running a hotel, even one as small as the Beach Lovers Inn.

Now back from her daily hospital visit, Kelly was furiously sweeping the sidewalk in front of the inn when a taxi pulled up honking its horn. Her father sat hunched in the rear of the cab. She set the broom against a concrete bench and hurried to the curb. She pulled open the taxi door. "Dad!"

Ben Walsh, several days' growth on his face and Florida Marlins ball cap on his head, grinned at his daughter. "I told you I'd be here quick."

"I see that." Kelly stepped aside as her father struggled out of the cramped quarters of the compact taxi. A cast ran up his left leg, from ankle to knee. "What happened to you?"

"This?" Ben grabbed a rubber-tipped aluminum crutch from the backseat and balanced himself on the sidewalk. The cab driver popped the trunk and pulled out two black hardshell suitcases. "A little accident. It's nothing really. It happened a couple of weeks ago."

"A couple of weeks ago?" Kelly gaped. "Why didn't you call me?"

"I didn't want you to worry. I knew you'd have your hands full with this place. Besides," he added, brushing away her concerns, "I was in and out of the operating room in no time."

Horrified, she grabbed his free arm. "Come on. Let me get you inside, Dad."

"Wait, let me get a look. It's been a long time since I've seen the old place." Her father stood a tad under six foot. He'd lost weight since Mom wasn't around to cook for him, subsisting mostly now on instant meals and sandwiches.

Ben Walsh's sharp blue eyes looked up appraisingly. "It's holding up nice. I always thought this property was a beauty."

Kelly smiled. "It is, isn't it?" She was so glad Aunt Ruth had not allowed the landmark pink stucco inn to be torn down and replaced with something more pedestrian and imposing.

Constructed in 1955, the Beach Lovers Inn had been conceived during the height of what one author had termed the Populuxe period of design. The word *populuxe*, Aunt Ruth had explained, was a synthesis of the words populism and luxury.

It made sense.

The Fifties had been an era of prosperity, opulence and fun; with cotton-candy colors, cars with tailfins that tapered to infinity and an optimism not to be diminished by the specter of atomic war. A time when every American thought that every appliance could be operated with the push of a button and every problem solved that very same way. Vacuum cleaners were designed to look like race cars and kitchens were filled with sleek, high-tech appliances, just like the kitchen of the Beach Lovers Inn.

The façade of the inn emulated that time period, too, as did the guest rooms. Kelly loved every inch of the place.

It was like living in a bit of a time warp.

And now it was hers.

"You'll be sharing a room with me, Dad."

"No problem. It will be like old times. You slept in that crib in our room for better than a year."

"Very old," Kelly said.

She led her father out to the pool patio and seated him under the shade of a six-foot blue umbrella that fluttered in the light breeze coming over the ocean and rising over the wax myrtle and bayberry-covered dunes. She tapped her fingernail against the cast. "Let's hear it, Dad."

"Can't a man get a drink first?"

"Fine." Kelly went to the kitchen and returned with

two cans of beer. Glass bottles were frowned upon around the swimming pool.

"To Ruth's recovery." He tapped the side of his can with his daughter's.

They both drank.

"I bought a motorcycle."

Kelly turned up her nose. "A motorcycle? Really, Dad? What happened to the motorhome?"

"I traded it in for the Indian. I always wanted a bike. Your mom always forbid me. She told me it wasn't safe. Can you believe that?"

"You can ask that with a straight face when you're sitting here with a broken leg?"

"This?" He extended his leg. "It's nothing. I'll be good as new in another couple of weeks."

"I hope you got rid of the motorcycle, Dad." One tragic accident was enough. She didn't need another one in the family.

"Get rid of the motorcycle? No. I'm having it shipped up here. I hope you don't mind. She needs a little work." Her father explained how he'd slipped in a patch of sand near the beach. The big motorcycle had gone into a slide. When bike and rider came to a stop, his left leg was beneath the engine.

"Me and the Indian did a little *pas de dirt*, you might say." Ben chuckled at his little joke.

Kelly pressed the cold beer can to her chest and gawped. Her father could have been killed although he seemed to be in denial of the fact.

"See? No big deal." Ben chugged his beer. "By the way, what's all this about attempted murder?"

Kelly stiffened, her hands putting a death grip on the arms of her chair. "Attempted murder? What murder?"

"While you were gone to get the beer, some kid came by. Nice boy. He told me somebody tried to murder Ruth."

Kelly narrowed her eyes and craned her neck up at room 209. "There was no attempted murder, Dad. Aunt Ruth had an accident. I was here, remember? She fell down the stairs."

Kelly stood. "But if it's murder you want, stick around, there's about to be one."

6

Saturday night, the courtyard at the Beach Lovers Inn was buzzing with activity. As a goodwill gesture and to clear the gloomy pall that had arisen after her aunt's spill down the stairs, Kelly had decided that the inn would host a barbeque for all the guests.

Above the courtyard, Kelly and George had strung lines decorated with colorful pink, blue and orange paper hibiscus flowers and lanterns. Practically all the guests showed up.

Kelly glanced up at the sky. The weather was cooperating. The air was balmy and not too humid. The breeze was light and the stars twinkled as if on a director's cue.

The mouth-watering smells of flaming burgers, hot dogs and corn on the cob permeated the courtyard.

Kelly had hired a friend of Drew's to tend bar. Too late, she realized she should have hired a live band.

"How are you doing, Kelly?" Ben wrapped a heavy arm over his daughter's shoulder.

"Okay. I was just thinking that I should have hired a band."

"Yeah. That would have been a good idea." He patted her arm. "Next time. For now, how about if we use my phone?" He hung onto his daughter with one hand and fished his phone from his cargo shorts with the other.

"I've got a portable Bluetooth speaker up in our

room," he added to sweeten the deal. "It's in one of my suitcases." Father and daughter were now sharing a hotel room.

Kelly studied the phone dubiously. "What kind of music are we talking about?"

"The classics," said Ben. "The Stones, the Beatles, the Grateful Dead, the Guess Who." He scrolled through his song list.

"Any Ed Sheerhan?"

Her father looked confused.

"Adele?"

"Who?"

"Never mind. Sounds great."

Ben tapped his crutch against the ground. "I'll be right back, honey."

Kelly skirted past the swimming pool. A handful of youngsters thrashed about in the shallow end, banging a big red, white and blue beach ball between them. Several adults sat along the coping, plastic cups in hand, dangling their feet in the water.

George was manning the barbeque in the corner near the sand's edge. White smoke rose upward as he flipped a row of burgers.

Kelly got in line at the bar. She was paying for this to-do. She may as well get a drink or two out of it for herself. She waved to Drew. She had volunteered to waitress and was bearing a tray, piled high with crab cakes, prosecco grapes, melon bites and Caprese tomatoes stuffed with mozzarella, from table to table.

Irwin stood whispering to Vivian Rochester under a slender palm tree cloaked in shadow. The Rochesters, Vivian and Jill, were part of the reunion group booking.

The strains of *Love Potion #9* cut through the air. Ben

Walsh had set up his portable speaker on a low wall near the lobby and cranked up the volume. Thumping music washed over the crowd.

Kelly shook her head. She was going to have to tell him to turn it down a bit.

After she got her drink.

A sprinkle of laughter came from the crowd as couples began shagging. The shag, or Carolina Shag, was the official state dance. Despite its proponents and practitioners boasting that anyone could easily perform the six-count, eight-beat, up tempo dance, Kelly had never gotten the hang of it. The dance looked so easy when she watched others perform it, but the deceptively simple steps always tripped her up.

Ted Nelson started dancing with his wife, Jean. One hand gripping hers, the other his wine glass.

The line at the bar moved up. "One mojito, please," Kelly said.

"Why aren't you out on the dance floor?" the bartender asked as he handed Kelly her drink.

"Two left feet," she said, stuffing a dollar into his tip jar. She thanked him and squeezed through the crowd in search of her father.

A man barked out a laugh. This was followed by a loud splash.

"Excuse me. Excuse me." Kelly pushed her way to the pool's edge. One of her guests was treading water in the middle of the pool. "Dr. Barron! Are you all right?"

He laughed and slapped the surface of the water. "Yeah. A bit clumsy, that's all."

Everybody joined in. One of the kids in the pool batted the beach ball at him. Charlie Barron playfully returned the volley.

Desmond Dennis, one of his reunion buddies, extended his hand and pulled him out.

Charlie Barron's Hawaiian shirt and khaki shorts were soaked through. He squeezed his shirttails then shook himself.

Everybody around screamed as water sprayed over them and into their drinks.

"One too many drinks already, Charlie?" Ted Nelson joked, wiping droplets of pool water from his bare arms.

"Better watch where you step, Charlie," cautioned Mr. Dennis's wife, Bonnie. She hoisted a margarita to her lips.

"You had better get changed out of those clothes, dear." Mary Barron tugged at her husband's sopping wet shirt. "You'll catch your death."

"It's not that bad," Charlie grumbled, helping himself to his wife's glass of wine.

"Oh, no you don't." Mary snatched the plastic cup away. "You can drink all you want *after* you've changed."

Charlie pushed the sodden hair from his eyes. "Okay, okay." He rubbed his arms up and down. "I am getting chilly."

The crowd parted as Charlie waddled off to his room.

"I knew there would be trouble," a cool voice said from behind.

Kelly turned. "Hello, Mr. Leland." The troublesome guest was dressed in long dark trousers and a long-sleeved pale blue shirt. His only nod to the festive occasion was that he had unfastened the topmost button of his shirt.

It had to be eighty degrees outside. Why wasn't he sweating?

Jefferson Airplane was singing about white rabbits.

Kelly wished she could make herself small right then. And disappear. Better still, make Harry Leland disappear.

"What are you talking about?" Kelly said in response to Harry Leland's comment about trouble. "Dr. Barron slipped and fell in the pool. It's no big deal. He wasn't even hurt. In fact, he was a really good sport about it."

Harry Leland turned slowly in a circle then latched his disturbing dark eyes on her. "Can't you feel it?"

Kelly grinded her teeth then swallowed half her mojito in one gulp. "What you are feeling, Mr. Leland, is people having fun. This is a party. Relax. Have a drink," she admonished, noting his empty hands. "Eat some food. I ordered veggie burgers especially for you."

His eyes flickered toward George and the barbecue with momentary interest. But only momentary. "Yes, but can't you sense it? There's an air of danger."

"The only air I'm sensing at the moment is hot air, Mr. Leland." She pushed him aside. "Now, if you don't mind—"

The sound of rapid shots stilled the crowd. A moment later, a silver firework shot into the air from the other side of the dune near the beach. It exploded like a small star and was quickly followed by another.

"Fireworks!" several voices shouted with delight.

The partyers grabbed their drinks and moved quickly across the courtyard and up the sand path across the dunes. Kelly ran with them. Standing at the top of the dune, she watched as multicolored fireworks filled the sky with smoke and fire and multi-colored lights.

"This is beautiful," Drew said. "I didn't know you ordered fireworks, Kelly."

A dark figure near the ocean's edge scurried along the ground like a midnight crab.

"I didn't," Kelly answered.

"Oh." Drew shrugged. "Maybe they are really for one of the other hotels or beach houses."

Folks stood on the balconies of the nearby high rises and pointed admiringly at the fireworks display.

"Must be." Kelly stayed with the others. When the show was over, the figure on the beach gathered up his things and tossed them in the basket over the rear tire of a bicycle. He hopped on his bicycle, waved and pedalled off into the darkness.

Back in the courtyard, the music continued and the drinks flowed.

"Some fireworks, eh?" Ben Walsh remarked. He leaned on his crutch and scratched at his cast. "Darn thing drives me nuts sometimes."

"Maybe you'll think twice about fixing your motorcycle up and getting back on it."

Her father grinned. "Not a chance, dear."

"Has anyone seen Charlie?" Ted Nelson asked.

"I didn't see him on the beach," replied Desmond Dennis.

"How long can it take to dry off and change clothes?" Bonnie Dennis wanted to know.

"It's not like Charlie to miss a party." Jean Nelson was clutching her husband's elbow.

"Pity he missed the fireworks," replied Jill Rochester.

"I'll check on him," Mrs. Barron said. Charlie's wife set her wine cup down on the bar. "He's probably watching TV. Ever since retiring, the man is addicted to the news."

Harry Leland sat on a low stone wall at the edge of

the courtyard munching on a veggie burger.

Kelly sauntered over. "You didn't go see the fire-works?"

"I was hungry," Harry said. "I hadn't eaten all day."

That was true. She hadn't seen Leland at the break-fast buffet that morning, which was unusual. For a skinny guy, he normally sucked up food the way a Hoover sucked up dirt.

"Where's George?"

"I haven't seen him. I helped myself."

The booming beat of the Dave Clark Five's *Glad All Over* began echoing through the courtyard. Kelly never did tell her father to keep the noise down.

And now here came trouble.

Mildred McConaughey was five feet tall, pos-sibly three hundred pounds—definitely two-fifty—with buzz-cut black hair and black eyes that sliced through you like you were made of hot butter.

"Mrs. Green," Mildred McConaughey began, "this racket is wholly unacceptable!"

"Hello, Mrs. McConaughey. I'm sorry. I'll talk to my dad."

"Your dad?"

"He's over there." Kelly pointed over the animated heads and across the pool.

Mrs. McConaughey narrowed her eyes. "See that you do talk to him." She hitched up her dress, a purplish-blue muumuu that swirled in the breeze. Pearls the size of golf balls adorned her neck. "I have guests to con-sider."

Kelly apologized once more. "Would you care for a drink, Mrs. McConaughey?" The woman and her hus-band had owned the Golden Arms Hotel directly next-door for two decades. Mr. McConaughey had since gone on to his just rewards, as the widow liked to say.

The widow ran the Golden Arms like a warship and dominated the neighborhood the same way.

Kelly was more than a little scared of her.

Ben Walsh appeared. He smiled broadly. "Good evening. Great night for a party, isn't it?" "Ben Walsh." He held out his hand and Mrs. McConaughey was forced to be civil.

"Mildred McConaughey. I own the Golden Arms next door."

"You don't say?" Kelly's dad looked suitably impressed. "That's a great property. The pride of Myrtle Beach."

Mildred McConaughey mumbled a thanks and stuck a finger in her ear. "I can hardly hear. The music is rather loud."

"Yeah," Ben Walsh replied. "Great music, eh? The kind of songs we grew up with." Kelly thought her father was being generous. Surely, Mrs. McConaughey had preceded him to earth by a decade or so.

"The good stuff," Ben was saying. "Not like these kids are listening to."

"I suppose…" Mrs. McConaughey appeared off-balanced.

"I'd ask you to dance but…" Ben indicated his broken leg. "Buy you a drink instead?"

Mrs. McConaughey looked flustered for the first time since Kelly had met her. "Well, I suppose…just one." She clutched at her pearls and allowed Ben to escort her to the bar.

"Did I mention that purple is my favorite color," Kelly heard her father say as he ran his fingers lightly over

Mildred's sleeve.

"Thank you," mouthed Kelly.

Ben winked in reply.

"What a battle ax," Kelly remarked to Harry as he turned from the grill with another veggie burger piled high with pickles, lettuce and onion.

"Mrs. McC? I think she's very nice."

"You do?"

A spine-chilling scream cut through the happy sounds of revelry.

Mary Barron ran into the courtyard, bumping into Jill Rochester and spilling her drink down the front of her yellow sundress.

"It's my husband! Mary Barron screamed. "He's dead!"

7

"Get a hold of yourself." Kelly tossed the contents of her drink down in a southern bush honeysuckle and set her plastic cup on the ground. She grabbed Mrs. Barron's trembling hands. "Are you sure? Maybe he's only sleeping."

"No." Tears streaked down Mrs. Barron's sunburned cheeks. Her head shook. "Somebody has killed him. He's been murdered!" Her eyes flew wildly around the courtyard.

"Murdered?" Harry abandoned his half-eaten veggie burger. Wiping his greasy fingers on his trousers, he rose quickly like a dog responding to its owner's call.

The Dave Clark Five had finished their song.

Good because Kelly wasn't feeling glad anywhere, let alone all over. Although the Beach Boys, who had come on next, singing about their groovy surfin' safari seemed totally inappropriate to the occasion.

Kelly motioned for her father to cut the music. He excused himself to an agitated Mildred McConaughey and ran to the table where he'd set up the speaker and picked up his phone. The music stopped.

Everybody was talking at once.

"You stay here," I told Mary Barron. "I'll go check." The door to room 206 hung open. I glanced up nervously.

"Harry, would you—" Kelly was going to ask Leland to sit with Mrs. Barron but he was gone.

The Dennises came up on either side of Mary Barron and led her to a table. Bonnie Dennis handed her a stiff drink.

The tears on Mrs. Barron's face slowed but did not abate.

Kelly flew up the stairs to the Barrons' second floor room.

"I wouldn't come in here, if I were you." Framed by the row of lights atop the bathroom mirror, Harry Leland stood in the middle of the guest room. His face was whiter than usual. A bit of damp green lettuce stuck incongruously to his shirt front.

Kelly hesitated only for a moment then plunged inside. Like the rest of the rooms, this one had two beds separated by a night table. Beyond that was a counter with a sink. To the left of that was the toilet and shower.

Open luggage sat atop a long low dresser.

Charlie Barron was stretched out face down on the tile in the middle of the doorway. His arms extended outward. A white hotel towel was wrapped around his waist.

A heavy ceramic lamp from the nightstand now lay on the ground. The piece was an original Midcentury modern turquoise zigzag lamp with gold trim. Every room had at least one of the vintage lamps. This one's white lampshade was twisted and bent.

It was a wonder the lamp base had not broken.

The same could not be said for her guest.

An angry red spot was visible on the back of Charlie Barrons' head.

"Is he—"

"Dead, all right," Harry Leland said with what Kelly thought was remarkable coolness. "And it's murder."

Kelly's mouth went dry. She bent and examined the lamp. The base had a smudge of the same red as the back of Dr. Barron's head. She felt bile rise in her throat. "I think I'm going to be sick."

Harry Leland stepped over her and moved to the night table. "I'll telephone the police." His thin fingers hovered over the vintage blue and black Bakelite telephone. The phones were original to the inn, complete with rotary dials, although their innards had been upgraded to work with tone converters to keep them running in the digital age.

Kelly bolted upright. "No! Don't touch anything!"

Harry reddened. "Right. Sorry."

"Use your cellphone."

Embarrassment turned to sheepishness. "I don't have one."

"You don't have your cellphone?"

"I don't own one."

"Great. I left mine in my room." This being a pool party and BBQ of sorts, Kelly had opted for blue paisley shorts and a V-neck tee shirt and little else. She patted the pockets of her shorts just in case. Empty except for her room key.

"What's going on in here?" bellowed Ben, limping into the room.

"It's Dr. Barron, Dad," Kelly replied.

"Somebody has smashed his head in with that lamp." Harry pointed to the apparent murder weapon.

Ben Walsh loomed over the body of Charlie Barron. "Did you call the police?"

"We were just about to do that. Hand me your phone,

Dad."

"We'd better get out of here until the police arrive," suggested Harry. "We're contaminating the crime scene."

Kelly groaned as she dialled 911. Just what the Beach Lovers Inn did not need: a crime scene.

They scuttled out of the room onto the breezeway. All eyes in the courtyard gazed up at them. Waiting for answers.

Kelly reached for the door handle then quickly realized that she shouldn't touch it in case there were fingerprints leading to a killer.

Ben Walsh hobbled down the stairs. "The party is over folks. I'm afraid there has been..." He glanced up toward room 206. "A small mishap. You should probably all go to your rooms now."

"No," Harry called down. "The police will want to interview you all."

"Harry," admonished Kelly. "Not now."

Harry ignored her and planted his hands on the railing. "A man has been murdered. You are all suspects."

There were gasps from below. Mrs. Barron was sobbing in Bonnie Dennis' arms.

"Harry!" Kelly looked at him helplessly. "Harry, the police can knock on their doors and interview them in their rooms if they want to. You are scaring everyone needlessly."

"There's a murderer loose," Harry mumbled. "They should be scared."

Kelly pushed him away from the railing. She pasted a grim smile on her face and confronted her guests. "Please, everybody. There has been an *accident*." She glanced at Harry who had snorted. She couldn't blame him. Even she didn't believe her own words.

"The police will want to interview you, I'm sure," Kelly said. "In the meantime, feel free to return to your rooms or remain on the patio, if you prefer."

The parents in the group took their children and left quickly. Others stayed, including Charlie Barron's friends who huddled together in a semicircle around his wife.

Now widow.

Kelly's father passed through the entry and went looking for the police. They couldn't be far off judging by the sirens growing louder.

"But the—"

"That's enough, Harry," snapped Kelly. "Why don't you join the others?"

"I think I'll stay and guard the room."

"The room doesn't need to be guarded."

Harry looked down his nose at her. "The killer could still be inside."

A shiver ran quickly up Kelly's spine. She hadn't thought of that. And she'd been standing with her back to the room. Completely vulnerable to attack from the rear!

Kelly shot around and faced the room. The door hung open but the curtains were pulled shut. "Don't be ridiculous." She couldn't hide her nervousness. "I'm sure he is long gone."

"He?"

"Or she," Kelly allowed. "Besides, I can hear the police now." Thank goodness. She kept a nervous eye on the open door.

Harry reluctantly left his post outside room 206 and bounced slowly down the steps. He moved to the opposite side of the pool, his eyes never leaving the door of the room until the police arrived.

Three officers in navy blue uniforms followed by a man in a brown suit swept onto the courtyard.

"Up here!" Kelly waved.

The man in the brown suit gestured and said something to the uniformed officers. One accompanied him up the stairs. The other two approached the people gathered on the patio.

Ben Walsh led a team of EMTs across the courtyard next and they moved up the stairs quickly. Not that haste mattered. There was no doubt in Kelly's mind that Charles Barron was dead.

This wasn't like Aunt Ruth's accident because there was also no doubt that her guest had been murdered.

8

"Detective Michael Burns. This is Officer Lowe."

The man in the brown suit thrust his ID in Kelly's face but she barely saw it. Her eyes were swimming with tears and her brain swirled in confusion. Who would want to murder one of her guests? And why?

"Ma'am?"

Kelly blinked. "Yes?"

"I asked you if the victim was in here." With his left arm, Det. Burns indicated room 206.

"Y-yes." She sniffed and made an effort to pull herself together. "I'll show you."

Strong arms held her back. "You stay here." His voice was deep and commanding.

Officer Lowe slipped on a pair of gloves matching the detective's and went inside the room. He returned a minute later. "Mrs. Green, right?"

"I remember." Kelly focused on the officer's warm brown eyes. "You were here the other night. When my aunt..."

"That's right, ma'am. How is your aunt?"

"Still critical but the doctors say she is stable, thank you."

"That's good. I'm going to need you to come downstairs with me now. Forensics needs to check the room. Det. Burns will want to talk to you when he's done."

Officer Lowe led Kelly downstairs where she joined her father who was handing out free drinks. She took a glass of wine and sipped.

"You okay?" Ben asked his daughter.

"Hardly." Kelly glanced at Harry, who stood rigid as a soldier, keeping an eye on the police and their activities. "How's Mrs. Barron?"

"She's in shock. An EMT is looking after her."

Kelly noticed a young woman ministering to Mary Barron. "Who would want to do such a thing?" Kelly asked her father.

He wrapped an arm over her back. "I don't know. I just don't know. Here comes that detective."

"I'd better talk to him." Kelly slipped free of her father and handed him her cup. She walked carefully around the far side of the pool but before she could reach Det. Burns, Harry had intercepted him.

For the umpteenth time, she wondered what was up with the guy.

"Excuse me, sir."

Det. Burns stopped and appraised the man facing him. They were of a similar age but that was where the similarities ended. The detective stood a head taller and had fifty pounds on Harry. "Can I assist you?"

"Are you in charge?"

"You could say that." The detective clutched a small spiral notebook and red pen in the fingers of his left hand. "I am Det. Burns, Myrtle Beach PD. And you are?"

"Harry Leland."

"Mr. Leland, are you the one who found the victim's body?"

"No. I mean, I saw him but I didn't find him."

"I see." Det. Burns jotted something in his notebook.

"Are you the inn's owner?"

Harry shook his head.

"Manager?"

"No. I'm a guest."

"Right." Det. Burns tried not to roll his eyes like they'd been trained not to in dealing with the public. "If you'll take a seat over there," he indicated an empty seat at one of the patio tables. "I or one of my officers will be by to collect your statement as soon as we can."

Det. Burns tried to step around Harry but Harry matched his move.

"Of course, detective. I wanted to make sure that you were aware of the situation."

The detective's brow went up. "If by situation you mean the dead guy, yeah, I got that." He gave Harry a friendly pat on the shoulder and started walking.

Harry dogged his steps. "But are you aware that there was another murder here only a matter of days ago?"

Det. Burns came to a sudden stop. Harry crashed into him and excused himself. "Another murder?"

"Well, technically, no. There was an *attempted* murder to be precise."

"An attempted murder?" Det. Burns scratched his temple with the tip of his pen. It had looked like just another ordinary hotel at the beach when he'd driven up. Suddenly there were mysteries on mysteries. "Are you telling me that somebody tried to murder Dr. Brennan before today?"

"Barron," Harry corrected.

The detective frowned and glanced at his notebook. "Right, Charles Barron, Providence, Rhode Island. You're saying somebody tried to kill him before tonight?"

Harry shook his head in the negative. "No, detective. Somebody, probably the same killer, tried to murder Ruth Evans."

"Ruth Evans?" Det. Burns face showed his confusion. "That's not the victim's wife, is it? Or girlfriend?"

"No, no. Mrs. Evans owns the Beach Lovers Inn."

"I see." That gave the detective pause. "And somebody tried to murder her?"

"Pushed her savagely," Harry gave the detective a nudge to point him in the direction of the stairs. "Right down those steps. The police came. I'm sure there is a report somewhere."

"*Ri-ight*. You saw this, Mr. Leland?"

"No," Harry admitted. "But I think I heard something."

"You *think* you heard something." Det. Burns sighed heavily.

"That's correct, detective. You see, I was in my hotel room and—"

An officer called down from above that the crime scene techs had cleared the room so that the EMTs could remove the victim's body. The detective gave his okay then turned his attention to Harry Leland. "Thank you, Mr. Leland. If you'll just have a seat. We can continue this conversation later. Okay?"

"Sure. That would be fine. I only wanted to make you aware of the situation." Harry called after him. "If you don't believe me, just ask him." He pointed to Officer Lowe. "He'll tell you."

From across the pool, Det. Burns waved his notebook. He had written down Harry Leland's name and underlined it. "Believe me, Mr. Leland, I intend to."

"Here he comes." Kelly left her spot near the bar where she had been huddling with George, her father and Drew.

The detective stopped at the table where Mrs. Barron and her friends sat. The EMT pulled herself away and spoke quietly to the detective. She didn't think the victim's wife was ready to handle any questions. Det. Burns frowned as the EMT returned to Mary Barron's side.

Rebuffed, Det. Burns approached Kelly standing beside the dying embers of the cooling grill. "Are you the manager?"

"Yes." Kelly grabbed the wood-handled wire brush and began scrubbing the greasy black crud off the grates. She was nervous and cleaning gave her something to do.

With his tanned face, bright blue eyes and silky sun-bleached blond hair, the detective reminded Kelly more of a surfer than a police detective. All he needed to do was lose the suit and tie and shrug into a muscle shirt, a pair of board shorts and flip-flops.

"You have a name?"

"Sorry," Kelly sputtered. "Kelly Green."

"Well, Ms. Green, what can you tell me about the incident?"

Kelly paused. "I'm not sure. Nothing really. We were having a party. Dr. Barron fell in the pool and went upstairs to change clothes. When he didn't return, Mrs. Barron went to check on him. The next thing we heard was her screaming that her husband had been murdered. Harry and I—"

"Harry Leland?"

"Yes. We went upstairs together." She dropped the

wire brush and squeezed her temples between her fists. "No, that isn't right. He went up first. Then I went up." She smiled. "He probably told you that."

"No, he didn't."

"Really?"

"I wanted to get your statement first."

"Right. My statement."

"Are you okay?" He noticed she appeared a bit wobbly on her feet.

"It all sounds so otherworldly, doesn't it? Like something you see in the movies."

He stuffed his notebook down his pocket and placed a couple of fingers on her elbow. "Why don't we have a seat over there and talk about it?"

Kelly allowed herself to be led to a weather-beaten picnic table planted in the sand just off the courtyard.

Det. Burns sat down across from her. "Let's begin at the beginning, shall we?"

"Everything okay over here?" Ben Walsh stood six feet away, eying them carefully.

Det. Burns glanced over his shoulder. "Who is that?"

Kelly smiled wanly. "That's my dad. Everything is fine, Dad."

Satisfied that his little girl was safe and sound, Ben Walsh rejoined the others.

As Det. Burns suggested, Kelly started at the beginning. She explained more fully about the party for her guests, how Charlie Barron had fallen in the pool and how they'd all watched the fireworks from the beach. "It was all so very ordinary."

Det. Burns consulted his notes. "Dr. Barron fell in the swimming pool and went up to change while you all went to observe the fireworks?"

"That's right."

"Did everyone leave the courtyard to watch the fireworks show?"

"I guess so. I didn't notice really. I mean, my eyes were on the firework show."

"Of course." Det. Burns rubbed the nape of his neck. "And you never saw Dr. Barron after he went up to his room to change clothes? You are sure he was not at the beach watching the fireworks?"

"I'm pretty sure he was not with us on the beach. His friends were remarking that it was taking him a long time to change out of his wet clothes. Then the fireworks started." Kelly shook her head. She may have been getting the order of things messed up.

"You didn't notice anything unusual tonight?"

"How do you mean?"

Det. Burns laid his notebook on the table. "Did you see any strangers, for instance? Anyone who was not an employee or a guest lingering about the premises?"

"No, not that I remember. One of the other employees might have seen someone. You should ask them."

"We'll be talking to everyone that was here," Det. Burns assured her. "I want to get your account."

"Of course." Kelly felt chastened as she gave the question further thought. She was desperate to help the police solve the case and make this whole murder thing go away.

"Like I said, everybody that was here was supposed to be here. I mean, except for Mildred McConaughey."

"Which one is she?"

Kelly pointed to the large purplish woman with a drink in her hand flanked by her father on one side and George on the other.

"Who's the man on the other side of her? Her husband?"

"No. That's George Easterling. He works here at the inn."

"Is it unusual for this McConaughey woman to be at your inn?"

"I don't know if I would say unusual. But it's never welcome."

"I'm afraid I don't understand."

Kelly frowned. She wasn't explaining herself well. She probably came across like a fool to this nice detective. "Mrs. McConaughey is not an employee or a guest. In fact, she came to complain about the noise."

"So she lives nearby?"

"She owns the property next door. She and my aunt feuded a lot. But I can't see her killing anybody, especially Dr. Barron. I mean, why would she?"

"That's what we are trying to find out, Ms. Green." He jotted Mrs. McConaughey's name in his notebook. "Let's forget strangers for a minute. Did you notice anyone arguing? Guests? Employees?"

"Nope, not at all. Everyone appeared to be having a good time."

"What about before the party?"

Kelly merely shrugged helplessly. "Sorry. I guess I'm no help at all."

"You're doing fine," he assured her. "Is there anything else you can add that might shed some light on things?"

"No, sorry. I wish I could be more helpful."

"You've helped plenty." Det. Burns replied graciously.

"Will we have to shut the inn down?"

"No. Don't worry," Det. Burns answered. "Once we

are done taking everyone's statements, you can all get on with your lives and running your business."

"I appreciate that."

"Room 206 will be off-limits for the time being, however."

"I understand." She would have to figure out what to do with poor Mrs. Barron.

"There is one more thing."

"What's that, Det. Burns?"

"Mr. Leland tells me there was an attempt several nights ago on your aunt's life? Tell me about that." He held his pen poised over the paper fluttering in the breeze coming off the ocean.

"I can tell you that Mr. Leland is very much mistaken," Kelly said sternly. "My aunt tripped and fell downstairs. Thank goodness she wasn't killed."

Kelly wrung her hands. "Aunt Ruth is getting on in years. Since the accident, I've heard from other inn employees who have told me that she has taken an occasional tumble now and then. This was just the most serious."

"I see. She's the owner and you are the manager, then?"

"No. I mean, Aunt Ruth officially owned the Beach Lovers Inn up until a few weeks ago. I'm purchasing the property from her. Before that, she did everything herself, after Uncle Jim died. She's retiring, you see. She was supposed to leave for Arizona to live with her sister the day after her accident. I'm taking over the operations now."

The very thought of which was making her extremely anxious. It would be hard enough running the inn under ideal conditions. Accidents and murders weren't going to help things.

"I'm sure she's grateful to you for that."

Kelly fought the tears that pushed out the corners of her eyes. "Thanks."

"Thank you for your time." Det. Burns stood. Kelly followed suit. Her legs wobbled beneath her. She clutched the edge of the picnic table.

"About this Mr. Leland." The detective's eyes fixed on Harry who now stood alone. His hands were in his pockets and he was staring up at room 206 as an officer stuck crime scene tape in a crisscross fashion across the door.

"What about him?"

"You say he entered room 206 first? Then you?"

"That's right."

"How much time passed between the time he entered the room and you?"

Kelly bit her lip. "I'm not sure." She replayed the tape of events in her head. "Mrs. Barron came downstairs crying murder. I tried to console her and asked her what was going on. Then I said I would go check upstairs. When I got there, there was Harry."

"In the room?"

"That's correct, detective."

"In the doorway?"

"No. He was..."

"Yes."

"I guess you could say he was standing over the body." Kelly gasped. "You don't think Harry had anything to do with this?"

"Early days," quipped Det. Burns. "Or nights." He glanced up at the moon. "I'm just trying to get things straight in my head."

"Harry didn't go up until after Mrs. Barron came downstairs, detective."

"Right." He handed her his card. "If you think of anything else, give me a call."

Kelly numbly accepted the business card. Things in her head were getting very, very crooked.

9

Det. Burns narrowed in on Mildred McConaughey. Surely he didn't think she was guilty of anything?

Besides rudeness, that is, thought Kelly.

"I'll take your statement now, ma'am." The detective held his notebook and pen at the ready.

"But I'm not one of *them*," argued Mrs. McConaughey. "I need to get back to my guests."

"Please." Det. Burns held firm. "This will only take a few minutes of your time. I merely want to get everyone's impressions."

Mrs. McConaughey folded her arms across her imposing chest. "My impression is that this little inn is a hotbed of iniquity."

"Iniquity!" Kelly took a step toward the woman. Her father held her back.

"I've always said it was only a matter of time until something like this happened." She aimed her words at Det. Burns.

"Did you see what happened?" he asked.

"Why, no. I heard about it. What an awful thing to happen. Murder! Nothing like that has ever happened at the Golden Arms, I can tell you that." She nodded sharply. Her triple chins did the shimmy. "Never will."

"Of course, not. Did you know Charles Barron?"

"The victim? No, I don't think so."

"He was never a guest at your hotel?"

"We have had thousands of guests, detective. I really wouldn't know."

The detective nodded and jotted something in his notebook. "You came to complain about the noise?"

"That's right. I telephoned the police as well. They had the nerve to tell me that there was nothing they could do about it until after eleven PM." Mrs. McConaughey thumped Det. Burns in the chest with a sharp red fingernail. "You're the police. You ought to be able to do something about rowdy behavior."

Kelly opened her mouth to respond but her father clamped his hand over her mouth. Kelly decided it was probably for the best. She had been about to call the woman a name that would only strain their tenuous relationship.

"Yes, ma'am."

"And then those deafening fireworks!"

"You watched the fireworks?"

"You do know what fireworks are, don't you?" Mrs. McConaughey said condescendingly. "Impossible to miss them."

Ben Walsh cleared his throat. "Actually, I don't recall seeing you on the dunes, Mildred."

A red tinge climbed Mildred McConaughey's neck. "That's right. I forgot. I went to the ladies room." She glared at Kelly. There was a poolside restroom for guests near the barbecue. "I heard them though. It was like we were under air attack."

A low growl emanated from Kelly's throat.

Det. Burns took one look at Kelly and said, "Maybe we should continue this in private, Mrs. McConaughey."

As Det. Burns led Mrs. McConaughey to the very

same picnic table where he had interviewed her moments before, Kelly fumed. "Rowdy! She's got some nerve calling my guests rowdy."

"Calm down, Kelly."

And what does she mean by *little inn*?"

"I'm sure she didn't mean anything disparaging," Ben Walsh replied.

"Huh!" Kelly had had very little to do with the old battle axe since coming aboard the good ship Beach Lovers Inn. She hoped to have even less to do with her in the future. "Where's Leland?" She scoured the crowd for the only man at the party wearing long pants.

Even George, who generally wore overalls and a teal Beach Lovers Inn shirt had opted for shorts, albeit he was still wearing his sturdy lace-up leather work boots. Still, it was the thought that counted.

"Harry?" Ben scratched his cast. "He left. He said he had some things to do."

Kelly swung to face her father. "Things to do? What could be more important than being interviewed by the police after a murder has been committed?"

Her father could only shrug. He shifted, pivoting on his crutch. "Uh-oh. Here comes Mildred. The detective's cut her loose." It was a warm night. He was sweating.

Like a deer caught in the open, Ben surveyed the courtyard looking for the nearest and best hiding place.

Kelly held him in place. "Oh, no you don't. If you run, you're only bound to make her even angrier. I can't afford her to be any more difficult than she already is." Kelly could picture the pile of complaints the hotelier would be filing with the police against the Beach Lovers Inn. "I wouldn't put it past her to try to get us shut down for being a danger to the community."

"But Kelly—"

"You got yourself into this, Dad. Off you go." She gave him an ever so gentle push, mindful of his broken leg.

Kelly approached Mary Barron sitting stiffly in a patio chair. Her hands clutched the arms tightly. Her face was wan. Jill Rochester stood on her right side. Bonnie stood to her left. "Mrs. Barron, I am so sorry."

The woman said nothing.

"A doctor gave her a sedative before he left." That was Jill Rochester speaking.

"Poor Charlie." Mary Barron looked at Kelly. "It must have been a burglary. You should have better security, Mrs. Green." There was a hollowness to her voice.

Kelly didn't know what to say so she apologized again. "Was anything missing from your room?"

"I have no idea. The police asked me for a list of our things." Mrs. Barron clutched her head. "I told them as best I could. Charlie packed his own bags."

Kelly swallowed hard. "Det. Burns said that your room is off limits."

"You should sleep in our room." Bonnie laid her hand on Mary's.

"No, I couldn't." Mary sniffed.

"That won't be necessary. You'll take my room." Kelly felt it was the least she could do.

"Are you sure?" Mary asked.

"Yes. I'll have housekeeping make it up."

"Where will you sleep, Mrs. Green?" asked Jill.

"Ruth's still in the hospital. Dad and I will use her apartment." There was only one bed and one bedroom. Kelly would be forced to sleep on the sofa. She couldn't ask her father to dangle off it with his broken leg.

It was all agreed. Kelly hunted down Drew. Together,

they cleaned out Kelly's room and hauled everything over to her aunt's apartment in front.

It was not until after midnight that the police cleared out. All the guests had retired to their rooms. Kelly noticed the light was now on in Harry Leland's room. She hadn't seen him return from wherever it was he had disappeared to.

The detective's words still burned in her brain. There was something very suspicious about Harry Leland.

And she was going to get to the bottom of it.

After seeing that her father was settled in, Kelly folded herself up on the sofa. Attempting to stretch out, she realized it was much smaller than it appeared. Her father had put up a fuss about who got the honors of the bed but she won—if sleeping on a sofa could be considered a victory.

It wasn't often she won an argument with her father, so she took some pleasure in the small victory, despite feeling like an accordion in a too-small case as she shut her eyes and tried desperately to shut out the events of the day.

10

Kelly woke with a start. Sun was slanting through the blinds. She glanced at the clock. Rats. It was nearly midday.

She had an inn full of people to manage. And a death in one of her rooms to contend with. This was no time to be sleeping in.

Had Dad overslept too? She threw off the flimsy pale pink sheet to check. There was no need to knock on the bedroom door. It stood open. The bed was made. Her dad was gone.

Skipping her usual shower—which would have been both wonderful and therapeutic considering the low back pain that the cursed sofa had inflicted upon her during the course of the night—she pulled on a pair of sort-of-clean floral twill shorts and a Beach Lovers Inn polo shirt that surely she could stretch one more day— it didn't smell that bad and a little spritz of her aunt's perfume from the bottle she discovered in the medicine cabinet masked the stale odor.

George was sweeping the courtyard. Drew bustled across the patio pushing a cleaning cart.

Kelly glanced sourly at the yellow and black police tape affixed outside the door of room 206.

The now infamous room 206.

Taunting her. Scaring the guests.

The plastic tape crisscrossed the door as if to say *here marks the spot*. A reminder of a terrible tragedy that nobody needed reminding of. She intended to ask the police how long the tape needed to stay.

The sight of it was not going to be good for business.

Kelly imagined future Myrtle Beach ghost tours stopping and telling tales of hauntings while gullible tourists sucked up the macabre particulars, guidebooks sharing the gruesome details, stretching the truth to suit their stories.

It was a future she did not want. This murder needed to be solved ASAP and the guilty party brought to justice. If not, suspicion and rumor would run rampant like a fast-growing weed spreading through the petunia beds.

"Down here!"

Kelly looked over the railing. Her father sat under the shade of an umbrella at a table near the entrance. He had company. She hurried down.

"Have a seat, Kelly." Ben Walsh scooped the newspaper off the chair next to his. "Harry here was just telling us about the case."

"The case?" Kelly sounded skeptical. Her sacroiliac complained as she fell onto the patio chair. The chairs were original to the inn, although they had been repainted a few times over the years. Between the wind, the rain and the salt, the beach can be hard on metal. It can be hard on everything.

The blue retro-styled chairs had seashell backs and powder-coated white frames. Specks of rust were beginning to show through. Another season or two and it would be time to repaint them.

"Charlie Barron's murder." Ben Walsh had a cup of

coffee on a saucer in front of him and a cold slice of toast with grape jelly half-eaten on his plate.

His poor eating habits continued. Kelly vowed to do something about that.

Kelly laid her hand atop her father's. "Want to buy an inn, Daddy?" She batted her lashes with hope. "Cheap?"

"Not a chance." Ben chuckled. "I will give you a hand though. While I'm here."

"Thanks." She pulled away her hand and helped herself to his coffee. It was black, like her mood. "What happened to you last night, Harry?"

The young man fidgeted and moved his chair out of the sun. Was he wearing the exact same clothes she had seen him in last night?

"How do you mean? Nothing happened to me. It's Charles Barron who got his skull bashed in."

Kelly winced. "Don't be obtuse, Harry. And must you talk like that? And so loudly?"

Guests were coming out of their rooms, loaded down with beach blankets, coolers and inflatables, heading for the beach and the pool. Some had small children in tow. They were seeking fun and new adventures, not to revisit a murder scene.

Actually, Kelly was relieved to see the Beach Lovers Inn still had guests remaining. She was eager to get to the office and see if there had been any early departures.

"Sorry." Harry Leland pulled a notebook from inside his shirt. It looked identical to the notebook Det. Burns had been carrying.

"Where did you get that?"

"What?" His hand snaked down into his shirt again and came up for air with a pen bearing the inn's name.

"That notebook." Kelly pointed. "Did you steal that

from Det. Burns?" A gasp flew from her lips. "What did you do, pick his pocket?"

Kelly was mortified.

"Of course not. Don't be ridiculous. This is mine. I bought it this morning." Harry placed the small notebook on the table, wet his thumb and finger and turned the pages.

"You disappeared last night," persisted Kelly. "Det. Burns wasn't happy. He wanted to talk to you."

"He had already talked to me. He didn't seem much interested in what I had to say either," Harry said unhappily.

"Where did you go?"

"Looking for clues."

Kelly took a mental step back and eyed him with suspicion. "Looking for clues or burying the evidence?" Det. Burns wondered about Harry Leland. So did she.

"Hey!" Harry cried.

"You know, buying a matching notebook doesn't make you a detective, too." Kelly was being catty and she knew it. Figuring it could have been low blood sugar, she stuffed the remains of her father's cold toast in her mouth and chewed.

"Now, now," said her father. "Harry's only trying to help." He prodded the young man with his crutch. "Tell my daughter what you found, son."

Son? thought Kelly.

"I'll be happy to, Ben." Harry cleared his throat while running a finger under his starchy collar.

"Icamphwaiftofeer," Kelly said.

"Huh?" Harry gaped at her.

Kelly swallowed the lump of toast. "I said I can't wait to hear." She settled her hands in her lap.

"First, I examined the grounds outside the inn. You'll never guess what I found."

"You're right, I'll never guess," Kelly said, feeling very much at the end of her patience. "So tell us."

"This." Harry reached down to a small brown bag on the ground and set it on the table between them.

"May I?" Harry's hands hovered over Ben Walsh's napkin.

"Be my guest."

Harry wrapped the soiled napkin in his hand. Kelly watched as he pulled out a wrinkled, thick brown wallet. Two tiny gold initials, CB, were pressed into a corner of the leather. She leaned forward. "Is that—"

Using the same napkin, Harry opened the billfold, revealing a driver's license. "Charles Barron's wallet."

"How do you like that, Kelly?" Ben was beaming. "Harry did all right, didn't he?"

"Are you freaking kidding me?" Kelly was on her feet again. Guests stared at them curiously.

Her father gently eased her back down. She felt like a bobble head on a spring inside a jack-in-the-box.

"That's evidence, Harry. You should have left it where it was and called the police."

"I suppose…" He closed the wallet and returned it to the brown paper sack.

"But Harry said he heard the trash truck coming. He had to do something quick. That wallet could have been lost forever. I'd call that quick thinking."

"I'm calling that detective," Kelly said.

"Good idea," Harry and Ben said as one.

"Don't you want to know where I found it?" Harry baited her.

Kelly hated herself for her curiosity sometimes. This

was one of those times. "Where?"

"In the parking lot. Inside one of the trash barrels."

Kelly furrowed her brow. "How could the police have missed that? They searched out there last night."

"I don't know." Harry shrugged. "But they did." He motioned for Kelly and her dad to lean closer to him as he leaned closer to them. "And do you know who was in that parking lot last night when everybody was watching the fireworks?"

"No, who?" Kelly was the first to ask.

Harry glanced across the courtyard. "Your head of maintenance, George Easterling."

"George?" blurted Kelly.

"Yes?" George, working nearby, called in reply.

Kelly clamped her hand over her mouth. "Sorry, nothing, George. Good job." She sank lower in her seat and glared at Harry. What had she done to deserve him as a guest?

"Are you really trying to suggest Ruth's handyman is our murderer?" Ben asked.

"I only state the facts." Harry swirled a rapidly melting glass of minty ice tea and took a healthy swig. "There were plenty of credit cards in the wallet. However," he pontificated, "no cash."

"So, robbery then, you think?" Ben Walsh asked.

"Please, Dad." Kelly felt a doozy of a headache creeping up from her shoulders and twisting its way into her cerebral area. "You're only encouraging him."

"Did you know that George recently asked Mrs. Evans for a raise in salary?" Harry asked Kelly.

"I heard something about that from Aunt Ruth. I told her I would take it under consideration. And that's what I told George. I explained that with the transition it was too soon to make a decision like that. George said he understood completely. He wasn't angry."

"Ask him to show you his new cellphone. I saw it this morning. Top of the line."

"How would you know?" Kelly replied. "You don't even own a phone. It seems to me like you are trying to make a case for George being the guilty party," Kelly said. "But I don't buy it."

"I'm not meaning to implicate him for the crime," protested Harry. "Like I said, I am merely stating the facts." He closed the lid on his notebook and stuck his chin out. "Facts speak for themselves," he added maddeningly.

"Yeah? Well, listen to these facts." Kelly counted off on her fingers. "First, you remained behind when we all went to watch the fireworks."

"So?" Harry turned to Ben. "I was hungry."

"Nothing wrong with that," Ben said amiably.

"Humph. Second," Kelly tugged at her finger, "when Mary Barron ran down the steps screaming that her husband had been murdered you, Harry—" She turned her finger on him. "You, were the first on the scene. In fact, you were alone on the scene, alone with the victim until I showed up."

"I wanted to see what had happened." Harry fought back. "What took you so long to get to room 206? I would have thought you would have been as concerned as I was."

"Don't make this about me!" Kelly stood abruptly, tipping over her chair. Her father jumped to pick it up.

"Everything okay, Mrs. Green?" George called from the other side of the courtyard. He held a green garden hose in his hand. Water sprayed down on the flower beds.

"Fine, George!" Kelly waved. "Thanks," she said to her father who had tucked her chair back under her butt. "And you, Harry, you need to give *that*," she jabbed an angry finger toward the brown paper sack between his shoes, "to the police."

"Of course. I was intending to deliver the evidence this morning. I only need a ride to the police station."

"What's wrong with your car, Harry?" Ben Walsh wanted to know.

"It makes noises but it won't start."

"Probably the battery. I'll take a look." Kelly's father was always happy to lend a hand. Even to people like Harry.

"Good. That's settled. I have an inn to run." She slid back her chair and stood. "Speaking of which, don't you think it's time you looked for someplace more permanent to stay, Mr. Leland?"

Harry's face fell. "Are you kicking me out?"

"Kelly!" Ben Walsh scolded.

"No, no. I'm only suggesting that you might want to find someplace more comfortable. More affordable. Like an apartment, for instance."

Harry wrapped his fingers around his glass and stared at the dissolving cubes. "If you think that's best."

"Believe me," Kelly said. Feeling gracious and relieved that her most peculiar guest would soon be moving on, she patted him on the back. Wow, nothing but bony bones. "You'll be better off."

11

Kelly hurried to the lobby. Lee Hollister, a part-timer, stood behind the counter. "Anything new?"

Lee Hollister, a slender retired librarian who seemed aloof but was really just shy and used to talking softly from her thirty years working in a library in North Charleston, South Carolina, was quick to answer. "The police were here earlier. A Det. Burns wanted to interview Mary Barron about the murder. What a horrible thing to happen."

Ms. Hollister picked through the morning's mail, separating the bills from the rest. She placed the bills in a small wire basket for Kelly to dispose of later.

"You heard about the murder?"

"Who hasn't?" Lee replied, inching her brown bifocals up her long, slender nose.

Kelly frowned. The news had probably spread like wildfire. "Have we had any cancellations?"

"I have fielded several telephone calls from concerned guests about their upcoming reservations. I assured them that the police had the matter well in hand and that they had absolutely nothing to worry about."

"Thanks, Lee." Kelly helped herself to the pot of coffee on the low built-in sideboard in the lobby.

Having started with the good news, Lee added, "We did have four early checkouts this morning. Sorry."

"It's not your fault," Kelly said with a sigh. She might have checked out of an inn where a murder had occurred the night before herself if put in the same situation. "I wonder how Mrs. Barron is doing?"

"I can't imagine. If I lost Arnie, I don't know what I would do."

Arnie was Lee's husband, a retired firefighter.

Kelly ignored the growing stack of bills. "I am going to check on housekeeping. Then I'll go see how Mrs. Barron is doing. Maybe I'll take her some coffee and muffins."

"Good idea." Lee turned to the computer screen and scrolled through the system. "I noticed quite a bit of food left in the dining room."

Sure, thought Kelly, miserably, because the Beach Lovers Inn now had less mouths to feed. She sank behind her desk and got busy. After checking on Mrs. Barron, she intended to swing by the medical center to see how Aunt Ruth was doing.

"Let's go take a look at that car of yours, Harry." Ben Walsh snatched up his crutch.

Harry nodded. "I need to run to my room first. To get the car key. I'll meet you in the parking lot. Five minutes?"

Ben agreed and limped off.

Harry picked up the brown bag and climbed to the second floor. He didn't go to his room though. He went to Kelly's old room. The guest room she had relinquished to Mary Barron.

He knocked on the door of room 203 without hesitation.

"Coming." A moment later a bleary-eyed Mary Barron pulled the door open a crack. "I don't need any service this morning."

She started to push the door shut. Harry stuck out his foot. "I'm not here for housekeeping. I wanted to ask you about this." He stuck the bag through the door.

Mrs. Barron sighed and let him in. There was a towel wrapped round her hair. She was wearing a white bathrobe with her initials on it: MB.

An open suitcase sat on the floor between the two beds. The telephone on the night table rested atop a Dickens novel. The TV was off.

Mary Barron moved silently to the low dresser atop which stood an open bottle of Armagnac. "Would you care for a drink?" She poured liquid into a small tumbler and drank.

"No, thank you."

"What's in the bag?"

Harry slid the napkin from his trousers and used it once more to lift the wallet. "Do you recognize this?"

Mrs. Barron leaned against the dresser. "Charlie's wallet! Where did you get it? What are you doing with it?" She eyed him with sudden suspicion. "Who are you?" Her eyes flew to the open door.

"I'm Harry Leland. I'm a guest. Like you. I was here last night. You must have seen me, if not last night, on other occasions."

She shook her head. "Sorry, I don't remember. And last night is mostly a blur." She downed the rest of her drink and poured another.

The brown bag rattled as Harry dropped the wallet back inside. "Do you remember the last time you saw the wallet?"

Her question seemed to amuse her. "I don't know.

Probably when we were out shopping. We spent the afternoon shopping and had lunch at a restaurant along the boardwalk. Where did you find it?"

"In the parking lot on the side of the building. Somebody threw it in the trash."

"You mean the killer."

"It looks that way."

"The police need to get that," Mrs. Barron indicated the bag holding her husband's wallet. "It's evidence and might help lead them to Charlie's killer."

"I intend to give it to them." Harry returned to the door and pulled it open. "Do you have any idea who might have wanted your husband dead, Mrs. Barron?"

"I talked to the police this morning. They told me it was probably a crime of opportunity. A robbery gone bad. Someone broke into our room while Charlie was showering. He came out, surprised the intruder and…"

Mary Barron doubled over. Her drink spilled from her hand, cascading to the floor. Tears erupted from her eyes.

Harry stood frozen, unsure what to do.

"Harry!"

Harry, jarred from his frozen state by a now familiar voice, turned quickly.

Kelly Green stood in the open door shouting at him. She had come from the office to check on Mrs. Barron and pay her condolences. She expected to find Charlie Barron's grieving widow. She had not been expecting to find Harry Leland confronting the woman. Upsetting her.

Kelly dropped her tray holding coffee and muffins on a small table next to the window. She raced over to Mary Barron and wrapped her arm over the woman's quaking back. She led Mary Barron to the comfy reading chair in the corner and sat her down. "What did you do?" she asked Harry.

Mrs. Barron wept uncontrollably.

Kelly's heart bled for her and she almost felt like crying too. The woman had lost her husband. Kelly herself had very nearly lost her aunt. Six months before that she'd gone through a divorce. Her mother had died over a year ago. Her father had shown up with a broken leg because he thought he was sixteen years old and fell off some stupid motorcycle!

"Grrr!" Kelly's fist slammed the back of the chair.

"I-I'm sorry," replied Harry. "I only wanted to ask her a few questions. You see, I—"

"Get out!" Kelly pointed to the open door.

After comforting Mrs. Barron and promising to check in on her later, Kelly went looking for Harry. But Harry and her father were both gone and Harry's car, a faded old silver hatchback with bald tires, had disappeared from the parking lot.

The Nelsons were seated at a patio table under the shade of a blue umbrella. Ted Nelson waved as Kelly re-entered the courtyard from the street.

"Is everything all right, Ms. Green?" Ted Nelson peered at her over his narrow sunglasses. He held a can of Sprite in his left hand.

"You do look flustered." Jean Nelson held her fingers between the pages of a paperback romance novel.

Kelly pushed her fingers through her hair. "Sorry. Don't worry about me. How are the two of you doing?" Her aunt had mastered the art of putting the guests first and keeping her own personal travails well hidden. It was going to take some time for Kelly to develop those same skills.

Ted gestured to the empty chair beside him. "Have a seat, Mrs. Green."

Kelly obliged. She was exhausted and it was barely midday.

Jean Nelson set her book on the patio table. "How is Mary?" She reached for a tube of sunscreen and applied some to her legs.

"We saw you go into her new room a few minutes earlier," explained her husband.

"All right, under the circumstances. She's resting. The doctor gave her a prescription for a sedative."

"I'm sure it is for the best." Jean Nelson adjusted the brim of her floppy white canvas hat.

"I'm sorry that this has spoiled your reunion."

"It's not your fault, Mrs. Green" Ted said lightly. He reached into a bag of potato chips and pulled out a handful which he began popping in his mouth. He offered the bag to Kelly who declined.

"This whole reunion vacation was a crazy idea, anyway." Jean Nelson wiped her hands with a tissue.

"Why do you say that? What sort of reunion was it? University?" No one had explained and it hadn't been her or her aunt's business to ask. Kelly scooted her chair to avoid the sun which seemed intent on frying her eyeballs.

Not to mention, in her hurry to get out the door, she had forgotten sunscreen, a daily requirement this time of year.

"No, business. Old business." Ted Nelson took a slug of soda.

"We all used to work together in a medical practice. Ted, Charlie, Desmond and his wife, Bonnie."

"Don't forget Vivian," Ted put in.

"No. We mustn't forget Vivian."

Kelly didn't get the joke. "What about Jill Rochester?" Vivian and Jill Rochester were a friendly pair, with Jill the more outgoing of the two.

"No." Ted drained the last of his Sprite and set the empty can on the table. "Jill came later."

"After Attleboro Heart Associates broke up." Jean slid a chip onto her tongue and snapped her jaw shut. Her left finger bore a large diamond engagement ring and a smaller yet equally expensive-looking diamond-studded wedding band.

"Attleboro Heart Associates?"

Ted explained that AHA was the medical group that the Nelsons, Barrons and Dennises had formed near Providence, RI. "Our practice broke up after ten years. We all went our separate ways."

"The company broke up?" Kelly wiped a line of sweat pouring down her neck. "Why? If you don't mind my asking," she hurried to add.

"Ask Charlie," Jean quipped.

"Now, love. No need to be bitter." He ignored her scoff. "You see, Mrs. Green, our experiment in working together was ill-fated. We fought a lot. Big egos. Every one of us." He smiled. "So we went our separate ways."

"Yes, and Charlie and Mary made out like bandits."

Ted patted his wife's hand. "Now, now. We haven't done so badly ourselves, have we?"

Judging by their clothes and their jewelry, Kelly was pretty sure they had done just fine. And then some.

Mrs. Nelson looked around the courtyard "I could use a drink. Is there a bar here?"

"No, sorry, Mrs. Nelson," Kelly said. "We don't, as a

rule, serve alcohol. Last night was a special occasion."

"I'll say." Jean Nelson rose and picked up a designer handbag. "I saw a convenience store up the street."

"Did I say something wrong?" Kelly asked. "Should I apologize?"

"No, Jean's fine. Charlie's murder has upset her. We all may not have parted on the best of terms but to see an old colleague murdered like that…"

"I understand. I'm surprised you all haven't checked out and headed for home. Not that I'm not happy you're staying."

"That detective asked us to stick around for a few days. Jean was all for leaving. But since we planned on being here for several more days anyway, I can't see any harm in remaining." He angled his face upward and pushed his sunglasses further up his nose. "And enjoying the sunshine."

Leaving her guest to enjoy the blistering sun, Kelly drove out to the Grand Strand Medical Center. She sat with Aunt Ruth for an hour, reading to her from the local newspaper. Ruth always liked to keep up on what was going on around town.

"Don't let me interrupt." Nurse Warren came into the room as Kelly was reading. The nurse glanced at the chart at the foot of the bed.

Kelly lowered the newspaper. "How is Ruth doing?"

"Better every day. She's responding to stimuli and her doctor thinks she'll be coming around any day now."

Kelly felt tears well up in her eyes. "That's good." She patted her aunt's cool, dry hand.

The nurse winked. "She enjoys you reading to her. I can tell."

Kelly smiled. "Thanks. I hope so."

The nurse was a tall brunette with gray eyes. She fluffed Ruth's pillow then moved to the door. "Between you and her nephew, your aunt is in good hands."

"Nephew?"

"Yes." The nurse slid a hand into the pocket of her uniform. "Harry I think his name is."

Kelly crumpled the pages of the newspaper in her hands. "Harry."

The nurse nodded. "He comes everyday too. I hope I'm this loved if my time ever comes."

12

Harry had to admit Kelly's father was a whiz. After popping the hood of the Nissan and fiddling with a few alien-looking doohickeys, he'd gotten the car up and running.

Fact was, it had never run better.

Harry drove west with some trepidation to the headquarters of the Myrtle Beach PD, located near Kings Highway and the railroad tracks.

Det. Burns was out. Harry left the bag containing the wallet with the alert black woman in a sergeant's uniform behind the thick glass in the lobby. "What is this?" She took the sharp tip of her pencil and carefully inched open the top of the bag.

Harry wondered if she was afraid it might contain a bomb of some sort. Did he look dangerous to her?

"It's okay. It's a wallet. I found it," Harry explained. "I thought Det. Burns would like to have it."

"You found a wallet?" The officer eyed Harry with mistrust. "Why would Det. Burns be interested? Is it his?" He'd take some ribbing for that. She set the bag aside.

Harry explained. "Because it belongs to Charles Barron."

"Who's that?"

"He was murdered in his hotel room last night."

"Oh, that fella." The officer's right hand moved under the counter. She eyed him with new interest. "Where exactly did you find it?"

"You see, I—"

A beefy man in a tight blue uniform shot through from a room in back. His hand rested on the weapon hooked to a belt containing half a dozen other instruments of enforcement.

Harry didn't like the way this situation was evolving. He had written scenes like this plenty of times. He wasn't going to make the same mistakes his characters made.

It was time to go.

"Bye." Harry turned and started walking.

"Hey, wait a minute!" The officer pleaded.

Harry forced himself not to run. That would be a sure sign of guilt.

And he wasn't guilty of anything.

Once out the door and out of line of sight of the front door, it was another matter entirely. He ran to his car, which, again thanks to Ben Walsh, started right up. He gave the little Nissan some gas and bounced out of the police station's parking lot and onto King's Highway.

Begun in 1650 and completed in 1735, the original King's Highway had been built by order of King Charles II of England. He had wanted the colonies reliably connected from Boston, Massachusetts, down to Charleston, South Carolina. Much of the original 1,300 miles of road are gone now or covered by modern roads like the one Harry was on.

Harry wasn't sure where he himself was going at the moment. His heart pounded to get out of his chest. At a streetlight two blocks away, he noticed a police car following him.

His heart started beating double-time. "Drat." His fingers squeezed the steering wheel.

Deciding this might be a good time to take Kelly Green up on her "suggestion" that he search for new accommodations, Harry pulled into a small shopping center for a paper.

Myrtle Scene Magazine was a local arts, news and entertainment publication. The tabloid-format weekly magazine was distributed freely throughout Myrtle Beach, supported solely by advertising.

The magazine prided itself on its alternative coverage of local and regional events.

Harry grabbed a two-day old edition of the free news magazine from the rack outside the office's door and stepped inside.

Myrtle Scene Magazine's editor, Kiki Donovan, stood at her desk peering at a very large computer screen. The desk was one of those high tech jobs that could go up and down at the flick of a lever, allowing her to sit or stand at will.

Kiki, a tall blue-eyed blonde with a body kept well-toned with regular sessions of yoga, bicycling, hiking, surfing and whatever other tortures she put herself through, was not alone. A casually attired young man and woman were huddled in front of another computer fiddling with several photo images on the screen.

"Hi, Kiki."

"Hello, Harry." She smiled with genuine affection. "What brings you?"

He held up the issue. "I popped in for this." He glanced nervously out the big plate glass window. A lone police car idled in the parking lot. Harry recognized the driver as the officer who had come out when he was dropping off the wallet at the police station. "And to ask you if you'd given any more thought to the job."

If he was forced to move out of the inn, he would need a job. Badly.

"Sorry, the magazine can't afford to take anyone on right now." Kiki smiled wanly and pushed a hand through her long blonde hair. "I wish I could help, Harry. I really do."

Harry returned the smile. She was letting him down easy. He had asked her out on a date once. She had let him down easy that time too. "That's okay. Can't hurt to ask, right?"

"Right. Can't hurt to ask." She moved to a cluttered table in the corner and hoisted a carafe. "I can offer you a cup of green tea."

The small office contained several desks and rows of beige filing cabinets, multiple computers and printers, a wall map of the South Carolina coast with the Myrtle Beach city limits drawn in purple marker, a couple of corkboards and one big whiteboard filled with names and assignments.

"No, thanks." Harry slapped the paper against his open palm. "I have things to do."

He turned to go.

Kiki's boyfriend, Chad Cummings, bushy brown hair, even bushier brown eyebrows and hooded brown eyes, pushed through the front door looking all self-import-ant. He was toting a bulky black backpack. He was Myr-tle Scene Magazine's number one news writer.

Harry placed Kiki and Chad in their late thirties to early forties. He was thirty-six himself.

"Hey there, Bones." Chad slapped Harry solidly on

the back.

Harry tensed. Chad was forever slapping him on the back and calling him Bones, an uncomplimentary reference to his build. He hated both the action and the moniker. "Hello, Chad."

"Talk to the mayor?" Kiki asked Chad. "I've held room for an article in the next issue."

"Yep. Got a solid interview. Taped the whole thing." He set his backpack on his desk and pulled out a small digital recorder. He hit his keyboard, bringing the computer's screen to life.

Kiki moved to Chad's side and laid a hand on his shoulder. "No trouble?"

"Well," Chad said. "That personal secretary of his can be murder to get past." He smiled smugly. "But I managed."

Feeling forgotten, Harry stuck the magazine under his arm and pulled open the door.

"Wait, Harry."

"Yes?"

Kiki tapped the edge of her mug with her short yet immaculate fingernails. At the moment, those nails were painted white; each nail decorated with an intricate orange and green Tree of Life. "Aren't you staying at that hotel where the man was murdered last night?"

"Right," Chad said. "I heard about that. He was just some tourist." While tourists were the main engine of Myrtle Beach's economy, some locals, like Chad, didn't take them all that seriously. "We get millions of them."

Harry ignored Chad's commentary. "That's right, Kiki. His name was Charles Barron. The Beach Lovers Inn. Why?"

"Did you meet him?"

"We said hello once or twice."

"I'll make you a deal, Harry."

Harry felt a tingle as Kiki approached and planted her fingertips on his bicep.

"Write me a story on the murder."

"Huh?" Chad whipped his head away from his computer. "You want Bones to—"

Kiki shushed him. "I'm talking to Harry, Chad."

Harry's head had already taken off like a rocket. He could make some money, see his name in print once again. "What exactly are you looking for?"

Kiki shrugged. "You tell me. You're on the ground at the scene of the crime. You can talk to people. Suss them out." She arched a very lovely brow.

Harry went into a tailspin.

"Maybe even nail the murderer. Wouldn't that be a scoop?" Kiki winked playfully.

"This is ridiculous," snorted Chad. "You can't go poking your nose into an active police investigation. Besides, didn't I hear this was just some dumb robbery?"

"If that's what it was, so be it," Kiki answered. "It's up to you, Harry, to find out."

Harry bobbed his chin. "How many words are we talking about?"

"Whatever it warrants. I don't want *War and Peace*, mind you. Let's say, two to three thousand words tops. Chad's right. It may be nothing more than a simple break-in gone bad." Kiki threw her boyfriend a bone. Chad could be testy. And a testy Chad wasn't a good reporter.

"I'm not so sure," Harry told her.

"This is on spec, mind you, Harry. I can't make any promises. I'll give you a week."

"The police will probably have the perp behind bars before then," Chad just had to toss in. "We get several of these stories every year. Tourists come to town, flash their cash and expensive jewelry around. Then some crook tries to relieve them of it. Sometimes it's a picked pocket."

Harry couldn't argue with that. Myrtle Beach did attract its share of thieves, lured not by the beach but by the millions of cash-carrying beachgoers who passed through town annually.

Chad folded his hands under his armpits and pontificated some more. "Sometimes it is aggravated assault. Sometimes the victim doesn't like to part with their money or their jewels so easily and nasty things happen."

"Dr. Barron had his head bashed in with a lamp."

"How horrible," gasped Kiki. "Myrtle Beach is normally such a nice, peaceful town."

"It was. I saw it myself."

"Did you get a picture?" Chad asked quickly.

"No."

"Figures." Chad shook his head in disgust.

"So do we have a deal, Harry?" Kiki extended her right hand.

Harry quickly agreed. He was already interested in solving the murder and had even talked to some of the guests at the inn about the crime. To get paid for it was going to be a bonus.

Because, as far as he was concerned, the story was already written and printed on the front page of the next edition. And he'd have a fat paycheck in his pocket before long.

Elated, he didn't even mind the cop following him,

all thoughts of apartment hunting abandoned, as he drove back to the Beach Lovers Inn. It was practically a two-car parade.

13

Returning to the Beach Lovers Inn lobby after stopping for groceries, Lee Hollister informed Kelly she had company waiting.

"Who?"

"Bonnie Dennis. Since you called to say you were on your way back to the inn, I told her it would be all right to wait in your office. I hope you don't mind."

"Of course not." Pushing through the half-door, Kelly walked into her office. She minded a little but it didn't seem worth making a fuss over.

Bonnie Dennis was standing behind Aunt Ruth's sleek, midcentury modern desk. Her left hand rested on the back of the chair. The desk had elegant, tapered poplar legs and a long but narrow desktop. There was an open cavity for storage with a single drawer at each end.

Bonnie Dennis was a tall woman with broad shoulders and a narrow waist. Black hair curled thickly around her richly-tanned, diamond-shaped face. She was a sharp contrast to her smaller framed husband for whom each step seemed to be a challenge. Desmond Dennis's hair was also black streaked heavily with gray and thinning all around. Kelly estimated the pair of about the same height but Desmond Dennis's tendency to slouch made him appear the shorter of the two.

As Kelly entered the office, Bonnie moved out from

behind the desk. Kelly took a seat in the white molded plastic desk chair. Its shorter legs matched those of the desk.

"How can I help you, Mrs. Dennis?" The door on the right stuck out an inch. Kelly gave it a satisfying push.

"Your assistant has been asking lots of questions—"

"My assistant?"

"Yes. Mr. Leland."

"Harry Leland is not my assistant, Mrs. Dennis," Kelly was quick to reply. "He is not an employee of the Beach Lovers Inn in any capacity whatsoever."

"He's not?" Bonnie Dennis was clearly nonplussed.

"He's not." Kelly planted her elbows on the desktop with a resounding thump. "Harry Leland is a guest, like you and your husband."

Bonnie Dennis sank into one of the two opposing guest seats. "Nonetheless, he's been asking lots of questions. Desmond is quite upset."

"I can only apologize for Mr. Leland's behavior, Mrs. Dennis. Believe me, I will be speaking to him." Spreading her arms across the desktop, Kelly leaned toward her guest. "What kind of questions has he been asking?"

"He wanted to know about our relationship to Charlie."

"Did he now?" Kelly rattled her fingernails against the desk. Unfortunately, a bit too hard and the nail of her right pinkie broke off. She swept up the bit of nail and deposited it in the trash can under the desk.

Kelly stood. "Trust me. Mr. Leland won't be bothering you any longer."

Taking her cue, Mrs. Dennis rose. "Thank you. I don't mind for myself but Desmond's health has been rather fragile."

"I'm sorry," Kelly walked Mrs. Dennis out of the office. The sooner she found Harry Leland, the better. "Is there anything we at the Beach Lovers Inn can do?"

She shook her head sadly. "No, my husband had a stroke many years ago. He hasn't been the same since. I had hoped that coming on this trip would prove restorative for him. I always wished we could spend more time in the south. Northern winters can be so brutal."

Kelly commiserated. "I couldn't afford to stay here myself in peak season. We are a bit more affordable in the offseason. You should come back then."

"We are on a fixed income, I'm afraid. If it hadn't been for the Barrons footing the bill for this vacation, we would never have come." Mrs. Dennis took pause. "Then again, maybe that would have been for the best."

Kelly held open the lobby door for her guest.

"Life has been hard. But we manage." Bonnie Dennis carried a capacious straw handbag with seashells painted on each side. Bags like that were cheap and plentiful at the tourist shops dotting Kings Highway and Myrtle Beach's myriad malls, shopping and outlet centers.

"If there is anything I or the staff can do to make both of your stays more comfortable, please do not hesitate to ask."

"Thank you." Bonnie Dennis helped herself to some orange pekoe tea bags and packets of refined sugar on the refreshment cart then departed.

"What was that all about?" Lee Hollister stood sorting postcards on the small carousel at the end of the front counter.

"Can you believe that guy?"

"What guy?"

"Harry Leland. He's been bothering the guests."

"Bothering them how?"

"Going around asking them questions about the murder." Kelly fumed. "Probably suspects them all of killing poor Dr. Barron. Making them all feel guilty."

Kelly angrily karate chopped the red pillows on the small sofa in the corner, leaving deep creases in each.

"Ruth is very fond of Harry."

"I know. What I don't know is why."

Lee Hollister smiled benignly. "He's a nice boy. Give him a chance."

"If you ask me, he's had one chance too many." Kelly poured a glass of lemon water from the pitcher on the drinks cart. "The police think *he* might have something to do with Charlie Barron's murder, you know."

"Seriously?" Lee's hands flew to her cheeks. "I don't believe it. Not Harry."

"Why not Harry?"

"Because he seems such a gentle soul."

Kelly didn't want to offend the woman by arguing the point. "Anyone can be guilty of murder under the right or should I say wrong circumstances, Lee."

"Not me," Lee replied confidently. "You?"

Kelly turned pink. She had been picturing those pillows she had karate chopped as being Harry's head. "I'm just saying."

A guilty Harry Leland wouldn't solve all of her problems but it would solve many of them. The Beach Lovers Inn murderer would be behind bars and she'd have one of the inn's best rooms available once more for booking. This was peak season. She could get top dollar for that room.

"I for one refuse to believe it until they lock the handcuffs on him." Lee Hollister put the extra postcards back in a cardboard box and hid them in the storage closet.

"How much is Harry paying for his room anyway?"

From the storage closet, Lee Hollister muttered something unintelligible.

"How much?"

Lee Hollister shut the closet door and glanced outdoors. "Looks like we're in for a little rain."

"Didn't you hear me, Lee? I asked what the rate was on 207."

"Oceanfront rooms are two hundred a night, Kelly. You know that."

"Right." Kelly scratched the tip of her nose. "I wonder how he can afford it?"

The second floor end rooms had windows looking directly on the ocean. The first floor rooms looked out on the tall dunes. The dunes didn't do much to help the inn's bottom line financially but during a hurricane surge the inn would be in trouble deep if those dunes did not exist. A good storm could easily drown the entire first floor.

A harried looking young man in a striped shirt and wrinkled shorts pushed into the lobby. "Hi, Jim Cooper. I called earlier?"

"Come in, Mr. Cooper." Lee Hollister waved the man forward. "I have a room all ready for you and your family."

A blonde woman fiddled with her cellphone while two youngsters stuck their heads out the rear windows of the minivan at the curb.

"Great place you've got here," Mr. Cooper remarked.

"Thank you," Kelly said.

She wondered if he would still think so after he had

seen the crime scene tape in the courtyard.

14

Having promised to look in on her later, Kelly prepared a sandwich and a salad and carried it up to Mary Barron's room. She knocked lightly on the door and Mary Barron bid her to enter. Stretched out on the bed in a dark blue dress and nylon stockings with several thick pillows propped up behind her back, the new widow was watching a Southern cooking show with Paula Deen.

"You're looking better," Kelly remarked. She held out the tray. "I brought you something to eat. It's important to keep up your strength."

"Thank you, Mrs. Green. Can you leave it on the bureau? I'm not hungry now but I'll try to eat it later."

"Are you sure?"

"Yes. That nice young man, Harry Leland, brought me some lunch. You see?" She held up a white paper sack bearing the name of a popular local Mexican joint. "Taco salad."

"How nice." Kelly slammed the tray down on the bureau. "I'll be off then unless there's anything else you need?"

"No, nothing. Thank you."

Kelly hesitated in the doorway. The ocean breeze tickled her legs. "Have you heard anything further from the police?"

Mrs. Barron picked up the TV remote control from the night table. She raised it and the screen went to black. "I am very tired. If you don't mind, I'd like to rest."

She leaned into her pillows and closed her eyes.

Kelly had no choice but to go. From the breeze-way, she spotted Det. Burns crossing the courtyard. Her father was wheeling a trash can with one hand, moving in the opposite direction. A pair of black-headed gulls took to the air as her father disturbed their inspection of the ground beneath one of the tables.

She had questions for both men but those questions would have to wait.

"Detective!" Kelly waved from the railing.

He lifted his neck, putting his hand over his eyes. "Mrs. Green. Have you seen Harry Leland?"

"Not lately," she called. "Wait, I'll come down." She danced down the stairs, mindful that she wasn't looking her best. The detective wore no wedding band. "What did you want to see him about?"

Out of the corner of her eye, she saw George and her father now carting away the portable bar from the night before.

What was her Dad thinking? That was George's job. Not to mention he should be resting his broken leg, letting it heal, not abusing it.

She was going to have a stern word with both men.

"I wanted to have a talk with him about this." Det. Burns held up a small sealed, clear plastic bag containing a wallet.

Kelly had seen that wallet before.

"Oh, that." Kelly sank into the nearest deck chair.

The detective joined her. He set the wallet on the table. "You were aware of this?"

She gulped. "Sort of."

"And you didn't think to tell me about it?"

"I didn't know about it until earlier today. Harry showed it to me. He promised he would take it to you at the police station." She gave him a smile. "And he did, right? No harm done."

Kelly made to rise. Det. Burns requested she sit back down.

She sat, rubbing her hands in her lap.

"There has been plenty of harm done." Det. Burns planted his elbows, rocking the table. "Despite how much you and Mr. Leland have been interfering—"

"Me?" protested Kelly.

He held up his hand. "Let me continue."

"Fine."

"We've interviewed all of your guests and employees. You will be happy to know that Dr. Barron's death *looks* like a burglary gone wrong."

"A burglary? Here at the inn?" Why did people keep saying that? Kelly still refused to believe it.

"You sound surprised. You ought to be happy."

"Happy, detective?" She gave him a judgmental look.

"You know what I mean. Your employee," Det. Burns paused momentarily to flip through the pages of his notebook, "Drew Schiffer?"

Kelly nodded and he continued. "She told me you've had a few incidents. Indications that maybe vagrants have been sleeping on the premises occasionally, according to signs?"

Kelly frowned. More bad news and bad publicity. How was she going to cope? "Once or twice maybe. But burglary? That's the first I've heard. Aunt Ruth would have told me.

"Don't get me wrong. Sometimes a guest complains about a personal item gone missing. Usually it turns out they dropped whatever it is behind the dresser, kicked it under the bed or left it out by the pool."

"Like they say, there is a first time for everything. And this," Det. Burns indicated the bagged wallet on the table between them, "points to robbery too."

"I suppose," conceded Kelly. The conclusion seemed inarguable.

"There are just one or two little things that are bothering me." He leaned back in his seat.

"Such as?"

"First, there was no sign of a forced entry to room 206."

"Somebody picked the lock?"

The detective shook his head in the negative. "There's no evidence to indicate that happened. Your security system is antiquated. You really ought to be using electronic locks, Mrs. Green."

"I know that." There was a long list of upgrades the inn could have used. Kelly mentally moved switching out the locks up the list a few notches.

It was all a question of resources, i.e. money. The inn operated on a very modest profit. What little money was left over after paying the bills went into building maintenance. Aunt Ruth had no savings to speak of. That was why she was planning to move into her sister's apartment in Sun City.

"I checked out your lobby too. Keeping room keys in cubby holes behind the front desk is a security risk. At the very least, those keys should be kept under lock and key themselves. Anybody could snatch one. The lobby door remains unlocked frequently and the desk gets left unattended."

Kelly colored. "We haven't had any trouble before this, Det. Burns. Our guests are honest people."

"Let me show you something." Det. Burns reached into his pocket and pulled out a key chain with an attached plastic pastel blue Beach Lovers Inn identifying tag with silver lettering. A solitary key dangled from its ring. It was a copy of the key to room 103. He waved the key in front of her nose. "I got this in under a minute."

Angry and embarrassed, Kelly snatched it from him and thrust it in the pocket of her shorts. "I see your point."

"How many persons have a master key?"

"I'm not sure." Kelly did some mental math. "I have one. Aunt Ruth still has hers, of course. There's one at the front desk."

"Housekeeping?"

"Yes."

"Maintenance?"

"Yes, of course. George needs a key." Kelly bristled. "You don't suspect one of my staff?"

"An outsider or even a guest could have gotten hold of a master key, could they not?" Sharky chose that moment to snake his tail around the detective's right ankle and mewl. Det. Burns rubbed the back of the cat's neck for a moment.

"I suppose we both know the answer to that question. Although we don't leave master keys lying around in plain sight."

"I saw a set of keys hanging on a hook on Drew Schiffer's housekeeping cart."

Sharky wandered over and sniffed his bowl in search of the odd treat. Sometimes guests were known to leave him a morsel or two. No such luck today. Sharky lifted his tail and sauntered up into the dunes.

"Are you here to solve a murder or to point out all my defects?" Kelly was getting tired of his barbs and beginning to take them personally.

"Solve a murder," Det. Burns said with maddening calm. "Consider the rest a public service."

Kelly glared. "Any one of my staff would have noticed if their master key was missing and reported it to me or my aunt. Which they did not."

"The killer wouldn't need to have the master key for long. All they would have had to do was make a duplicate at any one of a dozen places around town."

Kelly frowned. It wasn't impossible. "But that would indicate some sort of premeditation, wouldn't it?"

Det. Burns agreed.

"That's an awful lot of planning for a burglary, detective. Couldn't Dr. Barron have let his killer inside?"

"Could be," Det. Burns conceded. "But then why was Dr. Barron found wrapped in a bath towel with his head bashed in coming out of the shower?"

Considering Mrs. Barron was downstairs with the others at the time of the murder, Kelly's first thought went to the sordid. "Maybe he hired an escort or he was having an affair."

"An escort? That would be gutsy of Dr. Barron considering his wife was downstairs not a couple hundred feet away," Det. Burns said. "As for a lover's spat...yeah, that happens. But who's the lover? Any idea?"

"Don't look at me." Kelly threw up her hands. "I barely knew Dr. Barron any more than I know any of my guests, for that matter. My relationship to the clientele is superficial at best. Besides," Kelly continued, "I don't understand. If you are saying Charlie Barron's death came about as the result of a robbery—"

"Stop right there," Det. Burns chopped the air with his right hand. "I'm not saying this was a robbery. What I am saying is that it has the looks of one."

"Meaning someone, the killer, wants us to believe the murder took place during a botched robbery."

"You got it."

Kelly let the detective's words mingle with her own thoughts on the subject. "You mentioned there were a couple of things bothering you. What was the second?"

"There is no way we could have missed this." He thumped the wallet inside its protective plastic baggie. "We scoured that parking lot. Including the trash bins."

"That's where Harry says he found it, detective."

"That's what your father told me, Mrs. Green."

"You talked to Dad?"

"He tells me you're single."

Was that a teasing note in his voice? "I am." The conversation had taken an unexpected twist. Where was it leading?

"Interesting," was Det. Burns enigmatic reply. He stood. "I want a word with Mr. Leland."

Kelly fought not to frown. The subject once again was murder.

"I noticed his car in the parking lot, so he's probably locked away in his room."

The detective followed her to the stairs. "Unless he's at the beach. It is a beautiful day," he said, a wistful note to his words.

It was late afternoon. The air was balmy and the threatening gray clouds had been pushed further inland.

Kelly laughed. "You don't know Harry, do you?"

"How do you mean?"

"I mean Mr. Leland wouldn't normally be caught dead at the beach. He prefers to sit at his desk in his room writing on the computer. With the blinds down and the curtains pulled tight, no less."

Kelly was beginning to wonder why Harry had moved to the beach at all.

"Crazy." Det. Burns laughed. It was a warm, pleasant sound. "I'd prefer to be catching a wave myself."

"Are you a surfer?"

"A beginner. At this point, I spend more time climbing back up on my board than I do riding it."

It was Kelly's turn to laugh.

Det. Burns riffled through his notes as he followed her. "What sort of writing does Leland do?"

"He writes detective stories."

"Heaven help me," muttered the detective, adding a notation to his pad.

They reached the end of the breezeway. Kelly knocked on Harry's door.

A moment later, she heard the sound of the metal safety chain falling.

Kelly tensed, waiting for Det. Burns to make some smarmy comment about the flimsy security device. Surprisingly, he said nothing.

Harry stuck his head out.

"Someone to see you."

Kelly stepped aside for Det. Burns.

The detective dangled the baggie holding the wallet. "I'd like to talk to you about this."

Harry smiled. "I see you got Dr. Barron's wallet. Good."

"Yeah, great." Det. Burns slid the wallet into his coat. "You want to tell me where you found it, Mr. Leland?"

"Of course, detective."

"Better yet." Det. Burns pushed Harry's door open wide. "How about showing me?"

Harry led the detective downstairs, out the front of the building and around to the Beach Lovers Inn private parking lot on the south side.

Det. Burns noticed Kelly tagging along but didn't seem to mind.

Three barrel trash cans sat evenly spaced along the wall behind the parking bumpers.

Harry walked straight to the one furthest from the street. Sand duned up along the bottom of the black composite barrel. "This one."

Det. Burns peered inside.

The collection crew had emptied it that morning but the cans still stank of fish bait, fast-food remnants, tanning oil and urine. A potent brew. Kelly pinched her nose and moved upwind.

Harry loomed beside the detective. "It was down there. Half-buried in the trash."

"You should have left it in situ and called the police."

"I would have but the trash truck was coming. I did the first thing I could think of."

"Still." The detective poked around some more and toed the can with his shoe.

"My first thought was to save the wallet," Harry said in his own defense. "I didn't even know it was Dr. Barron's wallet. It could have belonged to anyone."

"That's true," Kelly said. "For all Harry knew, it might have been an old wallet that somebody discarded."

Why was she defending Harry? Was it because he

looked so fragile and helpless? Having never had children, the men in her life often bore the brunt of her mothering instinct.

Det. Burns gave them both a stern look. "Except that it wasn't." He kicked the trash can again. "I'll call somebody to come collect the can. We'll check it for fingerprints. Who knows? Maybe we'll get lucky and find some prints that match up to someone on file."

"You mean someone with a known criminal record," Harry said.

"That's right."

"Were there any fingerprints on the lamp that was used to strike down the doctor?" Kelly asked.

"Not a one. Our killer must have worn gloves."

"And, if they were smart, those gloves are probably at the bottom of the ocean," replied Kelly.

"Very interesting." Harry pressed a finger to his lips.

The detective wiped his hands on his trousers. "The techs will probably turn up nothing but rat prints on this thing." He gave the trashcan a half-hearted kick.

"We do not have rats, detective!" protested Kelly. At least not anymore. Sharky kept them at bay, according to Aunt Ruth.

"No offense," Det. Burns answered, sounding not sincere at all.

"Are we done here?" demanded Kelly. She had an inn to run and guests to mollify.

"Yep, we're done. You can take down the crime scene tape."

"Thank you." That was a happy surprise.

"Are you sure that's a good idea?" Harry asked.

"We've got all we need," Det. Burns said with a note of irritation. "I'm hopeful that we'll get this thing solved soon. Room 206 is all yours, Mrs. Green."

Kelly grimaced at the thought of having to ask Drew and her crew to clean the room for new guests.

As Det. Burns drove off in an unmarked black sedan, Kelly turned her attention to Harry Leland. "I've been getting complaints about you."

"Complaints?" Harry took a step back. "From who?"

"The Dennises for one, Mrs. Barron, for another" she added for effect although it wasn't quite true, if not, in fact, an outright lie.

"I don't know what any of them have to complain about. I was only talking to them."

"Well, stop talking to them," ordered Kelly.

"But I'm writing a story."

Kelly groaned. "This isn't one of your stories, Harry. This is a real-life murder. Leave it be, can't you?"

"I suppose." Harry sounded unsure, torn between wanting to please Ruth Evans' niece and selling a story to Kiki Donovan and the Myrtle Beach Scene magazine. "Don't you at least want to know what I've found out?"

Kelly narrowed her eyes and cursed. She wasn't so much mad at Harry Leland as she was at herself. Her brain itched. She balled her hands into fists that she held firmly at her side. "Tell me."

15

And he told her. But not right away.

Like everything Harry did, from what Kelly had seen, he refused to make it simple or easy, preferring to cloak every action and word in mystery and intrigue.

Before answering her, he scanned the parking lot and scoured the dunes. Not convinced that they were free of observation, he planted a cool, unwelcome hand on Kelly's shoulder. "Not here. Not now."

"Why? Are the rats listening?" Det. Burn's comment about the nasty beasties still stung.

"Let's meet in my room. After dark."

"Fine." It was a weird request but it suited Kelly perfectly. That would give her time to take care of a little business. She could arrange that the Barrons' old room be made ready for occupancy, check on her guests and take care of a hundred and one other things that seemed to sprout up each day in the hospitality business.

Things which left unattended often spelled disaster.

She stumped back to the inn. Drew was winding up for the day. Kelly caught up with her in the laundry room. "Good news. The police have given us permission to take back room 206."

Drew visibly shuddered. "Ugh. That means I'll have to clean it." She folded clean towels and placed them neatly on a wire rack on the wall. The washer and dryer hummed in the background.

The air trapped inside the laundry room was humid and hot. Kelly wondered if she could set out a couple of teak lounge chairs and rent it out as a steam room.

"You saw right after, Kelly. Was it, you know? Bloody?" Drew asked.

"I'm afraid so." The ugly image of Charlie Barron lying lifeless on the ground in a small pool of blood filled her mind's eye. "You could ask one of the others to do up the room. Or we could call in an outside cleaning service, if you like. The detective mentioned that there are companies that specialize in this sort of thing."

As gross as that sounded.

"No." Drew refilled the supplies on one of the house-keeping carts, adding tiny bottles of soap, lotion and shampoo. "Those services are expensive."

"You think?"

"Yep." She referred to a clip board on the cart and made some check marks. "I've got a cousin on the police force. I don't think you've met him. Drake?"

Kelly shook her head no.

"He told me about a double homicide once. Big mess. The homeowner paid one of those companies a couple thousand bucks to put her house right afterward."

"Whoa."

"Yeah, whoa. Don't worry, I'll handle it," Drew said bravely.

"I'll help you."

The clothes dryer buzzed and Drew pulled out a pile of warm, clean, fresh-scented sheets. "That I'll take you up on."

Kelly hesitated at the door. "Do you think you could ask this cousin of yours to keep us in the loop if he hears anything about Dr. Barron's murder?"

"I'll try," Drew replied. "But I can't make any promises that he'll share. He's Mister By-The-Book. I think his grand ambition is to be chief one day."

"I understand." Kelly helped Drew fold the sheets and stack them on the shelf. The inn maintained three pars of linen. Aunt Ruth had explained to Kelly that a par was the total number of linens needed to stock each room of the inn once over. "Any more signs of vagrants camping out here?"

"Not since George reinforced the lock." Drew moved the wet laundry from the washer to the dryer and started another load going.

"Speaking of locks, that detective tells me we're lax security-wise. Do you have your master key?"

Drew's brow went up and her hand went to her hip. From a deep pocket, she pulled out a metal ring jingling with keys. "Right here."

"Good. The last thing I want is for anyone else to get hurt." The second to last thing was for anybody to file a lawsuit against the inn for negligence. Kelly made a mental note to feel out Mrs. Barron on the subject. "Has anyone on your staff reported losing their key?"

Drew shook her head in the negative. "No, but I can ask around tomorrow morning, if you like."

Morning was the daily ritual of the staff meeting. Aunt Ruth had always insisted on them and Kelly was determined that they should continue.

"Do that, please."

"Do you want to tackle room 206 now?" The housekeeper glanced at her slender gold wristwatch. "I've got time while this load washes."

"It can wait until morning." Kelly stepped aside as

Drew pushed the carts into a line. "Maybe the house-keeping fairies will come in the night and save us the trouble." And consequent queasy stomachs.

"We can only hope."

Kelly held up her crossed fingers. "I'm off to see Harry."

"Harry Leland, 207?"

"The one and only."

"Be careful of that one, Kelly."

The hairs on Kelly's arms vibrated. "Why do you say that?"

"Nothing I can put my finger on. It's the little things. They add up to one strange man."

"He's a strange one, all right."

Drew warmed to her subject. "He rarely lets house-keeping in his room. Which is probably for the best because none of the housekeepers like to step foot in there."

"I was only inside once briefly. It's cluttered but it isn't exactly a house of horrors."

"No?" Drew said. "Everything in that room is related to murder. He's got books and magazines on the subject. Books on poisons, methods for killing people, books on how to plot a murder, what to look for at crime scenes, how to get away with murder. Books and magazines on weapons. I could go on but you get the picture."

That she did. "He writes murder mysteries," explained Kelly.

Drew's brow went up. "My cousin Drake might tell you that it's a fine line between obsessing about them and committing them."

"Are you suggesting that he might have bashed in Dr. Barron's head?"

"He wasn't watching the fireworks. Not that I saw."

"He told me he was hungry so he stayed behind to fix himself a burger."

"How convenient. And no alibi."

"What would be his motive?"

Drew shrugged. "Money?"

"Possibly. But Leland can't be doing too badly. He's been managing to stay here at the inn for a couple of months now. Money can't be too big an issue. Or motive."

As Kelly talked, Drew's brow rose higher and higher until it could go no further. "Sure. Because it costs him nothing."

"Excuse me?"

"You didn't know?"

"Know what?"

"Ruth comps Harry Leland's room. Not to mention the free food."

"Aunt Ruth lets Harry stay here for free?"

Drew colored as she nodded. "I had no idea you didn't know." She worried her lip. "Maybe I shouldn't have said anything."

"Ruth never said a word about it." In fact, she'd had nothing but kind words for Harry. What was going on? "I'm getting to the bottom of this right now." Kelly stomped out of the laundry.

"Just remember what Drake said," were Drew's final words on the subject.

Kelly gave pause. This cousin of Drew's might have been on to something.

"If you don't see me tomorrow," Kelly said in parting, "you know where to find the body."

The sad thing was, she wasn't joking.

16

The Dennises, Rochesters and Nelsons left in a group. Harry watched from the balcony of his room, notebook in hand. He was intent on his prey and ignorant of the beauty of the ocean to the east and the calming breeze.

A pair of commercial trawlers were working their way up the coast, lights twinkling as if they were connect-the-dot figures. Gulls were settling down on the water for the night.

The reunion guests seemed to have other plans. As far as Harry was aware, Mary Barron was in her new room, Kelly's old room. Alone. Several of her friends had ventured up and paid visits. None had remained long.

They were an odd bunch.

Harry stuck his pocket-sized notebook down his pants. Grabbing his jacket from the chair just inside his open door, he tossed it over his shoulder. Pulling the door shut behind him, he hurried after the three couples.

Harry hung back, petting Sharky, as the group stood in the breezeway at the inn's entrance. Despite the hour, George was there, leaning against a broom in the corner of the courtyard near the outdoor shower.

Harry nodded a greeting.

George nodded back as he swept wet sand from the

concrete pad under the shower head that beachgoers used to rinse the salt and sand from themselves before diving into the swimming pool or returning to their guestrooms.

The group talked among themselves, looked up and down the sidewalk then began moving. With Ted Nelson in the lead, they turned left.

The parking lot lay in that direction, right around the corner. Harry checked his pockets to make sure he had his car key. Keeping his distance, he followed. Instead of turning into the parking lot, the group continued walking towards the center of town.

It was summer and the sidewalks were crowded with tourists and locals alike. Ocean Boulevard ran north-south through Myrtle Beach. The well-traveled boulevard extended through the Grand Strand, the name of the sixty mile stretch of Low Country coast of South Carolina.

The two-lane road was tight and congested here and appeared to have been squeezed in between high rises by its builders. To accommodate the large crowds, broad sidewalks, wide enough for strollers and bicyclists, flanked each side of the road.

Harry had no trouble remaining close yet unnoticed. He often felt he was unremarkable and barely visible anyway. With all these people around, he was an insignificant speck. No more remarkable than a grain of sand on the beach.

The strip of property along Ocean Boulevard between Tenth Avenue North and Ninth Avenue North marked the beating heart of Myrtle Beach's tourist center. This area was home to Plyler Park on the oceanfront, Ripley's Believe It or Not!, SkyWheel Myrtle Beach and a seemingly endless array of restaurants and shops lined the strip. Condos and hotels rose into the sky, pressed upward due to the lack of space on the ground. Beginning at First Avenue North and extending all the way up to Sixteenth Avenue North, the Myrtle Beach Boardwalk and Promenade stretched out above the sand and along the beach for over a mile.

This was the famed Myrtle Beach Boardwalk Entertainment District, which swam with a colorful assortment of visitors by day and glowed like a beacon at night, drawing tourists from across the country and around the globe.

As Harry passed beneath the light of a streetlamp, the Dennises stopped. Both Desmond and Bonnie turned around and seemed to look at him. Desmond was hunched over, short of breath.

Harry dodged into a wax myrtle bush looming at the edge of the sidewalk. Prying the stiff branches apart with his fingers, he peeked out. None of the others paid any attention to him. He was sure that Bonnie couldn't possibly have recognized him from that distance.

Harry felt a tickle under his collar. A spider had found him and was exploring his skin. He flinched and stifled a yelp. He disliked spiders. And he positively hated them when they crawled across his skin.

Harry clamped his jaw shut to prevent a scream as the spider suddenly appeared on his left arm. It was big and black and fat with long ugly legs. The spider was looking up at him, its sharp jaws moving with a clock-like rhythm.

Was it poisonous?

Harry's arm began to shake uncontrollably and he didn't know what to do. His feet were stuck to the ground. The spider turned in a circle on his arm and looked up at him once again.

Finally, taking hold of her husband's arm to steady him, Bonnie urged Desmond on.

Harry blew out a breath, tore off a small branch with his free hand, and swiped the black spider away. He leapt backward, untangling himself from the over-grown myrtle, one of several flanking the entrance to a twenty-two story timeshare high rise, and fell to the grass.

The spider raced off to a flower bed layered in thick orange mulch.

Picking himself up, he frowned at the jagged tear in his shirt where the pocket had caught on a branch and been pulled loose. This was one of his best shirts.

Brown and green streaks ran up, down and across his pants. Harry spit on his fingers and swiped worriedly at the streaks on his trousers, making the stains larger and uglier. The piquant scent of wax myrtle clung to his clothes. He was beginning to hate wax myrtles almost as much as he hated spiders.

Fearing that he might lose sight of the group, Harry straightened what was left of his clothing, plucked bits of green leaves from his cuffs, and started after them anew.

Before long, they slowed. Harry watched with frus-tration mixed with disappointment as they entered Captain Haddock's Fish House, a sprawling, ramshackle seafood restaurant, and were shown to a large table near the center. Captain Haddock's had been part of the Myr-tle Beach scene for decades although he had never been inside.

Once seated, the group ordered bottles of wine,

bounteous plates of appetizers and family-style portions of seafood. From his vantage on the sidewalk, Harry watched them for a bit, ignoring the frowning glares of diners seated nearest the big windows in front who found his presence off-putting.

Curious, Harry thought. It seemed more a celebration than a wake for a lost friend.

"You need to move on." A burly figure in black pierced Harry with a stern look.

"Excuse me?"

"No loitering." The man had short black hair and watched Harry through steady, wide-set eyes. He sounded firm but not dangerous. "I'm sorry. But some of the customers are complaining that you are making them uncomfortable. The manager told me to ask you to move on."

Harry gulped. "Okay."

There was nothing to be gained by staying anyway. He couldn't hear what they were saying and he couldn't read lips. This little misadventure had been an utter waste of time. Plus, he was supposed to meet up with Kelly Green later.

Harry took one last look at the group. Pulling his notebook from his back pocket, he made a note of the day and time and who was present at the table. He went to drop the notebook into his shirt pocket, forgetting that the pocket was torn. The notebook fell to the sidewalk.

The man from the restaurant picked it up and handed it to Harry. "Look, if you need something to eat, the manager said you should go around back."

"Excuse me?"

"The kitchen door is open. Knock and go on in. We'll

fix you up a nice hot plate." His eyes took in Harry's skin and bones figure, quiescent demeanor and tattered, old clothes. He gave Harry's bony shoulder a squeeze. "It's probably been a while since you had a decent meal, huh?"

Harry's empty stomach called to him. "Thanks, Mister?"

"Vincent Lorenzo. Call me Vince. You?"

"Harry." He thought it best to avoid giving a last name. There was no real reason except that he was trying to operate undercover.

Harry worked his way up the block and through the alley between two buildings as directed by Vince. He found himself in a second even narrower alley lined with dumpsters and trash cans. It stank of filth and refuse.

Harry pinched his nose and quickened his step. The blacktop was greasy and slick underfoot. Food debris, soggy crumpled scraps of paper and battered boxes lined the alley's edges. There were few windows on the backs of the buildings at ground level and those were barred.

Harsh light and the bright sounds of a busy kitchen spilled from an open doorway. The smell of seafood beckoned. As Vince promised, the door stood propped open, a five-gallon bucket of pickle chips served as the doorstop.

Harry peered inside. The kitchen staff was moving quickly, like hornets buzzing around a flowering pear tree. It all looked like a riot of activity but in truth was well-coordinated. A cacophony of clatter accompanied their movements like an orchestral soundtrack.

A short, thick Hispanic man carrying a load of

glasses on a big plastic tray asked him what he wanted.

"Vince told me I could get something to eat?" Harry stuck his nose around the corner.

"Vince!" the man bellowed over his shoulder in a thick accent.

Vince appeared bearing a heavy-duty paper plate. "What do you say to a nice softshell crab sandwich?" He smiled and held out the platter.

Harry stared in horror at the fried and crusty golden crab, slathered in tartar sauce, lying dead on an open bun. A thick slice of tomato sat on a bed of lettuce and a pile of slender fries filled the remainder of the plate. "I'm sorry. I'm a vegetarian."

Vince looked at him in surprise but managed to smile. "One of those, huh?" He scratched his head and looked toward the kitchen. Two chefs and four sous chefs were working madly over the grill. "We've got crab mac and cheese. I can get a plate of just mac and cheese. Does that work?"

Harry said it did.

"I'll be right back."

As Vince started to turn, Harry laid a hand on the plate. "Can I keep the rest of this?"

"You want the fries?"

"And the lettuce and tomato."

"Sure." Vince scooped up the crab burger and turned the plate over to Harry. "Why not? We've got to get some meat on you. Of course, being a vegetarian, that might not be so easy." He laughed at his joke as he retreated.

Vince exchanged a few words with one of the cooks. The cook regarded Harry a moment, then grabbed a Styrofoam takeout container. Dipping a long-handled ladle in a warm vat of mac and cheese, he quickly filled the container. Vince popped the lid on it.

"Here you go." Vince handed the mac and cheese to Harry. He set a rolled up paper napkin and plastic fork on top the container.

"Thanks. I appreciate this." Balancing it all in his hands, Harry took a whiff. "Smells great."

"No problem." Vince walked Harry out the delivery door. He glanced at the sky. "The weather's nice. You might want to find a nice bench along the boardwalk. You can see the beach and the stars from there. Real first-class dining."

Vince disappeared into the kitchen, leaving Harry alone with his meal. Or so he thought.

A cough erupted from a pile of trash a few feet further up the alley. By the glow of the light over the back door of Captain Haddock's Fish House, Harry could just make out the shape of a man. The slouched figure leaned against the brick wall, cross-legged on the ground. Harry hadn't noticed him when he arrived.

Beside the man, sat a plastic grocery cart. The bare foot of his right leg was propped up on the bottom rack of the cart.

The man sniffed. A crumpled gray cowboy hat sat atop his long head like a small granite monument. Scraggly hair hung over his ears and more covered his chin and cheeks. His fingernails were long. "Dinner time, eh?"

Harry inched closer. "Who are you?"

"Who wants to know?"

"I'm Harry."

The man hacked up some phlegm and spat it across the alleyway. "No, you ain't. You're Scarecrow."

"I know you. I've seen you before. At the Beach

Lovers Inn. Am I right?" Harry recognized the homeless man. The older man frequently walked up and down Ocean Boulevard, pushing a cart filled with his worldly possessions. The ten-gallon cowboy hat of his was unmistakable. An over-sized gray tee shirt bearing a silk-screen image of the US flag fit him like a tent.

The man dug in the pocket of his loose black trousers held up with a frayed leather belt and extracted a small package of after dinner mints. Ripping the plastic with his teeth, he plopped two shiny white mints onto his coated tongue.

"No," the man cackled. "You're not right. You," he pointed at Harry, "are Scarecrow."

The whoomp-whoomp of a helicopter descended on them, echoing through the alley.

"Hear that?" The man skittered back against the wall. He quickly pulled off his hat, which Harry now saw was lined with aluminum foil. "It's them." He held up the foil-lined cowboy hat. "Don't worry. I've got my shield."

He waved Harry over. "Quick! Get under!"

Harry doubled over and squeezed next to the man, who exuded a strong, stale odor. In moments, the helicopter had moved on down the coast.

"All clear." Relieved, he twisted the hat down on his skull.

Harry straightened. The helicopter was one of many cruising up and down the Grand Strand on a daily basis. Myrtle Beach helicopter tours were popular with the tourists and operators ran them day and night.

One deeply tanned finger tapped Harry's mac and cheese container. "Smells good."

Harry set the container at the man's side and the

plate of fries, lettuce and tomato on top of that. "It's yours."

The man thanked him and snatched the napkin and plastic ware from Harry's fist.

Harry watched the man ravenously attacking the restaurant food. "You do know the Beach Lovers Inn, right?"

"I knew Mr. Evans. He was nice to me. Miss 'em. But Mrs. Evans, she's nice too."

Mr. Evans would be Ruth Evans' deceased husband. Ruth often talked fondly of him with Harry.

The scruffy old man stuffed a handful of fries in his mouth and chewed savagely. He washed it all down with a swig of water from a plastic bottle he'd been holding between his legs. "Glad she didn't die tumbling down those stairs. Didn't die, did she?" He sniffled. "Nasty business, that."

Harry lowered himself to the homeless man's level. "Nasty business?" The man avoided his gaze. "What do you know about her fall?"

He took another sip of water before answering. "That nice old woman didn't fall," he said with certainty. "She was pushed." He licked the empty container of mac and cheese.

"By who?" Harry's blood quickened. "Did you see who pushed her?"

The man's arm shook as he peeled the skin off a slice of tomato. "It was awfully dark. Don't like skins." He threw the skin carelessly over his shoulder. It flew backwards and stuck to the wall behind him.

"Yes, it was dark. But do you think you would recognize him if you saw him again?"

He took a vicious bite, then another. "Who said it

was a him?" he said slyly.

"It wasn't?"

The man shook his head side to side and tossed the empty paper plate to the pavement. It bounced like a flying disc, skittering to the other side of the alley. It hit the wall and came to a stop. "Not saying it was. Not saying it wasn't."

"But this is important. If you know something, you should tell the police."

The man's eyes bulged in horror. "No police. No police!"

"Okay, okay." Harry waved his hands in a placating fashion. "No police."

"The police are working with them." His gaze went straight up to the patch of sky where the helicopter had passed only moments earlier.

"How about telling me?"

"Well…" He scratched at the sagging flesh on the side of his neck.

"I promise I won't say a single word to *them*."

"They have a space station on the moon. They watch us from there. You want my advice?"

Harry said yes, if only to stay on the man's good side.

He wagged his finger at Harry. "Don't get caught under a full moon. They'll lock you in their sights—if you don't have protection. Ask them for protection."

"How can I ask them for protection? I thought we had to avoid *them*?" Harry wondered if he was wasting his time trying to get information from him.

"Not them. Them." The old man pointed at the kitchen door. "That's where I get mine. They're okay. They're safe. They are fish people. Fish live in the ocean. The moon can't penetrate the ocean, Scarecrow." He tapped the side of his skull with a gnarly finger. "Remember that."

"I'll do that," promised Harry. "Now about Mrs. Evans' fall."

"It's gonna cost you."

"I fed you." Harry's entire dinner.

The man scoffed, exposing uneven yellow teeth. "They gimme food." He jerked his thumb toward the restaurant door. "I want money."

"Fine." Harry sighed. Money was one thing he did not have in large quantities. "How much?"

The homeless man appraised Harry like he was a fish on a hook. "A hundred bucks."

"A hundred!" Harry shook his head. "That's crazy."

"That's my price." He held out a scruffy hand. "I won't take a penny less."

Harry frowned. "I don't carry around that kind of money. I'm going to have to find an ATM."

"You can find a leprechaun at the end of a rainbow for all I care," said the man. "You just get me my hundred dollars." He cackled and slapped his chest.

"You'll get it," Harry said forlornly.

"Cash only, Scarecrow."

"Where will I find you?"

"I don't go far." The man settled his back against the brick wall, stuffing an old newspaper behind his spine for comfort.

17

Kelly banged her fist on Harry's door. It rattled but no one answered. The curtains were pulled tight and no light escaped.

It was nearly dark. Faint stars twinkled hello out over the calm waters of the Atlantic.

It was almost unbelievable to think that a murder had occurred only the day before on a night such as this.

"Harry? Are you in there? Open the door." Her fingers wrapped around the master key in her pocket. She was very tempted to go inside and check things out for herself.

She fiddled with the key while debating the matter.

"What's wrong, Kelly?"

"Oh, hi, Dad." Kelly hung over the railing. Her father looked up at her from the courtyard. "Have you seen Harry?"

He scratched his head and balanced his weight on his crutch. "Not lately. What's up?"

"Harry told me to meet him. He's been acting all mysterious and said he had something to tell me."

"Tell you about what?"

"Charlie Barron's murder."

"Interesting. Like I said, I haven't seen him." Noting her hesitation, he said, "Is there something else?"

"I think Harry might be a killer."

"Our Harry? That's crazy. What makes you say that?"

The curtain of the room next door opened and light spilled out. A guest holding a curling iron to her hair eyed Kelly with curiosity.

"Hold on. I'm coming down," Kelly said.

Kelly joined her father at a poolside table. He was dressed in baggy brown cargo shorts and a tee shirt and had a cold brew in his hand. "Can I get you one?"

"No, thanks." She needed to think straight and alcohol wouldn't help.

"Okay." Ben Walsh cleared his throat. "What's this all about?"

Kelly ran over what she had learned from Det. Burns about Harry Leland. "He stayed on the patio while the rest of us went to watch the fireworks. That gave him opportunity."

"Maybe but that's no reason to convict the boy. And remember, he thinks George might have had something to do with it. He wasn't watching the fireworks show either, according to Harry."

"That's crazy. Neither was Mrs. McConaughey and you don't see Harry accusing her of anything," Kelly said. "George has been here a million years."

"Have you asked George about it?"

"No." Kelly didn't dare. "I don't want to insult him." She needed George's help running the inn. Desperately.

"Yeah, I can see that."

"Besides, the police interviewed him. If they have any suspicions, it's up to them to follow up on them. What if," Kelly said, "Harry is throwing shade on George to divert suspicion from himself?"

Ben leaned back in his seat. "You really think Harry might have murdered Charlie Barron?" His eyes went to room 206. The police tape remained in place. "Why?"

"I'm not sure."

"Not sure?"

"Okay, I have no idea. Drew thinks it's because he is deranged."

Ben chuckled and sipped loudly from his can. "I admit I barely know the boy but I would hardly call him deranged." He sipped some more. "A bit harsh, don't you think?"

"Maybe. He is strange though. You have to admit."

"I do not." Ben smirked defiantly.

Kelly hated it when her dad acted all feisty. "Did you know he keeps all sorts of books on murder up in his room?"

"So?" Ben wasn't convinced of anything. "I've got books on fishing, plumbing, motorcycles." He crumpled the empty can in his strong fingers. "What does that make me, some kind of psycho? Does it mean I cruise around on my motorcycle bashing fish on the head with a short length of pipe?"

"Very funny, Dad." Kelly snatched the six-pack out of her father's reach as he grabbed for it. "Don't you think you are drinking too much?"

"A couple of beers is hardly too much, dear."

Kelly pulled a beer loose of the webbing and handed it to him. "One more. That's all." She popped the lid, took the first gulp then handed it across. "Harry could very easily have bashed Dr. Barron's head in."

Ben arched his brow. "Harry is hardly what you might call Mr. Atlas in the muscles department."

"Maybe not but he's strong enough to crack an un-suspecting person in the head and kill him."

"I can't argue with that. But as for Harry being

strange," her father began in a tone of voice that Kelly knew meant a lecture was coming on. "Everybody's strange. We're each one of us different. That's what makes life fun."

"Yeah, but Harry is stranger than most." Kelly argued back. "I can't imagine why your sister is so fond of him. Did you know she lets him stay in that guest room for free? One of our best rooms too."

"No," Ben replied, voice steady. "I did not know that. You can ask her about it yourself when she comes around and I pray that she does soon."

"Me, too," Kelly said fervently. She was beginning to think that running this inn alone was going to be beyond her abilities.

"What I do know is that Ruth is a good judge of character. Maybe you should try to see in Harry what Ruth sees in him. I'll bet you a day's pay she does not see him as a potential murderer."

Kelly frowned. "You're unemployed, Dad."

"I didn't say it was a good bet." Ben snatched his crutch from the table and stood. "Speaking of motorcycles, I need to get online and check with the shipping company. Katie should be arriving any day now." He looked like a boy on Christmas Eve waiting for Santa Claus.

Kelly stood too. "You named your motorcycle after Mom?" Her mother's name was Kathryn. Dad had always called her Katie.

"It's a way of honoring her memory."

"By naming the thing she never wanted you to buy —and almost got yourself killed on—after her?" Kelly giggled. "I take back what I said about Harry, Dad. You might just be the strangest person I know."

Ben smiled, grabbed the remainder of the six-pack before she could protest, and started up the stairway. "I'll take that as a compliment."

She cupped her hands around her mouth. "You would!" Out of the corner of her eye, she noticed George fiddling in the storage closet where he kept his tools. She wandered over. "Everything okay, George? I thought you'd gone home."

The handyman slipped something into his pocket and pulled the door closed, locking it with his own master key, which hung from a silver chain on his belt.

"Hunky dory." George wiped his brow with a blue kerchief. "You need me for anything else?"

"No." She eyed him thoughtfully. "Good night, George."

After he rounded the corner of the inn, Kelly pulled out her key and opened the storage room door. She flipped on the light and took a look around.

Everything looked perfectly ordinary. Tools, yard equipment, gardening supplies.

No how-to books on murder. No dead bodies.

Harry was out of his mind. Or very, very devious. George was as harmless as a puppy dog.

Harry veered across the street to the local branch of his bank only to discover he'd left his wallet behind.

A rough hand grabbed him as he turned off the sidewalk and stepped onto the Beach Lovers Inn courtyard.

"Where have you been?" Kelly had been in the middle of setting out some refreshments and snacks for guests in the anteroom when she spotted Harry shuffling home.

Harry pulled himself free. "Hello, Kelly. I don't have

time to talk right now. I have to get my wallet and—"

"What do you mean?" Kelly struggled to keep her voice under control. There were several guests enjoying the patio, pool and barbecue. The last thing she wanted was for them to see her arguing with a guest. Although considering the circumstances, *guest* was hardly the word for Harry Leland. "You told me to meet you after dark. Here. Now."

Kelly leaned down to pet Sharky who had crept between their legs. "You said you had something important to tell me."

"I do," Harry insisted. "It will have to wait. You see, I was following the others—"

Kelly threw up her hand. "Wait." She grabbed his arm and pulled. "Follow me."

She dragged him toward the office. It was empty for the moment. She unlocked the door and nudged him inside.

"Okay, what others, Harry?"

Harry explained how he'd been following the reunion party. "I couldn't hear what they were saying of course. They were too far away and the streets are noisy."

Kelly's blood boiled. "Let me get this straight, Harry. You were tailing my guests?"

"I've been following them, yes." Harry didn't understand what the problem was.

"You've been following my guests? You can't do that," complained Kelly. "What if they saw you?"

"They didn't but I saw plenty," Harry said smugly.

Kelly hated herself for asking. "What did you see? Where did they go?"

She gaped at him as he went on. What if they had

spotted him spying on them? She was too dumbstruck for words.

"Then I was asked to leave," Harry was saying. "Vince told me he'd give me a meal."

Kelly remained mum. She didn't want to even ask who Vince was. The way reality was twisting around her like a creeping vine, it could have been Vincent Price or even Vincent Van Gogh.

Noticing Harry's torn and rumpled clothing for the first time, she asked the question: "What happened to your clothes?"

"I had to jump in a bush."

Kelly raised her brow in question.

"Long story. Anyway, I went to the back of the restaurant like Vince asked me. That's when I met the homeless man."

"If you take any longer to get to the point of this little story, *you* are going to be homeless, Harry."

"The man I talked to told me that your aunt's fall was no accident," Harry said quickly.

Kelly planted her hands on her hips. "This Vince person?"

"No." Harry shook his head. "The homeless man."

"And what would he know about my aunt's fall? Did he push her?"

If the inn had been receiving late-night homeless visitors, one of them might have given Ruth a shove if she had confronted them. Not that Kelly could picture Ruth giving anyone down on their luck a hard time. No, she would ask them to leave but doing so, she would give them something to eat and a few dollars.

"No, he didn't push her. But he saw who did."

Harry stood maddeningly still while Kelly wore a

hole in the lobby rug with her pacing.

Could it be true? Could Aunt Ruth have been pushed rather than fallen down the stairs? She went behind the check-in counter and pulled the occupancy list up on the computer. There was only one empty room and that had police tape across its door, bloodstains on its floor and fingerprint powder dust everywhere else.

Everybody that was checking in for the night was already checked in and settled. There was no reason to remain in the office. "All right, what's the plan?"

"He told me he wanted a hundred dollars before he would talk. I told him I didn't have the money on me but that I would get it. I stopped at the ATM but I didn't have my wallet, so I came back here to collect it. Then I'll stop at the ATM, get him his cash and see what he has to say."

Kelly was shaking her head side to side as he spoke. "No, Harry. No."

"No?" Harry was puzzled. It sounded like a good plan to him.

"We, Harry." She clicked off the computer and turned off the office lights. "*We* will hear what your mystery man has to say. If, and I do mean if, this guy saw somebody who hurt my aunt, I want to know about it."

There were big, nagging doubts in her mind about the whole thing—especially since it all involved Harry —but even the remotest possibility that this homeless person could shed some light on her aunt's fall and Charles Barron's murder meant that she had to follow the lead up. "Get your wallet."

Harry took the stairs two at a time.

Kelly frowned as she looked at her watch. Finally, Harry reappeared but he didn't look happy. "What took you so long?"

"I can't find my wallet." Harry patted his pockets fruitlessly. "I don't understand it."

Kelly sighed. "Forget it. I guess I'll have to pay." She fished in her shorts for the key to the office. She went inside and borrowed a hundred dollars from the till.

Kelly waved the bills in Harry's face. "You owe me for this."

"Agreed," Harry said with reluctance. Kiki had said nothing about paying him back for his out-of-pocket expenses.

"Lead on, Sherlock."

18

Harry led the way. It was a balmy summer's night. The kind that brought the tourists and the locals down to the coast in masses.

A line stood outside Captain Haddock's Fish House.

Harry cut through the waiting customers as he headed for the alleyway.

"Hey, wait." Kelly pulled him to a stop.

"What?"

"Look inside the restaurant."

"Shouldn't we go see my guy first?" Harry dodged as a skate boarder hurtled past. "I don't want him to leave before we've had a chance to see what he knows." With no permanent address, Harry had no idea when or where he'd find the guy again.

"With the hundred dollars you agreed to pay him? Trust me, he'll wait. All night if he needs to." Heck, for a hundred bucks cash, she probably would too, at this point in her life. When she and Alan split up, she gave up the only real financial security she'd ever had in her life.

Harry made grumbling noises and glanced inside Captain Haddock's. "People eating dinner. So?"

"Look closer. But be subtle about it." She shoved him over to the corner of the window.

He grumbled some more and pressed his nose to

the thick glass. The couple at the table in the window weren't happy to see him. Harry's head was at eye level with the woman's crotch. She frowned. The husband bellowed for the manager.

"Let's go," urged Harry.

"Just a sec. You're not looking the right way." Kelly turned Harry's head away from the woman's legs and to the right center of the seafood joint. Harry's eyes swept the crowded room. "There's George."

"And that's Mrs. McConaughey with him." Kelly's breath tickled his ear.

"I didn't know they were friends." Harry narrowed his eyes.

"I didn't know Mrs. McConaughey had any friends."

"Mrs. C isn't so bad," Harry replied. "Give her a chance."

Kelly ignored the editorial. "What are they doing together?"

Harry's shoulders moved ever so slightly up and down. "A date?"

"You think?" They were of the same generation more or less.

"I don't know," Harry was forced to admit. "Maybe."

Two men, one dressed like a waiter, the other wearing a coat and tie appeared in the window.

"Time to go!" Kelly jogged off.

"Wait for me!" Harry pleaded as he followed suit.

"Down here." He cut in front of her and guided her between the buildings and then moved further up the alley. "Hello? It's me, Scarecrow."

Kelly gaped at him. "Scarecrow?"

"That's what he calls me."

"No comment," commented Kelly, thinking back to

the Wizard of Oz and Scarecrow's lack of a brain.

"I don't understand it." Harry squinted into the darkness. "He was right here."

"There's no one here now. Except possibly cockroaches and rats." She hated rats. She hated cockroaches even more. "I don't know why I let you drag me down here."

"I didn't drag you, you wanted to come," countered Harry. "In fact, you insisted."

The backdoor of Captain Haddocks remained open. Noises from the kitchen spilled out as if carried along with the fluorescent light.

Harry jiggled the grocery cart. "He can't have gone far. He would never leave this behind. It must hold everything he owns."

Kelly agreed and said so. "I'll look in this direction. Why don't you go that way?"

The shadowy silhouette of a man stepped out from the doorway. "Hey, it's Harry." Vince was grinning. "I wondered what all the commotion was." He looked Kelly up and down. "I see you brought a friend."

"Hi, Vince. This is Kelly."

Kelly said hello.

"You hungry too?" Vince inquired.

"I could eat," she replied. "It is late and I haven't had supper yet."

"No problem. Next time, come straight around back and ask for me." He scolded both of them. "Don't go peeping in the window and freaking out the customers, okay?"

"I am so embarrassed," Kelly said. "I don't usual act this way." She cast an accusatory look at Harry. He seemed to bring out the worst in her.

"You can't blame me for that. You told me to look!"

"At George, not between that woman's legs."

"I wasn't looking between her legs," sputtered Harry. "I wasn't looking between anybody's legs!"

"Okay, okay." Vince cut between them like a referee separating a pair of antagonists in the ring. "I haven't got all night. What can I get you, Kelly? Are you a vegetarian too?"

Harry answered before she could. "Actually, we are not here for food. We're looking for that older man. He was sitting right there before."

Harry pointed to the spot where he'd last seen the homeless man. Harry's empty food container, plate and plastic fork sat on the ground along with the water bottle. The open bottle was tipped over on its side.

"Cowboy?"

"Yeah. That's right. He had a big cowboy hat on his head. Did you see him? Where did he go?"

Vince frowned. "I don't know. It's not like Cowboy to leave his cart behind."

"I told you, Kelly," Harry said smugly.

"Do you have any idea where he might have gone?" Kelly asked.

"Not a clue. Sometimes we see Cowboy every day, other times he disappears for days, even weeks at a time. I wouldn't worry about it."

"Do you know his real name?" Kelly asked.

"Sorry, I only know him as Cowboy."

"I had some money for him," Harry explained.

Kelly held up the cash.

Vince looked at it in surprise. "Shucks, you don't need a meal. You can afford the best dish on our menu."

"He was going to tell me some things."

"What kind of things?" Vince pinched his eyebrows together. "Who are you two, anyway?" Seeing the money in Kelly's hands had forced him to revise his opinion of the pair.

Inside the kitchen, two men were hollering at each other. "Pay no attention. That's the chef and the manager. They get into each other's faces a hundred times a night."

Vince sighed and rubbed the back of his neck. "What's this all about? Why would you be offering Cowboy all that money?"

"You see—"

Kelly tugged Harry's sleeve to get his attention. She shook her head ever so slightly.

"Oh, just things, you know." Harry had gotten the message though why Kelly had sent it, he didn't have a clue. "I'm a writer. I'm interested in his story. He's colorful."

Vince laughed. "When you get his story, you let me know. I'd love to read about it. Cowboy is one colorful character, all right." He said he had to get back to work and left them alone in the alleyway.

Harry brushed his sleeve. "What was that all about? What were you shushing me for?"

"I'm not sure," Kelly admitted. "I don't think we should tip our hand more than we need to. And what do we really know about Vince?" She answered her own question. "Nothing."

Harry grinned ear to ear.

"What are you smiling about?"

"You're beginning to believe me, aren't you? You believe somebody gave your aunt a push, same as I do."

"No, I do not believe you. I'm merely trying to save

you from looking stupid in front of strangers."

"Too late for that," grumbled Harry, picturing the look the woman in the window had given him when she thought he'd been peeping at her private parts. She'd spend the rest of her life thinking of him as some sort of pervert.

Harry ran a finger along the rusty handle of the shopping cart. "Vince suggested I eat at the benches in the park. Let's try that way. Cowboy might be there."

Without waiting for an answer, he started toward Plyler Park located beachside at Ninth Avenue North and Ocean Boulevard. Comfortable benches constructed from recycled plastics had been placed along the edges and toward the center surrounding a children's play area with a swing set, a small merry-go-round and a couple of teeter-totters.

Kelly and Harry looked around. All but one bench was occupied and none of them held a man in a cowboy hat. Couples cuddled and parents rested while their energetic children played on the grass or ate ice creams from one of the many shops nearby.

A woman with a red tricycle-powered vendor's cart stood at the edge of the park nearest the street. A red and white umbrella was mounted over the cart. The pretty blonde attendant in tight white short-shorts and a pink tank top was diddling with her cell phone, looking bored.

A thin, long-faced man with a moustache wearing a private security company uniform sipped a tall drink from a straw. Another man in a tank top and shorts sat alone at the end of the same bench.

"What about him?" Kelly asked despite the missing hat.

"No." The man occupying the bench was too thin, too well-groomed.

Approaching the nearest family, Kelly asked if they had seen a man in a cowboy hat. The answer was no. She tried a couple of others and the answer was the same.

Kelly did a slow turn and yawned.

Harry yawned too. "I give up."

"Face it, Harry. Cowboy might not have known a darn thing. He may have been leading you on. Maybe he got cold feet or developed a conscience and decided to lay low for a while rather than try to spin some fantastical yarn that you'd see right through."

Harry was tired and dejected. "Maybe."

"Cowboy can wait for another day. I bet he shows up tomorrow. He's going to want this hundred dollars."

"I suppose." Harry couldn't think of anything better to do.

"Why don't we check the beach first then head back?" Seagrasses danced along the dunes. The moon and stars above twinkled. It was all very romantic if you weren't scouring back alleys for homeless people who might or might not know something about a fall that might or might not have been an accident.

"At night?" Harry looked like she'd just asked him to leap off the Chrysler Building without a parachute. "I don't think so."

"Hey, Tom! That's the man!" a woman shrieked from the edge of the park nearest the street.

"What?"

"The man looking at my you-know-what!"

Harry paled. It was the couple in the restaurant who had thought Harry was leering at the woman's private parts.

"Oh, yeah?" he growled. "Hey, you!" The big man lurched towards Kelly and Harry, fists raised.

"Come on, Harry!" Kelly grabbed Harry's hand and raced up the dune and down the other side. Harry took two steps and tripped, landing face first in the sand.

A black shape the size of a gorilla stood atop the ridge of the dune. "Get back here you lousy peeping tom!"

Kelly jerked Harry to his feet and ran. A string of curses followed them though the sound of outrage was soon lost in the wind.

19

"Now what?" Harry stopped, breathless. Sand clung to his lips and tongue. He spat repeatedly to no avail. Sand stuck to him like a million tiny sucking creatures. The ocean was a black beast with silvery overtones. With every wave, the Atlantic seemed to be reaching for them. Trying to lure them into its inky depths.

Kelly angled down toward the water's edge where the sand was more compacted and the walking easier. "We'll follow the beach up the coast a bit then veer over to the sidewalk."

She glanced over her shoulder, making sure the ape wasn't following them.

He wasn't.

She stepped around a melting sandcastle that had been attacked by the incoming waves. The air was beginning to cool and she wished she'd brought a light jacket. Her exposed arms and legs were growing cold.

Harry was behind her, panting like an old work-horse.

"Hey." Kelly paused. She narrowed her eyes and studied the moving water. "What's that bobbing on the surface over there?"

"Probably seaweed. Or flotsam." Harry didn't bother stopping.

"I don't think so." Kelly kicked off her sandals and

waded into the water. She hissed as the cold seawater embraced her legs.

The lights of the fishing pier extended out in the distance like a glittery finger. "It looks like—"

She thrust her hand in the water. A moment later, she held the soggy, dripping object up like a trophy. "A cowboy hat," she said smugly.

Harry stopped and hurried back. "You're right. It is a cowboy hat." He gently took it from her as she climbed out and retrieved her sandals from the sand. "In fact, this looks like Cowboy's hat."

"Are you sure?" Cowboy hats in Myrtle Beach weren't as common as she imagined they were in Texas but they weren't exactly exotic. Tourists came from all parts. Even locals, particularly those who kept and rode horses, had similar hats.

"I think it is." Harry frowned. "What's it doing out here?"

They silently looked up and down the beach. A hundred yards down, a couple walked slowly, shoulder to shoulder while their small dog raced up and down in the breakwater.

"Come on," urged Harry. Carefully avoiding the surf, he moved north. "I think I see something in the water."

They quickened their pace. A dozen yards further, Kelly halted. "I think I see something too, Harry."

"Where?"

"About twenty feet out. There." Her pointing hand locked onto the dark moving shape.

"What is it?"

"It could be a clump of seaweed." Kelly kicked off her shoes once more and set them above the waterline. "I'll check."

"Or a shark."

Kelly bristled. "Really, Harry. Did you have to say that?" She was now up to her knees in the water.

Something rough brushed her calf. Kelly screamed and jumped.

Harry thrashed into the water, heedless of his shoes and socks. "Are you okay?" He grabbed her arm trying to help.

"I'm fine." She fought to free herself but Harry held on. Whether it was because he thought it was the macho thing to do coming to her rescue or clinging to her for dear life, she didn't know.

What she did know was that she wanted him to let her go. "It was nothing." Or so she hoped. "Maybe some seaweed like I said or a manta ray. Let me go." She yanked her arm at the same moment Harry did as she asked.

Kelly lost her balance and fell with a splash. She jumped up cold and angry, spitting salt water. "Look what you made me do!"

Harry backed up to the shore. "You said to let go."

Kelly fumed. Salt stung her eyes. She pushed straggly hair from her face. Sopping wet, it felt like the temperature had dropped forty degrees. "You are too much, Harry, you know that?"

"Uh, Kelly?" Harry pointed a crooked arm in her direction.

Kelly discerned an ominous edge to Harry's voice. "What is it, Harry?" If he was going to tell her that she was about to be eaten by a great white shark, she was going to roll with it.

"You might want to—"

Kelly screamed as something hard brushed the back

of her knees. She shot her head around. A dead body floated against her bare legs, face down, arms and legs spread wide apart.

Kelly screamed again and ran from the body, raising her legs against the pull of the water. She banged into Harry. They went down together.

Harry ended up on top.

"Get off of me!" growled Kelly. She was cold, wet, hungry, wearing a sand suit and she'd been mauled by a dead man.

And Harry Leland was lying on top of her.

"Sorry." Harry climbed to his feet. "Was it Cowboy?"

"How should I know?" complained Kelly. "I didn't take the time to look. Besides, I've never laid eyes on him." She grunted, hating what they had to do next. "Come on, help me pull him out."

"Shouldn't we wait for the police?"

"And take the chance that Cowboy or whoever it is drifts away before they arrive?"

"Good point."

They waded out to the body. By unspoken agreement, they each grabbed an arm and gently dragged the man to shore.

It was hard work. Harry caught his breath. A dead body, even buoyed in the water, weighed more than he would have thought. "It's him, all right."

Harry studied the corpse. The face tilted to one side, lit by the reflection of the moon. He was lying on his stomach, arms stretched overhead, legs dangling in the shallow water. "That's Cowboy."

"Sorry, Harry." Kelly sank to the sand next to the dead man.

Harry stood stock still. His eyes locked on the silvery disc in the night sky. The moon was shining down on Cowboy. An unseen helicopter beat its wings somewhere in the distance.

"What's wrong?"

"It's the moon. It finally got him."

"You're nuts. You know that?" Kelly wrapped her arms around herself. "I'm freezing." She jumped to her feet. "I'll call the police." Harry had already admitted he didn't own a cell phone, as inexplicable as that sounded in this day and age.

Cowboy was too far gone to require the services of an ambulance.

"I hope they get here soon."

Kelly stabbed at her phone and frowned. "Nothing."

"What?"

"I said *nothing*. As in no signal, no nothing!" She waved the phone at him. "My phone is ruined. That tends to happen when somebody knocks you in the water." She thrust the phone deep in her front pocket. Why she didn't hurl it out to sea, she didn't know. It was useless now.

Harry bent and started going through Cowboy's pockets.

"What are you doing?" Kelly asked, horrified.

"I want to see what he had on him."

"You shouldn't be touching him." Kelly pulled Harry back.

"But I'm looking for evidence."

"Evidence of what? Leave it. One of us needs to go call the police." Kelly's voice quavered and she was shaking. It wasn't shock. It wasn't the dead man at their feet. It was the cold and wet. So she told herself. "And one of us needs to stay here with the body."

Harry nodded.

"Which do you prefer?"

"I'll get the police," Harry replied.

"That's what I thought you'd say." Kelly pointed at Cowboy. "You stay here and keep an eye on...things. I'll get the police." If anything, moving would warm her up.

She began walking without waiting for a reply.

Harry watched as Kelly hurried back the way they had come. He lost her in the shadows as she moved away from the beach and up towards the dunes.

Ignoring Kelly's warning, Harry resumed his search of Cowboy's pockets. They were empty. No wallet. No ID. No money.

Not so much as a seashell.

Harry would never learn what Cowboy was going to tell him. His story and his secrets had died with him.

20

The cavalry arrived like General Custer and his men charging over the Black Hills. Instead of horses, they road dune buggies and small pickup trucks. Bright spotlights shot like white spears from fixtures mounted on their roll bars and roofs. Those that weren't on four wheels were slogging up the coast on foot in shoes made for pounding the pavement, not the beach.

The roar of a helicopter caught his ears well before the chopper itself appeared from behind a wall of high rises sprouting from the dunes. A powerful beam of light skirted the dark beach looking for its prey.

Harry squinted and shielded his eyes with his arm as the spotlight captured him and Cowboy.

"Over here!" He waved.

Kelly climbed out of the back of a dune buggy belonging to the city's Beach Patrol. She was swaddled in a heavy olive green blanket given to her by a patrol woman who had pulled it from the trunk of her car. Det. Burns drew himself out of the front passenger side of the dune buggy. The driver remained seated and used his hand to adjust the lights on the scene.

"Hello, detective. I think—"

"We'll take it from here. Please go wait over there, Mr. Leland." Det. Burns pointed towards the dune buggy.

Harry and Kelly exchanged looks while the detective

and several other men and women in uniform cordoned off the area and went about their business.

Finally, a young officer approached. Kelly recognized him as Officer Lowe.

"Cold?" he asked.

"Freezing," shivered Kelly.

"Det. Burns asked the sergeant here to drive you back to the station, if you don't mind. You can warm up. Get some coffee. He'll be there as soon as he can to take your statements."

"Fine by me," Kelly said, climbing back into the dune buggy.

"I don't know." Harry pulled out his pen and notebook. "Is that the coroner?" He pointed the tip of his pen at a sour-faced man with round spectacles who looked like he might have been roused from his bed. "Does he have a preliminary cause of death?"

"Sir, if you don't mind." Officer Lowe gestured at the vehicle.

"Get in, Harry." She grabbed him by the shirt and tugged.

Harry tumbled into the passenger seat as the driver gunned the motor. "His name is Cowboy. That's his hat!" he shouted to Officer Lowe.

When Det. Burns returned, he led them to a small windowless office. A squat desk with a computer on it filled most of the space. There was only one extra chair in the room. "I'll be right back."

Det. Burns returned a minute later with a second chair, which he offered to Harry. The detective took a seat in an old walnut swivel chair. "You okay?" he asked Kelly who was already seated. "Can I get you anything?"

Kelly clutched a steaming mug of hot chocolate, her second. "I'm good. Can we get this over with? I'd like to get home and out of these wet clothes."

Det. Burns smiled. "Of course. We'll make this as quick as possible." He rummaged in his desk drawers while he talked. "Finding a dead body on the beach. That's a new one for me."

The detective pulled out a pack of gummy worms which they both refused. Grabbing several, he popped them in his mouth. "What were you two doing out there on the beach, anyway? Lovers' stroll?"

"What?" Kelly leapt out of her chair. "Don't be ridiculous."

Harry looked hurt.

"It was nothing like that. You see, Harry—"

Det. Burns held up his hand and pointed to Harry. "Why don't you start?"

Harry uncrossed his legs. "I'll be happy to."

The detective started a small digital recorder on his desk as Harry wove his tale.

Kelly didn't know about Det. Burns but as she heard the last couple hours replayed now she was finding the whole thing improbable and absurd.

What had she been thinking following Harry down to a dark alley to hand over one hundred dollars of her hard earned money to a homeless man who claimed he had information that would prove that her aunt Ruth had been pushed down the stairs?

She should be home, curled up in bed—or on the sofa for the moment—with David Copperfield. Not sitting on a cold, hard chair in a cold, hard police station with Harry Leland as he spun his fantasies.

"Mrs. Green?"

Kelly snapped out of her reverie. "Huh?"

Det. Burns tapped the eraser end of his pencil against his desk top. "I asked if you had anything to add."

Kelly looked at Harry for help. She got none. "Uh, no?" How could she admit that she hadn't been listening?

"Can we go now?" Kelly asked hopefully, nudging her chair back.

"In a minute."

Kelly sighed. She set her empty mug on the edge of his desk and pulled her blanket tighter across her shoulders and chest. "I don't understand what the big deal is. I mean, I am sorry the man is dead."

She left unspoken that she was equally sorry to have to have been the one to have found him. "But Harry and I have done our civic duty. Is there going to be a funeral? If there is, please tell us because—"

Det. Burns interrupted her babbling. "It's preliminary but I'm told there is evidence of a struggle."

"A struggle?" Kelly sagged.

"Yes. Bruises and marks on the back of the victim's neck and shoulders indicate that he may have been held underwater."

The detective watched each of them in turn for a reaction to his news.

Kelly spoke first. "Are you sure? Maybe Cowboy was swimming or washing up and drowned. Or had a heart attack. It happens."

"Maybe. But I don't think so." The detective laced his fingers behind his neck and grunted. "So, the question I have is who would want to kill the guy?"

Neither Harry nor Kelly had an answer.

"We know it wasn't robbery." Det. Burns prodded

them along. "What few possessions he owned weren't worth squat."

"Like I explained, Cowboy implied that he had seen whoever it was that pushed Mrs. Evans down the steps at the Beach Lovers Inn the other night."

"So you think the killer eliminated Cowboy to keep him from talking?"

"Yes, detective," answered Harry. "I do. How else do you explain his sudden death?"

"If that's the case, and if Cowboy did see somebody give Ruth Evans a push, it could mean that we are dealing with a single murderer." Det. Burns doodled on a notepad on his desk as he spoke. "The person who attacked your aunt, Mrs. Green, possibly being the same person who murdered Dr. Barron and Cowboy."

"If she *was* pushed," Kelly put in.

The detective nodded. "We'll have the answer to that question as soon as your aunt recovers."

"If Aunt Ruth was pushed and the person who tried to kill her is the same person who murdered Charles Barron, it means my guests are innocent. Because they didn't arrive until the day *after* Aunt Ruth's injury." Kelly directed those words at Det. Burns.

"It also means," she directed the next sentence at Harry, "that they don't need some wannabe Hardy Boy spying on them."

Harry blushed. "All of them?"

"All of the Barrons' friends arrived the same day, Harry."

Det. Burns interrupted, planting his knuckles on his desk and looming over them. "It also means that there is still a killer on the loose. A killer who may or may not be a current or former Beach Lovers Inn employee or even guest.

"I suggest you both be very careful. Keep your doors locked at night and keep off the beach after dark. And leave the police work to the police."

"Have you made *any* progress in finding Dr. Barron's assailant?" Kelly asked.

"We're continuing our investigations," he replied vaguely.

Kelly took that as a big fat no.

"Getting back to Cowboy," interjected Harry. "What about footprints? If there was a struggle, the killer must have left footprints in the sand." Surely Cowboy would have fought his assailant.

"Sure. Him or her and about ten thousand other people who visited the beach today," Det. Burns replied. "And depending on the time of death, we can't be certain yet where the victim entered the water. The body was drifting north with the current."

"Do you have any idea what his real name was?" asked Kelly.

"Not yet," said the detective. "We've been canvassing the area. Seems all the local shop owners knew the guy but only superficially.

"Several employees at Captain Haddock's have identified a pair matching the two of you. You, Mr. Leland, were one of the last people to have seen the dead man."

"And the killer," Harry retorted.

Det. Burns rummaged through his pockets and pulled out a wallet in a sealed plastic evidence bag.

"Another one?" Kelly said.

"That's my wallet," Harry said with surprise. He reached out to pick it up.

Det. Burns laid his hand over Harry's. "This is evidence, Mr. Leland."

"Evidence of what?" Harry demanded. "I lost it or someone took it. I didn't kill that man."

"Where did you find it?" Kelly interrupted.

"A tourist went to, uh, relieve himself in the bushes outside 1201 Ocean. He said he looked down at his feet and there it was."

"You mean he—" Harry looked at his wallet in horror.

"No," replied the detective. "Lucky for you, he saw it first. Now let's get back to your story."

"It's not a story, detective." Harry pouted.

"So tell me how your wallet ended up in that bush."

"May I have it back?" Harry held out his hand.

"All in due course," Det. Burns replied. "Talk."

Harry hesitated. "Fine." He looked uneasily at Kelly before continuing. "I was following some of Dr. Barron's friends. Two of them, the Dennises, stopped for a moment and looked back. They might have seen me."

"They saw you?" Kelly blurted. "You told me no one saw you!"

The detective shot her a look of disapproval. "Go ahead, Mr. Leland."

"I don't know for sure. I hid in the bushes."

The detective nodded as if this was normal behavior. Maybe for Harry Leland it was, thought Kelly.

"Why were you following Charles Barron's friends?"

"I'm writing a story about his murder for Myrtle Scene Magazine. I wanted some background."

"I don't believe this." Kelly folded her arms over her blanket and mumbled to herself.

"Why not just speak to them, instead of following them around?" Det. Burns pressed.

"I was hoping I might find something out." Harry licked his fingertips and wiped his hand through his hair. "There's something fishy about the lot of them."

"Fishy how?"

"They did not appear upset. In fact, they were drinking and having a good time."

Det. Burns pushed himself up from the table. "No crime in that." He loomed over Harry. "There is, however, a crime in stalking. I suggest you stop following people around and leave the police work to me."

"Yes, officer," Kelly answered for both of them. "Let's go, Harry."

This time, the detective did not object.

21

Upstairs in Aunt Ruth's small apartment the following morning, Kelly shared a light breakfast with her dad. He buttered up a slice of sourdough toast and dropped it on her plate. "Eat."

"Thanks." Kelly dutifully nibbled. She was worn out, mentally and physically. If there were any other ways to be worn out, she'd be those too.

Ben Walsh waited at the toaster for a couple more slices to pop. "I heard you come in pretty late last night."

Kelly yawned. "I was out with Harry."

"Oh?" Her father's eyes twinkled mischievously.

Kelly made a face. "Yuck. Please. It was nothing like that. You're as bad as that detective."

"What detective?" Ben grabbed the jar of peanut butter from the shelf and sat with his toast.

They worked their way through a strong pot of black coffee while Kelly filled him in on the night's adventure.

The landline at the edge of the kitchen counter rang.

"I'll answer it." Kelly's dad hopped to the counter and grabbed the phone.

"Great news," he said after hanging up. "Ruth has regained consciousness."

Kelly slid back her chair. "Let's go."

"Relax, Kelly. The doctors are examining her. We can visit her this afternoon."

Kelly sank down at the kitchen table. "Fine. That will give me time to get room 206 ready."

Her father's brow went up. "The murder room?"

"Do you have to call it that?" That was all the Beach Lovers Inn needed—for room 206 to become known around town as the Murder Room. This being the Internet Age, the name would spread like wildfire.

He chuckled. "Sorry, no. You want some help?"

"No, thanks. Drew and I, plus the crew, have it covered."

"Are you sure?"

She patted his hand. "I'm sure. If I need an extra pair of hands, I'll enlist George. You rest that leg."

"I am not an invalid," Ben grumbled.

"Yes, you are. A very lovable invalid, but an invalid nonetheless." Kelly rose, kissed his cheek and headed out to find Drew.

She caught up with her head of housekeeping in the laundry room.

"Hi, Kelly. I heard about the fireworks last night." Drew stuffed a foam pillow into a fresh cover.

"Fireworks?"

She glanced around. The coast was clear, only a family of five seated at the picnic table at the edge of the courtyard. "You finding the dead body on the beach."

"Oh, those fireworks."

"When Cousin Drake told me you and Harry Leland found the body of some vagrant floating out to sea last night, you could have knocked me over with a feather." She smirked. "What's up with that, anyway? You dating one of the guests? I thought that was a no-no?"

Kelly held her temper. She could see that her employee was teasing. "It is a no-no, and in the case of

Harry Leland, it's a never-never." She gripped Drew's shoulder. "Did this cousin of yours say if they had anything on the dead man?"

Drew shook her head. "Not even a name. He says it was murder for sure though."

Kelly shivered. She'd been hoping, against all odds, that it had been an accidental drowning. "I can't believe there's been another murder."

Drew maneuvered a laundry cart out the door. She rolled the cart down the breezeway with Kelly at her side. "You think the two murders are related?"

"I wish I knew. I can tell you this though." Kelly paused as one of the part-time housekeepers scooted past them to grab some bottles of shampoo from the side of the cart then left again.

"What?" Drew asked after the young woman had gone.

"The dead man last night was a homeless man nicknamed Cowboy. He told Harry that he saw Aunt Ruth get pushed down the stairs."

"No!" Drew clutched a pillow to her chest. "Seriously?"

"Yep. That's why I was with Harry. Cowboy wanted a hundred bucks to spill whatever he knew."

"Wow." Drew, despite her tan, looked suddenly pale. "Instead, somebody spilled the dude's blood." Her brow rose. "That would explain what I told you about it looking like maybe we had a night visitor camping out. It could have been this cowboy."

"I was thinking the same thing."

Both women fell silent.

"Do you suppose it's true?" Drew asked finally. "Was Ruth pushed?"

"I'll find out this afternoon. The hospital called and she's doing better. Dad and I are going to see her this afternoon. She'll have some answers."

"I hope so," Drew replied. "I don't like the idea of a murderer running loose here at the inn."

"Me either."

"Shall we get busy?"

Room 206 couldn't be put off any longer.

Harry peered down from the balcony outside his room. Irwin Brunner was stretched out poolside on a cedar chaise lounge with a thick taupe cushion. Brunner was a lanky man in his late fifties or so, with thick red hair.

A copy of the newspaper draped over Mr. Brunner's bare belly. Baggy red swim trunks started at his waist and ended at his knobby knees.

A boy and girl each wearing inflatable water wings on their arms thrashed in the shallow end of the swimming pool while their mother watched placidly from a chair placed strategically in the shade.

The Rochesters, Jill and Vivian, occupied a pair of chaise lounges near the diving board. They were holding hands. Vivian wore a floppy wide-brimmed white hat while Jill's head was bare and her face was turned idolatrously towards the bright midmorning sun.

Harry marched up to Irwin Brunner and cleared his throat to get the man's attention. "Good morning."

Mr. Brunner looked up. "Hello."

Harry was going to be blunt. "You weren't with the others at dinner last night, Mr. Brunner." He had set his investigative sights on Irwin Brunner for just that reason.

Irwin Brunner slid his big dark sunglasses down his long nose, revealing a pair of narrow-set pale blue eyes. "So?"

"Where were you?"

"What business is that of yours, Mister...?"

"Leland. Harry Leland. I'm working with the Myrtle Beach police on the murder of Charles Barron."

Irwin Brunner looked amused. "Are you now? Funny, I thought you were a guest here. Like me. Now, if you don't mind, I'm trying to get some sun." He flopped over on his stomach. His back was nearly hairless and pale white.

Harry repositioned himself at the head of the chaise lounge and bent down to Brunner's level. "There was a second murder last night."

Irwin Brunner shooed him lazily with his hand. "The light, Leland. You are blocking the light."

"Don't you want to know who was murdered?"

Brunner sighed. "I suppose if you really want to tell me." He positioned himself on his elbows. "Who?"

"A homeless man. He was known locally as Cowboy."

"Ah, the vagrant." Brunner snatched the newspaper at his side. "There was a mention in the back of the paper. A vagrant drowned or something." He sounded completely disinterested. "Nothing to do with me."

"All of Dr. Barron's friends went to dinner at Captain Haddock's last evening. It was quite a wake. I'm surprised you weren't there."

"Friends?" Brunner laughed. Jill and Vivian glanced at them. Brunner swung his legs to the ground. In a low voice, he said, "Charlie Barron had no friends. Tell me, Harry." He tickled Harry's knee with his fingers. "May I call you Harry?"

Harry nodded and Brunner continued talking. "Was Mary at Captain Haddock's last night?"

"No."

"Interesting." Brunner's bushy graying brow went up. "Where was she do you think, Harry?"

"Her husband was brutally murdered. I'm sure she was in her room. Dealing with her grief."

Brunner beamed, delighted with Harry's answer. "You would think that, wouldn't you?" He shook his head sadly. "but she wasn't."

"How do you know?"

"Because I went to pay a visit to the Merry Widow at her room yesterday evening. She didn't answer her door or her telephone, for that matter."

"She may have been asleep. Or bathing."

"Her rented car was gone. It's a blue Jag. Always the best for the Barrons. It wasn't in the lot."

Harry made a mental note to pay a call on the widow later. She seemed to like him. Maybe she would be willing to talk. Tell him things she wouldn't tell the police.

"Is there anything else, Harry?" Brunner scooped up a sweating can of diet soda from the slide out tray built into the lounger and drank.

"You say Dr. Barron had no friends. Why did you come to this reunion?"

"Because Charlie said he wanted to make amends."

"Amends for what?"

"For a lifetime of being an ass, I suppose." He offered Harry a sip. Harry declined. "Why don't we have a drink later, just you and me?"

Out of the corner of his eye, Harry saw Kelly and a woman from housekeeping attacking the crime scene tape stuck to the doorframe of room 206. "I'll have to get back to you on that."

"Of course." Brunner repositioned the lounge chair, angling it so his back was now to the sun. "Let me know. I could tell you stories, Harry."

Harry mumbled some words and hurried up the steps to the second floor. "What are you doing?" he demanded breathlessly.

Drew Schiffer eyed him curiously. Kelly's eyes flashed irritation and impatience.

"What does it look like, Harry?" Kelly grabbed the last of the yellow and black tape, balled it up and tossed it in a trash bag hanging from the housekeeping trolley.

Drew removed a plastic bucket from the cart into which she dropped a bottle of green cleaning solution. She grabbed a handful of clean rags. "I'll meet you inside, Kelly."

"I'll bring the vacuum." Kelly replied. She reached for the industrial strength machine. The room was going to need it and then some.

"Wait." Harry placed his fingers over Kelly's wrist.

"What is it now, Harry? I've got work to do."

"This is important."

"It's always important with you." She grabbed the canvas bag of vacuum hose attachments. "Whatever it is can wait." She started into the room.

"Let's reenact the murder."

That stopped her.

"What?"

"I said, let's reenact Charlie Barron's murder." Hope lit Harry's eyes.

"You want us to reenact Dr. Barron's murder?"

"Yes."

She blinked at him. "Why?"

"What's up?" Drew appeared in the entry still clutching her cleaning materials and curious as to what was going on. "Are we doing this or not?"

"Yes. Sorry, we are doing this." Kelly nodded for Harry to take a hike. Preferably off the pier.

"Good morning, Mr. Leland," said Drew with a smile that only went as far as her lips.

"Hello," mumbled Harry.

"Harry here wants me to bash him in the head with a lamp."

"What?" Drew gasped.

"Or vice versa," Harry added quickly. "I think we should reenact the murder," he said for Drew's benefit.

"Why?" demanded Drew. She shot a look to Kelly that she interpreted as suggesting that Harry was nuttier than a jar of peanut butter.

"It's important." A bead of sweat erupted on Harry's hairline. Like always, he was overdressed, long-sleeved shirt and long pants. "We might learn something about the crime."

"Shouldn't we be leaving that to the police?" Drew said. "I have a cousin on the force, by the way."

"I agree with Drew."

"Please? It will only take a minute. This is our only chance before you rent the room out again."

"If I say yes, do you promise to go away?"

Harry laid his hand over his heart. "I won't pester you again."

Kelly sighed heavily and set the vacuum on the ground. "Fine. Let's get this over with."

"Are you sure about this?" Drew laid a hand on Kelly's upper arm.

"I'm sure. In fact, I just may enjoy this." She gave

Harry a curious look. "Care to witness the show, Drew?"

"Not me. I've got rooms to clean." She tossed the cleaning materials back on the cart. "Call me when you're through."

"Wait a second!" Kelly called.

The two huddled. "Don't go too far," Kelly urged. "Just in case."

Drew nodded with understanding and wheeled away. Room 202 was empty and close enough to hear a distress call.

Inside room 206, Kelly moved uneasily towards the bathroom. A dark stain covered several tiles. Fingerprinting dust coated every square inch of the guestroom. It was going to take more than a little elbow grease to get room 206 back in order. She might enlist her father to lend a hand after all.

"What do you want me to do?" Carefully avoiding standing in the bloodstain, Kelly moved over near the microwave oven and mini-fridge.

Harry picked up the remaining lamp on the other night table. The one that had been used to bash Charlie Barron's head in had been removed by the police. He hefted the lamp in his hand. "Heavy."

"No kidding." She watched him curiously. If he was the killer, this would be his opportunity to bash her skull in. She wasn't about to give him that chance.

"Stand over there." He pointed to the bathroom.

Kelly took a steadying breath and did as asked. She stepped into the smaller room housing the shower/bath combo and toilet. "How's this?"

Harry sidled up along the vanity wall just outside the door to the shower. "Perfect." He steadied the lamp in his hand.

"Don't break that!"

"I won't." He gripped it with both hands. "Come on. Walk out. Slowly."

"You hit me with that lamp and you are a dead man, Harry." Kelly grumbled but complied.

"Ouch. That's funny."

Kelly stopped. "What's funny?"

Harry was holding the lamp with both hands. He set it on the vanity. "If I'm standing here against the wall like this and holding the lamp with both hands, it's too awkward. You see?" He moved his arm awkwardly up and down. "If I try to lift the lamp, I hit the wall."

"Try holding it in one hand."

Harry did so. "It's heavy. I can barely manage it." Holding the lamp base tightly around its middle with his right hand for fear of dropping it, he slowly moved his arm up and down.

"There you go. The killer used one hand. Dr. Barron stepped out of the shower and wham-o!" Kelly banged her fist into her palm.

Harry looked troubled.

"Now what?"

"If the murderer used his right arm, he couldn't have been pushed up against the wall. See?" Harry pressed against the wall. "I can't move my arm."

"So?" Kelly planted her hands on her hips.

"So it means either the killer stood away from the doorway—"

"In which case Charlie Barron should have seen him," Kelly said.

Harry nodded. "At the very least he would have been struck in the face not on the back of the head."

"I'll be darned." Kelly inclined her head. Harry just

might have been onto something.

"There is one other solution." Harry wrapped the lamp cord around the base of the lamp and returned it to the night table.

"Which is?"

"The killer was left handed. If he—"

"Or she."

"Or she," allowed Harry, "was left handed, they would not have had any trouble shouldering against the wall and bringing down their left arm on the back of Dr. Barron's head as he came out of the shower."

Kelly gave it a try, without the lamp. "It works."

"Told you," Harry said smugly. "I wonder if the police know."

"I'm sure they do." Kelly stepped around the stain on the floor and gave Harry a push towards the exit. "If you want to mention it to Det. Burns, be my guest."

Kelly had a feeling the detective was tired of both of them interfering in his investigation. She had no desire to antagonize him further.

Drew stuck her head in the door. "Everything all right in here?"

"Fine, Drew." Kelly turned to Harry. "Are we done?"

"Yes." Harry stopped halfway to the door and turned. "Do you suppose your aunt could be in any danger?"

"What are you talking about?"

"Suppose she really was pushed down the stairs and that it was no accident. And suppose whoever pushed her is the same person who murdered Charles Barron."

"What are you trying to say, Harry?"

"Don't you think now that Mrs. Evans is conscious that the killer—"

"Hypothetical killer," Kelly asserted.

"Hypothetical killer," Harry allowed. "Don't you think such a person might want to make certain that your aunt didn't talk?"

Kelly's eyelids fell. "Why do you do this, Harry?"

"Do what?" He was baffled.

"Do you hate me?"

"Hate you? No. Of course, not." He turned to Drew but the young woman was grinning. This was more fun for her than the soaps she usually watched while turning over the rooms when the guests were out.

"That's it. You hate me." Kelly pushed her fingers across her scalp. "I mean. That is the only explanation for why you are constantly saying things to scare me or annoy me."

"I don't mean to—"

"Shut up and come on."

Kelly bounded down the stairs and burst into the lobby. There was a pint-sized man behind the counter whom she had never seen before. She stopped short. "Who are you?"

"I'm—" The fellow's face contorted like he'd been caught with his pants down around his ankles.

Kelly threw up her hand. "Never mind."

She'd get to the bottom of the mystery of the diminutive man behind the counter later. Right now, she had more pressing concerns.

Kelly stepped around the stranger, snatching her car keys from behind the counter.

"Where are we going?"

"To see Aunt Ruth!"

22

Kelly led Harry to a shiny red Audi A4 and jumped behind the wheel.

"Nice car." Harry admired the late-model coupe. There wasn't a scratch on it. His wheels, a hand me down from his older sister, were a rust heap in comparison.

"Thanks. It's one of the few things I kept from the marriage. Hop in." Beyond the car and a few personal belongings, she had accepted a lump sum settlement from Alan and no alimony. The money had become her down payment on the inn—and her new life.

Harry pulled open the door and gaped. Trash, various makeup odds and ends of which he only recognized three as being lip gloss tubes and sand littered the sleek black leather sports seats. Ditto the floor. He stood there, unsure what to do.

"Hold on." Kelly hastily shoved some of the garbage to the floorboard and tossed the rest over her shoulder to the backseat.

"Thanks." Harry was still searching for the buckle of his seatbelt when Kelly surged out of the parking lot. She waved to her father standing at the edge of the inn, leaning on his crutch.

She got halfway down the block then hit the brakes.

Harry flew forward, throwing his hands against the

dash. "What are you doing?"

"Dad might want to come." She backed up quickly.

Her father hobbled up to the curb. "Kelly, what are you two up to?"

She ordered Harry to roll down his window. "We're going to see Ruth. Want to come?"

Ben glanced at his wristwatch. "Now? We're supposed to wait until this afternoon. The nurse on the phone said—"

Kelly gunned the engine. "I'd rather go now. Are you in or are you out?"

Ben shrugged at Harry. "I'm in."

Harry moved to the rear seat and Kelly's father hopped up front, settling his crutch between the seats.

They made it to the medical center in record time. Det. Nick Burns was spilling out from the automatic doors of the visitor's entrance as Ben and Harry, mostly Ben with his broken leg, struggled to keep up with Kelly. She seemed determined to do everything in double-time, like a fast-forwarding video.

It was all Ben and Harry could do to keep her in their sight.

Kelly stepped in the detective's path. "Det. Burns, what are you doing here?"

"A routine visit." He ran the back of his hand along his damp forehead and then made a show of check his watch. "I am in a hurry. I've got court in less than an hour."

"Wait," pleaded Kelly. "How is my aunt?"

"She's fine. Fragile. Resting comfortably." The detective was wearing an unremarkable brown suit and clutching a worn black leather briefcase. He pinched his brows together, noting the concern on all three of their faces. "Is everything all right, Mrs. Green?"

"Yes."

"We're anxious to see my sister. I assume we can visit her now?" Ben Walsh tapped his crutch on the sidewalk impatiently.

"Sure. You can go right ahead, as far as I am concerned. Unless the staff tell you otherwise."

"And Mrs. Evans is alert? Is she coherent?" Harry wanted to know.

"Like I said, she's fine."

"We think the murderer might want to silence her," Harry said bluntly.

Det. Burns jerked his head back. "You do? Why?"

"It's only a theory." Kelly backpedalled. In the light of day, out of the so-called *murder room* and standing in the blazing sun surrounded by friendly faces, the idea—Harry's idea—seemed absurd.

"Is Ruth in any danger?" Ben Walsh demanded.

"I think not. She's in a hospital room, not out wandering in a dark alley in the middle of the night."

Kelly and Harry shared a look. Those stinging words were meant for them.

Det. Burns shifted his briefcase to his left hand. "What's this all about?"

Harry explained that whoever bashed Dr. Barron's skull in could have been the same person to push Ruth Evans down the stairs. "And murder Cowboy. The killer might try to silence her."

"Over my dead body," swore Ben Walsh.

"Interesting," admitted the detective, a vague smile shading his words.

"*Was* Cowboy murdered?" Kelly asked.

"According to the coroner, yes. No doubt about it."

"So Aunt Ruth could still be in danger." Kelly and her father shared a look of concern.

Det. Burns shook his head. "No. I don't think so. You see, we have our killer."

"You do?"

"At least a very good suspect."

"Who is it?" asked Harry.

"One Frank Murphrey."

"Who's that?" Kelly asked. "I don't recognize the name. He's not one of our guests."

"No, he's not." The detective explained how a couple of the big chain hotels near the airport had been suffering a spate of guest room burglaries and parking garage holdups. The hotels had increased their security and surveillance efforts. Det. Burns moved to the edge of the walkway, setting his briefcase down on the ledge of stone seating wall running the length of the path from the parking lot. He popped open the briefcase. Papers spilled to his feet. Red-faced, he scooped them up.

The wind grabbed a photograph and gave it flight. Kelly snatched it before it could make its escape.

"That's Frank Murphrey," Det. Burns said. "Recognize him?"

"No." Kelly was looking at the picture of a nasty pug of a man with dark, deep-set eyes and a shaved head. A blue tattoo ran from beneath the collar of his shirt, up his neck, along his chin and up to his ear.

Harry and her father also stated they had never set eyes on the man.

"He looks like he'd just as soon take a bite out of you as say hello." Once seen, she could never have forgotten him.

Det. Burns laughed appreciatively as she handed

across the photo. "A security guard caught Mr. Murphrey exiting one of their guest wings through a fire door. He had broken into two rooms. Made off with a camera, a top-of-the-line cellphone and some jewelry in the first.

"He wasn't so lucky in the second. That room was occupied. The guest, a Mr. Plowman, is a bodybuilder. Arms as thick as my thighs. Murphrey managed to get away from Plowman but he's got a busted arm." Det. Burns didn't sound broken up about it.

"That's a relief," Kelly said.

Harry had a question. "Was Murphrey left-handed?"

"Yeah, as a matter-of-fact, he is. At least, he was until Plowman busted it for him. Why?"

Kelly's father provided the answer. The two had filled him in on the drive to the medical center. "Harry has a theory that Charlie Barron's killer was left-handed, detective."

Harry took over, describing to the wide-eyed detective how he and Kelly had reenacted the murder in room 206.

"Harry," Det. Burns said when Harry wrapped up his tale, and foregoing formality, "is a man of many theories. In this case, he may have proven to be right."

"Has this Murphrey killed before, Det. Burns?" Harry asked.

"He's been arrested on burglary charges a dozen times but never murder. But there's a first time for everything. And he's been known to be working in this area for some time."

"What does Murphrey have to say about Charles Barron?" The question came from Kelly.

"Nothing. He says he never met the man and

wouldn't bother waste his time and talents burgling at what he called a two-bit hotel like the Beach Lovers Inn." Embarrassment showed on his face. "Sorry, Mrs. Green. His words, not mine."

He made a show of looking at his watch once again. "Now, if you don't mind. I am in a hurry."

The detective went one way and the three of them went the other.

Ruth was sitting up in bed when they entered her room. Stopping first in the hospital's gift shop located strategically near the entrance, they bore gifts. A huge arrangement of roses, a large box of truffles and a stuffed panda bear.

Her aunt's face lit up. "I seem to be under siege. Ben? What are you doing here?" She squirmed and held out her hands. "Come here and give me a hug."

Her brother squeezed her carefully. "How are you?"

"Tired." Ruth folded her hands atop the sheets bundled around her.

"Can I get you anything?" Kelly handed her aunt the truffles.

"Can you make some room for me, Harry?" Ben bobbed his chin in the direction of the night table.

"Yes, sir." Harry removed a tray holding the remains of Ruth's lunch and placed the tray on a visitor's chair near the door.

Crutch in one hand, flowers in the other, Ben settled the bouquet of roses and baby's breath on the bedside table.

By unspoken consent, they kept their voices low. Aunt Ruth's roommate was sleeping on her side in the bed a couple of feet to their right.

Harry was clutching the panda bear's right paw in

his other hand. "Hello, Mrs. Evans."

"Hello, Harry." Aunt Ruth wriggled her fingers in his direction. "New pet?"

"Oh, sorry." Harry blushed. "This is for you."

"Thank you, Harry." Aunt Ruth placed the toy bear on the pillow beside her. "Now, would one of you like to tell me why my brother is walking around with a broken leg?"

"It's nothing, Ruth," Ben replied, balancing on his crutch.

"Nothing?"

"Compared to you. Let's review, you've got a broken elbow, hip and leg. Wanna race?" Mindful of the bandages, he gently tousled his sister's hair. "And let's not talk about the skull fracture. Tell me, did it knock some sense *into* or *out of* you?"

"Very funny." She pointed. "The leg, Ben."

"I slipped in the shower," Ben said, facing the window.

"Ha!" Kelly scoffed. "He fell off his motorcycle, Aunt Ruth."

"Motorcycle!" Ruth disdained motorcycles every bit as much as Ben's wife, Katie, had.

"Traitor."

"Overgrown child," Kelly replied with love.

Harry broke the convivial mood. "You are lucky to be alive, Mrs. Evans."

"I know that, Harry."

"I think somebody tried to kill you."

A look of alarm flashed across her aunt Ruth's face.

"Harry!" admonished Kelly.

"Do you remember?" Harry pressed on. "Did somebody push you? Did you see who it was? Did he have a tattoo? A shaved head?"

"Now, now, son." Ben hobbled over to Harry at the bedside and restrained him. Ruth was looking sallow.

"Pushed?" Ruth's voice sounded dry and cracked. "I-I don't remember." She shook her head in irritation. "I'm afraid I don't remember much of anything." She looked at the three of them with frightened eyes. "Murphrey? Who's that?"

A monitor near her bedside flashed green and emitted a steady beep.

"Was it a man with a blue tattoo on his face and neck?" Harry ran his hand up his own neck.

Kelly felt like strangling him.

"I'm sorry. The police asked me the same thing. They showed me a picture of a man. I think his name was Murphrey." She shook her head to clear the cobwebs. "He was ugly, Ben. Uglier than you," she softened her words with a loving wink.

"Ha-ha." Ben tapped his crutch against the tile floor.

"I'm sorry, Aunt Ruth. Don't mind Harry." Kelly shot him the dirtiest look she could summons.

A nurse and an orderly burst through the doorway. "What's the trouble?" demanded the orderly, frowning at the monitor.

The nurse rushed to Ruth Evans' bedside. "Are you okay?" She laid her fingers on her patient's bony wrist. She snapped her fingers. "Call the doctor, would you?"

The orderly departed quickly.

The nurse asked them to do the same and herded them towards the door.

"What about Cowboy, Mrs. Evans?" Harry cried. "Do you know Cowboy?"

"Out you go!" The nurse gave Harry an extra shove.

23

Back at the Beach Lovers Inn, Ben retired to their room citing fatigue. Harry followed Kelly into the lobby.

The little guy with the buzz cut was sorting mail behind the front desk. "Hi, Harry."

"Hi, welcome back." Harry helped himself to a glass of lemon water at the refreshment bar.

"Who's the chick?"

Kelly glared at the diminutive figure. She had nearly forgotten all about the stranger she had caught behind the counter earlier. It was unbelievable that he was still here. Why hadn't somebody tossed him out?

"The chick has a name and it is Kelly Green. Do you mind? Customers aren't allowed back there." Where was Lee Hollister? Shouldn't she have been on duty? Keeping riff-raff like this guy out?

"Sorry, no offense," said the man who Kelly pegged as being in his mid- to late-forties. "It's just the way I talk. People say I have a bit of a mouth."

He also had sloped shoulders, a round face and squinty gray-blue eyes. There was a familiar look to him.

The stranger winked as he came around from behind the counter and joined them. He wore a deep pink polo shirt with white pleated shorts held up with a brown leather belt with a shiny silver seashell buckle. Chocolate brown leather sandals exposed ten fat toes. "But I'm harmless. Ask Harry."

Kelly did have a question for Harry. But that wasn't the one. She finally figured out who he looked like. "What's Gilbert Gottfried doing here?" She and Allen had caught the comedian's act once while vacationing in New York City.

"Huh?" Harry was confused.

"I am not Gilbert Gottfried." The man spoke for himself. "I'm Rick Ramus."

Kelly snapped her fingers. "Right. I'm so sorry. Please, when I saw you behind the desk, I thought you were a guest or something."

"No offense, dear. Are you a friend of Harry's? Girlfriend, maybe?" He added with a leer.

"Yes," replied Harry.

"Friend," clarified Kelly. "In a manner of speaking. Aunt Ruth told me about you, Mr. Ramus. You've been on vacation, right?"

Rick Ramus was the inn's part-time assistant manager. Kelly was going to be needing him desperately. It was important to stay on his good side.

"If you call performing three shows a night for two weeks, while sleeping in cramped quarters with a snoring stranger for a roommate aboard a Christopher Columbus-era cruise ship with lousy internet service, a vacation, then, yes, that's where I have been."

He eyed Kelly with disapproval. "Who did you say you are?"

Mr. Ramus' voice was both shrill and raspy. It made her want to stick her finger in her ear and clear the wax out.

"I'm Kelly Green." She put her hand out and he reluctantly took it. "I'm taking over the inn from my aunt."

"Yes, Ruth mentioned you were coming. Welcome," he added reluctantly.

Rick Ramus tugged at his shirt collar but not before first wiping his hand on the front of his shorts. Kelly wondered if he had a problem with germs in general or her in particular.

"You sure look like Gilbert Gottfried. You must get that a lot, huh?"

"For the record, I look nothing like Gottfried. I'm taller. And funnier."

"Are you kidding me? You look exactly like him."

Rick turned to Harry and said forlornly, "Which is exactly why I never made it in show business. Casting agents and booking agents all say I look and sound too much like him." He sniffed. "It isn't fair."

"I know, buddy." Harry patted Rick on the shoulder.

Kelly poked her finger into his other shoulder. "Can you do the parrot from Aladdin?"

"No," Rick Ramus said flatly.

"That insurance duck?"

Rick waddled off, head forward, back bent, looking very much like a parrot more so than a duck in Kelly's opinion.

"Was it something I said?" asked Kelly.

"Rick is a little sensitive about the parrot thing. And that insurance company cancelled his policy." Harry excused himself to do some writing.

Kelly remained behind, dutifully tending to inn business for the next several hours, fielding calls and catering to her guests' requests.

The phone at the front desk rang and Kelly answered it. "Hello, Beach Lovers Inn where every day is a ray of sunshine and every night is a dream." She'd just thought up of the phrase and liked it. She jotted it down on the pad beside the phone and congratulated herself. It could be the inn's new catchphrase. It sure beat any slogan that included the phrase *murder room*.

Unfortunately, the man on the other end of the line was not so congratulatory. It was one of Ruth's team of doctors. He had heard about her visit with Aunt Ruth.

Kelly's face heated up as he gave her an earful and warned her to be more considerate of her aunt's condition in the future.

Kelly promised she would. Feeling lower than an earthworm, she slunk out of the lobby. She caught up with Drew in the courtyard as she was going off shift.

"How's Ruth?" asked Drew. She had exchanged her housekeeping uniform for a pair of shorts and a bright red tank top.

Kelly gave her the abbreviated version. "She's doing better. Still rough and the doctors want to keep her a bit longer. She doesn't remember anything about the accident."

"Give her my best. Do you think it would be okay if I visit her tomorrow?"

"Call first to be sure," Kelly replied, still stinging from her recent rebuke. She glanced up at room 206.

Drew smiled. "I know what you're thinking. Don't worry. Room 206 is ready to go."

"You cleaned it?"

"Me and George," Drew answered.

"George?"

"Yeah, he was a doll. He insisted on helping."

"Thanks." Kelly gave Drew a one-handed hug. "I can't say I regret not being there to assist. I'll have to thank

George."

"I tell you, if we ever need another housekeeper, he's our man. He's a natural. He went over that room with a fine-tooth comb."

Kelly laughed. "If I was a more skeptical person and I didn't know that Charlie Barron's killer had already been captured, I'd think George was the murderer and that he was afraid he might have left an incriminating clue behind."

Drew creased her brow. Her smartphone chimed an incoming text. She glanced at the screen. "That's my date." She stuffed the phone in her back pocket. "Are you sure the police have caught the murderer?"

"Positive." Kelly explained how they had met Det. Burns at the hospital and he had given them the good news.

"That's funny." Drew inclined her head. "I guess he didn't know at the time."

"Know what?" Kelly frowned. "Why do I have the feeling that whatever it is you have to say is the opposite of funny?"

Drew twisted her keyring in her fingers. "Drake stopped by about an hour ago to see how things were going here. Unofficially. He had just gotten off-duty. He said—"

Drew hesitated. "He told me, in strictest confidence, mind you."

"Of course."

Drew glanced around the courtyard. Nearly all the tables were occupied but no one seemed to be paying either woman any particular attention. "He told me that the man they thought initially might have been responsible for Dr. Barron's death has an alibi and couldn't have done it."

"Frank Murphrey?"

"That was the name Drake mentioned. And he said the man has a rock solid alibi."

"How rock solid?" Kelly's stomach felt all queasy.

"He was caught on one of those CCTV cameras going into a bar a block from the airport at the time of the murder."

"That's solid."

"Sorry."

"On the lighter side," Kelly was determined not to let the dark cloud of murder hang over her head, "the assistant manager is back from his vacation. At least we'll have some extra help around here."

"Rick? Yeah, I saw him earlier in the lobby. In fact, we caught his act a couple of nights ago. He's added some new material."

"You did? I thought he'd been out of town?"

"He was. Got back a little while ago. We saw him next door in the lounge."

"At the Golden Arms?"

Drew nodded. "Rick's hilarious. You should go see him the next time he's playing in town. Knows his way around a hotel, too." Drew made walking motions in the darkening air with her fingers. "Gotta run."

"Back to square one," Kelly said to her housekeeper's receding shadow.

And what was that about having caught Rick Ramus's show a couple of nights ago? Hadn't he told her he had only returned to town that day?

24

Ben was snoozing on the sofa with a baseball game on the TV in the background as Kelly entered Ruth's apartment. She shook him awake.

He came alert and rubbed his eyes. "What's up, Kelly?"

"Bad news, Dad. According to Drew's cousin on the force, Frank Murphrey has an alibi for the night of Dr. Barron's murder."

"That is bad news. For us." His mouth formed a cavern as he yawned. "Good news for him, I suppose." Like his daughter, he would have preferred to have this whole nasty business wrapped up in a neat package— the not-so-neat package that was Frank Murphrey. "Did Drew say if the police have any other leads?"

"She didn't mention anything."

"I want to know what happened every bit as much as you do, Kelly. A man's been murdered. More importantly to me personally is that somebody might have tried to kill Ruth." He squeezed his fingers under the edge of his cast and scratched. "But do you know how many times I got called in to fix a plumbing repair that some well-meaning do-it-yourselfer screwed up?"

"How many?"

"Enough to pay your college tuition," he chuckled.

"What are you saying?"

"I'm saying you call a plumber to do your plumbing, right?"

"I call you."

"Same thing. My point is, why not let the police handle the police work?"

"This is important, Dad. I want the inn to succeed. I need it to succeed. The Beach Lovers Inn has been around a very long time. I don't want to be the one who let it fail."

Ben Walsh eased his broken leg to the floor with his hand and patted the now empty square beside him. "Okay." He rubbed his whiskered face. "Let's think about this. Maybe you aren't asking yourself the right questions."

She sat and folded her legs under herself.

Reaching for the remote, Ben turned off the ballgame. The Cardinals were losing anyway. He stuck his hand in the bowl of popcorn resting on the end table and tossed a few kernels in his mouth. "Suspects." He wiped his salty, buttery fingers on his cast. "Who've we got?"

Kelly did the math on her fingers. "Harry, George, Gilbert Gottfried, each and every one of Dr. Barron's friends. His wife?"

"Didn't you say she was watching the fireworks show?"

Kelly clenched her jaw. "I think so. I mean, I was watching the fireworks. If I had known there was going to be a murder, I would have concentrated more on who was there."

"Or, in this case, who wasn't there."

"Right." Kelly sighed. "Pass the popcorn." She shoveled out a handful and munched. "There's also your new girlfriend, Mrs. McConaughey."

"Very funny." He pulled at a beer and offered it to Kelly who declined. "See if I throw you a lifeline the next time you are drowning, young lady." He scratched harder at his cast. "Do they stick itching powder in these things on purpose?"

Kelly giggled. "Remember this itch the next time you get an itch to ride a motorcycle."

"Very funny." He gave up. "And I'm dying to know what you think Gilbert Gottfried has to do with this. Do I have to ask?"

Kelly swallowed a mouthful of popcorn. Too much butter and too much salt. Just the way her dad liked it. Mom must be rolling over in her grave. "He's the assistant manager. He bears a striking resemblance to that comedian who voiced the parrot in Aladdin."

"Iago?"

"That's right! His real name is Rick Ramus. He's been on vacation. Got back today, or so he implied."

"But?"

"But Drew saw him a couple of nights ago performing in the lounge at the Golden Arms." She sidled up to her father. "I think you should go ask Mildred McConaughey about that, Dad."

He barked out a laugh. "I have a broken leg, in case you forgot. I'll leave the sleuthing to you." He pressed a cold finger against the tip of her nose. "Off you go."

He retrieved the TV remote and flicked the game back on. The Cardinals had made up two runs. "Let me know what you learn."

Kelly grabbed her purse and paused at the door. "You're milking it, old man. Using that broken leg to your own advantage how and when it suits you."

"I know." Her father was grinning ear to shining ear. "Isn't it great? I may never remove this thing." He knocked his knuckles against his cast. It was crowded with the signatures of well-wishers.

Halfway down the stairs, Kelly stopped, wrestling with herself. Harry got along great with Mildred McConaughey. Talking to the infuriating bulldog of a woman would go much easier with Harry to facilitate things.

She turned around and knocked on Harry's door. She received no answer. He was either out or so wrapped up in writing his next Great American Mystery Novel that he couldn't be bothered to come to the door.

It was going to be up to her.

Inside the resplendent lobby of the Golden Arms Hotel, Kelly couldn't help being impressed. And a little intimidated. The lobby had a golden rotunda ceiling, a glistening marble floor and plush velvet furnishings with gold accents.

A man in a navy suit with sharp eyes framed in silver eyeglasses smiled at her approach. "May I help you?"

"Is Mrs. McConaughey in?"

"Is there a problem?"

"No." Kelly drummed the black granite counter. "I was hoping to speak with her."

The man's smile was threatening to break down. "If you would tell me what the trouble is, I'm sure I could help."

Kelly took a deep breath. "Let me explain. I'm Kelly Green." She stuck out her hand. "I'm taking over management of the Beach Lovers Inn."

Understanding flashed in his eyes. "I heard Mrs. Evans was retiring. You are the niece." He finally extended his soft hand and shook with her. "James Aldridge. Mildred is supping." He nodded in the direction of the restaurant slash lounge.

"Thanks, I'll go say hi."

He laid his cool hand atop Kelly's. "I wouldn't do that. She isn't very happy with you, right now."

"She isn't?"

He wagged his finger back and forth. "She calls you the noisy neighbor."

"The fireworks? That wasn't me."

He arched a thick judgmental brow. "The music? The murder?"

Kelly felt defeat staring her in the eyes and fought it. "That's what I mean. I came to apologize."

He thought a moment. "In that case—"

Kelly didn't wait for the rest of his thought.

Mildred McConaughey sat at a table near the bar, alone. A half-empty breadbasket and a bottle of red wine kept her company. Solitary candles in crystal bowls flickered on each mahogany table.

Mrs. McConaughey had been drinking heavily. Her eyes and nose were as red as the muumuu draping her shoulders. The woman's eyes came into focus. "Mrs. Green? What are you doing here?" She looked over Kelly's shoulder. "Where's Ben?"

"He's resting." Kelly slapped the side of her leg. "Dad's leg is acting up. Hey, maybe you should go say hi. It might cheer him up." Okay, so it was a little cruel—but her dad could use a little shaking up. Mildred McConaughey was far less dangerous than a motorcycle.

"Is there a Mrs. Walsh?"

"My mother is no longer with us."

"I see." Mrs. McConaughey twisted the thick gold

band on her ring finger. I will think about it. I'm a busy woman." She fingered a warm garlic knot.

The woman was slurring her words. How much had she had to drink? Kelly figured that could work to her advantage. Liquor was said to loosen lips.

Kelly reached for a chair. "Do you mind if I ask you a few questions?"

"Leave," the hotel owner said heavily.

"It's about Rick Ramus."

"Now." Mildred McConaughey's swollen eyes bored into her head.

"And the fireworks."

"Leave now or there will be fireworks, young lady." Mrs. McConaughey raised her right hand and snapped her fingers.

A beefy man in a tight black shirt and trousers appeared at Mrs. McConaughey's elbow. "This woman is disturbing me."

"Sorry, miss. You'll have to go," said the man.

Mrs. McConaughey reached for the wine bottle and refilled her glass.

Sensing a protest was futile, Kelly went quietly. The big man led her out of the restaurant. Through the curtained entrance to Laff Trax, the hotel's comedy lounge, she noticed a small crowd seated around tables surrounding a raised platform. Onstage, a young woman in jeans and a frilly blue blouse paced while mumbling into a microphone clutched tightly in her hands. The sign on the easel outside the door proclaimed that it was open mic night.

Kelly could have used a few laughs but knew better than to try to stop.

"Don't mind Mrs. McC," said her thus far silent escort

as he held the street entrance door open for her. "She's been having a rough time of it."

"Oh?"

He stepped outside with her and pulled a pack of cigarettes from the front pocket of his trousers. He offered the pack to her. When she declined, he lit one for himself and shoved the pack out of sight. "You know that guy that got murdered next door?" He blew smoke in the direction of the Beach Lovers Inn.

"Yes?"

"He was in here earlier that day. He and Mrs. McC had quite a blowup." He sucked on his cigarette and released another cloud of acrid smoke. "It really shook her up. She's been upset ever since."

Interesting. "You don't say. Do you know what they were arguing about?"

"Not a clue." He took a last toke, crushed the rest of the cigarette under his heel then kicked it behind a thick shrub to join its mates.

Kelly had no clue either but it did raise a lot of questions.

25

There was a light on in Harry's window and, like a moth, Kelly made for it.

"Hello, Kelly. What are you doing here?" He was in his tuxedoed kitten jammies.

"A little early for bed, isn't it?"

Harry stepped aside to let her in. He moved to his desk where the screen of his laptop glowed. "I was working. I wanted to be comfortable."

Kelly read the screen over his shoulder. "Murderous Minions of Mars?"

"It's a working title," he said defensively. He lowered the laptop lid. "What do you want?"

"I want you to put some clothes on and go talk to your friend, Mildred McConaughey."

"Now? Why?"

Kelly explained about Frank Murphrey's alibi.

"So," Harry rubbed his palms together. "The killer is still out there." He went to the window and peeked out the drapes. "Interesting. But what's that got to do with Mrs. McC?" he asked, peering out the window. There was a man walking slowly across the courtyard. Passing a spotlight under the eave, Harry caught a glimpse of thick blonde hair.

"Rick Ramus led us to believe he was out of town at the time of Aunt Ruth's fall and Dr. Barron's murder. He wasn't. He was next door performing in the lounge."

"Which means he could have snuck over here and killed Charlie Barron."

"The question is why."

"Maybe they had a falling out."

"Maybe he heckled Rick's act," Kelly quipped. "Maybe he's just plain crazy." That was the impression she'd gotten from her brief interaction with the comic slash assistant hotel manager.

"He seems normal to me."

Kelly didn't think that was much of a recommendation. "Maybe Rick was angry that Aunt Ruth had sold the inn to me. Maybe he wants it for himself."

"That would mean he would want to eliminate you, wouldn't it? But why would he murder Dr. Barron?"

"Because Dr. Barron saw him push Aunt Ruth down the steps," Kelly suggested.

"Why wouldn't Dr. Barron have told the police?"

Harry had a good point but she wasn't about to tell him that.

"Just go get dressed and see what you can learn from Mrs. McConaughey," Kelly snapped. "She's alone in the bar. At least she was a little while ago. From the looks of her, I'd say she wasn't going anywhere anytime soon."

"How can you be so sure?"

"She's been drinking heavily. It looked like she'd been crying, too. Did I mention that the bartender told me that she and Dr. Barron had had a heated conversation at her hotel the same day Dr. Barron was killed?"

"No, you didn't."

"Well, they did. In fact, he said it was quite a blow-up."

Harry grabbed his pants and shirt off the bed and

headed for the bathroom. "What could Mrs. McC and Dr. Barron have to argue about?" he shouted from the other side of the bathroom door.

"Ask her, not me."

Returning in his street clothes, he laced up his shoes. Kelly grabbed his wrists. "Be subtle, Harry. I tried talking to her and she threw me out. But she's vulnerable, upset. Why? That's what we want to know."

"And if she is she hiding something."

"Exactly." Kelly opened the door and sent Harry on his way. She had other fish to fry.

Kelly could have kicked herself. She had forgotten to tell Harry to report back what he had learned. She hoped he had enough common sense to come to Aunt Ruth's apartment when he was finished.

Kelly drove out to a mini-mall where there was a cell-phone store that kept late hours. She selected the cheapest model they had and it was still pricey. She should have sent Harry the bill for it since she blamed him for the loss of her last phone. But what would be the use? He probably couldn't afford it anyway.

At the inn, she grabbed a sticky from her desk, jotted her cell number on it and stuck it to Harry's door along with a note telling him to call the minute he got back.

Passing her old room, now Mary Barron's room, Kelly's heart surged. She wondered how the widow was getting along. The lights in her room were out.

Kelly didn't dare knock. If Mary Barron didn't come down for breakfast in the morning, she would take her up a tray.

The sound of raised voices carried on the ocean breeze and echoed throughout the courtyard. Two people stood side by side at the apex of the path leading across the dunes.

On the other side of the dunes, came the boisterous laughter of beer-infused late night revelers. More typical during Spring Break but there were always a few partyers about. The beach atmosphere seemed to bring the high spirits out in people.

On the other hand, the beach seemed to be fueling someone's homicidal tendencies.

Kelly stared into the darkness. The two persons sounded like they were arguing. She could hear their muffled barks but not see them clearly or make out their words. They were two mysterious black figures, arms dancing, as if being propelled by the wind.

The sounds of confrontation stopped. The figure on the left let out a shout that morphed into a gut-wrenching sob.

The figure ran down the dune, disappearing behind the inn. The second figure remained atop the dune, standing like a statue, unmoving.

Kelly went to check on the woman who had disappeared behind the inn. The last thing she needed was more trouble on the property.

Propped against the wall of the inn, Kelly found a woman seated in the sandy soil. She was crying. "Hello?"

The woman let out a gasp of surprise. She brushed the tears from her eyes. Her bare feet dug into the soft sand.

"Mrs. Rochester?" Kelly said softly. "Are you all right?"

Jill Rochester sniffled. "Fine." She pounded the sand with her fist and let the sand drift through her fingers.

"Just fine."

"Are you sure? Is there anything I can do?"

Jill Rochester jerked to her feet. She brushed the sticky sand off her shorts and long legs. "You can mind your own business." With that, she turned and marched off.

Kelly looked towards the dunes. Whoever had been up there with Jill was now gone.

Harry woke with a hangover. He wasn't used to drinking so much. But Mrs. McC had encouraged him to keep up with her. She had continued to drink until she had passed out drunk. He and the bartender had assisted her to up to her penthouse suite where a housekeeper on night duty tucked her into bed.

The banging on the door wasn't helping his headache. Tossing back the sheets, he hurried to answer it. He was prepared to give whatever barbarian was crashing the gates an earful.

"Hold on, hold on." He fumbled with the security chain, finally managing to get it off its catch. "I'm coming."

"Finally." Kelly barged into his room. "What happened to you last night? You were supposed to telephone me the minute you got back."

Harry stood yawning, bare feet and tuxedo kitten pajama bottoms.

"I waited up half the night for you. You didn't show up for your free breakfast either. I was beginning to think something might have happened to you."

"You were worried about me?" Something like amusement flashed in his eyes.

"Don't flatter yourself." She pointed to the red light

of the room's telephone blinking angrily on the bedside table. "I left you three messages."

Harry groaned. "I need some coffee."

"I'll make the coffee," Kelly barked. "You make with the explanation." Walking briskly to the coffee maker on the ledge above the compact teal refrigerator, she snatched up the carafe.

Harry flopped down on his bed.

After filling the pot with cold water, she searched vainly for a packet of coffee in and around the tray beside the coffeemaker. "There's no coffee here. Or tea." She opened and closed the dresser drawers. Zip.

"I'm out."

Kelly sighed. "You wouldn't be out if you'd let housekeeping in to do their job once in a while." She planted her hands on her hips and glared from the foot of the bed. "You look a wreck. I'll go downstairs and get some coffee. You hit the shower."

Moving like a beaten dog, Harry literally rolled off the bed. He hit the floor on his hands and knees.

Kelly helped him up.

"Sorry," he mumbled with embarrassment. "I'm not used to drinking so much." And dinner had consisted of three garlic knots and nothing more.

When Kelly returned with a carafe of coffee and a couple of blueberry toaster tarts fifteen minutes later, Harry was looking better, not good, but definitely better. He had showered, shaved and traded his jammies for a clean yellow shirt and blue jeans.

He ate at his desk.

Kelly slid the ottoman close. She watched and waited as Harry fastidiously drank one cup of coffee and gnawed slowly at the first toaster tart. "Okay. Mildred

McConaughey. What did you learn? What did she have to say, Harry?"

Harry yawned loudly and refilled his cup. "She told me that she did not know Charles Barron."

"What? That makes no sense."

"That's what she told me."

"Did you tell her that her very own bartender reported seeing Dr. Barron in the Golden Arms earlier on the day of his murder? And that he had been seen having a heated discussion with her?"

"I told her someone had suggested that, yes," Harry said carefully. "I didn't mention names. I did not want to get any of her employees in trouble. I'd feel terrible if one of them lost their job because they gossiped about their boss."

"Fine. I get that." Kelly grabbed the last tart and took a bite. She'd had nothing but a gala apple for breakfast. "What did she say?"

"Mrs. McC said that a man had come into the Golden Arms and that he had been belligerent. She didn't realize at the time that it was the same man who was later murdered here."

Kelly grunted. "Why was she so upset then when I saw her? Huh? Answer me that." She chewed hard. "If there was ever a person who was drowning in her tears, it was Mildred McConaughey. I tell you, Harry, she's hiding something."

"I think it's because—" He interrupted himself. "Are there any more of those?" He looked forlornly at the last remnant of blueberry tart as Kelly slid it across her tongue.

"Oh, sorry. There are plenty more downstairs. We can get them in a minute." Kelly wiped the telltale crumbs of guilt from her fingers onto her shorts. "You were saying."

"I was saying that Mrs. McC talked a lot about her past. She's very lonely and she's really a nice person, if you give her half a chance."

Kelly was in no mood to discuss Mildred McConaughey's merits. "Right. Continue."

"She talked a lot about her husband. He's dead, you know. Over ten years ago."

Kelly knew that. "Did she say anything more specific?"

He laced his fingers behind his head. "No. I got one good line though."

"Line?"

"Wait. I wrote it down."

He snatched his notebook from the corner of his desk and flipped to the last written page. "Here it is. She said 'old wounds heal slowly but not completely.'" He closed the notebook. "Isn't that great? She said I could use it."

"Yeah, great. Did you ask her about Rick?"

"Yes. She wasn't sure but I double-checked with the staff. You were right, Rick was in town. But he has an alibi. He was performing at Laff Trax three nights in a row, including the night of Dr. Barron's murder and the night before."

Kelly climbed off the ottoman and threw open the curtains.

Harry winced. "What did you do that for?"

"You ought to let a little light in here once in a while. It's good for you." Sunlight spilled in like an army of hungry photon-sized ants entering a new and forbidden land. "As for Rick Ramus, why did he lie?"

Harry started to answer but she wasn't letting him.

"I'll tell you why, Harry. Because the comedy club is only a hop, skip and a skull bashing away from the Beach Lovers Inn. Rick could easily have slipped out of the club."

Kelly picked up Harry's lamp. "Rick could have slipped into room 206 and clobbered Charlie Barron as he stepped out of the shower." She banged the base of the lamp on the table. "Presto, he zips back to the comedy club and nobody's any the wiser."

"I suppose that is possible." Harry finished the rest of his coffee and stuffed his notepad down his front pocket. "But there's still no motive."

Kelly frowned while she paced the narrow space between the dresser and the bed. "Maybe Rick Ramus and Mrs. McConaughey were in it together?"

"Accomplices?"

"Maybe. She's rich. Maybe she paid Ramus to kill Dr. Barron."

Harry shook his head. "Still no why." He yanked his curtains shut.

"Maybe not for wanting Barron dead but suppose Mildred wanted Aunt Ruth dead?"

"Why would she want that?"

"Maybe so she could get her hands on the inn. Maybe she's thinking of expanding her hotel."

"You've already taken it over. Face it, you've got nothing on Mrs. McC. I'm telling you, she's harmless."

"Sometimes, Harry, you can be more irritating than both my ex-husbands rolled up in one." Kelly swept a pile of garbage off the floor and into the trash bin at the side of the desk. She compacted the over-brimming can with her foot.

She was going to send housekeeping in whether Harry liked it or not. "I'm going to have a word with Mary Barron. Maybe she can shed some light on this."

"That's a good idea."

"You've got my cell number, right?" The stickie was missing from the door when she arrived.

"Yes, it's here some place." He looked around the messy room and scratched behind his ear.

"Never mind." Kelly grabbed a fresh scrap of paper from his desk and wrote it down again. She thrust it in his shirt pocket. "If you had a cell phone you could store my number there. It's a great way to keep in touch with people, Harry."

"Cell phones are dangerous." Harry straightened the paper she had stuffed in his pocket. "They emit harmful signals that rearrange brain cells and disturb synaptic function. Not to mention, the NSA uses the network to snoop on everything we say and everywhere we go."

"Sounds boring," Kelly replied. "What about pictures? Cell phones are good for taking pictures, too."

"I have a camera."

"What, a Polaroid?"

Harry looked at her with surprise. "It belonged to my mother," he replied huffily. "Now, if you don't mind, I have to get going. I checked my messages while you were gone. Det. Burns called last night to tell me I could pick up my wallet at the station."

"Great. I'll give you a lift."

"I thought you were going to speak with Mary Barron?"

"It can wait."

"It really isn't necessary. I have a car."

"I know. What if you get stopped driving without a

license?" Kelly grabbed the door handle and pushed.

"I have a license."

"Yeah, in your wallet, right?"

Harry frowned and accepted his fate.

26

Kelly and Harry were left cooling their heels on a hard bench in the lobby of the police station for nearly a half hour.

"All I want is my wallet," Harry complained once again to the woman behind the glass partition. He did not like police stations.

The woman instructed them to wait. That was fine with Kelly. She wanted to talk to Det. Burns about the case.

Kelly used the down time to make a few calls, including one to the hospital. Ruth was doing well and was about to attend her first physical therapy session.

Ruth still had no recollection of her accident. The doctor had told Kelly that she may never recover her memory completely. Physically, given time, he said she should do nicely.

Finally, a female officer led Kelly and Harry to Det. Burn's small office.

The detective hung up his phone and dropped it on his desk. "Have a seat. What can I do for you?"

Whoever's chair the detective had borrowed last time had wanted it back. There was only the one chair. Harry stood next to a blue-green surfboard in the far corner.

"Is there any news on Dr. Barron or Cowboy's murder?" Kelly asked.

"Frank Murphrey has an alibi. Other than that." He threw out his hands.

"We heard." Harry tried lifting the surf board. It was much heavier than he had expected.

"Oh?" Det. Burns looked at him with interest. "You want to tell me where?"

Harry opened his mouth. Kelly cut him off. "Didn't you say that your editor at Myrtle Scene Magazine mentioned it, Harry?"

"What?" Harry frowned. "Right. Kiki. She told me all about it."

The detective wasn't satisfied but he let it go. "Is there anything else?"

Kelly pressed her knees up against his desk. "Have you interviewed Mildred McConaughey?"

"Just some routine stuff the night of the murder. Why?"

"I have my suspicions."

"Suspicions?" Det. Burns was amused.

"There is something funny about her." Kelly was annoyed at his reaction. "You'd know that if you interrogated her."

"I am not going to interrogate her, Mrs. Green. She is not a suspect. I can understand your feelings. I've been told that your aunt and she weren't on the best of terms."

Kelly shrugged. "By her own admission, she wasn't watching the fireworks with the rest of us, detective."

"She went to the bathroom. People do that on occasion." Det. Burns gave his phone a twirl. "Are we done here?"

Kelly looked in desperation at Harry.

Harry cleared his throat. "Irwin Brunner gave me the impression that Charlie Barron had no friends, including those attending the reunion. He also told me that the night Cowboy was murdered, Mary Barron was not in her hotel room and her car was not in the parking lot."

"So the distraught widow took a drive? That does not make her a serial killer, Mr. Leland."

"If they weren't friends, why the reunion?"

"Besides getting a free vacation out of the deal? The widow told me they had all been close once. Then drifted apart for one reason or another. None of them are getting any younger so they decided to get together."

"Whose idea was this reunion?"

"Her husband's. Anything else?" Taking advantage of their momentary silence, he pulled open the top left hand drawer of his desk and tossed Harry's wallet on the desk. "Here you go."

"Thanks." Harry examined the wallet then slid it in his back pocket.

"If that's all..." The detective pointed to the door.

"Det. Burns," Kelly said angrily, "someone tried to kill my aunt and succeeded in killing one of my guests. You've got to do something."

"Sorry, I'm underwater here." He shuffled papers from one side of his cluttered desk to the other. "There's been another murder."

"Do you think it's related?" Kelly asked.

"Not a chance. This one involved a couple of bikers and one of their wives. Bikers don't take kindly to other bikers borrowing their wives."

"But what about Aunt Ruth, Cowboy and Dr. Barron?"

Det. Burns shrugged. "We're stretched for resources here, Mrs. Green. We're doing the best we can. Right now, I've got one very mean and very desperate man to catch. The captain's worried this could erupt into a war between rival biker gangs if we don't nip it in the bud."

The detective snatched his coat off a hook on the wall and hustled them out the door with him.

Asserting that he needed to work on his book, Harry asked Kelly to drop him off at the Beach Lovers Inn. She planned to stop by the hospital then do some shopping for the inn.

He waited at the curb for her red Audi to disappear up Ocean Boulevard then entered the lobby.

Lee Hollister and Rick Ramus stood behind the desk. Rick was Lee's boss. This was George's day off and Harry wanted to pay him a visit. All he needed was the handyman's home address.

He had refrained from mentioning his plan to Kelly because she'd probably get angry, even forbid him from going. Fortunately, she was not his boss.

"Got a minute, Rick?" asked Harry.

"Sure." There wasn't much of Rick visible over the counter. "What's up?"

"In private?" Harry glanced at Lee.

"I suppose. Come into the office."

Lee gave Harry a wink as he dutifully followed Rick inside. Rick took a seat and laced his fingers. "Spill. No, wait." His face lit up. "Tell me what you think."

Rick cleared his throat. "Ready? Did you hear about the guy who came into town for a reunion and got a bash instead?"

Harry pushed his brows together.

"Get it, Harry? Reunion? Like the group we got here. Bash?" Rick bashed an imaginary victim with an invisible object in his left hand.

"I get it." Harry replied. "I wouldn't repeat it to Kelly though. I don't think she'll find it funny." So far, Kelly hadn't displayed much of a sense of humor.

Harry fiddled with the white-framed photograph of Ruth and Jim Evans on the corner of the desk. Funny, Rick hadn't said much about the murder. But if he questioned him now, he'd get mad and Harry wouldn't get the address he needed.

"Yeah, I suppose you're right. I'll try it out at the club." Rick assumed a thoughtful pose. "What's up?"

"I would like George Easterling's home address."

"What do you want that for?"

"I thought I would pay him a visit."

"It's his day off, Harry." Rick stood. "He'll be around tomorrow. You can see him then."

Harry blocked Rick's path. "I was really hoping to speak to him today."

Rick looked curiously up at Harry. "What's this all about?"

"It's personal."

Rick draped his hand on Harry's shoulder. "No can do. Giving out an employee's home address is a breach of security."

"Please, Rick?"

"Sorry, bud. No. Can. Do. The new boss lady might can me." He fished in his pockets. "What I can do is give you a pair of comp drinks tickets to tonight's show at Laff Trax. I'm the emcee."

The assistant manager stuffed the tickets in Harry's pocket, which already held the scrap of paper Kelly had put there earlier. Sticking things in his pocket unbidden was becoming an annoying occurrence.

"Thanks," Harry replied automatically. He had no intention of attending Rick's show. Definitely no intention of drinking alcohol again any time soon.

Rick guided him out of the office by the elbow.

Kelly's words nagged at Harry. Rick Ramus was in town, not on a cruise ship. He was next door at the time of both Ruth Evan's "accident' and Charlie Barron's murder. That meant he was also in town at the time of Cowboy's killing.

Now that Rick had refused him the address, it couldn't hurt to broach the subject of Charlie Barron's murder a little deeper. "You haven't said much about the doctor's murder, Rick."

"That Barron guy?" Rick shook himself. "I don't like to talk about death. Gives me the creeps." He grabbed his arms. "That's why I make jokes. You gotta laugh about things, Harry. You should give it a try sometime."

Rick returned to the desk.

Lee Hollister stopped Harry as he was leaving. She handed him a folded piece of paper.

"What's this?"

"I couldn't help hearing." Lee glanced toward the office. "It's the information you wanted."

Harry glanced at the address written on the paper, thanked her and stuffed it in his shirt pocket. Why not? Everybody else was doing it.

27

Harry could see why George Easterling preferred living off the premises. His cottage was modest but its north Myrtle Beach location was terrific.

The small cottage, one of several in a row, had a gray-shingled roof and pale blue siding. A red mailbox stood on a crooked post. The yard was sand and weeds with palmetto bushes scattered haphazardly about.

But that didn't mean it had come cheap.

How could a handyman afford an oceanfront home? Even a small one?

The screened-in porch tacked on the front contained several pieces of wicker furniture and carried a smell of mildew.

Up close, he noticed the blue paint was faded and chipped. The wooden door was warped and curling up at the bottom as if it had been soaking in water. Harry pulled the rope attached to a brass bell beside the front door.

George answered the door in his handyman outfit. The same way Harry saw him every day around the inn, except for the bare feet and the unshaven cheeks. "Harry?"

"Hello, George." A tongue-wagging Irish setter padded to the door and gave Harry a sniff. Satisfied, the dog turned and ran.

"What are you doing here?"

"I was in the neighborhood." Lame, thought Harry. "I thought we might talk if you aren't busy."

"No." George scratched behind his ear. Behind him, the dog did the same. "Come on in."

A sad-looking artificial Christmas tree colored an unnatural shade of green stood in the bay window blocking the view of the ocean. Dust had settled atop the fake leaves, tinsel and ornaments. The silver star on top drooped.

How long had the tree been standing there? A three-piece suite of wicker furniture with navy slipcovers did little to fill the living area. Blue pile carpet covered the white tile floor peeking from the edge of the wall.

The dunes were almost non-existent here. One good hurricane surge and George's cottage would be under-water.

"Beer?"

"No, thanks," replied Harry.

"Weather's good. Let's sit on the deck." George clapped his hands. "Come on, Billy." The dog jumped off the wicker sofa and beat them to the sliding door.

George offered Harry a seat. Billy raced off to the beach, making himself at home with a couple and their three kids who had claimed their own square of the sand with a giant multicolored beach blanket.

"I don't get many visitors." George kneaded his fingers. "What did you want to talk about? It isn't trouble at the inn, is it?"

"No." Not handyman trouble. "Not exactly." Harry stared at a fishing boat churning its way down the coast. In the foreground, several surfers lay stretched out on their boards, waiting for the waves that would carry them to shore. Back and forth, back and forth they'd go.

Harry didn't see the point.

"Do you remember the night of Charlie Barron's murder?"

"Are you kidding?" George lifted his feet up onto the weathered wooden rail. "In all the years I've been working at the inn, there's never been a murder before." He locked Harry with his pale green eyes. "Couples argue. Kids yell at their parents and vice versa. Nothing even close to murder. I'm glad they caught the guy."

"That's just it, George. The police have not caught him at all." Harry explained how the initial suspect had a perfect alibi. "So you see, the real killer is still out there."

"That's awful." George stood. "Sure you don't want a beer?"

Harry declined.

George went inside and came back with one for himself. He drained half the bottle in one gulp. "I've been thinking. There's no such thing as a perfect alibi, is there? Maybe this guy is lying. Maybe he is responsible for the murder."

"The police found surveillance videos. Murphrey is on them clear as day. Tapes don't lie."

"No, I guess not."

Harry shifted his chair into the shade thrown off by the house. The sun burned into his face, the sand attacked his eyes. He didn't own a pair of sunglasses. "Kelly is very worried, George. First, Mrs. Evans gets hurt, then a guest is murdered. It's not good for business."

"I spoke with Ruth today," George replied. "She's

coming along. Should be out of the hospital soon though she says she may have to spend a little time in one of those rehab facilities before going home."

One of the children on the beach tossed a stick of driftwood into the surf and Billy dove in after it.

"You're going to miss Mrs. Evans when she moves to Arizona, eh, George?"

"Yep." He took a slow pull from the bottle. His free hand tightened around his kneecap.

Harry had to explore the possibility that George might not have liked Ruth Evans selling the Beach Lovers Inn to her niece. He might have wanted the property for himself. "Did you ever think about buying the inn from Mrs. Evans yourself? You've been working there a long time. I'll bet taking over would be a breeze for you, given the chance."

"I like things just fine the way things are. I don't need more responsibilities than I've already got. Besides, she's got her niece to run things."

"Right, Kelly. Interesting woman, don't you think?"

"Seems like a good kid," he said with a slight shrug.

"Yeah," Harry agreed. "She's all right." He cleared his throat. "Where were you the night of Dr. Barron's murder, George? Did you see anything? Hear anything? It could really help Kelly and Ruth if there was any little thing you might recall."

"Where I was, was with you on the courtyard," George said truculently. "Working. Serving our guests."

"I know," Harry said, trying to be delicate. "But during the fireworks, there was a short time where you were gone."

"And you want to know where I was? You think I would harm a guest? Or Ruth? She isn't just my boss,

Harry. Ruth is my friend."

Harry felt terrible. "I know, George. I didn't mean to offend you."

"Sure, Harry." George squeezed his eyes shut. "Like I told the police, everybody was busy looking at fireworks. I went to have a smoke in the parking lot. Ruth doesn't like me smoking in the courtyard. Says the cigarettes stink the place up. She's right.

"I've been trying to quit. I'm smoking these silly things now." He pulled an electronic vapor cigarette from his pocket. "Nasty things." He shoved it away. "That's all there was to it."

George rose and banged his fist on the flimsy railing. "I wish I'd never left. Maybe Barron would still be alive."

"Don't blame yourself, George."

"And if Ruth had fixed up the stairs like I asked, maybe she wouldn't have fallen."

"If she fell," pointed out Harry.

George gaped at him. "What?"

Harry explained how he believed Ruth had been pushed. Why, he didn't know. He also shared his theory that the death of the vagrant named Cowboy related to the other incidents. "Did you know him?"

"Cowboy? Sure. He was harmless. Wouldn't hurt a soul. I can't imagine anybody wanting to kill him. He didn't have anything worth killing for. Know what I mean?"

"Cowboy may not have had *things*, George, but he had something."

"What's that?"

"Information."

"What sort of information?"

"He told me he saw who pushed Ruth down the

stairs."

George's face contorted. "Who was it?"

Harry could only shrug. "He died before I could find out."

George put his fingers to his lips and whistled shrilly. Billy looked up, barked and came running. George ran the spigot on the deck and filled the dog's water bowl. Billy lapped it up.

"The bathroom window of room 206 faces the parking lot," Harry said matter-of-factly.

"If you're asking if I noticed anything, the answer is no."

Harry had another question. He wasn't quite sure how to ask it without making it sound like another accusation. If George told Kelly about their conversation, she'd be furious. Maybe even throw him out.

Where would he go?

Thoughts of a payday for solving the murder and selling the story to Myrtle Scene Magazine gave him strength. "Have you known Mrs. McConaughey long?"

George thumped Billy's side and led him back in the house. "He gets over-heated if he stays out-of-doors too long. Dog doesn't know what's good for himself. I built him the dog house and he barely uses it except to store odds and ends he finds at the beach."

The compact gray dog house sat at the far end of the deck against the house. Its pitched roof was covered in tin.

George leaned on the railing. He pulled out his e-cigarette and puffed madly. "I've known Mildred a long time. I knew her husband too. So you might say we're friends."

"I saw the two of you together at Captain Haddock's."

"So?" Wrinkles surged up around his lips as he sucked at the e-cig.

"It was the same night that Cowboy was found drowned nearby."

"I wish I could help you, Harry." George dropped the disposable e-cig down the neck of his beer bottle. "I'd do anything to help Ruth. Kelly, too. I like the girl. But Mildred's not involved in this anymore than I am."

George pulled open the sliding door and Billy raced out once again. "Come on, boy. Let's get you some exercise."

George and Billy stepped off the deck and onto the warm sand. "You can let yourself out, Harry."

Harry watched as the handyman and his Irish setter angled their way up the shore.

28

One of the housekeepers let Kelly know that Mary Barron was in her room. Kelly bought her lunch from a deli up the street and knocked on her door.

"Come in."

Kelly let herself in. "Hello, Mrs. Barron. How are you feeling today?"

Mrs. Barron said a few soft words into her cell phone then cut the connection. She placed the phone on the bed beside her. "That was the children. Charlie's memorial is in three days. I'm so glad they can handle everything for me."

"Will it be local?"

"No, up north."

"Does that mean you'll be leaving us soon?"

"The day after tomorrow."

"I brought you lunch." Kelly showed Mrs. Barron the deli bag.

"Thank you. Put it on the desk, please." She wore an elegant charcoal gray silk shirt and trousers.

Kelly complied. "Have the police been able to give you any further news about your husband?"

"Only that their initial suspect was a false lead." A black leather purse lay open on the bed. The widow extracted a tube of deep red gloss and ran it slowly along her lips.

Kelly straightened the pillows on the second bed, force of habit. "I want to tell you again just how sorry I am about what happened."

"It isn't your fault, Mrs. Green."

"We've never had anything remotely like it happen."

"I'm sure."

Kelly picked up a damp hand towel off the floor and draped it over her arm. "Were your husband and Mrs. McConaughey close?"

Mary Barron's eyes twitched momentarily. "Who?"

"Mildred McConaughey. She owns the Golden Arms Hotel next door."

"Never heard of her."

"That's funny. She stopped by the night of the murder. Several witnesses saw Dr. Barron arguing vehemently with her earlier."

Mary Barron crossed to the bag of deli food and peeked inside. "Your witnesses must be mistaken."

"I don't think so."

"Charlie and I were together nearly the entire time."

"He was positively identified."

"Then Charlie must have wandered in by mistake. Because he wasn't a guest, she probably demanded that he leave. Charlie didn't like being pushed around." She unwrapped a roast beef sandwich on whole wheat. Iceberg lettuce leaves stuck out in all directions.

She sniffed at the sandwich then rewrapped it and put it back in the bag. "I don't have much of an appetite yet."

"I understand. It hasn't been much of a reunion, has it?"

"I'm not surprised." The widow sat on the corner of the bed, massaging her stockinged feet. "The whole thing was Charlie's idea. I told him it was ridiculous."

"Why?"

"Because none of these people were his friends."

Kelly's brow shot up. That was precisely what Harry claimed Irwin Brunner to have told him. "I'm afraid I don't understand."

Mary Barron's features creased in a smile. "Charlie was getting sentimental in his later years. He wanted everybody to like him. Including his old partners. You'll forgive me for saying so, but my husband, brilliant as he was at business and medicine, was a fool when it came to people.

"Oh sure, they accepted his invitation to this little so-called reunion. But only because he was paying." Her voice grew harder and harder. "And probably just so they could tell him to his face what they thought of him."

"So you were all partners at one time?"

"Partners and investors." She sniffed. "That was a lifetime ago. They hated it when Charlie left the practice and struck out on his own. They hated him for his success."

Kelly stilled. "Do you think one of them killed him?"

"No." Mrs. Barron said firmly. "I think a burglar killed him. Believe me, none of them would have shut him up permanently without first finding out why he asked them all to come. Greedy bastards." Her legs kicked the air savagely.

"Exactly why did he ask them all here?"

"To ask their forgiveness. Silly, isn't it? I told Charlie it was ridiculous." She wiped at her eyes. "But he had a scare several months ago. A serious heart attack. His cardiologist told him he was lucky to be alive and that if he wasn't careful, he wouldn't last much longer."

"I'm sorry. I didn't know."

"Besides none of them could have killed Charlie. Everyone else was with me, watching the fireworks." She paused a moment. "Ironic, isn't it? That a celebration of fireworks would be occurring at the same moment my Charlie was being..." She hiccoughed. "Was being..."

Mrs. Barron broke down and cried, burying her face in her hands. "If only Charlie had died of another heart attack. It would have been so much easier in a way, you know?" she said weakly. "Than to die so-so savagely."

Kelly quietly slipped out the door, her own eyes damp with tears.

"Kelly!"

She looked down. Her father was waving from the courtyard. He looked happier than she had seen him in years. "What is it, Dad?"

"The truck's coming." He glanced at his watch. "The driver called for directions. She's practically here." He waved his arm, balancing on his crutch with the other. "Come on down."

Kelly hurried down the steps.

Her father was already hobbling out the courtyard. She caught up to him on the street.

A red and blue tractor-trailer truck came humming slowly up the road. Ben Walsh leaned against a lamppost and shook his crutch in the air. Air brakes squealed and the truck came grinding to a halt at the curb beside him, its engine rumbling.

"What's here?" Kelly looked curiously at the big moving truck. Was her father planning on moving all his worldly possessions into Ruth's tiny apartment?

The driver, a svelte woman Kelly's age, introduced herself and handed her father some paperwork. He dug some papers of his own out of his pocket. The driver merely glanced at them.

Cars were forced to veer around the big vehicle. One driver honked. Kelly recognized Drew behind the wheel. The semi blocked the inn's parking lot. "Sorry, Drew. We'll be done soon."

Drew replied that she'd pull over to the side of the road and wait.

Kelly followed her father and the driver around back. "What's happening, Dad?"

"You'll see."

A forklift was attached to the rear of the truck. The driver methodically lowered the forklift. She next lifted the gate of the truck.

A large object draped in a heavy canvas cloth was strapped to a pallet just inside the door of the truck.

"What is that?"

"Step back, please," urged the driver. Several people on the sidewalk had stopped to watch. Rick Ramus stuck his head out from the office window.

The driver fired up the forklift and deftly captured the pallet which she slid onto the parking lot.

Like a kid on Christmas morning, her father hurried over and began undoing the heavy straps crisscrossing the canvas. With the assistance of the driver, they removed the cloth revealing a shiny black motorcycle lying on its side like a wounded beast. The frame was bent, the paint was scraped and the tires were flat.

"Are you kidding me?" Kelly gaped at her father. "That is *your* motorcycle?" She pointed. "The one you had a *little* accident on?"

Ben's teeth flashed a grin. "Isn't she great?"

"She is a great big hunk of twisted rubber and metal, Dad."

Ben ignored her. He signed a final document accepting delivery of the bike. The driver folded up the tarp and tossed it inside the trailer. Ben threw the straps in on top.

Kelly stood beside the pallet. Seriously, the motorcycle was a total wreck. There was a rumble as the truck started up and lurched away.

Ben was examining every inch of the bike with loving fingers.

Drew pulled into the parking lot and walked over. "What's this?"

"Dad's wreck."

"This is Katie," Ben said proudly.

"Well, hello, Katie." Drew quipped. "Cool, bike, Mr. Walsh."

"Thanks."

"It's not a cool bike, Dad. It is a total wreck."

"A little elbow grease and a few new parts and she'll be good as new. You'll see."

"The only way this motorcycle is going to be good as new is if you junk it and buy a new one." She grabbed her father's arm. "Which I am not suggesting you do."

"I wouldn't dream of it." He squeezed the handle bar. The Indian chief painted on the gas tank looked like someone had taken a tomahawk to him. "Come on, help me get her in the garage."

"And just how do you suggest we do that?" Kelly looked askance. "That motorcycle must weigh a ton."

"Nah. Only about half that," Ben corrected.

"Oh, really? What was I thinking then? Come on, Drew. You take one side and I'll take the other. On the count of three, we lift."

Drew laughed. "I'm game if you are."

"I am not." Kelly grabbed hold of Drew and started back to the inn. "Goodbye, Dad."

"Wait, Kelly. What about Katie?"

"Leave her."

"Leave her? Somebody might steal her."

"Wouldn't that be a shame," Kelly mumbled.

"Kelly!"

"Figure it out, Dad!"

"Are you really going to make him deal with that bike by himself? Your father does have a broken leg."

"No. I just want to see him sweat," Kelly answered. "And think twice, no, three times about keeping that death trap. Nobody's going to mess with it. Later, I'll ask George to give him a hand."

29

Kelly ran Harry to ground in his room that evening. She wanted to share what she had learned talking to Mary Barron. But the first thing she saw when the door opened was a strawberry version of Harry Leland.

"What happened to you?" Kelly examined Harry's cherry-red face. "Is that a sunburn? I thought you hated the sun?"

"Long story," Harry said wearily. "What's up?"

A takeout pizza box sat open on the bed with several slices missing. She helped herself.

"I talked to Mary Barron this afternoon." Kelly threw herself down on the bed while Harry retreated to the desk. "She's convinced a burglar conked her husband on the head."

"At this point, I'll believe anything."

"Well, believe this." Kelly chewed the cold pizza around in her mouth for a moment before recounting her conversation with the widow. "She told me that this reunion was her husband's idea. Get this, it was no fun-time reunion at all."

"Meaning?"

"They all used to be partners and didn't like it when he left the practice and went out on his own. She said they are all jealous of her husband's success. Apparently, Charlie Barron wanted them all to bury the hatchet and make amends."

"You think one of them buried the hatchet, so to speak, in Charlie Barron's skull?"

"I don't know. Like Mrs. Barron reminded me, everybody else was watching the fireworks."

"Exactly. Except for George."

"Plus Rick and Mrs. McConaughey. And you," she added pointedly.

Harry bristled. "Me? Why would I murder the man?"

"Relax, Harry. It was a joke."

"It was not funny."

Kelly bit into the dwindling slice of pizza and chewed thoughtfully. "Mrs. Barron believes it was a burglar. But, I tell you, Harry, Mrs. Barron is hiding something. I could see it in her eyes. When I mentioned her husband and Mildred McConaughey knowing one another, I'd swear she knew about it. Yet she denied ever hearing the woman's name."

"Mrs. McC wouldn't hurt a fly."

"I know, I know. You keep saying that but all roads keep leading back to her." She threw the hard, dry crust back in the box and licked her fingertips. "I think we should check her out again."

"Why?"

"I just told you why. Come on, Harry."

A frown worked its way onto Harry's face. "I told George we had seen him with Mrs. McC at Captain Haddock's the night of Cowboy's murder."

"What did he say?"

"He said they were friends and that he had known her and her husband a long time. That's all."

"Did you ask George about the money?"

"What money?"

"The money you told me and Dad you heard him asking Ruth about. You said you overheard him saying that he needed more money."

"No. I forgot."

"Your Mrs. McC has money," Kelly said provocatively.

"I really think you should let it go, Kelly." Harry pointed to the screen of his laptop. "I did some digging of my own."

"And?" She grabbed another slice of pizza. Plain cheese. Where were the mushrooms? The black olives? Was he too cheap to spring for even a single topping?

"Guess who Vivian Rochester used to be."

Kelly had no idea and said so. She popped open the minifridge in search of something to wash down the pizza. She was confronted with nothing but fruit punch juice boxes. She grabbed one and stabbed it with the attached little plastic straw.

"Mrs. Irwin Brunner."

Kelly squeezed and purple juice shot out the end of the straw and dribbled down her shirt. Running to the bathroom, she grabbed a towel at the sink, wet it and dabbed. "You are suggesting that the Vivian staying here at the inn, who is married to Jill Rochester, used to be Vivian Brunner?"

"I'm not suggesting anything." Harry picked up the little bottle of complimentary hand lotion on the bathroom counter. He squirted some into his palms and then smeared it gently over his burnt face. "I'm stating a fact. It's on the internet. I found divorce and marriage records. Mr. Brunner used to work in finance. Now he sells real estate."

Kelly's chest was wet and freezing. She adjusted the dial on the room air conditioner upward. "George is off today. When did you talk to him?" Snatching the blow dryer from under the bathroom counter, she blasted her shirt with hot air.

Harry had been fearing that question. "I stopped by his house. I happened to be in the area," he explained over the roar of the dryer.

Kelly shut off the dryer and groaned. "I hope you didn't make him mad, Harry."

"Not at all. In fact, he invited me in for a beer." Harry's fingers went to his face. "That's how I got this. We sat on his deck. Did you know George has a house at the beach? And I mean right on the beach."

"No." That surprised her. "I did not know that."

"Beach houses don't come cheap."

"All the more reason to ask him about the money you heard him talking to my aunt about."

"I'll ask him tomorrow."

"No. I'll ask him." She was afraid Harry would say or do something to drive her handyman away. "Then I am going to have a word with Rick. I still have my doubts about him. Do you suppose Rick and George could be in this together?"

Harry didn't want to believe it but the theory was intriguing. "I asked Rick what he thought about Dr. Barron's murder today."

"What did he say?"

"He made a joke."

"That's interesting. Who jokes about murder?" Rick Ramus was sounding weirder and guiltier by the minute.

"A comedian?" Harry patted his pocket. "He gave me a couple of tickets for his show tonight. He's emceeing."

"At Laff Trax?"

Harry nodded.

"Let's go, Harry."

"What about Irwin Brunner and Vivian Rochester?"

"What about them?"

"Don't you think it's odd?"

"Odd? Yes but I don't see what it has to do with either murder. Hold on a minute."

"What?"

"There is one thing." Kelly told Harry how she had seen Jill and another person arguing on the dunes late the night before. "I discovered Jill sitting alone behind the inn. She was upset, crying. I tried to talk to her. She told me to mind my own business."

"Who was the other person?"

"I couldn't see."

"Maybe she'll talk to me." Harry grabbed his navy windbreaker from the closet. "I'll try her tomorrow." The telephone on the nightstand rang. Harry tossed the coat over the TV and answered it. "Hello?"

Kelly paced impatiently. After several minutes, Harry hung up.

"That was Kiki, my editor. Chad told her he'd been doing some digging of his own. He's learned that Charlie Barron was an inventor. He held a number of patents. One of his inventions was some medical gizmo he came up with years ago."

"That's something."

Harry shrugged. "Not really. I told Kiki that I had found that out already myself. I don't see what it has to do with his murder. Nice fluff for an obituary maybe, but nothing that's going to lead to the killer."

"I suppose you are right."

The last thing Harry needed was for Chad to convince Kiki to let him publish a story on the murder. He'd not only lose his payday, he'd lose face. "I wish Chad would keep his nose out of my story. I told Kiki I had some hot leads and that I would deliver the real story soon enough."

Kelly smirked. "You lied?"

"It's called baiting the hook," huffed Harry.

"Grab your coat, Harry. Let's go."

He pulled open the door.

Kelly stepped onto the walkway. "Who's Chad?"

"Chad Cummings. Kiki's over-inflated boyfriend. He's the magazine's lead news writer."

"Am I detecting a whiff of jealousy?"

"Not even a little bit," lied Harry as they made their way downstairs.

Kelly knew he was being untruthful. Was he jealous that Chad was Kiki's boyfriend or that the man was a writer with a paying job?

Kelly stopped at the apartment to swap her stained shirt for a lightweight yellow sweater.

Laff Trax had pulled in a good crowd.

Harry slapped the free drinks ticket down on the black table in the corner near the curtain. Kelly ordered a Sea Breeze and Harry a lemon daiquiri. Both drinks arrived in souvenir *Laff Trax at the Golden Arms Hotel* plastic cups.

"Do you see Rick?" Kelly craned over the heads of the couple at the table in front of them. She peered into the corners offstage.

"He should be around here someplace." Harry sipped cautiously. The drink was strong and tangy.

The red-haired comedian on stage was doing a poor

imitation of Rodney Dangerfield.

"Poor Rodney." Kelly took a slug of her Sea Breeze. "Even in death the guy gets no respect."

Harry pushed back his chair. "I'll go see where Rick is." But Rick suddenly appeared on stage as if on cue.

The comedian slash assistant inn manager looked natty in a black suit, white shirt and polka dot bowtie.

"You think he made that tie himself out of a Wonder Bread bag?" Kelly said, eying the tie with its red, yellow and blue polka dots on a shiny white background.

Rick clapped his hand, thanked the sweaty comedian for his time.

"Do the parrot!" shouted a loud-mouthed woman clutching a beer.

"See?" Kelly whispered. "It isn't just me."

Rick glowered. "If you don't keep quiet, the next thing you are going to get, lady, is the goose, not the parrot!"

The audience roared. The woman blushed and stared into her pink drink. Rick told a couple of jokes then introduced the next act, a ventriloquist with twin dummies dressed up like a couple of farmer's daughters.

"Now." Kelly jumped up. "Time me."

Harry looked helplessly at his wrist. "I don't have a —" But Kelly was gone. "Watch."

When she reappeared some minutes later, Harry's eyes were fixed on the ventriloquist and his dummies. "How long was I gone?" she asked breathlessly. A sheen of sweat clung to her face like a mask.

"Huh? I don't know. Ten minutes maybe."

Kelly sucked at her drink. A second souvenir plastic cup sat beside Harry's empty one. "Okay."

She had walked quickly to the inn, climbed the steps

and entered room 206.

A minute or two later, giving the hypothetical killer time to lay in ambush for Dr. Barron, she had retraced her steps. Once again, she was careful to move quickly but not so quickly as to draw attention to herself. If she had run, if the killer had run, somebody on the busy street might have noticed and become suspicious.

She waved for another round of drinks. The wooden dummy on the left wrapped her hands around the other, locking her neck in a death grip. The appreciative audience hooted. Kelly cringed and wished for the return of the poor man's Rodney Dangerfield.

"Ten minutes or less." Kelly leaned towards Harry. "Rick could easily have done it."

"Why?" Harry asked, raising his voice over the applause of the audience.

"Because he and Mildred McConaughey want the inn. My inn."

"You don't have any proof of that, Kelly" replied Harry. "Besides, that might explain the attack on Mrs. Evans but it can't have anything to do with the murder of Charlie Barron." He drained his second drink. "Or Cowboy for that matter."

"I have an idea."

"What's that?"

"Let's go to Captain Haddock's for dinner tomorrow."

"What?" Harry colored. "Are you asking me out on a date?"

"Don't be ridiculous," Kelly said a little too loudly. "I'm suggesting we check the restaurant out, Harry. Think about it," she urged. "You saw them all dining at Captain Haddock's. Cowboy was last seen alive there. And you saw George and Mrs. McConaughey having dinner there. All in one night."

Harry had to admit she had a good point. "Good idea. You're on."

30

The next day, Harry woke with a headache and went straight to the shower. He stood under the hot spray until he could tolerate it no longer. Fortunately, his sunburn had dwindled to a mere inconvenience.

He felt out of sorts and it wasn't just the late nights and the alcohol. His work schedule was out of kilter. Normally, he banged out at least a thousand words a day on the new novel. All before lunch. Now, with the murders and subsequent investigative work he was doing for Myrtle Scene Magazine, his strict regimen had gone out the window.

He dressed and went downstairs to fetch some coffee and a Danish. He carried them up to his room and placed them on the desk, determined to write.

The novel in progress was getting nowhere. The hapless hero of his novel was stymied. A man had been slain in a Boston alley. A witness claimed it was aliens. To back up her claim, the victim's corpse had been drained of two pints of blood. Plus, several circular impressions in the asphalt had been found beside the body. The witness theorized the tracks were left by a compact extra-terrestrial transport device.

Harry's hero, Dirk Soul, had been hired by the dead man's wife to find his real killer. The police had no clues.

Unfortunately, neither did Harry. That meant Dirk

Soul didn't either.

Harry sighed and chomped on the warm cinnamon Danish. He washed it down with tepid coffee into which he had dumped a packet of hazelnut flavoring.

His hands hovered over the keyboard. Thoughts refused to come to his fingertips. He was saved by a knock on the door.

Harry brushed the pastry crumbs from his lap and pulled open the door.

"Good morning, Harry." Irwin Brunner, dressed in baggy blue shorts, a gray *Take It Slow In Myrtle Beach* tee shirt and black beach sandals, presented himself. "Mind if I come in?"

Harry glanced down the breezeway. Below, several guests loitered around the pool. "No, I guess not."

Irwin whipped a pair of dark sunglasses from his face and thrust one end into the collar of his shirt. He took in the clutter and the pulled curtains. "Nice room. I'll bet you've got a great view." He peeked out the drapery.

"I suppose." Harry carefully closed the drape. "I find it a distraction when I am trying to write."

"Oh. Sorry." Irwin bent over the desk, running his hands over printed pages bearing Harry's scrawled edits. "I heard you were some kind of writer. This won't take long. I don't want to keep you from your work."

Harry put himself between his desk and his visitor. He didn't like people, especially strangers, seeing his work before it was complete. "What can I do for you, Mr. Brunner?"

Irwin bared two rows of brilliant white teeth. "Irwin, remember?" He cleared his throat. "I'll get right to it. I was speaking with Mary earlier."

"How is Mrs. Barron doing? I've been meaning to pay her a visit."

"I'm sure she'd like that, Harry. The thing is, she said that Kelly Green, the owner, has been asking her a lot of questions about Charlie's death."

"Yes?"

"Well, it's upsetting her, you know?"

"I'm sorry. Why are you telling me this rather than Mrs. Green?"

"I thought I could talk to you, man to man like. I've noticed you two seem close." He waved his hand between them. "Mary's been through a lot."

"Yes, but I'm sure she'd like to know the truth about her husband's murder. Wouldn't she?"

"Of course. Of course. That's what the police are for." Irwin dug his fingers into Harry's bony shoulder. "Look, Harry, all I'm saying is that maybe we should leave Mary alone."

"I don't understand. The other morning I got the impression that you suspected her of something."

Irwin Brunner chewed his lower lip. "Do you know why we are here, Harry?"

"For the reunion."

Irwin gave an indulgent smile. He sat on the edge of the chair and planted his elbows on his widespread knees. "It's surprising we all came. Personally, I'd rather be vacationing in the Bahamas. Of course, if you had said we'd all get to come and witness Charlie's demised, I don't think any of us would have hesitated."

"What an odd thing to say."

Irwin chuckled. "Why? In the end, that's what it is, isn't it?"

"I don't understand what you are trying to say," said

Harry. The man was rambling. "This is all very interesting but I don't see a point."

Irwin's face turned serious. "The point is that we all came hoping to get something back from Charlie Barron. Don't get me wrong."

Irwin pulled his sunglasses from his shirt and twirled them in his hand. "I knew it was a longshot. We all did. But hope springs eternal, right?"

Harry studied his guest carefully. "What was it that you wanted?"

"Easy." Irwin's smile was beguiling. "I wanted my wife back."

"Vivian Rochester?"

Irwin's brow flew up. "You knew?"

Harry nodded.

"Well, well. You've been checking up on me."

"What did Dr. Barron have to do with you getting your wife back?"

Irwin jumped to his feet. "Nothing. I knew Vivian would be here with her wife, Jill. This was my chance to try to talk sense to her."

"You want her back."

"Yes, I do."

"What does Mary Barron have to do with you getting Vivian back?"

"Vivian and Mary have been friends for years. Vivian used to work as Mary's assistant. To be blunt, she's offered to put in a good word for me."

"I see." Harry wrote a few words in his notebook. "You no longer suspect Mary Barron of being involved in her husband's death?"

"No."

"Yet that was the impression you gave me the other

morning." Harry reread his notes. "You said she wasn't in her room the night of Cowboy's murder and hinted that she may have been involved somehow."

Irwin lifted his foot and fiddled with the strap of his sandal. "Mary told me she had gone for a drive to clear her head."

"And you believe her?"

"Yes. I'd probably have done the same thing. I lost my wife once. It is devastating. Still, I can only imagine how traumatizing it is to have one's spouse murdered."

"What do you think happened to Dr. Barron?"

"I think he had the misfortune of falling in a pool and being surprised by a burglar when he went to change his clothes, Harry. Can you come up with something better?"

Harry couldn't. Not yet, at least. "Did Charlie know Mildred McConaughey?"

"Who?"

"She owns the Golden Arms Hotel next door." Harry gave a generous description. "She was here the night of Dr. Barron's murder."

"Sorry, I've never heard of the woman. I couldn't say if he had. You'd have to ask Mary."

"According to Kelly, her husband did not know Mrs. McConaughey."

"There's your answer then." Irwin ran his sunglasses up his nose. "Thanks for your time, Harry." He threw open the door to a gash of bright yellow sunlight. The sounds of summertime rock and roll rose from the courtyard. A startled gull perching on the ledge outside Harry's door took flight.

"One thing," Harry said, looking up from his notes.

"Yeah?"

"Hypothetically, if a burglar was not responsible for Charlie Barron's murder, who might you guess would be?"

There was a long silence filled only by the sounds of Bruce Springsteen and the E Street Band singing about girls in their summer clothes.

Irwin Brunner's smile was almost as enigmatic as his words. "Nice couple, the Dennises, don't you think so, Harry?"

Kelly pulled her hair into a loose ponytail and wrapped a pink bandana across her forehead. The bandana matched her bubble gum-pink Beach Lovers Inn shirt. She was in a better mood than she had been for days.

Ruth had been moved to the medical center's rehab unit. Things were looking up. Aunt Angie had begun remodeling work on the second bedroom in her Sun City villa to accommodate her sister's arrival.

Kelly fed Sharky a large portion of kibble and refilled his water dish. What was it she had said to that phone caller? *Where every day is a ray of sunshine and every night is a dream.*

Hokey but catchy. She decided to have George paint up a small sign with the slogan. They could hang it over the entrance to the lobby.

Thinking of George reminded her that she wanted to speak with him before Harry did.

Drew was busy changing the sheets in 102.

"Have you seen George this morning?"

"He's with your dad." Drew tossed the bedsheets into the cart.

"Thanks. Where?"

Drew grinned. "With Katie."

"Oh," Kelly said on a groan. "I completely forgot about the motorcycle."

"What's the problem with your dad having a bike?"

"The problem isn't that he has it. The problem is that if he repairs it, he's bound to ride it again. Call me selfish, but I only have one parent left and I'd like him to be around a while longer."

"Sure, I get that."

"Any word from your cousin Drake?"

"About the murder? No, sorry. He seems to think this might end up one of those unsolved mysteries."

"Not if I can help it," Kelly said under her breath as she went off in search of her father and his folly.

The Indian Chieftain lay in a heap outside the open garage door. The pallet had been practically picked clean. A turkey vulture sailed high above as if considering whether or not it was worth picking at the bones of the bike for tidbits.

George and her father hovered over a gold-trimmed Cadillac in the small garage.

"I see you managed to move the bike, Dad."

"Huh?" Ben Walsh lifted his head from under the open hood. "Right, yeah. Had to do it in pieces but we got it in." He drew his daughter closer. "Would you look at this?"

Kelly wrinkled her forehead. "Okay." She planted her hands on the edge of the car. "What am I looking at? All I see is an engine and a bunch of attached doodads and doohickeys."

Her father laughed.

George stuck a rag in his back pocket. "What you are looking at is a 1955 Cadillac Fleetwood Eldorado Biarritz."

"With all the trimmings." Her dad was practically drooling.

"By the way, Dad. Ruth got moved to the rehab facility this morning."

"That's good news."

"You must be happy, right, George?"

"Yeah, that's great." George mopped his brow.

Did he think her road to recovery was great or did he think he'd have to try to get rid of her again?

Kelly shook the thoughts away. Harry was making her paranoid. "So what's this old convertible doing here? Dad, you didn't have this delivered too?" What was going to show up at the doorstep next, a fishing boat?

"No. This was here in the garage already. Tell her, George."

"It belonged to Jim." George gently lowered the hood. He rubbed the hand prints away with his red rag. "She hasn't been driven since he died. Even then, he barely drove it the last few years or so."

George kicked one of the sagging front tires. "I guess it belongs to you now."

He was looking at her.

"Me?" said Kelly. "I don't want it." The humongous alpine white automobile came with red and white leather interior. The outlandish exterior design featured all gold trim, a gold front grille and gold wheels. Front projections housing the headlights stuck out like bombs. Long, tall tailfins gave the impression the vehicle could fly.

Kelly moved around the car. "Maybe we can sell it." The paint was dulled and pitted in spots. The ocean can be tough on cars. "How much do you think we might get for it?"

Both men gasped.

"You wouldn't!" Ben said.

"We'll talk about it later, Dad. Okay? I need to talk to George."

"Can we talk while we walk?" asked George. "I promised Drew I'd fix the leaky toilet in room 105."

George fetched his tool belt from the garage floor and buckled up. Room 105 was deserted and George got to work.

"What can I do for you, Kelly?"

"I'm not sure how to say this, George." Kelly watched as George leaned behind the commode and attacked the U-joint with a big pipe wrench.

"Spit it out. That's what Ruth always does. That's why we get on so good."

Kelly took him up on it. "Okay. I heard you were asking my aunt for more money."

George peeked up from behind the toilet bowl. "Who told you that?"

"Actually, it was Harry."

George set his wrench on the side of the tub and pulled off the cover of the toilet. "He came to see me yesterday. Did you send him?"

"No. Absolutely not." Kelly literally backed up in the bathroom doorway. Her hand flew to her chest. "I would never do that."

George tried the flusher a few times. "The pipe was loose but this float is shot." He fingered a big, black balloony thing inside the tank. "I think I have one in the shop."

"Great." Kelly waited. Did he intend to evade her question?

George replaced the cover of the tank. Next, he slid his wrench onto his leather tool belt. "Harry is a nice young man but he lives in a fantasy land. The money wasn't for me. It was for her."

"Her?" Was there a woman in George's life? A woman with extravagant tastes? "Are we talking about Mildred?"

"Mildred?" George looked surprised at the mention of the hotel owner's name. "Harry asked me about her, too. I'll tell you the same thing I told him." He bent down and wiped a puddle of water under the toilet. "If you want to know anything about Mildred, you'll have to ask her. I don't tell tales about my friends."

Feeling chastened, Kelly left George to get on with his work.

31

Harry had no intention of waiting until nightfall to continue the investigation into the killing of Charlie Barron. The inn's guests would be leaving soon and would not be available for interviews. Plus, Chad might beat him to the story. Assuming the police didn't beat them both to the solution—killing his chances of getting his byline in Myrtle Scene Magazine and collecting a payday.

He decided to corner Rick Ramus first. Rick was not in the office.

"George and Ben corralled him into giving them a hand," Lee explained.

"Where are they?"

"In the parking lot. Wrestling a bear."

"I don't understand," said Harry.

Lee grinned. "You'll see."

Harry obediently went around the side of the building to the parking lot. There was no one in sight.

And not a single bear.

Irwin Brunner's last words echoed in his brain. Harry decided it was time to pay a social call on the Dennises.

An internet search had brought up little on Desmond and Bonnie Dennis. Hopefully, a pointed conversation would turn up more.

He knocked on their door only to be told by Drew that she had last seen them headed for the beach with a beach bag, towels and a cooler.

"Thank you, Ms. Schiffer." Harry gave an anachronistic half-bow.

"No problem, Mr. Leland, and you can call me Drew. You've been staying here at the inn so long, you practically feel like family."

Harry blushed. Was she chiding him for taking advantage of Ruth Evans' generosity? "It's only temporary. I intend to get a place of my mine just as soon as I can."

"Hey, I don't mind. Stay as long as you like. Mrs. Green did ask me to clean your room though." Her eyes cut to room 207.

"That would be fine." Harry knew he couldn't keep housekeeping out forever. He grabbed the handle of the cleaning cart and idly moved it back and forth. "On the subject of rooms, have you noticed anything odd in any of the rooms belonging to Mary Barron's friends?"

"Odd how?" Drew grabbed a cleaning cloth, squirted the window and wiped. There was too much to do around the inn to stand around idle. "You clean hotel rooms long enough, you see all kinds of odd. Trust me," she said, picking up the window cleaner and giving the pane another squirt. "You do not want to know."

"I'm not sure," Harry admitted in answer to her earlier question. "Anything suspicious?"

"If you mean a signed confession, the answer is no." Drew grabbed the cart from Harry and rolled it up the walkway to the next room.

Harry climbed the dune. Holding his hand over his eyes to shield them from the imposing sun, he scanned the yellow sand. Gulls big and small ran along the edge of the water.

Desmond Dennis sprawled in a blue canvas chair under a red canvas umbrella. The chairs and umbrellas were spread out each morning by the company that had the rental rights for this stretch of beach.

Harry trudged through the spongy sand. "Mr. Dennis?"

Desmond Dennis held an open paperback copy of *The Guns of Navarone* against his bare belly. "Yes?" He peered at Harry over a pair of cheap sunglasses with brown lenses. The glasses looked disproportionate on his long, angular face.

An open cooler held beer, soda and plastic-wrapped sandwiches from Dagwood's Deli on Chester Street.

"Harry Leland." Harry angled himself under the shade of the umbrella.

"Staying at the inn, aren't you?"

"Yes." Harry pulled out his notebook and pen. "I'm doing a story for Myrtle Scene Magazine concerning the murder of Dr. Barron."

"Myrtle Scene Magazine?" Desmond chuckled.

"It's a local news magazine."

"Right. I think I've seen `it around in some of those sidewalk kiosks." Desmond set his book on the blanket and helped himself to a soda. "Like anything to drink?"

"No, thanks. What I would like is to interview you."

"What for?"

"Like I said, I'm interviewing Dr. Barron's friends. Part of the background story."

Desmond took a slug of soda and burped. "I don't know what I can tell you, Harry. The great Dr. Barron and I weren't exactly close. In fact, I hadn't seen him in twenty years."

"Why did you come, if you don't mind my asking?"

"Because Charlie was paying. We weren't about to say no to that." He tossed the empty soda can in the cooler and extracted a second. He popped the top. A sweet, fizzy purple cloud erupted.

Desmond ground his heels into the sand.

"Apparently, Barron wanted to show there were no hard feelings. Maybe not for him," Desmond scoffed.

Harry wrote diligently. "Hard feelings for what?"

"For ruining everybody's lives."

"Hey!" An angry voice called out.

Harry turned. A tall, belligerent woman was shaking a fist and marching towards him from up the shoreline. It was Bonnie Dennis, a fringed straw hat atop her head.

"What do you think you are doing?"

"Mr. Dennis," Harry said quickly, "how exactly did Dr. Barron ruin everybody's lives?"

Desmond squirmed and retrieved his book. "I've said all I'm going to say."

"I'm warning you!" growled Bonnie Dennis, growing closer by the moment.

"Please, Mr. Dennis, whose lives did he ruin? And how?"

Harry felt himself being spun on his heels. He slid sideways. A fist hurtled toward him, making contact with his right eye.

"Keep away from my husband," bellowed Bonnie. "Can't you see he's ill?"

"I-I'm sorry." Harry scrambled on his hands and knees for his fallen notebook.

She stuck her foot against his butt and gave him a shove. "Get lost, buddy!"

Harry tumbled forward and didn't stop until he was

on the opposite side of the dune.

"What happened to you?" Rick had escorted a young couple to their room and was on his way to the lobby for their luggage.

Harry cupped his hand over his eye. "It's nothing."

"Nothing? You'd better get an ice pack on that eye, Harry." He hollered to Drew who was busy on the other side of the courtyard. She ran over, took one look at Harry's swelling eye and went to work. "Your eye looks like that angry red spot on Jupiter. Or is that Saturn?"

The housekeeper had filled a wash cloth with cubes from the stainless steel ice machine at the edge of the courtyard. "Here." She placed Harry's hand on the ice pack. "Better keep this on for a while."

"I saw you and Kelly at the gig last night," Rick commented as Drew departed. "What did you think?"

"It was very informative," Harry replied.

"Informative?" Rick scratched his head. "What the heck does that mean?"

"You were funny."

"Yeah? You think?"

"Very."

"Thanks."

"Were you emceeing the night of Dr. Barron's murder?"

"Yeah," Rick said. "I guess so. Why?"

"What about Mrs. McC? Was she at Laff Trax that night?"

"Huh? I dunno. She was probably around. I really don't pay much attention. Besides, didn't I hear she was here at the inn? Moaning about the fireworks?"

"Right. I forgot."

"You sure you're okay, Harry?" Harry's face was red

going on purple. His eye was bloodshot. "You don't look so good, buddy."

"I'm fine." Harry pressed the dripping ice pack lightly against his eye. "I'll catch up with you later."

Harry was not in the mood for conversation. His eye was throbbing. He had had enough and wanted nothing more than to lie down for a bit until dinner at Captain Haddock's with Kelly.

Kelly was working in the lobby when Rick returned. "Got a minute, Rick?"

"Sure, boss. What's up?" He shifted nervously from foot to foot near the pile of red luggage he had yet to deliver to some new arrivals.

Lee Hollister was off-duty. Kelly and Rick were alone in the lobby.

Kelly decided to ease into things. She didn't want to risk offending her assistant manager. He may not be guilty of anything. "I enjoyed your show last night."

"Thanks. I'm working up some new bits."

She flipped through the room cards. The inn was three-quarters booked. Not so bad. "Funny, you didn't mention that you were in town the day Ruth had her accident." She stood behind the counter facing Rick on the other side.

"Look, I had a gig in Orlando," explained Rick. "I got back two nights before but then Artie at the Laff Trax asked me if I could emcee for a couple of nights. He had an opportunity to play a joint in NYC. I said yes."

"So why keep it a secret?"

Rick fussed with his shirt collar. "No secret. It wasn't any big deal."

"No? Ruth ended up in the hospital and you didn't

even say you were in town, let alone pay her a visit?"

Rick frowned. "Okay, here's the thing. I can see it looks bad for me. I was afraid you and Ruth might think I wasn't taking my job seriously. You might even consider what I was doing moonlighting. But it's not. I mean, the emceeing thing doesn't pay much. I need this job."

The assistant manager wiped a bead of sweat trickling from his brow. "I'm sorry about your aunt, Kelly. I hear she's doing better."

"She is." Kelly noticed Det. Burns' unmarked sedan pull up at the curb.

"Can I take this luggage now?" Rick's fingers hovered hopefully over the handle of the nearest battered suitcase.

"Go ahead. I would like to continue our conversation later."

"Sure thing." Rick nodded to the brown-suited detective as he entered the lobby. Rick loaded up the luggage trolley and tootled off.

"Hello, detective," called Kelly. "What brings you here? I thought you had other fish to fry."

The detective helped himself to a mint from the seashell dish at the end of the counter. "I do. But I was in the area and thought I'd stop by."

"I don't suppose you have any news on the murders?"

"No." He smiled annoyingly. "I don't suppose I do. May I?"

Kelly nodded and he helped himself to a glass of lemon water.

"Even if I did," he said between sips, "I couldn't share with you. Tell me." He tossed the paper cup in the recycle bin. "Are you and the mystery writer still investigating?" His eyes danced with smug amusement.

"If you mean, are Harry Leland and I taking an active interest in who's been killing people around here, the answer is yes." She grabbed a paper towel and wiped the water puddle he'd left when filling his cup. "Somebody has to."

He ignored the jab. "What exactly is your connection with Harry Leland?"

"He's a guest, detective."

"Is that all?"

Kelly pulled the bandana from her forehead and shook out her hair. "Look, as much fun as this has been, Det. Burns, I have an inn to run." The man had a way of getting under her skin. What had he stopped by for? Free food and drinks? Was the Beach Lovers Inn going to become a refueling stop on his route?

"Of course, I'll let you get on with it." He tilted his head to one side as he eyed her. "What are you planning to do tonight?"

"Why, so you can try to stop me, detective? Are you afraid I might do a little investigating and show you up?"

Det. Burns thrust his hands in the pockets of his suit coat. "Actually, I was hoping you would say you had no plans."

"I'm sure you were." She yanked open the door hoping he'd get the hint and leave.

"And that we might be able to get a bite to eat?"

"Oh." Kelly felt a warm flush climb her neck. "Are you asking me out on a date, detective?"

"Nick is asking you out on a date, Kelly. Can I call you that? Det. Burns plans to stay home."

"Yes." Her mouth was dry as an unbuttered biscuit.

"Yes I can call you Kelly or yes you'll have dinner with me?"

"I guess you'll find out when you come to the inn tonight." Kelly went out the door herself. She started shakily up the stairs, gripping the handrail for support.

"Shall we say seven-thirty?" she said over her shoulder.

32

Harry flopped down on his bed and promptly fell asleep with the ice cube packed wash cloth balanced over his eyeball. Sometime later, he woke freezing. The ice had melted down his face and neck, soaking through his shirt and puddling in his chest cavity.

Shivering, he peeled off his shirt, toweled himself off and put on some dry clothes. He looked in shock at the man in the mirror. It had been no dream. Bonnie Dennis had punched him in the eye.

Harry glanced at the bedside clock. Replaying the afternoon's horror in his mind's eye, he had had a sudden vision. That vision was of a bicycle with a basket over the rear tire. He slipped into his shoes and exited his room.

Looking over his shoulder, in case Bonnie Dennis was still on the warpath and out for his blood, Harry climbed the dunes. From there, he surveyed the beach. The crowds had thinned, with few beachgoers remaining now that the red sun was settling down in the western sky. The dozens of chairs and umbrellas that had sprinkled the beach earlier had been chained up for the night at the edge of the dunes.

Harry had been hoping to have a word with the young man who tended the beach rentals. The man rode a black bicycle with a wicker basket on the back. If he had been the person setting off the fireworks, he might have seen something the night of the murder.

Harry retraced his steps to the Beach Lovers Inn. He would track down the rental guy tomorrow and see if he could add anything to what so far was proving a not very fruitful story.

Determined to crank out a few words of his work in progress, *The Murderous Minions of Mars*, before Kelly's arrival for dinner at Captain Haddock's, he sat at his desk. He needed to sell this book. He needed it to be better than good. It had been years since his last novel had been published. Publishers were not exactly clamoring for his work.

He reread the last couple of pages on the glowing laptop screen, hoping for inspiration. But the murders of Dr. Barron and Cowboy ate away at his brain like an infernal, insatiable parasite.

The internet beckoned, promising information, knowledge.

And he followed.

Kelly opted for a pale blue wraparound dress with a modest neckline. She draped a gold chain that had once belonged to her mother around her neck. Sexy yet practical low-heeled red shoes completed the look. At the last minute, she added a dab of perfume to her nape.

Nick Burns arrived promptly at seven thirty behind the wheel of a yellow convertible with black leather seats. He was waiting at the curb chatting with her father at the entrance to the inn.

Kelly smothered a groan. Forty-one years old and her dad was still checking up on her dates. She sent him on his way and joined Det. Burns in the car.

"Where would you like to go?" The detective was looking practically like a new man dressed down in a charcoal polo shirt and tan trousers.

Kelly had prepared her answer ahead of time. "Captain Haddock's," she said casually.

Det. Burns cast a suspicious eye in her direction as he shifted the car into drive.

"What?" said Kelly, smoothing her dress and planting her purse in her lap. "I hear the snapper is good. I've never been and always wanted to try it."

Whether he bought the story or not, he agreed. They parked in a public lot near the boardwalk and were shown to a table near the back of the dining room.

"Your dad is quite a guy," Det. Burns said as they shared a bottle of sparkling white wine.

"Yes, he is."

"He was telling me about his motorcycle. An Indian Chieftain, isn't it?"

"Yes, that sounds right." Kelly discreetly surveyed the room. Dr. Ted Nelson in the booth in the front corner canoodling with his wife, Jean. She was a stocky woman with dyed blonde hair, high cheekbones and gray-blue eyes.

"And that car of yours." Ted nodded appreciatively. "I'd love to see it sometime."

"That old Cadillac in the garage? I don't know what the big deal is. Frankly, I'd like to sell it. Then I can get my car inside and out of the elements. Salt is not a car's best friend."

"Wow. If you really do think of selling, let me know. I might be interested."

Kelly promised she would. "Captain Haddock's sure is popular with my guests."

"What do you mean?"

Their dinners arrived. She had ordered the snapper and he the blue crab.

"So, Mrs. Green, is there a Mr. Green?"

"Yes. Actually, two of them."

"Two? Should I be worried? You aren't a black widow, are you?"

"Very funny. Divorced twice, if you must know. And they are both still very much alive...I think." She had not been in touch with Tommy in years. "Frankly, I'm not so sure about husband number one. He's a surfer and could be anywhere. But I can give you Alan's phone number if you'd like to check up on him."

Nick chuckled. "I don't think that will be necessary. You know, I've taken up surfing myself."

"I'll try not to hold that against you." Kelly quipped. "What about you, detective? What's your story?"

"Never married." He grabbed a chunk of brown bread and buttered it. "Engaged once. Briefly." He folded the bread into his mouth and chewed. "I think marriage is over-rated."

"You could be right but not everybody would agree." Kelly pointed her knife over his shoulder. "That's the Nelsons over there. They seem to have made it work." Ted and Jean Nelson snuggled side by side in a dim booth. A bottle of champagne stuck out of the wine stand planted beside their table.

Nick Burns stole a look. "So it seems."

"Did you know that the Nelsons and the Barrons used to be partners?"

"Yes, I did." The detective dug into his meal. "Try the pilaf," he suggested. "It's very good."

Kelly idly pushed some pilaf onto her fork.

"Did you know that Dr. Barron asked everyone here to make amends?"

"The reunion, yes." He refilled their wine glasses.

"I found out that Rick Ramus, that's my assistant manager, he was in town the night my aunt was pushed down the stairs."

Kelly jabbed her fork at him across the table for emphasis. The candle flickered. "And he was performing at Laff Trax, that's the club in the Golden Arms Hotel, right next door to the Beach Lovers Inn, I might add."

Nick leaned back and frowned as he dabbed butter sauce from his chin. "I know where the Golden Arms Hotel is."

"Right. Anyway, Rick was emceeing at the comedy club the night Dr. Barron was murdered."

The detective carefully laid his napkin on the table and smoothed it. "So?"

"So while one of the other comedians was performing, Rick could have left, conked Dr. Barron in the head and been back in the club with no one any the wiser."

The detective sighed. "I know I'm none the wiser. Look." He laid his hands on the table. "I came here to have a nice dinner, some good wine and the pleasure of your company. I promised I would leave the detective at home, remember?"

He drained his glass. "I was sort of hoping you would do the same."

Kelly's cheeks warmed. "I know, it's just that I can't help wondering if Rick and Mrs. McConaughey are in cahoots."

"Cahoots, huh?" Nick Burns' blue-green eyes twinkled with amusement. "I tell you what. I'll make you a deal." He planted his hands on the table and laced his fingers together.

"What sort of a deal?"

"If I promise to check into the backgrounds of McConaughey and Ramus, will you promise to forget all about murder and mayhem? At least for tonight? There's still time to enjoy dessert. You do want dessert, don't you? I'm told they do a primo praline cheesecake."

"Deal." Kelly took a quick bite of her snapper. "Did I mention that Harry told me he overheard George, that's the inn's handyman, asking Aunt Ruth for money?"

"No." Nick eyed his plate. His food was getting cold. So were his emotions.

"George and Mildred McConaughey were eating dinner here the night Cowboy was, you know, drowned." Kelly stopped, holding her fork suspended in the air. "Sorry. I'm stopping now."

She zipped her mouth shut the way an eight year old would. "See?"

Det. Burns gently laid his hand over hers. "I'll take another look at George too."

"Thank you. Please don't tell him I said anything."

"I won't."

"Harry says George owns a beach house. How does a handyman afford a beach house? Oops." With a flourish, she zipped her mouth shut once again.

"Sorry, detective. I mean Nick. You can't expect me not to get involved in what's happening under my very nose in my own inn."

"I can see that," he said with an indulgent smile.

"Thanks for understanding." Kelly scooted back her chair.

"Where are you going?"

"Ladies. I'll be right back."

Det. Burns said he'd order the cheesecake and a couple of coffees.

Kelly found the restrooms in the rear of the restaurant opposite the kitchen at the end of a dark, narrow hallway. An exit sign hung over a black door at the end of the hall. There was no sign of a burglar alarm.

Kelly glanced into the crowded, noisy kitchen. If anybody noticed what she was up to, she'd say she got confused looking for the ladies room.

Kelly inched open the door. No alarms sounded. She pushed the door all the way open and found herself in an alleyway. The same alleyway she had been in earlier looking for Cowboy with Harry.

"Interesting," she muttered. Interesting because anybody could have sneaked out the back way, murdered Cowboy and been back at their table without anyone suspecting a thing.

33

Nine o'clock came and there was still no sign of Kelly. Harry dialled the number she had given him. She wasn't answering.

Harry walked down to Aunt Ruth's apartment.

"Come on in, Harry." Ben Walsh appeared at the door in baggy denim shorts and a Grateful Dead tee shirt. He had a book on motorcycle repair in his hand.

"I'm looking for Kelly. Have you seen her?"

"She's on a date with that Det. Burns." Ben set the book on the kitchen table.

"I see." Harry worried his lower lip.

"You know anything about rebuilding motorcycles, Harry?"

"Sorry. No."

"Oh, well. I'll figure it out." Ben pulled open the refrigerator door and tossed Harry a beer. "What's going on? Come up with any new leads for that story of yours?"

Harry had told Ben how he was writing a story for Myrtle Scene Magazine concerning Dr. Barron's murder.

"I think I've found a couple of interesting new leads." After hours of internet searching, he had found out some interesting facts concerning the histories and backgrounds of Charles Barron and Desmond Dennis.

"Say," Ben grabbed Harry's chin in between his

thumb and forefinger, "what happened to the eye?"

Harry gave Kelly's father the unblemished truth, embarrassing as it was.

Ben laughed. "If you ask me, it means you're hitting a nerve." He threw himself down on the sofa and motioned for Harry to sit. He tossed Harry the brass bottle opener.

"Sir?" Harry fumbled the catch. He bent to pick the bottle opener from the floor as Ben Walsh explained.

"Sure, you're getting close to pay dirt. Why else would the woman take a swing at you?" He chugged and Harry followed suit. "You struck a nerve."

Harry nodded thoughtfully.

"Know what you gotta do?"

"What's that?" Harry licked his lips.

"When you strike a nerve, you just gotta keep drilling." Ben pumped his fist. "Deeper and deeper. You know what I mean?"

"I think so." Harry had seen Bonnie Dennis downstairs, seated alone at the picnic table. He finished his beer and thanked Ben for his help. "Tell Kelly I stopped by." He stood and crossed to the door.

Ben slapped him on the back. "I'll do that. And come find me tomorrow, I'll show you the Chieftain."

Harry promised he would, although he had no idea what or who the Chieftain was. Did it have something to do with the bear that wasn't there? The one that Lee reported that Ben and George had been wrestling with?

There were a lot of strange goings on at the Beach Lovers Inn—and they didn't all concern murder.

When he had first met Ruth Evans at Bayside Books across town, he had had no idea it would lead to all this. He had been doing a signing at the bookshop. Hardly any customers stopped at his table near the door. Most had avoided eye contact, but not Ruth Evans. She had smiled encouragingly and asked him all about his stories. In the end, she had purchased both of his novels and gotten his life story thrown in for free.

Learning that he was living temporarily in an acquaintance's camper van, she had invited him to stay at the inn for free. When he asked her why, she said she liked him and wanted to encourage his work.

Harry had not known what to make of the offer initially. Who was this dainty older woman offering to let him stay for nothing in her inn?

He thought she might have been a bit crazy and said so to the bookstore owner. The next day, however, he had driven to the address she had scribbled on the back of a bookmark, expecting to find an empty field or a small cottage. To his surprise, instead there stood the funky Beach Lovers Inn, right on the beach, with Jim and Ruth Evans, listed on the sign as proprietors.

She insisted Harry move in that same day and he did.

Now he was trying to find out who had attacked and very nearly murdered her and then successfully murdered one of her guests. Finding that person, was the least he could do to pay Ruth Evans back for all her kindness.

Harry steeled himself. Bonnie Dennis sat drinking alone at the picnic table in the sand. A dark bottle of something sat within arm's reach. A cigarette glowed orange between her fingers.

Moths circled the spotlights at the corners of the inn.

Bonnie Dennis glanced sullenly at Harry as he approached. "Hello, Harry." She tilted her head and blew a cloud of smoke upward. "How's the eye?"

"Fine." Harry maintained a respectful distance.

She grinned and patted the wooden bench. "Don't stand there, Harry. Join me."

Harry reluctantly did so. He read the label on the bottle by the glow of the moon and stars: Old Crow Kentucky Straight Bourbon Whiskey.

The glass bottle scraped the wooden table as she inched the bottle in his direction. "Have a drink."

"No, thank you."

"Suit yourself." She grabbed the bottle around the middle and took a swig. This was followed quickly by a drag on her cigarette. She flicked the still-lit butt into the side of the dune.

Harry cringed.

"Where's your girlfriend?"

"Girlfriend?" asked Harry.

"Kelly Green. The owner of this lovely hotel. The two of you are shacking up, aren't you?"

"No. We're...friends."

Bonnie grunted. "You want something?" She looked at him expectantly.

"I know both you and your husband once worked for the Barrons."

"Worked with, Harry. Worked *with*." There was a vicious undertone to her response.

"Worked with." Harry gulped. The smoke mixing with the salt air irritated his tender, swollen eye.

"The bastard ruined our lives." She threw out her arms and looked heavenward. "Thank you, universe!" she bellowed. "For screwing us over. Thank you very much." She took a drink from the bottle and slammed it down on the table.

Harry bristled. "Where were you when Dr. Barron

was murdered?"

Bonnie swung on Harry. "You wanted to know where I was? I was watching the fireworks. Same as you, Harry."

Harry didn't bother to correct her.

"Little did we know the fireworks were to celebrate Charlie's death." She grinned. "We would have taken more pleasure in them. We all would have."

"Not Mary Barron," Harry said.

Bonnie merely shrugged.

"The Barrons flourished and the Dennises floundered. I guess that's the way things go." A small stream of tears flowed down her cheeks. "Poor Desmond."

"What happened to him?"

"He had a stroke. Years ago. After what happened with Charlie."

"What happened with Charlie? Did you and Charlie have an affair? Did your husband find out?"

Bonnie threw back her head and barked out a deep laugh. "Me and Charlie? Not on your life." She dug a pack of cigarettes from the pocket of her shorts and lit up with a disposable pink lighter. "Desmond was an electrical engineer and computer programmer. He was smart. Real smart."

Harry had discovered that in researching Desmond's background. The man had graduated at the top of his class from Rensselaer Polytechnic Institute. RPI was a top school, so that had been no small achievement. "Was?"

"After the stroke, he just couldn't do much of anything any longer."

"I'm sorry." Harry could only imagine what it would be like to have a long life ahead but nothing productive to do with that time.

Silence hung over them for a moment until Bonnie said, "That pacemaker was our golden ticket, you know? And Charlie snatched it away."

"Pacemaker?"

"The one Charlie invented." She sniffed hard. "Or so he said. Desmond deserved credit too. We all did. But Charlie took all the credit."

Bonnie sucked angrily on her cigarette then flicked it into the darkness. "And all the money."

"Why didn't you take him to court?"

Bonnie gaped at him, amusement written in her eyes. "Don't you know, Harry? When you are the one with all the money, you always win in court. That's the way the world works. This world, anyway. Who knows? Maybe the next one will be better."

Harry could think of no words to say in reply.

"Good night, Harry." Bonnie snatched the bottle from the table and carried it with her up and over the dune.

Trembling, Harry retraced his steps. Kelly had stood him up for a date with Det. Burns. For some reason he could not fathom, that fact got under his skin. Not that he was jealous.

Rough hands grabbed him by the collar as he turned the corner under the stairwell. "What were you doing with my wife?"

Harry stared into the inky shadows. "Desmond? Hello." After what his wife had said, he felt a newfound sympathy for the man.

"You are a nosy SOB, aren't you?" Desmond's hard little eyes squinted up at Harry. "Or are you hitting on her?"

"No, sir. We were only chatting," Harry said placidly. He extricated Desmond's hands from his shirt.

"See that you don't. In fact," said Desmond, rocking back on his heels, "here's a hit for you to see that you don't!" His left fist flew slowly at Harry's face.

Harry dodged but it was too late. Desmond's fist connected with Harry's eye. Both men yelped in pain.

"Everything okay down there?"

Harry recognized the voice of Ben Walsh. "Yes, sir. It's me, Harry."

"Well, it's late. Keep it down, son."

"Yes, sir." Harry turned to Desmond Dennis. "Listen, Mr. Dennis—"

But the slopped gray figure of Desmond Dennis was already skittering away across the courtyard.

Harry touched his throbbing eye. The good news was that Desmond didn't pack nearly the punch that his wife did.

Plus, Desmond had struck the same eye his wife had. At least he wouldn't have a second black eye to explain to the curious.

34

Kelly had not seen Harry all morning. He hadn't come down to the dining room for breakfast or made an appearance of any sort. His car was missing from the parking lot.

She had so much to tell him. First and foremost, how she had discovered that anyone of Charlie Barron's pals could have snuck out the back of Captain Haddock's and murdered Cowboy.

What was Harry up to? Did it have something to do with Charles Barron's murder? Was he working on the case and his story without her?

She was determined to read that story before he submitted it for publication. It was critical that the Beach Lovers Inn be shown in the best possible light. It would be disastrous if Harry made it out to appear like some sleazy motel that was home to a criminal element.

A reputation like that could destroy the business.

It was already wreaking a certain amount of havoc around the inn. The guests were whispering about the unsolved murder over breakfast. Rick Ramus seemed put out. Even George had been acting all standoffish.

When she finally returned to the inn after visiting Aunt Ruth in rehab, she spotted Harry crouched with her dad beside a heap of motorcycle parts at the edge of the garage.

"Hi, guys." Kelly gave her dad a hug. "Ruth says hello."

"How is she?"

"Doing well."

"Great. I'll stop by in the afternoon." Ben Walsh had forgotten to mention to his daughter that Harry had stopped by the apartment the night before looking for her.

"She will like that. I told her I'd pack a few changes of clothes. Take them for me?"

"Sure thing."

Harry fiddled with the bike's carburetor. He hadn't said a word beyond hello.

"Why the cold shoulder, Harry?"

"I don't know what you are talking about." His reply came out more stiffly than he had intended. "How was dinner at Captain Haddock's? Did you and Det. Burns have a good time?"

Kelly's father cleared his throat. "I think I'll take a break. Thanks for your help, Harry. I might do like you said and search YouTube. Maybe I'll find a video or two that will help with some of this stuff."

Ben wiped his hands on his blue jeans, leaving black greasy streaks. "The truth is, I know more about plumbing than I do motorcycles." He looked pointedly at Kelly and tilted his head towards Harry.

Kelly gnawed at her lip. She had forgotten until seeing Harry now that she had invited him to go to the restaurant with her so they could do a little snooping. "I messed up, didn't I?"

Harry pushed himself up from the garage floor. "I don't know what you mean." Big black sunglasses covered his face and hid his eyes.

"No, huh?" Kelly grabbed his elbow. "I didn't mean to hurt your feelings."

Sharky wound between them then ducked under a parked car to catch a nap in the shade.

"You didn't." Harry started back to the inn.

Kelly pulled down the garage door and followed after him. "When Nick asked me out, I completely forgot that we had talked about going together. I only said yes because I wanted to check out the restaurant and see if I could squeeze any information out of him."

"Makes sense."

Harry walked faster. She sped up.

"Guess what, Harry? Anybody could have snuck out the back of Captain Haddock's. There's another door in the back but this one is near the restrooms," she said as Harry passed the lobby entrance into the courtyard. "It opens out into the alley."

Harry stopped in his tracks. "Really?" He turned around.

"Yep. It's at the end of a dark hallway that isn't visible to the diners. The kitchen is on one side but barely visible and everybody there is too busy to pay much attention to the hall or the bathrooms."

She could practically see the wheels inside Harry's mind turning. She helped them along. "Think, Harry. They all saw you: the Nelsons, the Dennises and the Rochesters. Maybe George and Mildred. We don't know what time they got to the restaurant."

"Maybe they were curious what you were up to. Maybe one of them saw you talking to Cowboy. Then they figured he might talk, so he had to go. Anyone of them could have lured him away and murdered him after you left."

Harry had to admit it wasn't a bad theory. "Did Det. Burns say whether the police had any new suspects?"

"No." Kelly glanced at the guests in the courtyard. None of them were members of the reunion. "He did agree to look a little deeper into the backgrounds of Mrs. McConaughey and Rick."

"Yes?" Rick had stepped out of the lobby door. He was loaded down with a case of soap in his arms. "You call my name?"

"No." Kelly's forehead turned pink. "Harry and I were just talking."

"Okay." Rick smiled. "I better run this box up to the laundry room for Drew before my arms drop off." He lurched awkwardly up the steps.

"Speak of the devil."

Kelly followed Harry's gaze as he adjusted his sunglasses. A black sedan rolled to a stop at the curb.

The window slid down as Kelly approached. Det. Burns leaned across the center console. The AC was humming and ice cold air spilled out. "I'm on my way to a meeting. I stopped to let you know that I checked up on Mildred McConaughey."

"And?"

"And maybe there is something."

"And that something is?"

"Mildred McConaughey filed a ten million dollar wrongful death and negligence lawsuit against the Barrons and their firm about ten years ago."

"Whose death?"

"Her husband Moe's. Moe had a heart condition and it was one of Barron's gizmos that was attached to his ticker. It failed. Moe died. It would have been the end of the story but the widow next door was dead sure it was malpractice and that the device was defective. It took a year and a half for the case to play out in court."

"Hear that Harry?" Kelly said over her shoulder. But Harry had gone. "With what result?"

"Charles Barron and his company were exonerated. That cost Mildred McConaughey plenty. She not only had to live with the verdict, she had to pay her attorney fees and court costs plus the defense's fees."

"Ouch."

"Ouch is right." He glanced at the clock on the dash. "I'm off. I just thought you'd like to know."

Kelly gripped the edge of the windowsill. "Wait. Do you think she might have wanted revenge?" Her eyes went up the towering Golden Arms Hotel as it cast a shadow over the Beach Lovers Inn. "They were seen arguing in her hotel the day of the murder."

"So I remember." The detective's radio chirped. "Gotta roll. I'll keep you informed."

Kelly wasn't waiting for the detective to get around to talking to Mrs. McConaughey. She marched behind the front desk of the Golden Arms, ignoring the baffled look of James Aldridge who was speaking in soft tones to a guest checking out on the other side of the counter.

Mrs. McConaughey sat regally in a tall leather chair behind an ornate mahogany desk the size of a small yacht. The opulent office had plush purple velvet curtains, an antique Oriental rug and a stone fireplace.

"Mrs. Green?" She glanced away from her computer screen. "What are you doing here?"

A pair of manicured hands locked onto Kelly's upper arm. "I'm sorry, Mrs. Green," James Aldridge said emphatically. "But you will have to go."

He wore his navy blue suit and bore a woodsy scent.

Kelly figured that the bottle of cologne was as close to the woods as James Aldridge ever got.

"I wanted to ask about your lawsuit."

"Lawsuit?"

"The one you filed against Charles Barron."

Mildred McConaughey's left hand flew to her temple as if she'd been hit with a hammer. "It's all right, James." She shooed him off.

"Have a seat, Mrs. Green."

Kelly adopted one of the two dark leather chairs across from the desk.

"So you know about the lawsuit." She turned off her computer screen.

Kelly couldn't help feeling sorry for the woman behind the desk. "Why didn't you say something?"

The woman shrugged helplessly, rustling the folds of her butter yellow dress. "It's not something I like to remember. How did you find out?"

"The police told me."

She groaned. "I suppose it will all have to come out now."

"I'm afraid so," Kelly said quietly. "Do you want to talk about it?"

"There is not much to say, Mrs. Green. I loathed the man."

"Somebody told me that you were seen arguing with Dr. Barron the day he was murdered. Here in the hotel."

"After all these years." Mrs. McConaughey heaved herself up from her seat and began pacing. "You can imagine my surprise. Charles Barron showed up in the hotel. Asking for me. I barely recognized him at first. He had lost a lot of hair. And weight."

"What did he want?"

"He said he remembered that we, my husband Moe and I, owned a hotel in Myrtle Beach called the Golden Arms and wasn't it a funny coincidence that he should be staying at the hotel next door after all these years." She fluffed her hair. "I said it wasn't so funny and threw him out."

"That's all?"

Mildred McConaughey bored her beady eyes into Kelly's. "That's all, Mrs. Green. If you are thinking I murdered the man, while I might have taken great pleasure in throttling him…" She feigned a strangulation with her bare hands. "I did not. And I defy the police to prove otherwise."

She looked out the office window toward the Beach Lovers Inn. "How much longer are they all staying, may I ask?" She viciously pulled the curtains shut. "I'm sick of looking at them, even knowing they are all there is upsetting to me."

"You know all of them?"

"Each and every last one." She thumped back in her leather chair. "They were all in court at one time or another during the trial." Her lips curls into a sneer. "They all hated the Barrons as much as I do."

"Why?"

"Because he cheated them all, of course." When Kelly looked at her with confusion, she continued on. "He cheated them of money, of jobs, of their futures." She planted her elbows on the table and pushed her palms into her cheeks with a sob. "Cheated Moe of his life."

Kelly watched in silence as Mrs. McConaughey cried. She reached into a silver tissue box on the corner of the desk and handed her one.

Mrs. McConaughey blew her nose loudly. "Did you

know the Nelsons were staying here?"

"What do you mean?" The Nelsons were guests of the Beach Lovers Inn.

She held up her fingers. "For three nights before the murder."

"That's odd."

"I thought so too. I never spoke with them, although I recognized them right away. I did not know if they had recognized me or not. I'll tell you something else that I haven't told anyone."

Kelly leaned closer. "Yes?"

"The night Ruth got hurt?"

Kelly's heart froze in her chest and her mouth dried. "Yes?" she croaked.

"I saw Mrs. Nelson running up the dunes."

Kelly furrowed her brow. "What do you mean?"

"I heard a commotion. Yelling, sirens. I went out on my balcony. I looked down. There she was."

"Jean Nelson?"

Mildred McConaughey nodded solemnly. "She came running up over the dunes towards my hotel in a short white dress."

"Are you certain it was her?"

"She came right across the patio and pool deck. We keep the lights on late. It was her all right."

"Harry thinks somebody pushed Ruth down the steps. I think so too."

"Harry is a bright young man."

"But why would Jean Nelson want to hurt my aunt Ruth?"

"I have no idea." Mrs. McConaughey's phone rang but she chose to ignore it. And why had the Nelsons stayed at the Golden Arms Hotel prior to their checking in at the Beach Lovers Inn? "Do you think Jean Nelson and Charles Barron might have been lovers?"

"I wouldn't put anything past that bunch. I'll tell you something else but you have to promise it stays between us."

"Okay."

"At your place the night of Dr. Barron's death, when I was going into the bathroom, Jean Nelson was going out."

"You didn't tell the police this?"

"No. And you aren't going to either. You gave your word."

Kelly did some serious thinking. "Are you suggesting Jean Nelson might have murdered Charles Barron?"

"If she did," Mrs. McConaughey said, "and the police find out? I'm hoping they pin a medal on her, not a murder rap."

35

Harry was frustrated.

His day had been unproductive. His novel was stalled as was his investigation. Kiki had left two messages on his room phone inquiring of his progress. She was still holding space for him in the next edition of Myrtle Scene Magazine. Harry had called back promising to deliver.

How he would live up to that promise, he had no idea. He had tried interviewing a handful of other homeless persons around town. They had treated him with suspicion and disdain. None had been willing to share any information about Cowboy.

Harry had also checked out the restrooms at Captain Haddock's. Kelly had been right. Rather than narrowing the list of suspects, it only seemed to expand it.

The only thing good to come out of his day was that Vince at the restaurant had given him a free lunch in exchange for sharing what he knew about Cowboy's murder. Since Harry knew so little, he had gotten the best of that deal.

Returning to the inn after dark, he knocked on Kelly and Ben's door. Ben had answered and explained that Kelly was with Det. Burns once again. "Two nights in a row." Ben smirked. "How do you like that?"

Harry wasn't sure if he liked that at all. He kept his

opinion to himself. He went downstairs. The courtyard was occupied by a number of guests, including a couple of young families splashing around in the pool with a plastic baseball bat and a beach ball. Harry helped himself to tea and cookies in the alcove, which he intended to eat at his desk.

"Harry." Mary Barron waved from the far end of the courtyard. A tiki torch flickered behind her. "Join us."

Harry reluctantly joined the intimate group. They had gathered a number of chairs from the surrounding tables and formed a loose circle with the widow in the center.

After hellos were exchanged, Ted Nelson explained what they were up to. "We're planning a memorial for old Charlie."

"That's nice." Harry grabbed a chair and pushed it nearer their table.

"What's with the sunglasses, Harry?" asked Irwin Brunner loudly. He teetered as if he had been drinking heavily. "Afraid you will turn into a werewolf if you look directly into the moon?" He tilted his drink up at the half moon loitering overhead.

"Give the kid a break," Ted said.

"I hear he's been asking everybody questions about Charlie's murder. Although he hasn't gotten around to me yet." Harry squirmed as Jill Rochester poked fun at him as if he wasn't there.

"Maybe he's working undercover and the sunglasses are part of his disguise." Jill Rochester laughed wickedly. Only Irwin joined her.

Harry rose. "I should go."

"No, stay, Harry," said Mrs. Barron. "Please?"

"Yeah, come on. Harry knows I'm only teasing,"

Irwin rose and jostled Harry's shoulder. "We're friends. Right, Harry? No offense."

Harry slid back into his chair, smoldering.

"I'm composing the eulogy." Mary rolled a ballpoint pen over her tongue. "You are a writer, Harry. Maybe you can help." She thrust a yellow legal pad at him.

Harry scanned the words. It was the usual sentiment, doting husband, loving father. Harry hadn't even thought about whether the Barrons had children or not. "It's lovely," he said. "How many children do you have?" He handed her back the legal pad.

"Two. They are in Rhode Island."

"Are they coming down for the memorial?"

"No. We'll have a proper service back home once we can make arrangements." Mary jotted something further to her eulogy.

"This is just for us," explained Ted Nelson. "A reunion send off." He patted his wife's knee. She smiled wanly.

Harry stole a glance at the Dennises. Their faces unreadable masks. He was surprised they were participating.

Bonnie caught his look. "We're holding it at the beach at sunset. We all plan to say a few words." She was wringing her hands. "It's the least we can do."

"It's a shame a cloud of murder still hangs over," Ted mentioned.

"Yes, too bad." Irwin slumped in his chair, having gone from brash to morose.

Harry noticed Irwin had positioned himself close to his ex-wife, Vivian.

"Don't worry," Harry said brazenly. "Kelly Green says she knows who the killer is."

"What?" Several voices rose at once demanding an explanation.

"Who?" Jean Nelson was the first to ask.

"I can't say." Harry held up his hands. "She is waiting for one piece of crucial evidence. That will tie the whole thing up."

"What is it?" asked Mary.

"She wouldn't say. She's been working with that Detective Burns, you know."

"Yes," Jill Rochester had a drink in her hand. She appeared listless and her face sagged. "We all saw them leave together this evening. That detective of hers is quite handsome, wouldn't you agree, Viv?"

Vivian merely wet her lips and glanced quickly at her ex-husband.

"Kelly hinted that housekeeping may have stumbled on a clue in one of the guestrooms." There were hisses of amazement as Harry continued to lay it on thick, praying that poking a sharp stick into the hive would lead one of these killer bees to make a mistake.

Finally, he stood and fabricated a yawn. "Hopefully, we'll find out tomorrow for sure who killed your husband, Mrs. Barron. Good luck with your memorial."

Harry felt a dozen or more inquisitive eyes on his back as he retreated.

It was after midnight but Kelly was anxious to share what she had learned with Harry. Besides, the light was on in his room. If he kept regular hours, she had yet to figure out what those were.

Kelly and Nick Burns had gone to the movies but she had been too occupied with her own thoughts and concerns to pay very much attention to what was showing on the screen. She had hesitated to go out with him again so soon. She had no interest in a relationship with anyone. She didn't have the time or the energy. The Beach Lovers Inn was going to take every bit of energy she had—and that was without the addition of mayhem and murder.

Kelly had only agreed with the hope that he would share any updates in the investigation. Unfortunately, Dr. Barron's murder was still taking a backseat to more pressing crime.

As she climbed the steps, she heard a plaintive mewling. "Sharky?"

There was no sign of the cat down in the deserted courtyard below.

"Sharky?"

The mewling came louder and faster. A crack of light showed from beneath the laundry room door. "Oh, poor Sharky. Somebody accidently locked you in, didn't they? Don't worry, I'm coming."

The new padlock hung open on the hasp. Kelly wasn't too concerned. She knew it was going to take some time for everyone to get into the habit of securing the lock each night at the end of the day.

Kelly reached for her key and unlocked the laundry room door knob. The minute she did, Sharky flew out, tail raised and meowing angrily. "Well, you're welcome," she whispered as the cat bounded silently down the stairs.

A rumpled brown paper bag from the grocery store sat in the far corner of the laundry room. "What's that doing here?" It wasn't like housekeeping to leave trash lying around.

The door slammed behind her. She yelped and spun

around. "Hey!"

A loud explosion shattered her eardrums. She turned around. The grocery bag had exploded and was now a hot ball of shooting flames.

Kelly tried the door handle. The door wouldn't budge. She jiggled the handle and threw her shoulder against the door. It was no use. She was trapped inside.

"Help! Help! Fire!" she cried, coughing as the smoke rapidly filled the laundry room and seared her lungs.

Harry didn't know what had prompted him to look out the window. Looking back, he put it down to another of his premonitions. Like the one the other day when he had tried to warn Kelly that something bad was going to happen to Ruth Evans.

And it had.

But when he heard the broken glass and saw the flames shooting out the laundry room window, he raced from his room. Grabbing the fire extinguisher from the wall halfway along the corridor, he ran.

"Is somebody in there?" he hollered. By now, other guests were peeking worriedly out of their rooms.

"Harry?" coughed Kelly. "It's me!" She banged the door in frustration. There were security bars on the window. The door was her only hope.

"Hold on." He tugged at the padlock that had been secured to the hasp. "It's locked. Stand back." He slammed the butt of the fire extinguisher repeatedly against the door. After several strikes, the edge of the door nearest the lock splintered. Kelly came flying out, landing in his arms.

He turned the extinguisher on the flames. Ben appeared with a second extinguisher. Together, they fought the flames valiantly until the police and fire department arrived and put out the remaining fire.

Harry's face and clothes were black.

Kelly glanced at Harry. "What's wrong with your eye?"

His hand flew to his face. "I must have got some ash in it."

"But it looks swollen—"

"It's nothing. Here comes Det. Burns."

Harry and Kelly sat at one of the patio tables with Det. Burns grilling them. Ben Walsh was pacing, tapping his crutch on the courtyard deck, muttering to himself. Practically every room of the inn was lit with the curious watching from their windows.

"What happened up there?" Harry asked. "Was it an electrical fire?"

"No," Kelly said. "There was a bag. I saw it. There was an explosion."

"A bag?" Harry didn't understand.

Det. Burns explained. "It's early days but we think somebody set off a bag of fireworks in there."

"Why would they do that?" asked Harry.

"Fireworks?" Kelly said. "How could they? I was alone."

"The fire marshall says he found remnants of an electronically-triggered incendiary device."

"An incendiary device," repeated Harry. "That's pretty sophisticated." The work of Desmond Dennis perhaps?

"What exactly happened?" Det. Burns laid a hand over Kelly's.

"Sharky got locked in the laundry. I heard him meowing. I went to let him out and got locked in myself. The next thing I knew, kaboom!" She threw her hands in the air.

Det. Burns wrote furiously in his notebook. He was in his street clothes. "I'd say somebody locked the cat up on purpose, possibly to lure you there."

"Then they lock you in," said Harry, not wanting Det. Burns to get all the credit for brains, "and set off the explosion. I don't want to alarm you, Kelly, but I think they meant to kill you."

"Harry!" Kelly shrieked.

"I'm afraid Mr. Leland is right. Whoever planted that incendiary could have killed somebody."

The detective looked around the courtyard. "Heck, they could have burned this whole inn down."

"Oh, that's a pleasant thought," Kelly coughed and took a sip of water from the bottle one of the firefighters had brought her.

Det. Burns smiled. "Lucky thing Mr. Leland was around to save you."

Harry didn't like the tone of the detective's words. "What's that supposed to mean?"

The detective pocketed his notebook. "Nothing. Just lucky, wouldn't you both agree? You say you were in your room working when you heard the commotion, Mr. Leland?"

"That's right." Harry shifted uneasily in his seat.

"I see." Det. Burns turned and went back upstairs to confer with the fire marshall.

"I don't like that man," grumbled Harry.

"He's only doing his job." Kelly patted his arm. "Thanks for rescuing me, Harry." She planted her lips on his smudgy cheek. He tasted like soot but he deserved a kiss.

36

It was two in the morning. Because of the lateness of the hour, the police had decided to wait until the next day to interview her guests, for which Kelly was grateful. At the rate things were going wrong, there soon wouldn't be any guests.

"I've had enough excitement for one night," Ben said through a yawn. "I'm off to bed. Coming Kelly?"

The big fire hoses had been rolled up and the last of the fire trucks had rumbled off into the night. The guests had retreated to their respective rooms. Yellow warning tape crisscrossed the damp and blackened laundry room entrance.

"In a minute, Dad."

Harry turned to go.

Kelly put her hand on his arm. "I need to talk to you, Harry."

"Yes?"

"Not here." Standing there in the middle of the courtyard, Kelly suddenly felt like she was in the center of a fishbowl. Being watched. "Your room."

Harry led the way. Pushing open the door, he grabbed his sunglasses from the dresser and slid them up his nose before hitting the light switch.

Kelly turned on a second lamp. She helped herself to a glass of cold tap water. "Can you believe this?" She sank onto the edge of his unmade bed. She sniffed her shirt. She reeked of smoke. So did Harry. "I could have been killed."

"The laundry room was locked." Harry sat at his desk, facing his computer. "How did you get inside?"

Kelly explained how she had used her master key. "I left it in the keyhole."

"I didn't notice it when I arrived," Harry said.

"And you didn't see anybody?"

"Not a soul." Harry opened his notebook and doodled on the page, drawing shooting flames. "Whoever planted that bag knew that it would take somebody with a key to open that door."

"That makes sense." Kelly rose and refilled her glass. She had never felt so thirsty in her life. It was as if she was on fire herself and it was going to take all the water in the world to quench the flames inside.

"Being late at night, that leaves only you, Kelly. Everyone else with a key is gone for the day. Everybody knows you are the only one of the staff living on the property."

"Oh my gosh." Kelly's hand flew to her chest. "Somebody really wants me dead." She thought again how she would have been burnt alive if not for Harry. She came up behind him and swept her arms over his chest. "Thanks again, Harry."

Harry was torn. Should he mention that he had boasted to the reunion guests that Kelly knew who killed Charlie Barron? His words might have put her in danger. "You know, Kelly—"

"What's that sheet doing on the wall?" Kelly approached a bedsheet that had been taped to the wall on the far side of the bed. She had been so intent on her near-death experience that she hadn't noticed what Harry had done to the hotel room.

"And is that permanent marker?" Names, times, dates, and locations had been scribbled all over the sheet. Some had lines connecting two or more of them together.

Harry doodled a cat. He liked cats. "Don't be ridiculous. I used washable ink."

"It had better be," Kelly mumbled, her fists clenched. "What are you writing that is so important? And all that on the wall?"

"I think better when I can visualize things concretely."

"Why didn't you simply type it on your computer screen?"

"I wanted to see the big picture."

Kelly gaped. Was he joking? No, knowing Harry, probably not. "Would you turn around, please?"

Harry complied, turning around quickly then back to his doodle just as quickly.

"Can't you please look at me when I'm talking to you?" Kelly stomped over, jerked his chair around and yanked off his sunglasses.

She gasped. Harry was nursing a black eye.

"That's not from the fire. What happened to you?"

Harry snatched the sunglasses from her hand and put them on. "One of your guests took offense to my talking to his wife." He suddenly didn't feel like confessing to Kelly that the black eye had initially been the work of a woman. She seemed to think little enough of him as it was.

"Which guest?"

"Desmond Dennis."

"What did you say?"

"To his wife? I merely asked her a few questions."

"Like?"

"Like where was she when Charlie Barron was murdered. And was she having an affair with him."

"Harry!"

"What?" He looked hurt. "I took a shot."

Kelly folded her arms over her chest. "Yes, and you almost got yourself shot in the process. You cannot go around asking people, especially my guests, such offensive questions." She huffed. "I'm surprised somebody tried to kill me rather than you."

Harry decided this was definitely not a good time to mention that he might have put her in danger himself.

"Maybe Nick is right. Maybe we should leave this to the police."

"Det. Burns told you himself that the killer might never get caught. Everybody is leaving in a couple of days. They told me they are planning a sunset memorial for Charlie Barron," Harry said. "After that, they will all be departing. What are the odds of finding out the truth then?"

Kelly looked at the writing on the wall—literal writing on the wall. Harry Leland was nuts. "And I must be nuts too," she said aloud. "I'm beginning to wonder what the odds are of getting through the week alive."

"I understand how you feel." Harry sympathized. "But even if you no longer care to find out who murdered Dr. Barron and Cowboy, you do want to know who tried to kill your aunt Ruth, don't you?" And he wasn't going to have a publishable story if that story had no ending. That ending was going to require a solution to the crime.

"Darn you, Harry." Kelly flopped back down on the bare mattress, hard. "Of course, I do." She pounded the pillow with her fist. "In fact, I've been thinking."

"I'm listening." Harry lowered the lid of his laptop and turned his chair around to face her.

"It's the fireworks." Drew's recent comment about fireworks had been niggling inside her brain. She finally knew what it was. The question that remained un-answered.

"The ones somebody planted in the laundry room?"

"All of them. Those plus the fireworks the night of Dr. Barron's murder."

"What about them?"

"Think about it. The murder might not have hap-pened if it hadn't been for that fireworks display."

"You can't blame yourself for that. You didn't know that ordering a fireworks show was going to result in a man's murder."

"What are you talking about, Harry?" Kelly pulled at her ruined shirt. A washing wasn't going to save the shirt or the skirt. Both were destined for the trash heap. "I didn't order any fireworks."

"You didn't?"

"No. Why would I?"

"I don't know. I assumed you had ordered the display for your party."

"I didn't."

"So who did?" asked Harry. "I was thinking of having a talk with the person who put on the show. I wanted to find out if they might have noticed something."

"I don't know but it wasn't me. I don't have money to spend on frills like that."

"You know, none of this could have happened either

if Charles Barron hadn't fallen in the pool."

"Or been pushed," noted Harry.

Thinking back to the night of Ruth's spill down the inn's steps, Kelly thought that with the way Harry's mind worked somebody was always pushing somebody else. But this time he could be right. Kelly's head throbbed. She squeezed her eyes for a moment, reaching back in time. "I remember Ruth was going to tell me something the night of her accident."

"What?"

"I'm not sure. We were in the kitchen." Kelly pressed her fists against her temples. "She saw somebody."

"Who? Cowboy? The killer?"

"I don't know," she said in frustration. "I just don't know."

"We need to ask Ruth."

"I don't think that's a good idea. I don't want to upset her further, Harry. Not now, she needs her strength."

"If you don't ask her, a killer might go free," said Harry. "Or worse."

Kelly frowned. "What could be worse?"

"They could kill again."

Kelly lurched to her feet. It had been a seriously long day with an almost seriously dead ending. "I'm going to bed. Correction." She raised her finger. "First," she said with a tug at her shirt, "I am taking a shower, a long hot shower. Then I am going to bed."

She looked pointedly at Harry. "I suggest you do the same, stinky."

"Good idea. What about the murder?"

Kelly opened his door. Sharky went puttering down the corridor. "Maybe we can find out who set off those fireworks on the beach."

"I have an idea about who might be responsible for tonight at least."

"Yes?"

"Desmond Dennis."

"Why him? He seems harmless." She grinned. "Except for punching you in the eye. You sure you don't need some ice on that?"

"I'll be fine," Harry insisted. "Mr. Dennis has advanced degrees in electrical engineering and computers."

"Interesting. I'll mention that to Nick." Kelly yawned loudly. "There's lots more to talk about but it's going to have to wait until tomorrow. Thanks again for coming to my rescue."

"Forget it," Harry said. And he really wished she would. "It was no big deal."

37

"Can you believe he said that, Dad? No big deal. The guy single-handedly saves my life—" She waved a crisp triangle of toast at her father. They sat across from one another at the small kitchen table.

"Hey, I helped," Ben said.

"Okay, practically single-handed." She chomped down and chewed. "Then he says forget it like it was nothing."

"He's a good kid. I've been telling you." Dark bags hung from his eyes. Like Kelly, he'd had little sleep and plenty to worry about. He had dressed expecting to get dirty in a pair of old denim shorts and a Daytona Beach Bike Week tee shirt. If he wasn't roped into cleaning up the wrecked laundry room, he planned to work on his wreck of a motorcycle.

Kelly refilled their coffee mugs at the counter then returned to her seat. "Yeah, Harry's not so bad, I guess."

"Have you checked out the laundry room yet?" asked her father.

"Not yet." Kelly frowned, remembering how she'd almost been burnt to a crisp. "I can only imagine."

"Me and George took a look before you got up."

"And?"

"There's no other way to say this."

Her dad dumped way too much sugar in his cup.

303

Mom would have screamed at him, thought Kelly.

"Total disaster."

Kelly groaned. "I'll have to call the insurance company right away. But what are we going to do in the meantime? The inn can't run without clean laundry."

Ben tilted back in his chair, pushing against the floor with his crutch. "You could always ask Mildred if you could use the Golden Arms facilities."

"Ask Mrs. McConaughey? Are you crazy? That woman hates me." She had told her father all about her latest conversation with Mrs. McConaughey and how she had learned about the lawsuit she had filed against Dr. Barron and company.

If Mrs. McConaughey hadn't hated her before, she surely must now. She certainly had not been doing anything to endear her to the woman.

"Suit yourself." Ben carried his cup to the sink. "It would only be temporary. It's either that or somebody is going to be running back and forth all day long to the laundromat."

Kelly tilted her head and flashed a grin. "You busy today, Dad?"

"Oh, no." Ben turned on the faucet and rinsed margarine from his fingers. "I am not going to sit in a laundromat with a bunch of women, watching wet laundry tumble round and round all day. I'd rather do anything than that."

"Actually, I'm glad you said that, Dad." Kelly rose and gently bumped her father aside with her hip to rinse her own dishes at the sink. "I was thinking you could step next door and ask Mildred for that favor."

Ben groaned and wrapped his fist around his crutch. "Can I change my answer?"

As much as she was dreading it, Kelly went to take a look at the laundry room after dressing. Like her father had said, the room was a burned up wreck. The linens were soggy and black. The shelves were melted and the washer and dryer were large black lumps of steel. A smoky stench filled the air.

Guests would be rising and starting their days. Those guests would expect clean sheets and fresh towels.

She prayed that her father worked his magic with Mrs. McConaughey. It would be far more practical and cheaper to use the Golden Arms laundry facilities rather than have to haul loads of dirty laundry out to a laundromat.

Not to mention, her housekeepers would need fresh linen pronto. Would Mrs. McConaughey loan them some? She texted the question to her dad so he could broach the subject with her.

Lee Hollister and Rick Ramus sat side by side at the small seating area in the lobby's street-side bay window.

Rick leapt to his feet, throwing his arms around Kelly. "Oh my dear, are you all right?" He stepped back as he looked her up and down.

"We heard about last night's fire." Lee stood now too. "Are you okay?"

"I'm fine." Kelly straightened her blouse.

"Heard about it?" exclaimed Rick. "We saw it."

"You saw it?" Kelly asked.

"We saw the damage this morning when I got in. Didn't we, Lee?"

Lee nodded. "What are you going to do?"

"Call the insurance company first. Please tell me

we're covered."

"Absolutely, Kelly," promised Rick. "Ruth was strict about making sure we had full coverage. Don't you worry about a thing."

"Tell that to Drew, Rick." Lee retreated behind the front desk. "She is going to have a heart attack when she sees the laundry room." The head of housekeeping was due in soon. "She's going to wonder what housekeeping is supposed to do."

Drew liked everything neat, tidy and orderly. All good qualities in a housekeeper.

"No problem," Kelly replied as she made her way to the office behind Rick. "My dad is working out a deal with the Golden Arms." Fingers crossed.

Lee's brow went up in surprise.

"The insurance papers are in this cabinet here." Rick moved to a long, low cabinet behind the desk and rolled it open. "I'm sure glad you're okay, boss."

"Me, too." Kelly sat on the edge of the desk while Rick riffled through the file folders.

Rick ran his fingers across the dome of his head. "I mean, when Harry told all those people that you knew who the killer was...I mean, anything could have happened."

Rick scratched himself behind the ear. "I thought it was in here. It must be the next one." He slapped the cabinet closed with his knee and yanked open the one below it. "Watch your foot," he cautioned.

"Exactly," Kelly said, imagining all the things that might have happened if the fire had spread. She dutifully moved her feet to one side.

"Ah." Rick raised a thick green folder. "Here it is." He slid the folder on the desk. "So who is it?"

"Who's who?" Kelly flipped open the folder and began reading.

"The killer, silly." Rick pressed his butt against the filing cabinet. His mouth hung open.

"Wait? What killer?" The file folder fell from Kelly's hand to the floor.

Rick bent to retrieve it. "Are you okay, Kelly?"

Kelly accepted the folder from her assistant. Rick's previous words finally struck home as if they had arrived from far away. "Did you say that Harry told everybody that *I* knew who killed Dr. Barron?"

"That's right."

"When?" The file folder bent in her hands.

"Yesterday night."

Kelly twisted the file folder.

"Careful there," cautioned Rick, reaching for the file. "We need those records."

"Was this before the fire?" Before someone had tried to burn her to a crisp? And maybe the Beach Lovers Inn?

Rick prised the file folder from her stiff fingers and pressed it flat on the desk. "I suppose. Why?"

"Why?" she growled. "Because I'm going to murder him. That's why."

Rick wanted to ask who his boss wanted to murder and exactly why but she was gone before his lips could form the question.

Harry drove to the Myrtle Scene Magazine offices where he found Kiki working at her desk. Chad was huddled over her. Both sets of eyes were on her computer screen.

"Good morning, Harry." Kiki flashed him a smile. "Got something for me?"

"Yeah, what's the word, Bones?" Chad folded his hands under his armpits and smirked. He was wearing a short-sleeved plaid shirt and gray trousers.

"I read in the newspaper this morning about that fire last night at the inn you're staying at. You know anything about that?" Chad had moved within arm's reach of Harry.

"The police think it was arson."

Kiki fielded a phone call then joined them as Harry explained to Chad what Det. Burns had told them about the incendiary device. "That's interesting. Did the paper mention that, babe?"

"There was a quote from the fire chief suggesting arson."

"Do you think the fire and the murder of Charles Barron are related, Harry?" asked Kiki. She handed him a cup of hot tea without his asking. She placed the steaming cup in front of him at the counter.

"I think they could be." Harry did not want to commit one way or the other. Nor did he want to mention that his words might have led to the perilous event.

"Was anybody hurt?"

"No. Fortunately, not."

"What's with the shades, Bones?" Chad reached for Harry's sunglasses.

"My eyes are sensitive. That's all." Harry fought off Chad's groping fingers. "From the smoke."

Kiki's pupils dilated. "You witnessed the fire?"

"Actually, I helped put it out." Harry stuck his chin forward.

Chad whistled. "Good for you, Bones. You're a real hero. Hey, maybe we ought to take your picture and put it in the mag. What do you think, Kiki?"

Kiki placed a hand each under Harry and Chad's arms. "I think you two should stop posturing and do your jobs. We have a news magazine to get out, remember?"

The editor released them. "What brings you here, Harry?"

Harry sipped his tea before answering. "I was hoping to use your computer."

"What happened to that antique laptop of yours?" Chad couldn't resist saying.

"Nothing. You have access to databases I don't. I was hoping to do a little research." Harry knew that they subscribed to several fee-based news sources. He explained about Mildred McConaughey and her lawsuit with Dr. Barron.

"Wow." Chad slapped Harry on the back a little harder than necessary. "Good job, Bones. You got some real dirt there."

"Help yourself, Harry," Kiki answered. "Susan's away from her desk this morning. You can use her PC."

"You let me know if you need any help," Chad said before returning to his own desk. He picked up his backpack, planted a kiss goodbye on Kiki's forehead then departed.

Harry dug around on the internet, aware of Kiki's eyes on the back of his head now and again.

None of the others who knew Charles Barron had police records. In fact, all had led fairly mundane lives. Only the Nelsons seemed to have thrived after the breakup of Attleboro Heart Associates though. Ted Nelson had a thriving practice and a million dollar home, according to the tax records. He even looked into George and Mildred's backgrounds but found nothing helpful.

Finally, Harry gave up. He stood and stretched his arms overhead.

"Anything?" Kiki smiled at him from her chair.

"No. There is going to be a sunset memorial for Dr. Barron at the beach tonight."

"You should cover it. In fact," the editor followed him to the front door, "I was thinking you might want to do another story."

"Another story?" Harry was intrigued. Another story would be another potential paycheck. "What sort of story?"

"A story on this hotel owner. What did you say her name was?"

"Mildred McConaughey?"

"Yes, that's the one. Maybe there's a story there. Medical malpractice, big money."

"Maybe. That was a long time ago." Besides, Harry wasn't sure he liked the idea. Mrs. McC had always been nice to him.

Kiki said, "Did I mention you should get pictures?"

"Pictures?" Two house sparrows pecked eagerly at the bread crumbs surrounding an overspilling sidewalk trashcan outside the bagel shop next door. Harry stepped aside as a delivery man in khakis shot past him carrying a load of parcels inside.

"Of the memorial. The other members of this reunion group. Mrs. Barron, if she doesn't object. We can't run any photos without permission. Hey, how about a picture of the room where the murder was committed? Do you think the innkeeper would mind?"

"I'll see." Harry didn't think Kelly Green would go along with it.

Noting Harry's contorted face, Kiki asked, "Is there a

problem?"

"I don't have a very good camera." Kelly's comment about his camera had stung. "Will a Polaroid do?"

"A Polaroid? You mean like one of those old instant cameras?"

Harry felt the blood climb his neck.

"Wait right there." She returned a minute later with a sleek digital camera dangling from a black nylon strap. "Here you go. We've got several."

Harry turned the shiny camera over in his hands. He didn't recognize any of the buttons. He didn't even see a view finder, just a dark screen on the back of the smooth flat rectangle.

"Do you need me to show you how to use it?"

"No." Harry tucked the camera into his pocket. "I used to have one exactly like this."

Rather than confess his ignorance, he decided to look up the model on the internet and read the user's manual before the time came to use it.

38

"What the heck is wrong with you, Harry?"

"Huh?"

Harry took a step backward. Kelly managed to poke her finger into his chest nonetheless. "Are you trying to get me killed?"

"No. Of course not." He took a second step back, bumping into the wall, leaving him nowhere to go. Kelly had trapped him in the courtyard of the inn near the lobby on his return from town.

"Is it true? Did you tell everybody that I knew who killed Dr. Barron?"

"Well." Harry swallowed hard. "I didn't tell everybody exactly." He was well aware that wasn't what she meant but he was trying to buy himself some time. Kelly was mad, really mad.

"You told all his friends."

"I was hoping to lure out the real killer." He slid sideways, moving towards open space. "I was trying to help."

"You almost got me killed, Harry." Kelly matched him step for step.

Harry teetered at the edge of the pool, one foot on the patio, the other dangling precipitously over deep water. He caught himself in the nick of time. If he had fallen in, not only would he have gotten a soaking, the fancy camera in his pocket might have been ruined. Kiki would not be happy about that.

"What are you talking about," he managed to say once he'd righted himself. "You are the one running around like a young Jessica Fletcher."

"Jessica who?" Kelly asked. "Is that the sexy, curvaceous bombshell in that old Roger Rabbit movie?" Not bad. She'd been called worse. Much worse.

"No. No." Harry shook his head. "That's Jessica Rabbit. You're thinking of *Who Framed Roger Rabbit?* I'm talking about Jessica Fletcher, the old lady who solved murders on TV. *Murder She Wrote.*"

Kelly narrowed her eyes. "Are you calling me an old lady?" Murder was exactly what she was about to commit. "I am not old." Well, she wasn't that old. No more than a few years older than him anyway.

"And you know what?" She suddenly realized who Harry looked like. The black and white image of an odd man in a dark suit sprang to mind from the back of an old omnibus edition of the author's work. "You remind me of a young Edgar Allan Poe."

"I'll take that as a compliment." Harry pulled himself straighter. "Besides, there was no *old* Edgar Allan Poe."

"Excuse me?"

"Poe died of consumption or some other ailment—some say murder—when he was forty, I believe." Harry looked at her smugly.

Kelly paused and caught her breath as a guest passed swinging a cooler which he proceeded to fill at the ice machine. "How old are you, Harry?"

"Thirty-six. Why? How old are you?"

"That's not important," Kelly snapped. "The point is that I would like to live to a ripe old age."

"I can understand that." Harry wiped his smudged sunglasses on his shirttail then placed them back on his nose.

"Good. So I am asking you please to stop doing and saying things that might jeopardize that goal."

"I know. I am sorry." Harry looked up at the blackened laundry room. "I'll pay for the damages..."

Kelly threw her hands in the air. "Pay? With what? Do you have any money? You don't even pay for your room."

Harry turned bright red. "You-you know about that?"

"Yes, Harry. I know about that. I don't know how you conned Aunt Ruth into it but, yes, I know all about it."

She clutched his wrist in her vise-like fingers. "As a matter of fact, I had been thinking that you and I were going to need to have a long talk about that. And now is as good a time as any."

"Is there a problem?" a deep, stern voice demanded.

Harry and Kelly turned. It was Det. Burns.

"Hello, detective," mumbled Harry.

Det. Burns ignored his greeting. "Is Mr. Leland disturbing you, Mrs. Green?"

"What?" Kelly looked at Harry. "No. We were just talking."

The detective nodded. "Mr. Dennis called in a complaint about you, Mr. Leland."

"What?"

"He said you were harassing him and his wife. And impersonating a police officer."

"That's ridiculous!"

"Harry would never do that. Besides, it was Mr. Dennis who hit him. Harry's the one who ought to be issuing a complaint." She turned to Harry. "You should file assault charges, Harry."

"Mr. Dennis struck you?"

"It was nothing," muttered Harry. "I'd rather forget the whole thing."

Det. Burns shrugged. Sweating profusely, he pulled off his suit jacket and flung it over his shoulder. "Fine by me. Saves me some paperwork. But take it as a sign that you should keep your nose out of police business, Mr. Leland. Both of you should."

Harry turned and walked off.

"Did you have to be so rude to him?" Kelly felt a pang of...something...for Harry as he slouched off. "He did save my life." Even if he had been the one to put her in danger in the first place.

"There is something odd about Harry Leland." The detective eyed Harry's departure. "I'm not convinced he is as innocent or clueless as he appears."

"Is there any news on the fire?"

"Nothing concrete. Definitely arson. Not a clue as to the perp. It is being looked into. Maybe Mr. Leland?"

"No," gushed Kelly. "He would never. He's the one who came running to extinguish the fire."

"It wouldn't be the first time that some nut case didn't start a fire just so they could turn around and play hero putting it out afterward."

"Not Harry," Kelly insisted.

"Speaking of fire, I really came by to ask why you didn't tell me about the fireworks."

"What do you mean? I told you, I saw a bag in the laundry room and—"

Det. Burns interrupted. "Not those. The fireworks display the night of Charles Barron's murder."

"I am sure I did, detective," Kelly replied. He was really getting under her skin. She hadn't liked the way he had spoken to Harry, nor his belligerent attitude towards her now.

"Okay," allowed Det. Burns, slipping off his dark sunglasses and sliding them into the pocket of his coat. "But I had a long chat with Mr. Ramus. In the course of our conversation, he told me that there is no record of the inn ordering any fireworks show the night of Dr. Barron's death."

"That's right."

"You didn't tell me that it wasn't you who ordered the fireworks display."

"No. I guess I didn't. Do you think it is that important?"

"It could be," was his cagey response.

Kelly glanced at the sleek towering rectangle next door. "Maybe it was Mrs. McConaughey at the Golden Arms who ordered the show."

"No. I interviewed her myself. She would have mentioned it if she had."

Unless she was behind the murder, thought Kelly.

"Besides," the detective added impishly, "she seemed rather put out about the fireworks display, if I am remembering correctly."

He was and Kelly said so. "If she didn't order them and I sure didn't order them, who did?"

"That's what we are trying to find out. You have no idea?"

Kelly shook her head in the negative.

"One of your guests maybe?"

"Maybe." It was certainly a possibility, although no one had mentioned it that night. "I could ask them if you like."

He held up his palm. "Leave it to me. I'll give you the same advice I gave Leland, stick to running the inn and leave the investigating to the professionals."

"All right," she said stiffly. Once again, Kelly felt chastened by this detective.

"Dinner tomorrow night?"

"Sorry," Kelly said sharply. "I have plans."

She left Nick Burns standing there drowning in his own perspiration and smug sense of superiority.

Kelly hadn't had plans earlier but she most definitely did now. She was going to find Harry and together they would find out who ordered the fireworks and why.

If it led to a dead end, so be it. If it led to discovering who killed Charles Barron before that condescending, irritating detective did, so much the better.

She marched up the stairs and banged on Harry's door. No answer. She fumbled with her master key and went inside, praying not to see him stepping naked from the shower or lying dead in a pool of blood—the killer's next victim.

She threw open the door and peeked. There was no sign of him. The bathroom door was ajar and not a peep came from that direction.

No evidence of violence although she still felt like strangling him for writing all over the bedsheets.

Still fuming from Det. Burns' words and manner and too restless to focus on the inn, she decided to go for a drive and see if she could find the fireworks store herself. She needed her purse and keys.

"Harry!" Kelly exclaimed, entering her apartment. Harry and her dad were sitting at the kitchen table.

Her laptop sat between them along with two open bottles of beer and a bag of pretzels that looked like it had been disemboweled. How many times had she asked her father to open bags carefully along the top like they were meant to be?

Harry flinched, spilling beer down his shirt.

Ben had seen and heard Kelly scolding Harry and invited him up for a beer. He grabbed the dish towel and tossed it to Harry. Harry dabbed at his light blue shirt.

"Pretzel?" Ben lifted the bag, pretzels tumbled from the gash in the bag to the table.

"How many times, Dad? How many times?"

Ben winked at Harry. "Looks like you aren't the only one in trouble, son."

Harry struggled to his feet. "I'd better go."

"Yes." Kelly snatched her purse from the hook by the front door. "You are coming with me."

"Huh?" Harry hovered by the open door. "Where are we going?"

Kelly ignored him and his question. "And you," she told her father, "are going to clean up this mess."

"Yes, dear." Ben began scooping up pretzels from the table and tossing them back in the torn bag. "Don't worry about a thing. Everything here is under control."

Sadly, Kelly knew that wasn't true. Absolutely nothing was under control in her life or at the inn.

39

"Where are we going?" Harry repeated as they reached the parking lot.

"Climb in." Kelly unlocked the Audi and jumped behind the wheel. The black leather was red hot. The interior of the car felt like it was a million degrees. She cranked the AC down as low as it would go.

Harry shivered and turned the vent as far from himself as possible. "Do you mind telling me what we are doing?"

"Looking for a store that sells fireworks." Kelly gunned the gas pedal impatiently waiting for a red light to turn green.

"Your dad and I were looking online. There are only three stores in the area selling fireworks. Two are a bit distant, one further north, the other farther south."

"Where's the closest one?"

"Fireworks Warehouse. It's out near the interstate."

Following Harry's directions, Kelly drove west over the Intracoastal Waterway.

"You know, Irwin Brunner told me something interesting the other morning" Harry tried not to let Kelly's erratic driving rattle him.

"What's that?"

"He pointed out that Mary Barron was not at Captain Haddock's with the others the night Cowboy was murdered."

"So? Neither was he, right? Besides, she was probably mourning up in her room."

But Harry was shaking his head no. "Mr. Brunner said he knocked on her door. He received no answer. He looked for her rental car in the parking lot. It was gone."

"Meaning she went somewhere and could have murdered Cowboy."

"Or he could have been lying to me."

"Why would he do that?"

"Because he's the killer and wants to shift suspicion to Mrs. Barron." Harry checked to make sure his seatbelt was properly fastened. "Everybody knows the spouse is always the most likely suspect."

"Except in this case that spouse was standing elbow to elbow with me."

"Are you sure?"

"I remember distinctly. She was squealing with delight watching the fireworks show. She couldn't have been more than a couple of feet away." Kelly squeezed her eyes shut. "And Dr. Nelson was right here." She pointed to her left.

"Then Brunner reversed course. He came to my room after you spoke with Mary Barron."

"What did he want?"

"Basically, he wanted us to leave the widow alone. He assured me she was innocent."

"Strange."

"He said that Mary and Vivian were old friends. She offered to help him win her back."

"Maybe that was why I saw Jill crying the other night. Maybe Vivian said she wanted to break it off."

Kelly had already shared with Harry how the Nelsons had been staying at the Golden Arms prior to checking in at the Beach Lovers Inn. She had also told him that Mrs. McConaughey had claimed to have seen Jean Nelson running back to the hotel around the time of the attack on her aunt Ruth.

"I don't see how that could have anything to do with Dr. Barron's murder."

Kelly didn't either. "Maybe Jean Nelson was having an affair with Dr. Barron and he decided to break it off."

"So she killed him?"

"If she couldn't have him, nobody could."

"Sounds extreme." Harry dug his fingernails into the dashboard as Kelly careened around a corner and landed in the gravel parking lot of Fireworks Warehouse.

Harry breathed a sigh of relief as she killed the motor.

"Do you have a better idea?"

"We still don't know much about George. I'd still like to know how he can afford a beach house. And he did ask your aunt for more money." Harry tumbled to the ground. "Plus, he says he was having a smoke in the parking lot at the time of the first murder. There are no witnesses. He could easily have killed Charlie Barron."

"And he has a master key." Kelly hitched her purse over her shoulder. She had to admit, her handyman was beginning to look rather suspicious.

The fireworks store was a dead end.

The clerk claimed he knew nothing and further stated that he had told the police the exact same thing.

Back in the car, Kelly cursed and banged the steering wheel with her fist. "That was a complete bust."

"Maybe not," Harry said. "You know that guy that

runs the beach concession across from the inn?"

"What about him?"

"I noticed his bicycle the other day. I think it matches the one you described as being the one used by the person who set off the fireworks."

"Are you sure?"

"No but it has a basket on the back, like the bike you described. And he does run the rental concession right there in front of the inn. It stands to reason that—"

The rest of Harry's words were swallowed as the car lunged forward once again.

Ben Walsh waved his cap at Kelly and Harry as they pulled into the lot at the Beach Lovers Inn. He was sitting on a short-legged swivel stool next to his motorcycle, wrench in hand. "Good news, Kelly. Mildred has agreed to let you use her laundry room and linen until you can make other arrangements."

The front of his tee shirt was soaked in perspiration. By the looks of things, he had made little progress putting his bike back together—if that could even be done.

Big if.

Kelly kissed her father on the cheek. "Thanks, Dad."

"She's really not bad once you get to know her. Mildred is one of those people who keep their defenses up." He placed his wrench on the stool. "I don't think she murdered Dr. Barron."

"Neither do I," Harry said.

"I'm not convinced yet," Kelly replied. "She had plenty of reason to want him dead."

Ben eyed Harry and Kelly with curiosity. "What are you two up to?" The pair had been at each the other's throat only a short time ago.

"We are trying to figure out who ordered the fireworks display the night of Charlie Barron's murder," Kelly said.

"You think that has something to do with things?"

"We aren't sure," Harry put in. "But we won't know until we figure out who ordered them and why."

Ben wished them luck as they scurried off. "Hey, Kelly," he called after his daughter. "The insurance man is due at four today to inspect the laundry room damages."

Kelly promised to be there.

They trudged up and over the dunes into a sea of sun and beach worshippers smothered in tanning oil or sunblock as per their personal taste.

"That's him over there." Harry was already perspiring heavily. Sweat dripped from his forehead, stinging his eyes.

A lean shirtless man in red swim trunks with a golden tan and chiseled abs was seated in a low beach chair. Ear buds were planted in his ears. A pair of mirrored sunglasses hid his eyes.

"Excuse me." Kelly nudged the edge of his chair with her toe and he perked up.

"Yeah?" He lifted the corner of his sunglasses and gave her the once over. His eyes were as blue as the ocean.

"Are you the guy that set off those fireworks here on the beach the other night?" While it had been night time at the time of the fireworks display, the silhouette of the bicycle matched that etched in Kelly's memory.

A half-frown formed on his thin lips as he extracted the black ear buds and let the cord dangle over his glistening, hairless chest. "What if I am?"

Kelly rolled her eyes. "Are you?"

Harry stepped forward. "Who paid you?"

The attendant climbed to his feet. "What's it to you? You the police or something?" His jaw moved quickly as he chewed on a piece of peppermint-scented gum.

"Look," said Kelly, realizing that belligerence was going to get them nowhere, "I'm Kelly Green. I own the Beach Lovers Inn." She pointed at the blue roof just visible over the dune.

"What happened to the old lady that owns the joint?"

"You must mean my aunt, Ruth Evans. She is retiring."

"Gotcha." He punctuated his remark with a snap of his gum.

"A man was murdered at the inn the night of the fireworks display."

He scratched his head. "Yeah, I heard about that. Wild." Suddenly, he grinned. "Hey." He pointed at Harry. "And you're the one that got punched by that—"

"We simply want to know who hired you," interrupted Harry.

"Yes. Please."

The attendant let out a long-suffering sigh. "Listen. I got the fireworks from a store."

"Fireworks Warehouse?" Kelly asked.

"Yeah. I got a call from a pal of mine who works there. He said somebody came in, plunked down some cash for a load of fireworks."

Kelly and Harry looked at one another. "He lied to us," Harry said to Kelly.

"Was it a man or a woman?" asked Kelly. "Do you know?"

The attendant rolled his neck. "I think he said it was

a couple. You know, a man and woman."

"That lets out Jill and Vivian," noted Harry.

"Yeah, but it lets in a load of others," replied Kelly. "How did you get involved?"

"They asked him to find somebody to do the actual show. He called me and, boom, the deed was done."

"What exactly was the deed?" Harry pressed.

"To set off a bunch of fireworks here."

"By here you mean across from the Beach Lovers Inn?"

"That's right."

"Not the Golden Arms or Sun Towers." Sun Towers was a row of three tall condo buildings south of the inn.

"Look, I was paid to put on a show. He told me where and he told me when. So I put on a little fireworks show at the beach?" his voice rose. "What's the problem, anyway? It's fireworks, not freaking nukes."

"Somebody got killed," Kelly pointed out again.

"Didn't get killed by fireworks, did he?" The attendant released a string of expletives.

"No," Kelly was forced to admit.

"Then what's the big deal?" He stepped away and dealt with a new customer for a moment, then flopped back down in his chair. "You still here?" He stuffed his buds in his ears.

"What about the mysterious bag of fireworks in the laundry room?" Kelly demanded.

"What about the tooth fairy?" He popped the lid on a plastic cooler and extracted a dripping bottle of iced tea. "What are you talking about, lady?"

"Somebody planted a bag of fireworks in the laundry room of the inn. I was lured there and then the bag exploded. I could have been killed."

"You accusing me?"

"Maybe. Where were you?"

"What time?"

"After midnight."

"Then it couldn't have been me."

"Can you prove that?"

"Me and my band were playing from nine o'clock on in front of a hundred people. I didn't get home till three in the morning." He spat out the name of a local beach bar. "Check it out."

"We'll do that," promised Kelly.

"Did you know a homeless man known as Cowboy?" Harry asked.

"I saw him around. Heard he's no longer with us. Good riddance. I caught the bum huddled up in our umbrellas and chairs on more than one occasion. Had to kick him out. I warned him he was going to get himself in trouble one day."

"You're a real humanitarian, aren't you?" Kelly found the attendant distasteful. "What happened? Did you catch him and decide to see that he never did it again?"

The attendant leapt to his feet, his hands tight fists. The cords on his neck bulged. "Are you accusing me of murdering the bum?"

Harry stepped between them. "So you never saw who ordered the fireworks?"

The attendant glared. His hands remained clenched. "Like I said, my buddy called me. I picked up the fireworks with the instructions on where and when. That's it." He sliced his hands through the air. "Over and out. Sayonara." He dropped back into his chair.

"The police will want to talk to you," warned Harry.

"I can't hear you," answered the attendant, cranking

the volume on his earphones. "Rent an umbrella or take a hike."

"Come on, Harry." Kelly pulled Harry by the arm.

"I don't think there's anything left to learn here."

"Even if he was on stage last night, he could still be responsible for blowing up the laundry room," Harry said as they walked.

"How?"

"Det. Burns said an electronic device of some sort was used to trigger the explosion, remember?"

"Meaning it isn't impossible that our friend set it off remotely." She vowed to keep an eye on the disagreeable attendant.

"And he's admitted to having fireworks."

Desmond Dennis stood planted in the sand at the edge of the courtyard as they plunged back towards the inn.

"You two still playing detective?" snorted Desmond Dennis. He clutched a beer can in his hand and teetered. His wife was staring from behind one curtain of their room.

"Harry boasted how you were going to solve Charlie's murder, Mrs. Green." Desmond Dennis spat between their feet. "You haven't got a chance in hell."

"Is that what you think?" Kelly was disturbed that she was losing her cool with a customer but could not seem to stop herself. "Let me tell you, Mr. Dennis, not only do I know who the murderer is, soon the world will know."

"You're bluffing." Desmond tipped his beer can to his lips and drank. "If the police can't figure it out, neither can you."

"Speaking of police," interjected Harry. "You've got a

lot of nerve calling the police and complaining about me." Harry shook his fist.

Kelly had never seen Harry so worked up. Tensions were rising dangerously. The last thing the inn needed was another ugly incident. "Okay, Harry. Maybe we should all take a collective breath." Guests were staring, transfixed.

Harry ignored her. "You and your wife both punched me in the eye and you didn't see me report you."

Kelly's mouth fell open. "His wife hit you?"

Harry ignored her.

"You're nuts." Dennis belched. The smell of sour beer filled the air. Kelly waved her hand in front of her nose. "You both are. And this inn stinks and it ain't just the smoke from the fire."

"Did you start the fire?" accused Kelly. "Were you trying to burn the inn and me to ashes?"

"I can't wait till we can get out of this place and go home." Dennis stormed off.

The curtains of his room fluttered shut.

"What's this about Mrs. Dennis punching you in the eye?" Kelly asked.

Harry pressed his sunglasses to his face. "I'd rather not talk about it."

Kelly giggled.

"Hey!"

"Sorry." She suppressed a second giggle. Tension was swooshing through her veins and all her anger was being converted to absurdity.

Harry bit back a retort. Sweat trickled down his collar. "I'm going upstairs," he said wearily. "Maybe we'll learn something tomorrow."

"What? No, you're not."

"Yes, I am. I've had enough for one day. The memorial is tomorrow. I told Kiki I'd cover it." He patted the camera in his pocket. It might be his last chance for the story.

"We can't wait until tomorrow, Harry. You heard Mr. Dennis. Everybody is checking out and going home soon. If that happens, I'm afraid these murders will never get solved."

"I don't see that we have much choice," he said morosely.

"Yes, we do."

Rick Ramus hollered from the upstairs railing, trying to get Kelly's attention. George was standing silently beside him. "If you two are done putting on a show for the guests, I wanted to mention that the insurance man called a few minutes ago. He's on his way."

Kelly groaned. "He's not due until four."

Rick shrugged. "Well, he's coming now."

"I can't now, Rick," shouted Kelly. "I've got to go out."

"Right now?" Rick said. "Can't it wait, boss?"

"No." Kelly grabbed Harry and dragged him across the courtyard.

"What about the insurance man?" Rick called. "What do you want me to do?"

"You're the assistant manager, Rick. Assistant manage!"

"Now where are we going?" Harry demanded as Kelly took to the wheel of the Audi once again. He wasn't so sure he was up for another car ride with the wannabe race driver.

"I have an idea." Kelly gunned the engine.

"Don't you ever start a car engine without revving it?" Harry quickly struggled into his lap belt. What he needed was a racing helmet, harness and roll cage. "What is your idea?"

"First let's go see Aunt Ruth."

40

"I hope this works." Kelly surveyed the beach from the top of the dune. Warm wind blew her hair in every direction. Mrs. Barron, Irwin Brunner, Jill and Vivian Rochester, Ted and Jean Nelson and Desmond and Bonnie Dennis stood together at the shoreline.

"I hope this chair works." Harry struggled with the awkward and alien-looking beach wheelchair. He was several steps behind Kelly, struggling to push the wheelchair through the loose sand.

"Can I give you a hand, Harry?" Ben Walsh was struggling up the dune himself. The crutch wasn't much use in the shifting sand.

"No, thanks. I've got it, sir." Harry was anxious to show that he could handle anything. What would it look like if he asked for help from a man with a broken leg?

Ben worried that Harry would lose control and that Ruth would go tumbling backward down the dune. It may have been only sand but his sister didn't need further injuries added to those she still suffered. He took Ruth's hand. "Are you okay, sis?"

"I feel silly in this contraption." Ruth was securely belted into the purpose-built, all-terrain beach wheelchair. They had rented the bulky chair from a medical supply store.

The chair's frame was sturdy, bright white furniture grade PVC and sat on four balloon tires. The big, fat tires were bright blue like the cushioned seat on which Ruth was perched.

"Are you sure we shouldn't have told the police what we are doing, dear?" Ruth asked.

"And have that detective jeer at me?" replied Kelly. "Not a chance." She held down the corner of her skirt as it billowed in the wind, wishing she had worn something more practical but it was too late to change now. The reunion guests had seen them and were watching avidly. "Besides, Drew promised her cousin would be here."

Unofficially, of course.

Drake had warned Kelly and Drew that, if his superiors knew he was helping them, he might get in serious trouble. A reprimand could be the least of his worries if they learned he was assisting civilians in an active police investigation without authorization.

Kelly casually scanned the sparsely populated beach for a sign of Drake. A few strollers moved lazily along the water's edge. Drew's cousin had promised to be at the beach at sunset to discreetly keep an eye on developments. That meant he'd be out of uniform and dressed to blend in.

Kelly couldn't spot him but that wasn't a bad thing. It meant the others wouldn't be aware of his presence either should anything go wrong.

"There's Kiki!" Harry called as he reached the crest of the dune. He waved to a young woman in a bright red halter top and matching terry shorts, all of which highlighted her smooth, bronzed skin. Kiki returned the wave from a small rainbow-colored beach towel up near the dunes.

"You told her?" Kelly gaped at the impossibly sexy woman and instantly felt two decades older than she actually was.

"Yes. She mentioned today that she might swing by. Just to observe." Harry was happy to see no evidence of Chad. "She was curious to see all the players."

"Pretty," commented Ben. "Have you asked her out yet, Harry?"

"Why, no. I—"

"Would you please wipe that silly grin off your face, Harry," complained Kelly. "We're supposed to be attending a wake. And if all goes according to plan, somebody's figurative funeral," she added under her breath.

Mildred McConaughey sat in a chair high up on her balcony looking down on the proceedings. Kelly wondered what she was thinking.

The beach attendant watched them with a sullen expression on his face. He was in the process of shutting down for the day. Stacks of folded chairs and umbrellas were arranged near a small storage shed with its back against the dune. A bicycle leaned against the side of the shed near the open door.

A heart-shaped ring of white flowers, twelve feet in circumference, was laid out in the sand near the mourners.

A thunderstorm had crawled through earlier in the day. Both Harry and Kelly had worried that the guests would change their plans. Perhaps moving the memorial service to another location, leaving them out and their own plan in ruins.

But the weather had turned. The sun had forced its way through the clouds as it sank slowly to the west in a red ball of fire. And now they had gathered together at the beach.

Harry, Kelly and company intended to crash the party.

Harry ever so slowly guided the beach wheelchair down the slope. This part was trickier than going up. If he didn't hold on tight, Ruth Evans would tumble to the ground.

Kelly reached the group first. Ben hobbled up behind her, followed by Harry wheeling Ruth through the sand.

"What are you doing here?" demanded Bonnie Dennis. "This is a private affair." An ill-fitting, cheap cotton navy blue dress hung off her wide shoulders.

"We came to pay our respects," Kelly answered.

"We didn't think you would mind," Ruth said gently.

"I'm not sure this is a good idea." Irwin Brunner stood to the left of Vivian, his ex-wife. Jill stood on the opposite side, her face expressionless.

Vivian herself looked like she had been crying. Her eyes were puffy and red. Kelly was surprised she was getting so emotional over Charles Barron's death now.

"How are you, Mrs. Evans?" asked Irwin. "You are looking well."

"Thank you." Ruth touched a hand to the brace around her neck. "To tell you the truth, I'm a bit frustrated with my progress. The doctors say I need to be patient."

"Healing is a slow process, especially as we get older. Give it time," said Dr. Nelson.

"Do you remember your accident?" Desmond Dennis wanted to know. He had dressed for the occasion in a loose black tee shirt and brown trousers with an old pair of penny loafers on his feet.

"Bits and snatches," Ruth said vaguely.

A pair of laughing gulls flew lazily past. Long gray shadows cast by glittering high rises marched towards the shore.

"Are we going to have this service or not?" Bonnie Dennis demanded. "We've got packing to do. Let's get on with it. Why don't the rest of you take a hike?" She glared at Kelly, Harry, Ben and Ruth.

"Oh, let them stay." Mary Barron was clutching a slim dark blue book of poetry by John Keats. "I was about to read a poem: *Bright Star*. It was one of Charlie's favorites."

Harry's words carried on the ocean breeze. "'Pillow'd upon my fair love's ripening breast, to feel for ever its soft fall and swell, awake forever in a sweet unrest, still, still to hear her tender-taken breath, and so live ever —or else swoon to death.'" He lowered his head at the finish.

Kelly was staring at him. So were the others. Harry remembered the words of an obscure three hundred year old poem? He barely remembered to tie his own shoes.

"That's right," whispered Mary Barron, holding the page open in her hand as the breeze tugged at the corner of the paper. She silently closed the book.

The widow wore a simple black silk dress—it appeared new—and matching leather sandals. The white carnation in her hair matched those that formed the heart in the sand. Kelly felt a pang of sadness.

"I agree," said Ted Nelson. "Let them stay. There is no harm." Ted's wife stood off to the side. She had chosen to wear a simple green shift dress and flats. The ocean lapped at her feet. She did not appear to mind.

"You aren't fooling me none," said Desmond Dennis with a sniff. "You don't give a hoot about saying good-bye to Charlie. You're here because you're thinking you know who bopped him." He smelled like he had been drinking.

"Is that true?" Mary blinked at them.

The air was beginning to cool. Kelly laid a hand on her aunt's shoulder. "Yes."

Of course, she was bluffing. But they didn't know that.

A collective gasp came from the mourners.

"I think it was that handyman of yours," Desmond said. "I caught him snooping around in our room."

"He's a handyman, Des. He was probably doing maintenance," Irwin replied.

"I don't care who it was," Jill Rochester said suddenly. "I only want to go back home. Back to the way things used to be." She reached out and squeezed Vivian's hand.

Irwin frowned. "No offense, Mrs. Green, but I came to pay my respects to an old friend, not be subjected to wild accusations."

"I think it was that woman who runs the hotel." Kelly was surprised to hear Vivian express that opinion. "She sued him and lost."

"Yes, that's right." Mary Barron clutched the book of poetry to her chest.

"Mildred McConaughey did file a lawsuit against Dr. Barron," allowed Harry. "And she had plenty of reason to hate him."

"She sued him for millions," Irwin said.

"She kept ranting that Charlie killed her husband." Desmond said. "What was his name, Bonnie?"

"I don't remember." Bonnie stood behind her husband.

"But Mrs. McConaughey isn't the killer." Harry glanced up at Mrs. McC. She had refused to come and had chosen to watch events unfold from her balcony. "It was one of you." He had left the sunglasses at home. The eye was healing and they would have been useless in the dwindling light.

"Are you daft?" Desmond Dennis sneered.

"The killer couldn't be one us," Vivian said softly. "We were all together."

"Watching the fireworks, yes." Kelly patted Ruth's hand. "But is that really the case?"

"It wasn't just Mildred McConaughey who had a reason to hate Charles Barron," Harry said. "You all wanted Charles Barron dead for one reason or another."

"One of you ordered those fireworks."

"And one of you killed him."

"Those fireworks quite conveniently went off just as Dr. Barron was being murdered in his room."

"Sheer coincidence," said Irwin Brunner. "It can't mean anything. Charlie fell in the pool. If he hadn't, he wouldn't have gone to his room at the time the fireworks went off." Neither Kelly nor Harry missed the dark look he cast his ex-wife.

"Did he fall in the swimming pool?" Kelly asked. "Or was he pushed?"

"Pushed? You think somebody pushed Charlie in the pool on purpose?" That was Vivian Rochester.

"Knowing that he would go upstairs to change out of his wet clothes." Harry pulled the collar of his shirt tighter.

"And the killer was waiting." Kelly slowly circled the others like a lion circling its prey.

"But nobody pushed Charlie into the water," re-asserted Bonnie Dennis. "He fell."

"Are you sure?" Kelly asked, coming to a stop beside Bonnie Dennis. "It was a party. The music was loud and everybody was dancing."

"Let's get back to you, Mr. Brunner." Harry turned to Irwin. "You say you came here to pay your respects to a dead man."

"That's right." Irwin thrust his hands in the pockets of his trousers. His loose button-down, short-sleeve white shirt fluttered in the breeze.

"Is that really the case?" Harry asked. "You had invested heavily in Attleboro Associates."

"I provided the startup capital, that's true."

"In exchange for a share in the profits. And then Charles Barron left the practice and started a competing one. Attleboro eventually shut its doors."

"And Dr. Barron got rich on the profits from his medical device," added Kelly.

"You lost a bundle," noted Harry. "Then you lost your wife."

"The stress led to fighting. We separated. I always hoped we'd get back together once again." Irwin looked longingly at his ex-wife.

"Those profits should have been ours too," Vivian said venomously.

"Quiet, Viv," Irwin urged.

"That's right. You and Irwin were married. You worked for Attleboro Associates too, didn't you, Mrs. Rochester?"

"Vivian has nothing to do with any of this," Irwin said sternly.

Harry swung around. "What about you, Mr. Dennis?"

"What about me?"

"You will leave my husband alone, if you know what's good for you, buster." Bonnie pushed in front of her husband.

Harry ignored her warning. "You and your wife both worked for Attleboro Associates. Unfortunately, things didn't go so well for either of you once the business closed its doors."

"Desmond suffered a stroke." Bonnie's eyes were clouded with hate and pain. "It wasn't his fault. It was Charlie's. All the stress. The strain." She patted her husband's arm. "Desmond did his best."

"You also know a thing or two about electronics, don't you, Mr. Dennis?" Harry pressed.

"What of it?"

"A remote electronic ignition device was used to detonate the bag of fireworks that nearly burned down the inn."

Kelly planted her hands on her hips. "And nearly killed me in the process."

"It wasn't me and you can't prove different."

"Maybe."

"Which leaves you, Dr. Nelson." Harry stepped nearer the doctor and his wife.

"The only one in the group who is successful." Ted Nelson adjusted his necktie. He had dressed in a dark suit for the occasion. The expensive leather shoes on his feet were meant for carpet and fancy tile, not sand.

"So why would you want Charles Barron dead?" Kelly wanted to know.

"Exactly. I wouldn't."

"Tell me, why were you and your wife staying at the

Golden Arms Hotel next door prior to checking in here at the Beach Lovers Inn?" Kelly continued.

"It's no big deal. We wanted a few days alone first. No offense, Mrs. Green, but we wanted something more spacious, more luxurious. We had reserved an ocean-front suite."

"That's right," Ruth leaned forward. "I remember now. I saw you when I stepped next door to have a word with Mildred. That's what I started to tell you, Kelly, in the kitchen the night of my accident. Then I forgot."

"You forgot because somebody interrupted you." Kelly scanned the rapt audience.

"No," Ruth squeezed the arms of her wheelchair. "That wasn't it. It wasn't *somebody*. It was *something*. I remember now. Dr. Barron had a spill at the table."

"He broke the water pitcher." Kelly filled in the details.

"I don't see what Charlie breaking a water pitcher can have to do with his murder." Mary Barron spoke up. "I mean, you didn't kill him over it, did you, Mrs. Evans? Or you, Mrs. Green?"

Kelly ignored the taunt. "Did your husband drop the pitcher or did you, Mary, cause him to?"

Ruth leaned forward. "He said you bumped his elbow."

Mary Barron gaped. "Don't be ridiculous. Why would I do that?" She took a step back. "And even if I did, it would have been an accident."

"I don't think there were any accidents. I believe everything was well-planned. Wasn't it, Dr. Nelson?" Harry turned his gaze on Ted Nelson.

"You probably saw my aunt talking to Mrs. McConaughey," said Kelly." You were afraid she would say something that would alert your husband to the fact that the Nelsons had been staying next door. You wanted to keep Aunt Ruth from telling. That might spoil your plans."

"So you created a distraction," Harry said.

"This is crazy." Ted Nelson smirked. "Are you sure it isn't science fiction that you write, Harry?"

A troubled look passed between Mary Barron and Ted Nelson.

"Yes, this is preposterous. Forget what I said earlier," said Mary. "I want you all to leave. Now."

"Face it. We may not love one another but you're way off base. We were all together on the beach watching the fireworks," Desmond Dennis contended. "What you're suggesting is just not possible."

"He's right," asserted Jill Rochester.

"I'm afraid so," agreed Irwin Brunner.

"I disagree," said Kelly. Harry cleared his throat. "We both do."

"Here's what we think happened," began Harry. "Ted and Mary were having an affair."

Mary Barron scoffed. "Never!"

Harry ignored the interruption. "The two of you were tired of living apart."

"You wanted Charlie out of the way," Kelly put in. "The two of you planned the whole thing. In fact, I over-heard your husband saying this entire reunion wasn't even his idea."

Mary bit her lip.

"I remember. I heard that too," Ruth said. "When he broke the pitcher."

"Ted Nelson came to see you the night before the official start of the reunion," theorized Kelly. "You were both afraid that Mrs. Evans might let slip something about the Nelsons being next door, so you pushed her down the steps."

"I'm guessing that Cowboy was camping in the laundry room. He must have seen who pushed Mrs. Evans. That's why he had to be eliminated next."

"You arranged for the fireworks to go off at a predetermined time," Kelly said.

"And then you arranged for Charlie to fall in the pool."

"The same way you arranged for him to break the pitcher," said Kelly.

"It wouldn't take much with everybody dancing to give him a little shove in the right direction." Ben Walsh leaned heavily on his crutch next to his sister.

"And then you insisted that he go upstairs and change out of his wet clothes." Kelly directed her words at Mary Barron.

"Hey," blinked Desmond. "She did do that. I remember."

"Then when we were all supposedly watching the fireworks, Ted snuck back and murdered Charlie. It wouldn't have been difficult to steal a master key." Kelly now knew how painfully easy that could be.

"You can't prove any of this," Ted insisted. "I was up on those dunes watching the fireworks the entire time and nobody can prove otherwise." He pointed up at the sandy barrier.

"Let's think about that," said Kelly. "Mrs. Barron, you were to my right."

"Exactly." Her face was mottled red. Her eyes darted to Ted Nelson.

"Let's all think back. Tell me who was standing near

you, Mr. Dennis."

He frowned. "My wife, of course. And those two." He pointed to the Rochesters. "That one was lurking around them like a ghoul."

Irwin colored.

"And you, Mr. Brunner?"

"Vivian and Jill. I remember seeing the Dennises."

"Who else?"

"It was dark. Darker than it is now." He shrugged in frustration. "I was looking at the sky, not the people around me. That's all I remember."

"That's okay. What about you, Mrs. Nelson?"

Jean Nelson stood statue-still.

"Mrs. McConaughey, that's her up on the balcony." Kelly pointed up at the Golden Arms. "She saw you running back to the hotel from the direction of the inn the night Aunt Ruth was pushed down the stairs."

"I didn't do it." Jean Nelson looked at her feet, half-buried now in the wet sand. "I just wanted to see."

"What did you want to see?"

"What Ted was up to."

There was a long, ominous pause as two surfers trotted past with their long boards.

Jean Nelson's eyes blew up with tears. "Why did you do it?"

Ted blustered and reached for his wife. "What?"

"I followed you to the inn. I wanted to know what you were doing. Why did you have to push her down the steps? I saw you and Mary together the next day, on the beach. You kissed her. You swore to me that it was over."

"And then you killed Charlie. Why, Ted? Why?" Jean Nelson's hands clutched at her chest.

As Ted came closer to his wife, she backed away. "You

told me you loved me. You told me it was over between you and Mary. You promised!"

"Jean, shut up. You don't know what you are saying."

"You killed them!" Her arm trembled as she pointed her finger at him.

Ted slapped his wife across the face. Jean's head spun sideways and she cried out in pain and fell towards the ground.

Harry lunged forward, grabbing Ted around the waist.

Ted wrapped his strong fingers around Harry's neck and squeezed. Harry teetered and his eyes rolled back in his head.

Ben pushed forward. He began striking Ted repeated on the head with his crutch.

Ted's grip on Harry loosened and he spun around. Unfortunately for him, he had put himself right in Bonnie Dennis's path.

She closed one eye as she drew her arm back and landed an expert punch on Ted Nelson's jaw. A loud crack split the air. Ted Nelson looked startled for a moment, then sank to his knees.

Harry and Ben held him there.

Kelly glanced up towards the dunes. Drake was too busy talking up Harry's friend, Kiki, to have been any use at all. She patted herself on the back. They had managed to solve the case with no help from the police at all, official or otherwise.

Then Aunt Ruth began shouting. "She's getting away! She's getting away!"

Kelly looked over her shoulder. Mary Barron was scuttling awkwardly up the beach. Kelly took off, catching the woman in three strides. Mary slammed the book of poetry down on the bridge of her nose. Kelly cried out in pain as tears welled up. Mary clawed her arm and twisted to pull free. Kelly stuck her foot between the widow's legs and plowed into her midriff. They both tumbled to the ground in a tangle.

The widow kicked and punched venomously but Kelly managed to roll on top and pressed her elbows into the sand. Mary Barron shuddered then stopped moving. Her breath came out hard and heavy.

Harry appeared and offered Kelly a hand up.

"Thanks." Kelly pulled Mary to her feet.

The widow was cursing up a storm. "It was all Ted's doing," she insisted. "I had nothing to do with killing Charlie or hurting your aunt. Then he killed that homeless man."

"She's lying!" Ted scrambled to his feet and would have lunged for her but Kelly's father threatened him with his crutch and he held back.

"He told us that he had seen Ted push your aunt. He asked us for money," Mary Barron wailed. "Ted took him down to the beach and murdered him. I'm innocent. I was in the restaurant. He tried to kill you too by burning you alive. I begged him not to do it."

"Tell it to your lawyer," Kelly grumbled.

Vivian cradled Jean Nelson in her arms. Jill appeared to be in shock.

Harry picked up the book of Keats and dusted it off. "Are you okay, Kelly?"

Kelly rubbed her nose. Three police officers were tumbling down the dunes and Drake moved to intercept them. Somebody must have called the cops. Finally. "Yeah, I'm fine. But talk about your poetry slam."

As Kiki approached, Harry quickly pulled out the

camera and snapped a picture of her.

"Hey!" complained Kelly as the flash momentarily blinded her.

"I promised I'd get pictures."

Kelly shoved the camera away from her face. "Then take some of Ted and Mary, not my nose!" She covered her swollen nose with both hands.

41

It was a time for celebration. Earlier in the day, George had strung extra fairy lights all along the courtyard. The underwater light at the deep end of the swimming pool went from red to green to blue to magenta and back again. Ben had brought down his Bluetooth speaker and the Beach Boys provided the festive soundtrack to the evening.

Kelly smiled and closed her eyes, a glass of dark and fruity sangria in her hand.

This was the first chance she'd had to relax in what felt like eons. The beer and wine were flowing and the stars were shining. Except for the plywood barricade covering the door to the laundry room upstairs, one would never know that a mere twenty-four hours earlier the Beach Lovers Inn had been hosting a reunion—a deadly reunion.

Maybe this new life of hers was going to work out okay after all.

"What are you thinking?" Ruth interrupted, nestled in the wheelchair with a blanket on her lap. Sharky lay snoozing in the center of the blue blanket. In a couple of days, Ruth would be on her way to Arizona with her doctor's blessing.

"Absolutely nothing." Kelly smiled. "And, believe me, that's a good thing for a change."

George and her dad sat on a stone bench near the fire pit talking motorcycles and drinking beer. Kelly had learned from her aunt that the handyman hadn't been asking her for money for himself. He had been asking her for more money toward the inn's upkeep. As for how he could afford an oceanfront cottage, Aunt Ruth told her it was neither of their business.

She was right. It wasn't.

There were only four guest rooms occupied at the moment and even that didn't stress Kelly out. Ted Nelson and Mary Barron were the only two of the reunion guests left vacationing in Myrtle Beach. And they were only here because the police was holding them for murder.

Ruth nudged her niece with her elbow. "Is that the cute detective you told me about?"

Kelly forced one eye open. "Yeah. That's him." She ran a finger over her nose. The swelling had gone down and a bandage covered the cut that Mary had inflicted on her with that book.

Kelly would never look at poetry the same way again, especially Keats. "Hello, detective."

"Hi, Kelly. Nice seeing you again, Mrs. Evans." The detective inquired as to her health.

"I'm much better, thank you." Sharky stirred and leapt from her lap, off on his nightly rounds.

Det. Burns had been late on the scene the night before. According to Drew's cousin, he'd been on a date.

"Have a seat." Kelly offered the detective a chair around the table.

"No, thanks. I can't stay."

"Another date?"

The detective bristled. He was in civilian clothes,

cargo shorts and a baby blue polo shirt. "I promised my mom we would stay in and watch a movie tonight."

The beginnings of a smile appeared on Kelly's lips. "You live with your mother?"

"I *do not* live with my mother," Det. Burns said stiffly. "My *mother* lives with *me*."

"Right." Kelly rolled her eyes.

"So what does bring you here, detective?" asked Ruth.

"I thought you would like to know that Dr. Nelson and Mrs. Barron are talking up a storm. Each is accusing the other of being behind the murders and both are trying to make a deal with the prosecutor in exchange for their testimony.

"It seems Charles Barron had grown soft in his later years. He felt badly about some of the things he had done. He was preparing to give the bulk of his money to charity."

"I can't imagine his wife would have been very happy about that." Kelly had noted that Mary Barron looked every bit the part of the wealthy wife.

"Yeah. Ted and Mary were long-time lovers. Charles Barron knew all about the affair. Rather than confront his wife, he left the practice."

"So he left the practice not to cheat the others but to get his wife away from Ted Nelson."

"He tried anyway. It didn't work." The detective shifted back and forth on his feet. "Glad you are okay," he added finally. "You, and Mr. Leland, are very lucky you weren't hurt pulling a stunt like that. You should have called me to let me know what you were planning to do."

"Why? So you could stop us?"

"So I could do my job and keep you alive."

Kelly frowned. "Yes, well, I'll take that into consideration next time."

"Next time?" Det. Burns thrust his fingers into his pockets and glared down at her.

"It's a figure of speech," Kelly replied vaguely before lifting her glass and drinking.

"So sad," Ruth said softly as the detective wandered off. She twisted her head.

"What's that?"

"All these years, we've never had a murder before." Ruth draped the blanket over her legs.

"Are you sure? Because I remember Harry saying—"

"Mrs. Evans!" Rick Ramus skipped up to the table and threw his arms around Ruth. "It is so good to see you!"

"You, too, Rick." He offered his cheek and she kissed him with affection.

Kelly felt like a heel. "I'm sorry for thinking you might have been involved in Ruth's accident. And the murder," Kelly said. "Forgive me?"

A smile was plastered all across the assistant manager's face. "Sorry? Are you kidding? I think it's great. I'm writing a whole new bit based on it." Rick's eyes glittered with excitement. "Rick Ramus, the Killer Komedian. That's killer with a capital K."

Kelly and Ruth shared a giggle. "Have a seat."

"No, thanks. Can't stay. Emceeing next door."

"Okay. Are you sure we're good?" Kelly waved her finger between them.

"We are great. We are going to get along famously, dear." Rick smacked his moist lips against Kelly's forehead then tossed his hand in farewell.

"Killer Komedian with a K?" Ruth chuckled. "Can you

believe it?"

"Sounds more like Corny with a capital C," Kelly whispered to Ruth as Rick left the courtyard.

Kelly caught movement at the stairs out of the corner of her eye. "Harry!" She waved.

Harry approached and said hello.

"Sneaking out?" teased Kelly. Harry had on a pair of rumpled black trousers and a white button down shirt with what appeared to be a tea stain the shape of Michigan at the beltline.

"A friend is picking me up." Harry glanced towards the entrance.

"Hi, Harry." Ben and George joined them at the table. Ruth asked George to wheel her to the kitchen and they trundled off.

"How are you holding up, Harry?" asked Ben. "Didn't see much of you today."

There were ugly purple marks around Harry's throat. Ted Nelson hadn't been kidding around.

"I was writing."

"Finish your big story?" Kelly set her empty cup on the table.

"Yes. I should be getting a check in the next day or two." Harry leaned back on his heels. "I've already begun packing. I expect to be out of your hair by the end of the week."

"Right." Kelly toyed with her cup. "Glad to hear it. That's one of our best rooms you are in."

"I know," Harry said. "And I appreciate that you've let me use it."

"Now, now. Don't be so hasty, Kelly." Ben winked at Harry. "I could use some help around here."

"We've got George."

"George is semi-retired. You said so yourself."

"Harry here is young, strong—"

Kelly snorted. "I've seen him with his shirt off, Dad. Strong isn't an adjective I would use to describe him."

"Hey," complained Harry. "I'm plenty strong. I just don't believe in showing it off with a load of clownish muscles like some people." Det. Burns came to mind.

"Anyway," Ben continued. "You really could use an extra hand around the inn."

"I've got you, Dad." Her father had already agreed to stick around indefinitely. Kelly leaned forward, her elbows on her knees. "No offense, but can you do anything?" Kelly asked Harry. All she'd seen so far was that he was good at writing and finding crimes where there were none. Well, mostly none.

"I fixed my own toilet, didn't I?"

Kelly frowned as she recalled the mess that George and Drew had described to her. The repair had cost fifty dollars in supplies, not to mention George had had to caulk, sand and repaint behind the toilet. "That was you?"

Ben sent his daughter a cautionary look. "That sure was brave of you last night the way you went after Nelson, Harry. Wasn't it brave of Harry, Kelly?" He prodded her in the ribs with the tip of his crutch.

"Yes. Yes," she admitted. "It was brave of you."

A car honked at the curb and flashed its lights.

"That's my ride." Harry turned to go. "Like I said, give me a couple of days and I'll be out of your hair." He looked toward the kitchen. "Say goodnight to Mrs. Evans for me."

Kelly promised she would. Harry hadn't taken three steps when she heard herself saying he could stay.

Why?

For the longest time, all she wanted was to be rid of him. Now, the thought of him actually walking out of her life left her feeling...what?

Kelly wasn't sure. But there was something deep inside of herself that wanted him to stay.

Harry turned. "You mean it?"

Kelly hesitated. There was still time to renege but she didn't. "Yes. But I'm putting you to work," she added sternly.

Harry grinned. "No problem."

"And you'll have to move to another room. Room 101." That was a room on the ground floor near the street. It rented for far less than Harry's current ocean view apartment.

"I understand."

"Happy now?" Kelly whispered to her father as the car at the curb honked impatiently and Harry once more began his retreat.

"The boy saved your life. And helped save your inn and your reputation." Ben picked his crutch up from the table and stood. "But if that's all he's worth to you is some tiny little room, well, that's your decision to make."

He shifted his crutch side to side, balancing on his good leg. "I expect it's going to crush his creative spirit. And after that wonderful write-up he said he's going to give you in Myrtle Scene Magazine, too. I'll bet that'll boost business around here," Ben droned on.

Kelly groaned and narrowed her eyes at her father. "Harry, wait!"

"Yes?"

"I just remembered. Bed bugs."

"Bed bugs?"

"Big ones." Kelly spread her hands a foot apart. "You won't be able to move into room 101 until they're gone."

Ben nudged his daughter. "And the plumbing."

"Don't you have someplace to be, Dad?"

"Nope," he said, nudging her a second time.

"Right. The plumbing will need replacing too, Harry." She supposed that was sort of true. Her father had inspected the inn's plumbing and found it deplorable. His word, not hers.

"What am I going to do?" Harry looked troubled. "Where will I write?"

Kelly gaped at him. Leave it to Harry to be more concerned with where he would write rather than where he would sleep.

"I guess you'll have to stay where you are," Kelly answered. "For now." Her jaw ached from the strain of speaking.

Harry appeared unsure. "I suppose. If you say so."

Ben whispered in his daughter's ear. "Ask him if he'd like to get a late dinner."

Kelly shot her head around and locked eyes with her father.

"Go ahead," urged her father. "Ask him." `

"There's some leftover broccoli casserole," Kelly found herself saying. What was her father suddenly? Some sort of Svengali? "Would you like to join me?"

Kiki Donovan strutted up from a silver coupe at the street in a slinky red dress and metallic silver high heels. "Hi, Harry. Didn't you hear me honk?"

"Hello, Kiki. You remember Kelly and her father."

"Of course, good evening, Mrs. Green. Mr. Walsh, isn't it?"

Ben smiled and shook her hand. "Yes. Good memory."

"I was beginning to think Harry had lost his memory and forgotten all about our date."

"Date?" Ben and Kelly shared a look.

"It's not really a date." Harry squirmed. "Kiki invited me out to supper to celebrate my article on the murder."

"The least I could do. It's wonderfully written. A real scoop from an insider's perspective." The editor patted Harry's shoulder. "We may have some more work for you."

"Have a nice time." Kelly watched as Harry followed Kiki to her car and sped off.

Ben turned on his heel. "I'm famished. Broccoli casserole, eh?"

Kelly remained at the curb watching the passing headlights.

"Coming?" Ben asked.

"Right behind you."

Ben walked back and led her by the arm. "You like him, don't you?"

"Who? You mean Harry?" Kelly's voice crescendoed. "No, Dad. I am mad at myself for not being able to get rid of him when I had the chance. I mean, I was this close —" She pinched her thumb and finger together. "This close." She squeezed harder, watched the blood drain from her fingers.

"What stopped you?"

"Really, Dad? You mean besides you giving me the guilt-trip of a lifetime?"

"Yeah, besides that."

"I wish I knew," she mumbled.

The weekly edition of Myrtle Scene Magazine hit the stands two days later with a not-so-flattering picture of Kelly on the front page—an ill-composed close-up highlighting her bulging eyes, sand peppered face and swollen nose—above the caption: *Startling Conclusion To Local Murder.*

With the hot-off-the-presses news magazine rolled up tightly in her left hand, Kelly banged repeatedly on the door of Room 209.

Wisely, Harry did not answer.

HI, THANKS FOR READING!

If you enjoyed this book, please support me by sharing your positive review online and on your favorite social media platforms. Trust me, every little bit helps.

And, don't forget, if you enjoyed BOOKING A KILLER VACATION, please check out some of my other books.

Thanks again!

J.R. Ripley is also the bestselling author of A Bird Lover's mystery series, the Maggie Miller mysteries, the TV Pet Chef mysteries (writing as Marie Celine), the Todd Jones comic thrillers and other novels; also writing as Glenn Eric Meganck and others.

Visit www.GlennEric.com and connect with JR at Facebook.com/JRRipley & Twitter @JRRipleyAuthor.